Prepare for takeoff! *Ransom in the Rock* launches you into another universe, peopled by characters you grow to care about.

Ransom in the Rock is a wonderful read. Once you return to Gannah you don't want to leave. This story is so well written, so tight you zip right along and suddenly the book is ended and you lean back waiting for the next one.

A must-read for Christian sci-fi lovers – or anyone wanting a great story!

I'm impressed with the author's ability to craft such lifelike characters-without whitewashing them. A VERY intriguing read.

I was pulled into the drama and engaged by the writing.

With more twists and turns than a Gannah underground tunnel, the author skillfully weaves the elements of a story that sings of the peace that can only come when we trust in Almighty God, whatever the circumstances.

Once you've set foot on Gannahan soil, you'll want to come back!

Well told and engaging.

I enjoyed all of the characters as they were made to seem like they could live right around the corner from me here in Oklahoma. I enjoyed the book so much I have in fact already purchased the other two books from Amazon. They are awaiting their turn in my reading queue.

Ransom in the Rock

Book 3,
Gateway to Gannah

Gannah's Gate

RANSOM IN THE ROCK

Gateway to Gannah 3

Second Edition

Yvonne Anderson

Ransom in the Rock (Gateway to Gannah #3)
(Second Edition)

Scripture quotations are from the Holy Bible, King James Version.

This novel is a work of fiction. Characters, plot, and incidents are products of the author's imagination, and any similarity to people living or dead, whether on Earth, Karkar, or Gannah, is pretty much coincidental. Except for the Yasha, of course, who is very real.

ISBN-13: 978-1-946985-03-3

Cover design
By Ken Raney
Clash Creative

For who is God save the LORD?
Or who is a rock save our God?

Psalm 18:31

1

𝓗ER chest tight with dread, Lileela opened the closet.

She could only bring one outfit. One outfit? How insane was that? No way in Karkar could she narrow her wardrobe to one item. It was almost enough to make a girl scream. But, tempting though it may be, fifteen was a little old to be throwing a tantrum like a toddler.

She chewed her lip, trying to think.

It should be a multi-piece ensemble. Though technically one outfit, she could wear separate parts on different occasions, making it seem like more.

But she'd have to coordinate it with something Gannahan, and that would putrefy the entire look.

She'd never survive this.

Swallowing a sob, she climbed the stepstool to reach the control that activated the display. One by one, each item in her closet appeared on the screen, then faded away to reveal the next.

This was going to be a tough decision.

"Lileela?"

Great. Aunt Skiskii was here already.

"We need to get to the shuttle bay."

Ignoring her, Lileela watched the delicious parade of apparel march past her vision. If she took the knee-length brushed yueeed jacket and the Eutarian silk blouse—no, not that silk. The paler one, with the little flecks of—no, maybe the solid would be better.

"What's this?" Skiskii's voice could cut through glass.

Lileela limped down from the stool and exited the closet, leaving the display running. "What's what?"

"These cosmetics in your case. What are they doing here?"

Lileela tipped her head back to look her aunt in the pale yellow eye. "I'm taking them. What else would they be doing there?"

Skiskii's ears tilted back. "Weren't we told they don't wear cosmetics on Gannah? And you've scarcely left room for clothes. You said you were bringing one civilized outfit, but I don't see it."

"I haven't packed it yet." Lileela slipped between Skiskii and the suitcase. "Still trying to decide which one I want."

Skiskii's exasperated sigh reverberated around the room. "What have you been doing all day, buying every eyeliner on the ship? You've got a lifetime supply in there."

"That's the plan. If they don't wear cosmetics on Gannah, that means I can't buy it there, which means I'll have to bring my own. Because I'm not about to walk around with a naked face the rest of my miserable life."

Skiskii's lips parted as if she was about to shriek again, but then her ears tipped outward. "Well. Well. I suppose it can't do any harm. But we do need to get to the shuttle bay, so let's grab whatever else you're bringing." Two swift, long-legged steps put her in the closet. "Let's see..." Pressing an icon, she changed the display to one that showed thumbnails of the entire contents.

Row after row of miniscule images filled the wide screen. Lileela was proud of her wardrobe, but it did make choosing difficult.

She watched her auntie—actually, her cousin; Skiskii was her father's first cousin on his mother's side—scan the selection. She'd miss the old thing. More than she cared to admit. That was one reason she had such a hard time deciding what to bring. It wasn't just clothes she'd be leaving behind.

"Here." Skiskii pressed a selection. "This is perfect." She chose the very jacket Lileela had been thinking of, along with fashionably snug trousers and a filmy but triple-layer ruffled blouse, the color of which picked up the mauve of the jacket's piping. To Lileela's delight, she added a floor-length skirt besides.

Lileela couldn't have chosen better herself. "Oh, grab that cream-colored sash, too. And I've got the most darling bangles to match the jacket buttons." She scurried to her jewelry armoire and flung it open.

That was another thing she would sorely miss. What sort of accessories would she find on Gannah? Trying to remember if her mother wore jewelry, all she could recall was a ring. The signet of her authority as toqeph.

The closet rack whirred as it spit out the clothes Skiskii selected. While she removed them from their hangers and folded them, Lileela boxed the earrings and brooch, along with a neck chain.

Her hands trembled, and she took a slow, deep breath, trying to calm herself. The breath turned into a sob.

Skiskii left her folding and reached for Lileela, pulling her into a long-limbed embrace. The grinding noise in her throat was supposed to be comforting, and to a Karkar child, it might have been. But it only made Lileela's tears flow more freely. She was no longer a child, though on Skiskii's planet she was the size of one. And she was only one quarter Karkar, though she could barely remember living anywhere else.

"I don't want to go, Auntie!"

Skiskii's dinner-plate-sized, six-fingered hand stroked Lileela's dark, curly-bobbed head. "I know you don't, dear one." She crooned like a Cephargian alley cat yowling in pain. "I know you don't. But Gannah is your home. You were born there, your family's there."

Lileela pulled away. "You're family, and you're not there. I don't remember my parents anymore, and I've never seen my younger brothers and sisters. Why do they even want me?"

Skiskii's ears wobbled. "Your parents love you. They've missed you. The family's not complete without you."

"That can't be." Lileela pulled out a tissue and wiped her eyes. "There's got to be some other reason."

Skiskii sat on the vanity bench, but she still had to look down at Lileela. "They do love you. You've been gone for so long, and they want you home so they can get to know you again."

For a moment, Lileela felt her auntie's sorrow at never having had a child of her own. But that moment was short, fleeing before her greater self-pity.

"Your neurological treatment has been a considerable expense to them, you know."

Lileela pouted, a feat that never failed to impress the blank-faced Karkar. Especially when she managed to produce a few tears in the corners of her eyes, like she did now. "Why should that worry them? They're rich, they own all of Gannah, but people there don't use money. It wouldn't burden them to keep me on Karkar the rest of my life."

Skiskii's answer was cut short by an urgent beep followed by a whistle from the speaker above the door. Then an electronic voice intoned in tinny Karkarish, "Lileela Pik. Please report to Shuttle Bay Three immediately. Lileela Pik. Shuttle Bay Three."

Skiskii hopped up and turned back to the half-packed suitcase. "We've got to scoot. We should have been there a quarter hour ago."

Lileela slammed the jewelry box into the bag. "All right. If you don't want me any longer, I'll go down to that awful planet. But—"

"That's not the case, and you know it." Skiskii's ears twitched in irritation. "Stop acting like the spoiled brat I've allowed you to become." She snapped the bag shut.

Lileela let out a shriek. "Wait, I need shoes!" As fast as her labored, deliberate gait allowed, she moved to the closet and up the stepstool. "I know which ones I want, it'll only take a sec."

When the shoes she selected emerged, she tossed them to her auntie, who stuffed them into the suitcase and closed it again with swift movements.

Skiskii snatched the case with one hand and ushered Lileela out the door with the other. Lileela went, but she scowled all the way. "This is the most ridiculous thing I've ever heard of. Just one decent outfit, one real pair of shoes, and no cosmetics. They're going to make me dress like a barbarian—"

In the hall outside, Skiskii slid the bag into the rack in the back of the scootercart. "Yes, yes, just get in. I'll drive."

"Oh, my tote!" Lileela limped back into her room, grabbed her purse and returned to the scootercart while continuing her rant. "A barbarian, I tell you. They'll have me dressing in scratchy old sacks and eating with my hands."

The cart lurched forward, slamming Lileela into the seat. "Eating nasty roots dug out of the filthy, wormy ground, and then picking my teeth with a stick. After all you and Uncle Ogliziizl have gone through to teach me how to be civilized, they're going to want me to go back to—"

"That's enough, Miss Lileela." Skiskii's stern voice would have sent Lileela cringing to the far side of the scootercart if she hadn't known her auntie was all bark and no bite.

Skiskii pulled the horn, and people in the hall moved out of her way. "I know you don't want to go, but we have no choice. The arrangements have been made, and it's out of our hands."

Lileela crossed her arms and scowled at her shoes. They were cute shoes, too. She was certain never to find anything like them on Gannah. "So what am I, a commodity to be traded by agreement between planets?"

Skiskii sighed. "We've been through this, Lileela, and I won't explain it again. Your finally come up with the means of paying for your care. And it's a king's ransom. You should be touched that they'd—"

"Pay so much for my release? Some release. They're buying me from Karkar so they can use me for a slave. My father used to beat me, did you know that? He beat me with a rod, then made me sit in a drab, gray room for hours on end, just because he didn't like the way I was dressed, did I ever tell you that?"

"He did not. Don't expect me to believe that."

"He did! And I was little then. How do you think they'll treat me now? They're Gannahan, they'll do terrible things to me!"

Skiskii cornered a little too abruptly, and Lileela had to grab her tote to keep it from flying out of the cart.

"They're your parents, they love you. The League of Planets has ordered us to turn you over to them now that they're able to pay off their debt. I have no doubt you'll be well cared for there."

"Humph." Lileela smoothed a curl back from her forehead. "I'll remember you said that when I'm imprisoned and forced into hard labor."

Skiskii negotiated another turn, a little more carefully this time, onto the last hall before the shuttle bay elevators. "It will be nothing like that, and you know it." She patted Lileela's leg. But her worried ears and tearful eyes belied her comforting words.

⁂

ADAM watched through the glass as the last truck pulled up behind the others at the edge of the landing field.

Try as he might, he couldn't grasp why those rocks dug out of the ground were so special. Why the League had refused to allow his sister to come home until Gannah agreed to provide a sufficient amount of them.

Nor why they were worth a man's life.

In all his twenty years, he'd never known anything so perplexing.

The drivers left their trucks and crossed the grass to the building where Adam and the others waited. Steamy air poured into the lobby as they filed in through the entrance.

One of them approached Adam's mother and bent forward in a respectful bow. "It's all here, Madam Toqeph. Five tonnes of raw zahab ore, five tonnes of nechosheth, and a hundredweight of uncut green keliystone."

"Thank you, Jax. The transport is expected in ten minutes, so you're here in good time." Emma turned from Jax and looked up at Adam. "Do you hear anything from your sister?"

He shook his head. "She doesn't seem inclined to communicate with me."

Adam glanced at his father by Emma's other side. Abba's waxen Karkar face revealed nothing, but his ears quivered with suppressed anticipation, and tension radiated from his whole being in almost visible waves.

It was Abba who had put Lileela on that starship for Karkar after her spinal cord injury, and it was Abba who felt responsible for her return.

Adam and his sister had been close as children, and their separation had been difficult to adjust to. But at least he had the ability to maintain contact with her through what Abba called meah telepathy.

Adam wasn't sure if telepathy was the right word, because there was nothing extra-sensory about it. But since only native Gannahans possessed the gland that performed the function—and since only Emma and her children were native Gannahans—and since Emma's meah had been damaged in an accident—it was, in fact, a rare ability.

An ability that Lileela lately chose to not use.

She didn't want to come home, that much was clear. But Adam didn't mention that to his parents. Since he didn't understand her reluctance, he couldn't explain it to them.

Why would anyone not want to live here? Yes, Karkar was the planet of their father's birth. Beside the superior medical services she'd been sent there for, it had many other interesting things to offer. But when he tried to imagine being cut off from his beloved Gannah, Adam felt suffocated. Lileela should be eager to return and breathe freely again.

The trucks' drivers mingled in the lobby, their voices joining the other eager murmurs humming throughout the room. A visit from Outsiders was a rare event, and never had they brought such precious cargo.

He reached in his meah toward Lileela, but she still shut him out. The last time he'd seen her, she'd been fighting for her life, breathing with the help of a respirator, a terrified five-year-old who'd never known anything but Gannah. Now she was, under Gannahan law, only a few months away from the age of adulthood, and with Outerworld experience that Adam could only imagine. Was that why she was cutting him off? Was she ashamed of his ignorance, embarrassed by his provincialism?

Or was she once again a frightened little girl facing a great unknown?

He wished she would let him in. He wanted to comfort her like he used to, help carry her fears. He was also eager to learn from her, for the things she'd seen in the past ten years could be a great benefit to Gannah.

After more than twice the ten-minute estimate, a rumble filled the ears, first of the native Gannahans with their keener senses, and then the others as well.

No one spoke as the ship drew closer. No one could have heard their words if they'd tried. Before the gigantic vehicle began its final, hovering descent, many covered their ears with their hands, even though they'd all inserted earplugs as the transport's approach grew louder.

The thunderous noise, the ground-shuddering vibrations, the massive size and flashing lights of the mechanical monster that eased itself onto the landing pad in clouds of smoke and flame both excited and repulsed Adam. This beast was a marvel of engineering, nearly magical in its abilities, but it was a dirty, foreign thing. A violation of Gannah's air and soil, a threat to the purity and stability of the planet.

But it carried Lileela home. For that, he would forgive it anything.

2

CLENCHING her teeth against nausea, Lileela avoided looking out the triple-paned porthole.

Entering the atmosphere was more stressful than she'd expected. The jostling and slamming of her strapped-in body seemed calculated to beat her into submission before she ever set foot on this forsaken place.

But she wouldn't let it. Closing her eyes and controlling her respiration, she endured the abuse without a murmur—as she would continue to do until she found a way to escape. Among the Karkar, she was vocal, because the Karkar were vocal. On Gannah, she'd be stoic as a Gannahan. But in no case would she surrender.

Auntie's ears were still flat against her head from terror, but she'd ceased her shrill keening by the time Lileela opened her eyes to the Gannahan sunlight sifting through the soot-dimmed windows.

Lileela swallowed hard. "I'm about ready to throw up. I don't blame Uncle Ogliziizl for not coming to the surface with us."

Skiskii grabbed a bag from the seat pocket and noisily emptied her stomach into it.

Lileela wrinkled her nose and stared out the porthole until Auntie's retching ceased.

Some ten meters above the ground, the window provided a fine view despite the film of grime. The land spread toward the hazy horizon in gentle waves of green. Dark stripes that Lileela knew to be roads, though they wouldn't be deemed that by civilized folk, marked the fields into plots shaped more by the lay of the land than by any intelligent designer.

In the far right corner of her view, barely seen, sprawled what appeared to be a jumble of rock. Lileela, however, recognized it as the architectural disaster known as Gullach. Designed to blend in with the landscape, the former palace of the toqephs was now the home of the New Gannahan settlement and the place of her birth.

"It's not the travel sickness." Skiskii wiped her mouth on a napkin. "Your uncle just couldn't bring himself to set foot on Gannah. No offense to your people, my dear, but—"

"None taken." Lileela studied the tiny moving figures in the scene below. Like it or not, they were her people. As the smoke and dust from the landing cleared, she could see them moving toward the airfield from different directions. Coming to greet her, she assumed. Great. She'd rather they'd ignore her, as she planned to do to them.

"—but it's hard for him to overcome his ingrained prejudices."

Once Skiskii disposed of her bag of nastiness in the nearest refuse tube, Lileela turned toward her. "I know, Auntie. It was generous of him to take me into his home the way he did."

"I left him no choice." Skiskii downed the remainder of the nutrawater in her bottle. "I'll admit, it did bother him at first. But you're family, and after your grandfather died, I wasn't about to leave my cousin's child in an institution, to be treated to who-knows-what indignities professional caregivers might give a mongrel such as yourself. I simply would not allow that to happen."

Though Lileela knew the Karkar way of expressing a thought without regard to how hurtful it might be, the words stung like a slap.

Unmindful, Skiskii patted Lileela's leg. "Karkar professionals are the finest in the galaxy, of course. But personal prejudices can taint even the best. And with that curly hair and those glowing green eyes, not to mention your silly lack of digits, you do look rather frightful until one gets used to the differences."

Reminding herself of her vow to keep her dignity, Lileela forced a smile. "I appreciate all you've done for me, Auntie. And I've enjoyed getting to know you."

Skiskii's ears lifted in the Karkar excuse for a smile. "Ogliziizl and I have both enjoyed the experience as well. You've become very dear to us."

Lileela was tempted to ask, "Then why can't I stay?" But she knew the answer. Her cousins were citizens of some influence, but the decision had been made above their heads. Instead of complaining, she rubbed her forearm against Skiskii's in a Karkar gesture of affection. "You're dear to me as well."

The transport pilot's squawking voice over the intercom interrupted, obviously reading from a script. "Ladies and gentlemen, we are now on the planet of Gannah. As you know, this planet is not a member of the League of Worlds. If you choose to disembark, you will be an alien here with no protection or rights under League Statute. However, the government of Gannah has extended us the freedom to set foot on the planet, communicate with the residents, and travel about as we choose.

"This freedom comes with some warnings. The food and water are pure and untainted. Nevertheless, ingesting it is known to cause intestinal distress for those who aren't accustomed to it, and you are advised to limit your consumption to things you have brought with you."

Lileela yawned as the Karkar voice shrieked on. "No part of the planet is off-limits during your visit. You may browse in the local stores, but be aware that Gannah does not follow the League Standard monetary system. It is illegal for any male to touch a female, even to shake hands, unless they are related by blood or marriage. No alcohol or spirits in any form are permitted anywhere on the planet. Failure to comply with these laws will result in immediate expulsion."

Skiskii looked at Lileela, ears stiff. "What's all that about?"

Before Lileela could answer, the pilot continued. "That's the official statement. Personally, and on behalf of Karkar Space Aeronautics, I would like to thank you for allowing us to transport you to this exotic place. Enjoy your visit, but please be sure to follow the guidelines they suggest so you can return safely. None of us, I'm sure, wants our journey to end here.

"This transport's departure is scheduled for three days from now, at 0800 on the twelfth of Sjklxxk, or League Standard Date 2923.05.12. The cabinets on the lower level are stocked with ample beverages and travelrations for the duration. You may return to this ship whenever you choose, for as long as you choose. The seats convert to cots, if you wish to spend the nights here. However, the people of Gannah have indicated that accommodations are available for any brave souls who choose to use them.

"You are now free to disembark. Watch your backs, ladies and gentlemen. This might be the New Gannah, but it's still Gannah. Again, thank you for your patronage, and enjoy your stay."

The flight carried few passengers. Most Karkar had better sense than to visit the land of the galaxy's most fabled villains. The only people who shared the transport with Lileela and her aunt were the shuttle crew and attendants, a geologist who was to inspect the ores being exchanged in payment for Gannah's debts, two finance ministers, and two League advisors who were authorized to oversee and certify the exchange.

They unfastened their safety restraints at the close of the announcement, chattering at shrill Karkar levels. "No alcohol?" "What was that about not touching a female?" "Shop without money, how does that work?" "I wonder what language they speak here." "This is a city? Where are the buildings?" "For that matter, where are the people?"

Lileela listened mutely to their jangling. She enjoyed knowing more about Gannah than the most educated among them. But the thought that they would be leaving in three days while she must remain put a damper on any gloating.

She and Skiskii waited in their seats until all but the attendants had exited the transport. Then they rose. Lileela, heavy with dread, moved more stiffly than usual as they made their way to the gaping mouth of the doorway.

"Are you all right, dear?" Skiskii asked.

Lileela nodded. "I've just been sitting too long. I'll loosen up soon."

Hot, moist air wrapped them in smothering arms as they approached. Lileela thought she remembered summer's heat, but its oppressiveness took her by surprise as she descended the steps to the sizzling tarmac.

Skiskii gasped. "By the blessed Kankakar Jewels, what's wrong with their climate control?"

"Auntie, there is no climate control. This is weather." She answered absently, hardly hearing Skiskii's sputtering as her attention seized on the group assembled to meet them.

A faceless rabble of drably clad bodies peppered the area, but four at the center drew her eye.

A tall blond man towered above the rest, of Karkar size but with the grooming of a savage, clad in the long skirt and coat that on Gannah passed for formal attire. That would be Abba.

On his right stood a younger man, not quite as tall but similarly bearded and dressed, with the face of her brother Adam, now grown. Lileela greeted him in her meah and his meah responded with joy.

On Abba's left stood a small, sturdy woman with black hair braided and wrapped around her head. Her emerald trousers and tunic intensified the color of her eyes, which were the same brilliant green as Lileela's. And though those eyes were fixed on the delegation that preceded Lileela and her aunt, Lileela knew the woman's focus was on her and her alone.

Lileela's head swam and her legs felt weak. The pavement beneath her radiated the heat of the sun overhead, making her sympathize with a patty on a grill press. But the woman in green—her mother—drew her onward. Despite her mother's damaged meah, she connected with Lileela in a way no one else ever had, nor ever could.

Walking beside Lileela, Skiskii tamed her shrieking complaints to a croaking stage whisper, then quieted altogether as they drew nearer at a dignified pace. Even she felt the power of the toqeph of Gannah.

Emma greeted the officials with a smile and a bow. Abba touched fingertips with them in a twelve-point, the Karkar equivalent of a handshake. Adam bowed like a Gannahan and performed a twelve-point as well.

Emma directed the Karkar visitors to follow two other men—who were they? One looked vaguely like one of the councilmen who used to meet with her parents, but who was the other? Was it that ship captain who took her to Karkar when she was injured? What was he doing back here on Gannah? Once the officials moved away, the toqeph turned her piercing green gaze on Lileela.

No breeze stirred to cool Lileela's perspiring forehead as she forced herself to look her mother in the eye. "Hello, Emma."

Abba and his cousin Skiskii exchanged greetings in their native language. The Outlandish display probably drew almost as much attention from the onlookers as did Emma's and Lileela's long embrace.

"Welcome home, my daughter," Emma murmured in the Standard tongue. "We've missed you so."

"Thank you. It's good to be back."

Wrapped in her em's arms for the first time in more than ten years, Lileela felt a sharp stirring within, like a hammerstrike to her conscience. She'd just lied to her mother. And a Gannahan didn't lie.

3

*F*ARIS paid close attention to his instructions.

He always did. Schooled to catch and retain every detail, he could recite his captain's words from last month or last year, or the inconsequential chatter of his men upon arising yesterday morning. He could even repeat the bawdy banter amongst Mustafa's unit at dinner last week—if he permitted such coarse words to cross his lips.

But those words were nothing compared to what he heard now.

Captain Abdul-Malik's orders made the stuffy briefing room feel chill. Planted a bitter nut in his belly that sent roots downward and branches upward and filled his whole being with dread.

He was a warrior. Trained from birth. A machine with a heartbeat. But he was afraid.

The captain's dark eyes drilled from beneath black brows. "Is that understood?"

"Aye, sir." Faris held his gaze.

Abdul-Malik's lean face hardened but his voice remained silken. "Do I detect resistance, Commander?"

"Sir, I do not question. I hear and obey." The mantra Faris usually chanted with pride nearly stuck in his dry mouth.

The captain nodded. "See to it, then."

"Aye, sir."

Salutes exchanged, Faris turned, ramrod straight, and left the room.

He passed through the corridors, firm footfalls echoing with more confidence than he felt. When he touched his messenger and spoke to Safiy, his voice betrayed none of his concern. "We depart tonight at 0300. Notify the team to meet me in fifteen in Strategy Two."

"Aye, commander."

Disconnecting the call, he strode into the restroom, nodded to Barakat at the sink, and entered a stall. Only then did he allow his shoulders to slump as he closed his eyes and released a long breath. There were evil forces at work. Greater, blacker wickedness than even he, with his dark history, had previously seen.

League Special Starforces Central Headquarters—its unofficial address jokingly listed as One Middle of Nowhere, Planet Earth—lay more than a hundred meters below the desolate sands of Rub' al Khali. Elbows on knees and head in his hands, Faris felt the weight of those countless tons of blistering desert sand pressing upon him.

He lifted his eyes to the glowing diode panels above. A gentle mockery of the sun that blazed one hundred fifty million kilometers distant, they provided sufficient light for human vision without the blinding intensity or vaporizing heat of the star they were created to emulate. Earth's sun, in its turn, was a fairly modest power in the universal pantheon of stars.

His skin prickled at the realization that there was a Light greater even than their sum. A Light that promised to dispel all darkness.

He couldn't pray aloud. Not here. But no one monitored his thoughts. *Oh, Light of the World, show me the way.*

The diode panel in the ceiling still mocked. The weight of the desert still oppressed, and the captain's orders still rang in his ears.

He inhaled the faintly putrid, faintly chemical-scented air. What did Hell smell like? Thankfully, he'd never know. But Earth held plenty of previews.

He flushed, washed, and left the room, heels clipping, shoulders straight beneath their load.

In the strategy room nine minutes later, the eight-man team stood when Faris entered. "Good morning, gentlemen. We have an assignment."

Always the eager one, Ishaq asked, "Where're we headed, sir?"

Faris nodded. "Be seated. We're going to Africa." Turning to the display screen on the wall, he brought up a map of the northeastern quadrant of that continent. "Ethiopia." He drew the focus in closer. "Our target has been located here, in a compound outside the town of Soddu."

Satellite images depicted a fortress crumbling with age. "The defenses are not formidable. I'll get more details in the next couple of hours, but I'm told it'll be just the usual surveillance cameras, standard force field, and a small cadre of guards."

Safiy nodded. "What's our objective, amir?"

Faris pulled up a headshot of a handsome African in his thirties. "Philip Dengel, a leader of the Jeshi Samaki, organizer of a loose confederation of renegades scattered in pockets across Northern Africa. The group's origins stem from long before Dengel's time, but under his leadership, the number of cells are multiplying like cancer. We've recently learned this fortress is his base of operations. He's there now, preparing to launch his next recruiting campaign tomorrow, so we have to move quickly."

"Jeshi Samaki?" The workings of Omar's mind showed in his expression. "Aren't they mixed up somehow with that big Asian mob they call Singsong Gundy?"

"Saengseon Gundae," Faris corrected "We're not sure how they're affiliated, or even if they are. But they share many characteristics. The Asian group is gaining in numbers, but their impact so far has been more positive than anything. Though HQ Asia is monitoring them closely, they've chosen to not interfere at present.

"But that's in Asia. What we have here with the Jeshi is a different matter entirely. They infiltrate businesses, schools, neighborhoods, and places of worship and sow the seeds of anarchy wherever they go. HQ Central East wants them weeded out."

Faris's hand felt like ice as he brought up more images of the fortress. "Until we get the data about their security systems, we won't be able to map out the details. But in general, we'll Mini-Stealth in under cover of night, landing in this open area a half kilometer out. We'll move to the fortress, neutralize the defenses, apprehend the target and his family, and take him to the detention colony on Station Two. He knows the locations of every cell in northern Africa, and that's what we want him to tell us."

"His family, sir?" Safiy's brows lifted.

Faris swallowed. "That's right, Lieutenant. Our orders are to transport Dengel to the detention colony on Station Two for questioning and his family to the Multicultural Pleasure Center on Station Six."

He felt the men's disapproving stares. Or maybe the twinge came from his own disapproving conscience. Whatever the source, he stifled the pang. "It's hoped that once Dengel learns of the destination intended for his wife and daughters, he'll cooperate in order to spare them. If he does, it will save everyone a good bit of grief. But that's not our concern. We're not to speak to him or to his family. Just detain them as wards of the League, transfer them to whatever ship we're assigned, and keep them on ice until we get to Station Two. The Wardens will take it from there."

"We hear and obey," the others returned as one.

"Once I get the pertinent intel about the fortress security, you'll be briefed. Dismissed."

"Sir!" They saluted and filed out without a look of reproach. The task of accusation was left to the image of Philip Dengel staring down from the screen.

Philip Dengel, the man who, just over a year ago, had introduced Faris to the Eternal Light.

4

TRYING not to stare, Adam watched the visitors with fascination. Photos and video calls hadn't prepared him for the sight and sound of a group of Karkar in the flesh.

It must have been a wonderful experience for Lileela to live among these people. It must also have been deafening. Abba had taught Adam a few words in his native tongue, but he hadn't warned him that, when spoken in ordinary conversation, the language defined cacophony. The unique facial musculature of the Karkar limited their ability to form the subtle nuances of sound required for other languages. Their language added variety to the syllables with anything-but-subtle growls, hisses, clicks and shrieks.

Now, as they assembled around the long, oval dining table in the toqeph's suite, the visitors connected their translators. They could understand Standard speech, but since they weren't able to pronounce it, they relied on technology to communicate with non-Karkar speakers.

The Outsiders' food waited on serving carts smelling like vials of chemicals. The aroma of the Gannahan food wafting from the kitchen was more to Adam's liking.

Earlier, Emma had worried how to deal with their guests. A search of the records to see how her forefathers handled similar situations revealed no precedent. A Gannahan toqeph had never entertained alien dignitaries of any sort, at any time, in any circumstance.

"I guess we'll treat them like anyone else," Emma decided. Abba agreed, making suggestions for how best to make them comfortable.

According to Karkar protocol, the transport personnel were of too low a social level to be included, so the Ruling Council entertained the pilot and crew elsewhere. Here in the toqeph's dining room, Abba addressed the remaining eight guests.

"Welcome to my home." Abba spoke in the Standard tongue, extending his hands and bowing slightly in traditional Gannahan hospitality. "It is our pleasure to share our midday meal with you. Or at least, share your company, as you've wisely provided your own meal."

Ears lifted in smiles as the guests acknowledged the welcome.

"Gannahan tradition seats diners in order of age rather than status. Since I don't know all your birthdates, I must ask you to arrange yourselves." Abba placed his hands on the back of a chair. "Eldest will go here, then in this direction around the table, so the youngest—that would be you, Lileela—will sit beside the eldest."

After some questioning glances amongst themselves, everyone found a place. Groaning and choking with good-natured Karkar chuckles, everyone found a place that was, if perhaps not entirely honest, at least agreeable to all concerned.

Noting that the toqeph remained standing behind her chair, the visitors did the same. From their questioning ear movements, it was apparent they wondered why they'd been asked to choose seats if they weren't going to sit in them.

Without explanation, Emma lifted her hands and head, closed her eyes, and began to sing the afternoon blessing.

Abba and Adam joined her, but Adam couldn't resist sneaking a peek at the others around the table. Their faces, of course, were expressionless, but their ears twitched, showing their discomfort at the scene. According to the signals his meah picked up from Lileela beside him, her feelings ran more toward embarrassment.

Did Emma sing all seven verses out of gratitude for her daughter's return, or a desire to irritate the Karkar? Whatever her purpose, the guests were left standing until the last note was sung.

Finally Emma lowered her hands. "Thank you for your patience, ladies and gentlemen. It is our tradition to thank our Creator for His abundance before we partake of it. Which we may now do, if you'll be seated."

As they pulled back their chairs, Emma smiled at Lileela further down the table. "And we truly have much to be thankful for today."

It was obvious Lileela didn't share their mother's enthusiasm, and Adam couldn't figure out why. He looked forward to the opportunity to get her alone to talk. They had much to catch up on. And why was she blocking him from her meah? They'd been so close when they were kids.

But there were too many other things to think about for him to dwell on those questions.

Abba poured Gannahan blend into goblets for the family. Not everyday blend, but some of the best from the old toqeph's collection. While he did that, servers poured filtered water into the guests' glasses and set before them small dishes of the appetizers they'd brought. The stuff was a pale, translucent yellow, and oozily gelatinous.

The Gannahan meal began with a mixed platter of summer fruits, some of which had been brought all the way from Ayin. Lileela refused the fruit, asking for the slimy appetizer instead.

Watching a Karkar eat was enlightening. Adam always considered his father a typical example of the race, but now he could see Abba was exceptional. He not only pronounced the Standard tongue far more clearly, and occasionally even smiled, but he also had less difficulty eating.

Not that the guests considered themselves handicapped. They seemed quite comfortable sucking their food through their oddly curved spoons. They probably thought the Gannahans undignified for opening their mouths wide and taking whole bites, then chewing. Lileela's meah reflected disgust at the sight and sounds the Gannahans made. When Adam reminded her mentally that this was the way most humans ate, she turned and gave him a withering look as she dabbed her lips daintily with a napkin.

Course followed course. The Gannahan food was fresh, whole and delectable, and Lileela refused it all, opting for the soft Karkar fare. How could she live on that stuff?

Not very well, from the look of her. She was small even by Gannahan standards and had an unhealthy appearance. Though darker than any Karkar, her complexion was sallow, an effect accentuated by the film of cosmetics coating her face.

Hard to believe Abba used to wear make-up too. Adam had seen photos from the old days and thought them laughable, but every Karkar around the table, man and woman alike, wore cosmetics.

Naturally powder-pale, their faces were made smooth and glittery by the application of a substance tinted to coordinate with the colors of their clothing. Their lips were slashes of purple or red outlined in contrasting shades. The thin black lines rimming their eyes extended out from the corners in elaborate designs that covered their temples, and the irises were embellished with decorative contact lenses.

The men wore neither beard, mustache, nor sideburns. And their hair—all the men were blond, but the women apparently dyed theirs, for each sported a different unnatural color—was short and sculpted.

They ate slowly and with great dignity, reserving most of their conversation for the lull between courses. Kughurrrro, the eldest of them— or at least, the one who sat on the other side of Lileela, though Adam suspected Neen, the woman with the pink and lavender hair, was older— commented on the palace's architecture. "When we first arrived, I thought the only building in town was the airport terminal, and the rest of you lived underground like rodents. Your residence has quite a unique design."

Emma nodded. "The Old Gannahans liked to make as little impact on the environment as possible."

"But it's lovely nevertheless." Neen gazed around the room. "I wouldn't have thought so, seeing it from the outside. I expected it to look like a musty old cave."

Aunt Skiskii waved her arm, drawing a circle. "I'm intrigued with the shape of the rooms. Did your architects not understand the concept of straight lines and right angles?"

Abba poured himself another glass of blend. "Squares were considered ugly and unnatural. Gannahan architecture employs circles, ovals and arcs both inside and out."

"How quaint."

More small talk followed, during which the visitors demonstrated unabashed ignorance of everything Gannahan. Some of the guests, having spent their entire existence on a planet whose atmosphere was so poisonous that food came from factories or high-rise hydrofarms, didn't even understand the basics of weather. They seemed to think it remained unchanged year round and expressed amazement that water sometimes fell from the sky.

The ears of the woman beside Aunt Skiskii lifted with amusement. "Well, of course. Haven't you ever heard of rain?"

The youngest official's ears stiffened. "I thought that was a myth, like snow."

Just when Adam thought their foolishness had reached its zenith, the finance minister named Zidz, whose contact lenses made his eyes look like stars, addressed Abba.

"I confess surprise, Dr. Pik. Other than your slovenly appearance and bestial table manners, your condition seems to be under control."

Adam stopped eating to stare at the man.

Abba set down the slice of roasted powlroot he'd been about to bite. "My condition?"

"Your mental illness, of course." Sakakkak, the official wearing the glittery blue face powder, answered for him. "I've been thinking the same thing myself. You almost seem to be in your right mind."

Lileela's and Emma's meahs sent out shock waves, and the servers paused, wide-eyed, as if frozen in place. But the Karkar guests seemed oblivious to the impropriety of the comments.

Hglk, the youngest official, nodded at Abba. "It's gratifying to see you so functional." Her eyeliner extended to her hairline in dizzying geometric patterns. "Though it's still a shame. You wouldn't consider coming back with us, would you, for treatment? I hear they're doing some interesting brain experiments at the research center you founded years ago, before you lost your faculties. They might like to use you as a test subject."

"Do you think?" Zidz wiggled his ears thoughtfully. "I expect the poor fellow would be too far gone by now, having lived under the unhealthful influences of this savage place for so long. They'd have to do a lengthy detox—"

Emma burst out laughing, and everyone—Gannahan and Karkar—turned and stared.

She seemed to try to control herself, but failed. Stifling giggles, the servers left the room in a hurry. When Adam exchanged glances with Abba, they both laughed.

Lileela's face puckered with tears.

"By the Jewels, it's worse than we thought." The woman with the geometric temples shook her head.

Zidz's starry eyes widened. "You don't suppose it's contagious, do you?"

"I'll bet that's why they warned us about drinking the water." Pink Hair's eyes widened.

Adam couldn't stop laughing. His mother buried her face in her napkin, and Abba's guffaws sounded like a series of small explosions.

The visitors stared from one to the other, ears sagging in speechless confusion. When Lileela rose to flee, Emma waved her hand and motioned for her to sit.

Lileela paused as if trying to decide whether or not to obey, until Emma brought herself under control enough to speak. "You have not been excused. Don't be rude to our guests." Then she sputtered into a new peal of laughter.

Skiskii reached over and, putting a bejeweled hand on Abba's arm, spoke his full name. "Pikpeeeekpiktootakpikkakazghaghanmattsson. Why is your wife in distress? And what is this awful noise you're all making?"

"Don't you see, auntie?" Lileela burst out, sobbing. "She's laughing. They're all laughing. At all of *you!*"

Emma wiped her eyes. "Yes. It's true, I was laughing. And I apologize." She took a deep breath. "But your words required a response of some sort, and I chose to laugh rather than take offense."

Taking a cue from the toqeph, Adam brought his mirth under control, and Abba's eruptions ceased as well.

Zidz's ears frowned. "Offense? Whatever for?"

"Put yourself in my place." Emma picked a seed from between her teeth. "If I were a guest at your table and accused your wife of being insane, wouldn't you be offended?"

"Not at all." Zidz's ears swiveled in a Karkar shrug.

"His wife *is* insane," said Kughurrrro.

Adam almost laughed again but caught himself.

Zidz was unfazed. "She's presently residing in the Mental Wellness Dome. But I see your point. If my wife *were* of a sound mind, I doubt I'd appreciate your suggesting otherwise." He cast a glance at Abba.

"And why would you think my husband is not?" The edge to Emma's voice made Adam uncomfortable.

The visitors glanced at one another a moment before Skiskii answered. "Because he's here, of course. No Karkar in his right mind would move to Gannah."

Emma nodded. "Of course not. Nor marry a Gannahan."

"Obviously," said Sakakkak.

Pink-and-Lavender tipped her head in a Karkar nod. "That goes without saying."

"When he first left the planet and went to Earth," Skiskii said, "the family didn't think too much of it. It was bizarre behavior to be sure, but, after all, his father was an Earther, so it almost made sense."

Kughurrrro leaned forward, speaking earnestly. "But then, years later, when he came back with the Kankakar Jewels—the Kankakar Jewels!—you have no idea what that meant to us as a people. They were the symbol of our identity, of our achievements, of our worth. Taken from us by the filthy horde that defiled— Well, anyway, when Dr. Pik went to Gannah and rescued them after they'd been gloated over as trophies by the invaders for centuries—"

Adam watched Emma's face, fearing her response to that gross misrepresentation. But she didn't bat an eye. Just let the man continue.

"When he brought our Jewels back after they'd been on Gannah for eight hundred years, why, he was a hero. The richest, most powerful man on the planet."

Emma gazed at Abba, a smile playing at her lips. "And then, when he threw it all away and ran off with me, you figured he'd cracked."

All sixteen Karkar ears lifted in smiles. "Yes," several of them said together.

"So you *do* understand." Zidz's ears wiggled with pleasure.

Emma smiled back. "Of course. How silly of me to not see it sooner." She turned to Abba. "I hadn't thought about it before, but they might be right. *Are* you insane?"

"If I am, I'm incurable. Perhaps I'd better stay on Gannah where I won't do my fellow-Karkar any harm."

"Do you think you contracted the illness when you first visited this awful place?" Skiskii's voice was full of concern.

Abba's ears stiffened thoughtfully. "It's possible. I did drink the water."

5

Flashing his friendliest smile, Broward gazed up at the visitors assembled in the airport lobby. "Welcome to Gannah. I'm Edwin Broward, member of Gannah's Ruling Council and retired starship captain for the League of Planets. And this is my wife, Marianna."

The towering row of expressionless faces staring down at him unnerved Broward a little.

Having known Pik for decades, he thought himself familiar with the Karkar. But Pik was only half-Karkar and had lived much of his adult life off the planet. These were the real deal, and Broward wasn't sure what to make of them.

"The toqeph has asked us to be your guides. With my background in space travel, and you being the transport crew, I seemed the logical choice for the job."

They each took out translators and put them in position. Apparently they planned to speak.

Marianna smiled, and Broward's tension eased a little. If anyone could charm them, she could.

She spoke pleasantly. "As you know, our people are preparing to serve you a meal in the airport lounge. We'll give them a few minutes to bring the food from your ship. While they're getting set up, do you have any questions?"

The pilot squawked something, then made some adjustments in his translator and tried again. "How safe is it here? Should we be armed?"

Broward and Marianna exchanged puzzled glances. "I'm afraid I don't understand. You're perfectly safe here."

One of the Karkar women asked, "The criminals aren't dangerous?"

Marianne's brows rose. "What criminals?"

"New Gannah is a penal colony, isn't it?" said the pilot. "Weren't the settlers expelled from Earth for political crimes?"

Another woman cocked her head. "That's what I heard too."

Broward tried not to look as surprised as he felt. "I'm afraid you've been misinformed. We're here because we chose to come. Each of us had our own reason, but none of us have ever been incarcerated."

The pilot made a gesture with his head, something between a nod and a nervous tic. "Our apologies. No doubt a misunderstanding on our part."

"No need to apologize." Broward exuded conciliation. "We know there's been tension between your people and Gannah for centuries. That's one reason we've invited you to visit with us for a few days. Since Pik, our founding father, so to speak, is a Karkar by birth, we hope to put old animosities aside and allow our two planets to enjoy friendly relations."

The pilot's ears tilted backward. "So you do not accept our apology?"

Broward's heart rate quickened. "Of course I accept it. I only meant that your misunderstanding didn't offend us, so no apology was necessary." He used to have a gift for keeping interplanetary relations moving along smoothly. Were these people that difficult, or was he losing his edge? "But your question is valid. When visiting an alien culture, it's wise to proceed with caution. If it will help put things into perspective, permit me to ask: are you familiar with Earthers and their ways?"

The visitors tipped their heads and made some sort of a noise that he interpreted as an affirmative, though the translators produced only static.

"It might help you to realize, then, that for the most part, the New Gannahans are Earthers by race and birth. The children were born here, but their parents are Terrestrials. The only exceptions, as you know, are the toqeph and Pik. The toqeph and her children are the only settlers of native Gannahan blood."

One of the crewmembers asked, "How many of those mongrel savages did she spawn?"

Marianna gasped, but Broward swallowed his anger and kept his voice calm. "You've met Lileela, of course. Is she a savage?"

"She is a most unique individual." The pilot gazed down at Broward. "Surprisingly intelligent for one who's only one-quarter Karkar. But she's had the rare privilege of spending her formative years in a civilized culture. Our concern—and I think I speak for all of us—" His translator faded in and out, and he paused a moment to adjust it. "I think I speak for all of us when I say our concern is primarily about those growing up without proper training. Not only the aberrant native Gannahan progeny of your toqeph—"

Marianna's face flushed, and Broward laid what he hoped was a gentling hand on her arm.

"—but also the youth of Terrestrial descent who are being raised in this unhealthful environment. Will they and their offspring eventually become true Gannahans and endanger the peace and safety of the galaxy?"

Marianna, though not one to keep her thoughts to herself, was apparently speechless with fury. Broward took the opportunity to answer. "I can see you're concerned, and for good reason. Your planet once suffered greatly at Gannah's hand, and that has understandably colored your thinking. But, ladies and gentlemen, when was the last time Gannah was a danger to the galaxy?"

He gave them a moment to think, then answered for them. "No warship from this planet has flown for almost nine hundred years. And the only overtures Gannah has made toward the rest of the planets in all that time have been peaceful ones."

The visitors' ears tipped back and they all began speaking at once. The din was alarming, especially with the translators functioning erratically.

Broward heard something about a wanton slaughter decades ago at the Galaxy Games, but that was all he could make out. He raised his hands. "Ladies and gentlemen, please. If you're referring to the incident some years back where a Eutarian athlete was killed in a bar fight during the Games, let me say this: that was one incident between one Eutarian and a lone Gannahan. It was hardly a slaughter, nor did the Gannahan government condone it. In fact, if I recall, the entire Gannahan team withdrew and returned home in order to avoid further disruption to the Games."

"What did they do to the murderer?" One of the crewmen squawked. "Pin a medal on him?"

Marianna found her tongue. "As a matter of fact, no. According to the historical record, the athlete was brought home in shame and subsequently executed by the toqeph."

That shut them up.

"But not for murder," she added. "A Gannahan is permitted to kill to defend himself, which is what that man did. He was executed for drinking alcohol, which has always been a capital offense on this planet. I trust none of you smuggled in any beer?"

Broward clenched his jaw against a smile as the visitors glanced back and forth, their ears twitching nervously. "If so, you may flush it away in the restrooms and dispose of the containers in the proper receptacles."

Their eyes darted around the terminal as if they sought out the restrooms. One of the settlers gestured from across the room, and Marianna nodded her acknowledgement, then turned to the guests. "But now, your meal is ready. So if you'd like to freshen up, we'll meet back here in ten minutes and take you to the lounge. After lunch, we'll begin our tour. Lavatory facilities are directly behind you and around the corner. They're marked with the universal symbols, so you should have no difficulty finding them."

The guests turned and headed the direction she indicated. Broward took Marianna by the hand and led her to an upholstered bench. "Nicely done, Mrs. Broward."

"Thank you, captain. We make a good team."

"We do indeed." He kissed her. "This tour is going to be interesting."

JAX muttered under his breath. What was with this guy?

Kughurrrro, the Karkar geologist, inspected the ore as it was loaded into the transport. Every minute and a half, or so it seemed, he'd halt the process in order to take another sample. It was hot and putrid in the underbelly of the ship, and Jax was in a hurry to get out into the fresh air.

After Kughurrrro stopped the conveyor for the eighth time, Jax approached him as he bent over the ore. "You'll find it's all the same. Five tonnes of our purest zahab. All high grade stuff."

The giant tipped his head to the left and removed his monocle. "It is of excellent quality."

Or at least, that's what it sounded like. Jax couldn't be sure, because his translation device wasn't working.

"You're saying you're satisfied?"

The geologist's head bobbed and he made a sound something like, "Jshsss." Then he stood upright, ears stiffening. "Waaa tisdat saaaaahnd?" The last word, whatever it was, rose to a high, ear-ringing pitch.

Wiping sweat from his forehead with a grimy hand, Jax paused, trying to translate. "Oh, 'what is that sound?'"

The head bobbed again. "Jshsss."

"That rumbling? It's thunder. I've been hearing it for a while, but it's getting closer."

The ears made some sort of movement, and the big man stood straighter. "Tun dur?" The syllables that followed were unintelligible and heartfelt.

"Yes, thunder. And probably whatever else you said, I'm not sure. It's just an ordinary summer storm." Jax remembered the Karkar cities were all under domes. "Ever see one before?"

The geologist's head cocked to the right and his ears stiffened. "Nuh."

"Would you like to watch it? I love a good storm. They're exhilarating."

With surprising energy for a man his size and age, Kughurrrro strode toward the exit exclaiming something loud and incomprehensible.

Jax trotted with him and looked out when they reached the loading dock doors. "It's just arriving. We've got time to run to the terminal and watch it through the windows, where we'll get a better view than we would from here. You game?"

The big guy's head bobbed eagerly.

"Then let's go!"

The wind tried to blow them away as they raced an oncoming wall of rain across the tarmac toward the terminal. When another thunderclap shivered the air, Kughurrrro let out a blood-curdling whoop. The rain outpaced them, smattering them with big, warm drops as they scooted into the terminal. By the time they'd turned around to face the windows, water streamed down the glass in giddy furrows.

The geologist's ears lifted in what must have been glee as he stared, wide-eyed, at the scene. Like a weird monster child, he gasped and pointed at the lightning, clapped with the thunder, and pressed his face against the glass as if hoping to feel the rain through it.

Jax laughed. "You like a good storm too, I see."

"Loffit. Loooofffit."

Jax kept his distance for fear of being knocked over by his companion's long-limbed exuberance.

When the most violent wind and lightning had passed but the rain still poured, Kughurrrro moved to the door, hesitated a moment, then went outside to stand in the torrent.

Head bowed against the onslaught, he watched the rain fill the broad hollow of his cupped hands. He lifted his head, its careful coif now carelessly flattened, to the sky. He said something Jax couldn't understand, then erupted in guttural laughter.

When the rain tapered off to a misty sprinkle, Jax ventured onto the glistening pavement. He stood beside the dripping Karkar, who inhaled deeply. "Snells gud. Snells… lack no-tink ah edda snell dafforr."

"It does smell good, doesn't it?" Jax took in the scent of hot pavement breathing in relief, the thirsty ground soaking up the life-giving water, and the rain-washed air. "I suppose it's true, you've never smelled anything like it before. You must miss a lot, living indoors all the time."

The sun broke through the last of the dark clouds, and Kughurrrro pointed, nearly jumping up and down with excitement. "Trissn! Uh dig trissn!"

That made no sense to Jax at first, but then he understood. "A prism? Yeah, I guess you could say that. But it's not a big prism, it's a whole lot of little ones, a trillion water particles suspended in the air. The sun's light refracts through them, breaks down into the whole spectrum, and spreads across the sky. Pretty awesome stuff, huh?"

Kughurrrro stared. Ears stiff, he lifted both huge palms and made a long, slow arc in the air, as if tracing the rainbow's course, and murmuring something that might have been, "Such beauty. Such amazing beauty." After several minutes of silent delight, he turned and looked down at Jax. His wonder-struck eyes stared from a mess of melted cosmetics. "Jshou see sotch tinks heerrr effey day?"

Jax smiled. "Yes, sir. We see such things here every day. Maybe not rainbows every day, but wonders are all around us. Gannah's the most beautiful place in the galaxy."

Kughurrrro turned and reached toward the rainbow, now fading. He took a step closer. "Ah! It goes! Ah jhood haff taakn a pic-churrr."

"If you don't get another chance before you leave, I'll make sure you get a picture of a rainbow to take with you. But no photo can do it justice."

The Karkar's head tilted left. "Jshsss. Ah haff sin pic-churrrs dafforr..."

"And they're nothing to compare with the real thing," Jax finished for him.

They watched together as the rainbow faded into the pale blue sky. Then Jax noticed the big man was shivering. "You're soaked. Do you want to change your clothes?"

Kughurrrro's head tipped right and said something that sounded a like, "No, I will wear the rain." He took one more deep breath of the sweet air. "Ah!" Then he headed on long legs toward the transport.

Jax followed. "Back to work, then?"

"Jshsss. Dack to duuurk. Till notch tu dee hex-hananned."

Jax scratched his head, trying to translate. "Oh," he said under his breath. "'Still much to be examined.'"

At the rate the big guy worked, the inspection would take the whole three days. But that prospect no longer seemed quite so unpleasant.

6

*L*ILEELA sat beside Aunt Skiskii on an ample couch. She remembered the sitting room as being cavernous. But after living on Karkar, things around here seemed miniature, except for Abba's special-made furniture.

And except the vast, frightening outdoors. Hard to believe she used to enjoy the open air. Harder yet to believe that, as a five-year-old, she'd run off into that immensity alone and injured herself in a sledding accident. She remembered lying cold and helpless in the snow, staring at the unending sky above. The thought sent a shiver through her.

She studied the little dark-haired girl leaning against Emma in a chair opposite. The child watched Lileela with equal interest through brilliant green eyes.

"Ra'anan." Emma bent and spoke to the child. "This is your Aunt Skiskii and your sister, Lileela. They've come all the way from Karkar to see us."

Holding onto Emma's arm with both hands, the little girl gazed up at her mother. "Abba is from Karkar. That's why he has six fingers."

Emma smiled. "That's right. Your Aunt Skiskii has lived her whole life on Karkar and has never been to Gannah before. Aren't you happy she was able to come to visit and bring your sister back to us?"

Ra'anan didn't answer. She just stared back and forth between Auntie and Lileela.

As far as Lileela was concerned, she didn't need to speak. Without exchanging a word, she knew the child was enthralled with the visitors and loved her big sister at first sight.

That was good. Being the object of idol worship could be used to advantage.

"Come up here with us." Lileela patted the couch. The child grinned and scampered over. After climbing up between Lileela and Skiskii, she sat and kicked her feet, looking first at one and then the other.

Skiskii stared down at her. "She's very small, isn't she?" She spoke Karkar because her Standard language pronunciation was incomprehensible. "And even funnier to look at than you are. Such a shame to taint good Karkar breeding with all that foreign blood. First Terrestrial and now this. I'm glad Pik's mother didn't live to see it."

Speaking to Ra'anan, Lileela translated. "She says you look just like me. And that we look more like Emma than we do Abba."

She felt Emma's eyes boring into her. Her translation wasn't really a lie. And how would Emma know anyway?

Ra'anan giggled. "I don't think you look like Emma at all. Your eyes do, but just the insides. Outside, they have all that stuff drawn around them." She got up on her knees and leaned toward Lileela, extending a broken-nailed finger toward her face. "Does that dark stuff come off?"

Recoiling from her touch, Lileela grabbed Ra'anan's exploring hand. "Yes, I wash it off at night and reapply it in the morning."

"People on Karkar like the look," Emma said. "They find us strange because we don't wear cosmetics."

Ra'anan turned to Skiskii. "Your curlicues are pretty. Could you give me some like that?"

Auntie's ears lifted. "Why, thank you, child. I suppose—"

Emma interrupted. "Aunt Skiskii's adornments are very artistic, aren't they? But they're a little fancy for an eight-year-old."

The sound of someone pressing the door opener distracted Lileela's attention. Emma turned too. "Oh, look, Ra'anan, would you like to introduce your sister to the rest of the family?"

Ra'anan slid off the couch. She made a little bow to Skiskii, then followed Emma, who had risen to greet a stout, gray-haired woman entering with three more children.

The woman seemed familiar, but Lileela couldn't place her.

"Sylvia," Emma said, "you remember Lileela?"

That's it. Sylvia Dmitry. She'd sometimes taken care of Adam and Lileela when Emma was busy running the planet.

Lileela rose from the couch, straightening slowly. Moving with deliberation to hide her clumsiness, she imitated Ra'anan's bow. "Mrs. Dmitry. I remember you."

"And I certainly remember you." The woman passed the children to Emma, then turned to Lileela, her eyes filling. "We're so glad you're home! And even more glad to see you healed. Oh, what a time. We were afraid you'd never walk again." She embraced Lileela, then stepped back to take a closer look, shaking her head. "I never would have known you, you've grown so. And walking on your own two feet! Thank the Yasha!"

"Thank the Karkar Neurological Commission." Lileela turned to Auntie, who remained seated. "This is my father's cousin, Skiskii. I've been living with her since Abba Lars died."

Auntie tipped her head and lifted a hand. Looking uncertain, Sylvia approached and pressed fingertips with her, though Skiskii's sixth finger had nothing to connect with. "I am happy to meet you."

Skiskii spoke to Lileela. "Pudgy little thing, isn't she? Tell her it's a pleasure."

Lileela nodded. "She says she's happy to meet you too." Turning to Emma, she retained her smile, but her stomach felt queasy. Her mother had borne all these children while she was gone? She'd never felt so irrelevant.

Emma turned to Sylvia. "We hope you'll stay and visit."

"Thanks, I'd like that." Sylvia took a seat on the couch, and Lileela sat beside her. Sylvia gave her another hug. "I'm so glad you're home!"

Emma gestured to a moppet half-hiding behind her. "Meet your brother, Hushai. He's five. And"—she bounced the toddler on her hip—"your sister Tamah. And this"—she put her hand on the head of a boy clinging to Ra'anan's hand—"is Ittai. Tamah here is almost two, and Ittai is three."

Emma sat with Tamah in her lap and, with Ra'anan's help, herded the boys in front of her. "Children, this is your sister Lileela. She's been away since before you were born, but she's home to stay now. Isn't that wonderful?"

Wonderful. Why did they bother bringing her home, if they had all these others? Such wanton procreation was disgusting.

From the way Skiskii's ears jerked, she didn't approve either. Lileela got the impression she viewed the children as vermin.

"They are—" Lileela paused. What Emma would want her to say? "They're—" She couldn't think of a proper response, so she went with honesty. "There are so many of them!"

Emma chuckled. "We are abundantly blessed, to be sure. But I hope you're not worried that I'll expect you to care for them all the time. You'll have responsibilities, of course, because everyone does. But we brought you home because this is where you belong, not to use you as a babysitter."

Studying the stair-step array of curly, dark heads, Lileela wondered about the feasibility of stowing away when the transport departed in three days. Could she hide in the cargo hold? No, there were no atmospheric controls in there. If she survived the violence of the thrust, she'd freeze and/or suffocate once out of the atmosphere.

But that certain death might be preferable to the tragic life she saw spreading before her.

Skiskii's squawk drew her out of her daze. "Where is the sire of this litter? I'd hoped to see more of my cousin while I'm here."

Lileela told her mother, "Skiskii asks where Abba is." She turned to her aunt, who could understand the Standard tongue even though she couldn't speak it. "But Auntie, he had to go with the financial officers to complete the negotiations. He told us he'd be busy for a while."

"Why can't the toqeph do that? Isn't she the one in charge around here?"

Lileela opened her mouth, but Emma spoke before she could translate. Did she know what Skiskii had said, or would she have explained anyway? "Due to cultural as well as language issues, it seemed best for Pik to deal with the officials. Once all the documents are finalized, I'll sign them."

Skiskii's ears frowned. "I thought everything had already been arranged."

Lileela translated, and Emma answered. "For the most part, it is. The officials need to inspect the material we're submitting as payment and agree that it's sufficient."

"Speaking of the language issue," Skiskii said, "is there something we can do about these translation devices? Why are they all going on the blink?" She tapped the useless device, which she still wore like a gaudy necklace.

Again, Emma either understood or guessed the question and answered immediately. "Electronic devices brought in from off-planet seldom work on Gannah. One of our best technical minds is looking for a solution, and we hope to be able to get them functioning soon. In the meantime, we have two Karkar speakers who can translate." She nodded at Lileela.

Joy. They were putting her to work already.

"If we can't get the gadgets working, we'll probably issue tablets to each of you visitors so you can communicate through writing."

Overcoming their shyness, the little ones came near. It made Lileela nervous, and she rose. "Aunt Skiskii, would you like a tour of Gullach?"

Emma stood too, holding Tamah. "That's a good idea. You'll be interested in the changes since you were here last, Lileela. Besides making renovations to the palace, we've moved several families to the first chatsr at Qatsiyr now, so you'll want to see the town as well." She waved the other children toward her. "Come along, let's go for a walk."

Skiskii's ears sagged with a question. "Sjhaat-zhurr?"

Lileela explained. "A chatsr is a neighborhood."

"Yes, sort of," said Emma. "In ancient times, every village was built in a circle or oval, with a courtyard in the center and a wall surrounding the entire thing. This was for protection against attack by animals, not people. Unlike other planets, Gannah's past is not marred by human wars."

She and Sylvia herded the nursery crew out of the apartment, Lileela and Skiskii following, while Emma continued. "As a community grew, new chatsrs were added. Large cities have many, small villages have just one or two.

"Qatsiyr is the city nearest the palace. Before the Plague, it had twenty-some chatsrs, and we're in the process of revitalizing the central one. You might call it the downtown neighborhood. A dozen families live there now, and they're busy developing a variety of businesses to serve the New Gannah."

Despite herself, Lileela's interest stirred. In her first five years, she'd never been anywhere but the palace of Gullach and its immediate environs. She'd never seen a chatsr except in pictures. But she remembered photos, drawings and films of Old Gannahans going about their daily lives in those lovely little communities. Filled with trees and gardens and courtyards, every chatsr was unique, reflecting the purpose and personality of the community, unlike the sterile, angular uniformity of the domed cities of Karkar. The chatsrs reminded Lileela of many diverse cells making up the living organism of Old Gannah.

The thought that those dead cells were being brought back to life intrigued her.

But she hoped to be a million light years away when it happened.

7

*T*HE Ministealth slipped through the rainy night as silent and unseen as a black cat.

Faris unfastened his restraints as soon as the purring little craft settled onto the wet Ethiopian ground. At his word the men rose, gathered their equipment, and exited the plane.

Sensors revealed no watchers on the scene, neither electronic nor human. But with their cloaking camo rendering them invisible and the steady rain muffling sound, only the most fine-tuned surveillance could have detected them.

Leaving Esam to guard the Mini, Faris led the other six men through the dark savanna, guided by the GPS read-out in his night-vision goggles. A few minutes after disembarking the aircraft, they took up positions at the fortress.

Faris murmured a reminder into his mike. "Nonlethal only."

They nodded silent *aye, sirs* and moved forward at his signal.

The restriction against use of lethal force was the only thing about this mission that wasn't routine, and it was Faris's stipulation, not Abdul-Malik's. But as commander of this team, he had the freedom to make the rules, provided the mission was accomplished.

He'd anticipated little resistance and got even less. The outdated security systems weren't fully functional. The dozing gatekeepers, taken by surprise, wilted within seconds of being shot with seda-darts.

The informant's directions led the team straight to the targets' unguarded sleeping quarters, where it took them no time to dart the subjects, bind them, and carry them out. Dengel was a big man, and it took two to carry him. The woman and two girls were no burden for three men to each carry one over his shoulder.

A mere half-hour after landing, Esam lifted the Ministealth off the soggy plain and flew out on silent wings.

Safiy removed his goggles and headgear, shaking off the rain. "That was too easy, amir."

Binyamin peered at the monitor as if expecting pursuit. "I've seen better security at the movie theater."

"With that sorry excuse for protection, I can't believe Dengel's never been apprehended before." Ishaq smoothed his hair. "Didn't you say he's been hiding for a couple of years?"

Faris nodded. "That's what they tell me."

"It is the will of Allah," said Omar bin Ibrahim.

"What, that he wasn't caught before?" Faris glanced toward the back of the plane, but couldn't see the prisoners from where he sat. "Or that we were able to pick him up so easily now?"

"Both, sir." Omar wiped the splotches off his goggles with a handkerchief. "Everything that happens is the will of Allah. Why try to make sense out of it beyond that?"

Ya'qub snorted. "You Normals, conceived by chance and raised in the primitive family model. You're victims, you know that? Your minds are held prisoner by the old superstitions. It's a handicap the League was wise to breed out of us."

Faris would have been surprised if Ya'qub really meant that. Ever since he'd learned of the family concept, he'd been intrigued by it. He used to wonder if the lack of that fundamental human element was why he felt such a void in his soul.

"You don't know what you're saying." Omar shook his head. "My family makes me rich."

Binyamin leaned back in his seat. "Your pay rate sure doesn't."

They laughed. Faris joined in, but without mirth. The League took good care of him, and always had. But he was just a tool to them, valuable only because of the investment they'd made in him. He was an asset, not a beloved son.

The Ministealth's flight having leveled off, he unbuckled his safety restraints and rose. "Gonna check on the prisoners." He made his way to the back of the plane, where Dengel and his family lay like baggage.

None of them showed any signs of awakening, though each pulse was strong. Noticing the wife's restraints were digging into her flesh, he loosened them. Then he checked the others' to make sure their circulation wouldn't be cut off. Finally, he went back to Dengel. Resting his hand on his friend's neck as if checking the carotid, Faris closed his eyes.

He didn't dare pray aloud, but his men couldn't hear unspoken thoughts. "I cannot deliver this good man and his loved ones to the torturers. Father, what must I do?"

Ya'qub and Omar continued their discussion, and now Ishaq chimed in. "Let me get this straight. It's okay for you to practice your religion, but we arrest people like Dengel for doing the same?"

Omar sounded offended. "It is not the same. Islam is the true religion, and Dengel maligns the one true God. Of course he is a criminal."

Ya'qub's brows lifted. "So if I don't embrace your Allah, it's a crime? You saying I should be lying back there with our guests?"

Adil laughed. "I wouldn't mind lying back there with the female."

"Maybe you can, once she's delivered to the Pleasure Center." Safiy grinned. "If you can afford it."

"Allah would not approve of that." From Omar's tone, it was apparent he didn't either. "But League law does not require you to embrace the truth. It's only illegal to declare it a lie."

Faris rose and returned to his seat. "So that's the man's crime? Criticizing your Allah?"

"Not merely criticizing him." Omar's brow creased. "Leading people away from him, away from the truth. Teaching them to believe that the religion of their fathers is in error."

Faris cringed inwardly, yearning to speak up for the real Truth. But hearing such treason from their commander would put his men in a precarious situation.

"I don't get it." Binyamin leaned forward. "What difference does it make if you believe in Allah or Jesus or Buddha or whatever they get into on other planets? Isn't it all one and the same?"

Omar nodded. "Exactly. Allah is the one true God. To say otherwise is not only foolishness, but it threatens the peace of the League. The law is wise to forbid it."

"If that's the way those Jeshi Samaki people want to be," said Ya'qub, "they should find themselves another planet to live on where they won't bother anybody."

"Yeah." Ishaq plucked a wet piece of vegetation from his boot. "Like that Gannahan woman. They say she had rebel leanings, and that's what she did. Got together a bunch of followers and took them all back to Gannah to set up her own little kingdom."

Faris had only been half listening, but that caught his full attention. "I've heard that, too." It was Dengel who'd told him, but Faris didn't mention the source of his information. "That was more than twenty years ago. Anybody know what happened to them? Did they ever make it to Gannah?"

"Who cares?" Safiy shrugged. "Good riddance, I say. I never heard anything good about Gannah."

Piloting the plane, Esam interrupted them on their headphones. "We're approaching Addis Ababa."

"Acknowledged," said Faris. He turned to the men. "Seats, gentlemen, and buckle up. I'm not sure I trust Esam's landings."

"What're we doing at Addis Ababa, Commander?" asked Ishaq.

"Picking up our ride to Station 2. They're giving us a new little Photuris."

Binyamin whistled. "The ship that shrank the universe."

The other men echoed their approval. The Photuris's propulsion technology was so cutting-edge, it almost made one bleed.

The standard League vessels' systems facilitated travel along cosmic time/space channels. But now, by incorporating new Pyetronium technology into the hull of the craft as well as the engine system, the Photuris series was able to slide more smoothly along the channel. It could travel many light years in less time than a standard clock could measure.

Esam's voice came through the headphones. "Those are fast little suckers. I test-drove a prototype, did I ever tell you that?"

Binyamin fastened his restraints. "Only six or eight times."

"Per day," added Ya'qub.

Faris chuckled. "What's the range?"

He could hear the grin in Esam's voice. "That little baby'll take you as far as you want to go, sir. You thinking maybe we could highjack it and take it for a joyride?"

"I'll get back with you on that." Faris didn't dare pray aloud, but God heard his silent praises.

8

KUGHURRRRO took the bottle of Karlson's that Zidz handed him. Here on the transport vessel, they were legally on Karkar soil, where having a beer didn't make you a felon.

Despite Gannah's repressive laws, the evening's entertainment had been pleasurable. At intervals throughout the long, drawn-out meal, the settlers demonstrated an array of talents running the gamut from instrumental music and *a capella* singing to a poetry recitation accompanied by dance.

At first, the Karkar found it a little off-putting to carry on like that while dining, but the fun was infectious. Halfway through the evening, Kughurrrro's people stamped their feet and pounded the tables in approval along with the Gannahans. Uncouth custom though it was.

After the gaiety, Skiskii remained in the palace to spend the night with the family of that traitor, Pik. The rest of them would sleep here on foldout cots. It wasn't the most comfortable arrangement, but the surroundings were familiar and safe—and secure from prying ears.

"You're sure we're not being monitored?" Kughurrrro glanced around, looking for anything out of place.

"Positive, sir." The pilot, Klao, reviewed the information coming through his scanner, which—for the moment—functioned perfectly. "No bugs planted in here, and no long-range listening devices directed this way."

"Do they even *have* eavesdropping capabilities?" asked Neen, the finance minister with the lovely pink and lavender hair.

That wasn't all that was lovely about her. But, always the

professional, Kughurrrro would resist the temptation to dwell on her most desirable features. At least until they returned to the starship, where, as leader of this recon team, he enjoyed the privilege of a private cabin.

While the others laughed at her question, Kughurrrro enjoyed watching the muscles flex in her long, shapely throat. "They appear quite backward," he said, "but it's superficial. They're hiding something."

Sakakkak snacked on a slurp of salt xax. "I agree. We should not underestimate them."

Hglx, the young agent who, like Sakakkak, doubled as a League advisor, twitched his ears. "For a people whose forerunners were so violent, they don't seem very combative."

"I'm not so sure about that," said Liilo, who posed as a flight attendant. "The female they gave us for a tour guide has a feisty streak."

"And what's with that League starship captain?" Kaakaan snorted. "He's a sharp one, by all accounts. Besides multiple degrees from Milky League schools, he has a long and exemplary service record. He could retire in comfort on any planet or space station in the territory, so what's he doing here?"

Kughurrrro growled. "There are many questions, many things yet to be investigated. But some key points are abundantly clear. Gannah's resources are rich and untapped. The atmosphere and soil are unsullied, almost primordial. And if, as it appears, they have no military defenses, the New Gannah is ripe to become the New Karkar. It will be beautiful justice to take over the home of the people who plundered our own."

Klao tipped his head in assent. "Even if they had the means to repel an attack, they haven't the manpower. What did they say the population was, something like fifteen hundred on the whole planet, including children? More people than that live in my apartment building in Kinkakakinkadon."

"So must they all go?" Liilo dabbed a bit of beer foam from her mouth. "Skiskii and Ogliziizl are inordinately fond of that half-breed cousin of theirs."

"The Oglis are weasels." Zidz's starry eyes flashed. "Haven't so much as a jot of Karkar pride. The idea, taking in that five-fingered aberration and trying to turn it into a normal person. Pure foolishness."

Kughurrrro savored his mouthful before swallowing. "Who's spared and who's sacrificed is not our decision. We're here to gather intelligence, make our report, and leave the planning to others."

He allowed a discreet belch to escape. "I've persuaded that smiling Jax fellow to give me a tour of the mines. While we're out and about, I'll see what else I can get him to show me. That will take the next two days. While I'm gone, Klao, you and your flight crew will show an interest in the planet's technology. See if you can get in good with that techy who's working on the translator problem. Stroke his ego and let him boast about what he knows. The rest of you, examine as much of the palace and that sorry excuse for a village as you can. Try to gain access to the abandoned parts of the town, too. Who knows what they might have hidden away in those old buildings."

Sakkakak pulled out a second beer. "Too bad we don't have time for a thorough search. And that underground tunnel system. What I wouldn't give for a week to explore down there!"

Kughurrrro agreed. "Have any of you had an opportunity to do enviroscans?"

Hglx nodded, her ears tilting outward sadly. "Yes, but those gadgets work about as well as our translators."

Neen laughed. "Maybe if we ask nicely, the little idiots will be gullible enough to fix our surveillance equipment."

Kughurrrro's ears frowned. "These people are not idiots. They're up to something fiendishly clever, and doing a masterful job of masking it. Whatever their plot, I feel honored to play a role in putting a stop to it before it gets out of control." He lifted his bottle in a toast. "To Gannah's final and complete defeat."

"Blessed Kankakar," they shrieked in unison, "we shall avenge thee."

LILEELA stared at the page, but the words were incomprehensible. She backed up a page to refresh her memory, but she had no recollection of having read it, either.

She shut the book and laid it on the bed beside her in the halo of light that shone from above. A book, bound at the top. Not a sensible electronic reader, because sensible things didn't work in this forsaken place.

Leaning back, she closed her eyes while her mind and meah chased each other in dizzying circles. Her stomach churned with them.

What was she doing here?

She nourished a healthy Karkar aversion to everything Gannahan, and that was a good thing, right? It proved she was civilized.

But it was beginning to smack of self-hatred.

She loved Karkar. Loved her Ogli relatives, appreciated all they'd done for her. She was grateful for the efforts of Karkar's skilled neurological specialists to heal her body. She admired the gritty spirit of the Karkar people, their determination to maintain their dignity despite their hardships, and their creativity in surviving against all odds. Odds that were steeply tipped against them, thanks to the Gannahan invasion. But they survived, and prospered, and now enjoyed the richest, most cultured human society in the galaxy. What was not to love?

But she couldn't deny it: though her mind and heart were Karkar, she had Gannah in her blood.

And it was curdling.

At least, her stomach was. She tensed against a cramp. Why had she drunk that blend tonight?

Because it was delicious. And because sooner or later, she'd have to eat the food. She might as well ease into it now and get it over with. Emma assured her that if she started slowly, it would minimize the distress. Just have one glass today, another tomorrow, and the third day you should be over the hump. By the end of the week, you can eat and drink anything without a problem.

As if she'd have the appetite.

A faint suggestion of light filtered through the thin curtain that closed her off from the rest of the room.

Like everything else on the planet, Gannahan beds were barbaric. Resembling animal dens, they were recessed into the fabric-cushioned walls. They pulled out like drawers for changing the linens, which were stored underneath. When the bed was in place in its nook, a curtain covered the opening.

On the other side of the drapery, Skiskii's snores sawed the air. Her seven-foot frame wouldn't have fit into a bed nook, so they'd brought in a foldout couch and rigged an extension to accommodate her length. After going through the expected routine—grousing about the miserable accommodations and wondering if she wouldn't be better off in the transport with the others, then being reassured that Lileela needed her auntie with her—she'd settled down with the hand-held personal theater she'd brought down to the planet.

Which quit functioning after five or six minutes. No surprise there. It was just as well, though. The video was full of the typical anti-Gannahan humor, which tonight rubbed Lileela the wrong way.

It was a relief when Skiskii shut it off. Auntie seemed glad, too, as it gave her more to gripe about. But once she'd gotten that rant out of her system, she fell asleep in half a minute. The physical exertion of touring the palace and the village, not to mention the emotional stress of being on this alien planet, must have done her in.

Lileela was exhausted too. She felt drained. Of everything. Including sleep.

She shut off the overhead light, plumped her pillow, then lay on her side, trying to unwind.

Songs and sights from the evening's entertainment jostled one another in her mind. The show had been a numbing combination of familiarity and strangeness. Then, just when she thought she'd endured all she could, her fellow Karkar started banging on the tables and stomping their feet like the Gannahans.

She'd headed for the restroom as quickly as she could make her legs move. It wasn't just the foreign drink that upset her stomach.

How was she supposed to handle this? How could she be a Gannahan and a Karkar at the same time? Her brothers and sisters didn't seem to have a problem with it, but what did they know about being a Karkar?

To his credit, Adam was hungry to learn. He seemed drawn to the visitors, and he was certainly drawn to Lileela. She knew he wanted to spend time with her, to hear what she'd learned on their father's planet. But she was uncomfortable with him. The little boy she'd known was replaced by a stranger.

Just like everyone and everything else. The few memories she retained from her early childhood were proving to be twisted reflections of the present realities.

Except for Emma. Despite the years, and having borne four more children—four!—her figure was shapely, her black hair untouched by gray, her skin unmarred by wrinkles, her eyes bright and all-seeing. Her right arm didn't extend fully anymore, the only visible sign of the injuries she'd sustained in that shuttle crash that had turned Lileela's world inside-out and backward. Other than that, she was the same Emma who had left the planet surface to visit the League starship *Promontory* ten years ago. The last time Lileela had laid eyes on her until today.

Tears spilled onto the pillow. Never had she known such love as what she sensed pouring from Emma's broken meah. That was another thing that was different about her. Like eyes dimmed by cataracts or a mind dulled by drugs, Emma's meah had lost its clarity. But what remained pumped love into Gannah like a heart pumped blood.

Her joy at Lileela's return was evident and unfeigned. But it was wrapped in an inexplicable, multi-pronged grief. Was Emma happy to see her or not? And if not, why had she insisted she come back?

Even more perplexing, Adam's joy was mixed too. His meah being clearer, she could see that his sorrow had something to do with the ransom of precious ores and gemstones Gannah was paying Karkar. But why would Gannahans, who had no use for money, worry about a little thing like that?

Trying to figure it out made her head hurt.

Lileela sat up slowly, reaching to feel how much headroom she had. These beds seemed so much bigger when she was five. She opened the curtain.

There was no window, but dim light glowed from the baseboards. This illuminated the room enough to maneuver across it without bumping into things. But it also cast long shadows upward. They mingled in the gloom and turned the domed ceiling into a deep, black pool. Fear of what swam there used to keep little Lileela huddled in bed all night, safe behind the curtain, until Emma came in and opened it.

Until Emma came in no more.

Why had she gone up to that starship? Didn't she know Lileela needed her?

Skiskii's long bulk beneath the sheet stirred, coughed, and resumed its snoring.

Careful to not look up at the shadows, Lileela eased out of the bed. The hard floor felt cool on her feet as she lifted the robe from its hook and wrapped it around herself, then slid into the slippers that lay waiting. Karkar slippers. She never went barefoot on Karkar like she used to do here. Her feet were an embarrassment, having only five toes each.

She crossed the room, then eased through the door, shutting it softly behind her. After visiting the bathroom, which provided little relief for her all-over discomfort, she shuffled down the curved hall to the spiral stairs.

Steps were still a bit of a problem, but she could manage them. She simply didn't have much practice, since they had nothing so primitive on Karkar. At least these had a handrail. She smiled, remembering how she and Adam had raced up and down this steep, tight spiral until they were panting and dizzy.

Downstairs in the dark, the children slept, but as she climbed toward the light, she heard muffled voices.

That was another memory. Emma and Abba holding meetings of the Ruling Council in the dining room. As a child, it had seemed normal, ignorant as she was. Later she learned that other people's rulers had whole buildings to meet in, vast complexes of offices, official residences, and who knew what all. The visiting officials would never believe this planet was run from the very table they'd sat around for the midday meal.

She flushed with humiliation at that fiasco. The way Gannahans ate was disgusting, picking up food with their hands and gnawing it like animals. And she couldn't believe her family would be so rude as to laugh at the Karkar officials.

On the other hand, the officials had been rather insulting to Abba.

True, he looked ridiculous. She shrank in shame when she looked at him, with that handsome Karkar face covered by a horrid beard, and his powerful frame wrapped in oversized Gannahan rags. Yes, his appearance was mortifying. But he spoke perfect Karkar with a sharp wit, and his eyes sparkled with intelligence. How could they think him mad? It was outrageous. Emma's laughter, shocking though it was, had defused what might have become a volatile situation. Had she done it deliberately?

But the most mortifying thing was Lileela's own tears. Crying like a six-year-old, right there at the table in front of family and distinguished guests. Neither Karkar nor Gannahan should behave like that, and she was both.

Or was she neither? The purity of both races was defiled. She was a genetic blot, unfit to live on either planet.

The Terrestrials were a mix of breeding, and therefore tolerant of all sorts of differences. She was one-quarter Earthish. Perhaps she could move there. Or maybe one of the League's Space Stations, some of which were said to be beautiful, bustling places.

But how would she get off the planet? And how would she afford to live? She'd have to find a way somehow, because she certainly couldn't stay here.

The voices drew her toward the dining room. The heavy doors were closed, but if she stood near the doorway, just out of sight in case someone glanced through the sidelight, her sharp Gannahan ears could pick up bits of the conversation.

She listened. And what she heard made her Karkar ears stand out with horror.

9

ADAM took a seat at the dining room table. He wasn't a member of the Ruling Council, so why had he been asked to attend?

Emma called the meeting to order and began the recording. "It's been a long, interesting day, and I'll try to make this quick. I merely want to gauge your impressions of our guests, those of you who've had an opportunity to interact with them." She turned to Captain Broward. "Captain, how did your tour go?"

Broward smoothed his beard. "Well enough, I suppose. Communication was a bit awkward, but they managed to get their questions across. And they had plenty. About everything."

"Such as?"

"At first, at the airport, they kept asking where things were. Weapons room, satellite controls, where we house our defensive missiles. Why they saw no flights coming in or taking off, where the real airport is, why did we bring them here to show them an obvious decoy. You know, the usual polite queries."

Adam and the council members laughed.

"When we piled into the bus to drive them to Qatsiyr, they asked about the bus and its capabilities, why the highway was so small and why there was no traffic. They just can't conceive of a place that isn't teeming with people." Broward shook his head. "I understand their confusion. It was a shock to me at first, too."

The others agreed. Except for Adam. This was all normal to him, for Gannah was all he'd ever known.

"We took them into Qatsiyr, drove around the elevated perimeter past the empty chatsrs, then went down and parked below the First Circle. That's when their ears really perked up. The tunnels seemed to fascinate them. Then up on the ground level, we showed them the hotel, the restaurant, and every store and workshop. A couple of people even took them through their homes. Two things they kept asking about. First of all, not surprisingly, was the subject of money. They couldn't figure out how we can function without it."

Abba nodded. "That was one of the hardest things for me to grasp."

The others agreed. Adam wondered again how lifeless items like cold metal, glittery stones—or, worse yet, flat figures on a computer screen—could be afforded such worth in other societies.

"The second thing they asked about," Broward said, "concerned the children, why they weren't in school. Or, if they were off on holiday, why we refused to show them the school buildings. I don't think they believed us when we insisted we have no schools."

"They haven't met Jerry yet," Emma said. "Maybe he'll be able to explain it to them."

Adam listened quietly while the Council went on. Why was he here, when he obviously had nothing to contribute? He might be part Karkar, but he was unfamiliar with the people and their customs.

"The weather threw them for a loop too." Broward chuckled. "Good thing the thunderstorm hit when we were in the underground parking, or they'd have been in hysterics. I'm pretty sure they thought the whole thing was staged for the purpose of scaring the feathers off of them."

"Did they ask a lot of questions about the tunnels?" Jax asked.

"Matter of fact, yes. Once they got over huddling together in fear, they wanted to go exploring in the tunnels. So when we left Qatsiyr, we took them back to the airport through the underground rail."

"I wondered," said Jax, "because the geologist guy, Kughie, seemed really interested when I told him about the old subterranean system."

Emma listened to the discussions but didn't say much, until Jax finished telling about Kughurrrro's intense interest in everything he saw.

"He's a scientist," Abba said. "I would expect him to be inquisitive."

That's when Emma turned to Adam. "What do you think? Or rather, what does your meah tell you?"

She could have given him a little warning. What, exactly, was she looking for? He probed her mind for clues, but as usual, her meah was clouded.

He swallowed. She might be his emma, but she was also the toqeph of Gannah, and she awaited an answer.

"I think—" Racking his meah for overlooked data, he licked his lips. "I think they're legitimately overwhelmed by the things they see here. It's all completely out of their realm and they're struggling to understand. But I get the impression—"

He stared at an invisible spot on the table, concentrating. What *was* his impression? It took form even as he searched for it, and its shape alarmed him. His glance rose to meet Emma's, then bounced to Abba, then back to Emma again, who held his gaze. "Their curiosity is genuine, but their intentions are not."

Everyone in the room seemed to let out pent-up breaths. Had that been each of their suspicions as well?

"What do you mean?" Emma asked, though he sensed she already knew.

"I think they came here for the reason they claim. To bring Lileela home, and to settle the debt. But I get the impression that's only part of their mission. Their curiosity isn't idle. They're gathering information for a purpose, and I don't believe that purpose is benign."

As he put it into words, the impression solidified into certainty. "They hate us. With an unreasonable ferocity. They've been taught this hatred for generations. It's such an integral part of their race, they're no more able to give it up than they could—" He glanced at his hands on the table in front of him. "—remove their sixth finger. Hatred of us is part of who they are, and they wear it proudly."

Abba's pale face grew ashen, reflecting a pain Adam hadn't realized he bore.

"Knowing you grew up there," Adam said to him, "I marvel you were able to overcome that resentment. How did you do it?"

Abba shifted in his seat, looking first at Broward and then at Emma. "That's a long story. The short version is, only by the Yasha's grace. He was moving me in that direction long before I knew him. A complete turn-around like that is a miracle, a gift from God. It cannot be brought about by human intentions."

Emma smiled at Abba, then turned back to Adam. "Based on what your meah tells you, then, what is your recommendation?"

Adam blinked. "*My* recommendation?"

"Yes. It's customary for the toqeph to receive recommendations from various advisors before making decisions."

"Yes, of course." But she'd never asked his advice before, and Adam was more comfortable being an observer. Invisible, like this afternoon, when he sat in while Abba negotiated the terms with the finance ministers and League advisors. "Yes. Well, I recommend that we be careful."

"Do you think we should send them home in the morning?"

Adam wished everyone would quit looking at him. "With all due respect, Madam Toqeph, I don't know."

Emma glanced around the table. "How about the rest of you? Do you agree that our guests are not all that they seem? Do you think we should insist that they shorten their visit?"

Councilman Ras Tewodros, who hadn't had much opportunity to interact with the Karkar other than greeting them upon their arrival, addressed his question to Adam. "What is it they want from us, what are they looking for?"

"I think they want to ascertain our strengths and weaknesses. To see where we're vulnerable. To decide how to take what they want from us."

Abba had been watching and listening with such sorrowful intensity, it caused him to slump in his seat. Now he sat up, his face almost Earthish in its expression of comprehension. "And I know what they want."

He had everyone's full attention.

"Adam's dead-on about their hatred. Every Karkar blames Gannah for everything that's wrong with their world, whether it be illness, the state of the environment, rebellious youth, economic conditions, or what have you. It's all Gannah's fault, in their minds.

"One of the most serious problems the Karkar face, of course, is the pollution of the water, soil and atmosphere, and the depletion of raw materials. They've managed to get along by constructing domes, conserving and recycling water and other resources, and manufacturing artificial foodstuffs or growing natural ones in high-rise hydrofarms."

Abba leaned forward. "But there's a limit to how long you can sustain that kind of thing, and Karkar is nearing the end. It's taking a toll on nutrition and health, both physical and psychological. Manufacturing of anything other than edibles is at a near standstill, and the cost of imported goods is spiraling out of control. For many decades they've been exploring abandoned parts of the planet, testing the toxicity of different locations in hopes of building new population centers in fresh sites, and searching for new solutions to their other problems. But after meeting serious obstacles everywhere they look, they're running out of options."

Dortius Dmitry gasped. "You mean they're looking for another planet?"

"And they want to take ours?" Ras said.

Abba looked grim. "The more I consider it, the more likely that seems."

That couldn't be. Adam hoped Abba was misunderstanding all this.

"Why, that's—" Jax's eyes widened. "They wouldn't!"

"It has long been Karkar's dream to do unto Gannah what Gannah did unto them," Abba said. "It's been a favorite plot of literature and films, as well as the subject of serious speculation, for centuries."

"Small wonder," Emma said. "It's the Karkar version of the most fundamental human theme of all time. The struggle of good and evil climaxing with the hard-won triumph of good. With Karkar as the good guys, of course, and Gannah as the devil."

Jax's brows lifted even higher. "But that's not true."

"What's not true?" Emma's green eyes latched on Jax. "That good will triumph? Or that Karkar will be the ultimate victor?" She shifted her gaze from one to the other. "The underlying theme is found in every planet's culture because it is universally true. People tend to forget, though, that it's not a human conflict, but a spiritual one. We're not the players, we're the pawns.

"Unlike the pieces in a game of Karkar hmmmjckt, though, we each have the freedom to choose which layer of the board we move on."

"I understand that in theory," said Broward, "but how does it tell us what to do in this situation?"

Adam wondered the same thing, but Ras spoke first. "That's what I want to know. All of us in this room have chosen to follow the Yasha, and he has transformed each of us, much as Dr. Pik said." He nodded at Abba. "But does that tell us how to deal with these lying Karkar?"

"I think it does." Emma turned again to Adam. "What do you think?"

His mouth went dry and his heart pounded. Then his mind went back to the morning's communion with the Yasha. That passage he'd read and contemplated—was it relevant to this situation? "I'm thinking of something in the Earthers' Book of God."

She waited, and he continued. "King Hezekiah of Judah was healed of an illness that nearly killed him, and the king of Babylon heard about it. When Babylon sent ambassadors to congratulate him on his recovery, Hezekiah took the visitors all over the palace, showed them all his treasures."

Emma nodded. "And—?"

"And afterward, the prophet Isaiah told him that in the future, Babylon was going to conquer Judah and take all those treasures for themselves. So does that mean we shouldn't have let the Karkar come? Are we wrong for showing them what we have here?"

"I've been thinking about that same passage myself," said Emma. "But let's consider what happened earlier, before the Babylonian ambassadors came."

She looked at Adam, waiting for him to fill in the blank. And he did. "Another country, Assyria, tried to attack them."

Emma nodded. "Tell me about that."

Usually they served beverages at these meetings. Why not tonight? He could use something to wet his throat. "The Assyrian army surrounded Jerusalem and sent messengers to demand their surrender."

"What had happened even before that?"

Adam reviewed the scriptures in his mind. "Oh, yeah. The first time the Assyrians came, they demanded a ransom. Hezekiah paid it, and the armies pulled away. But then they came back. That's when the messengers told them they might as well surrender, because Judah was already as good as conquered. They said they'd beaten everyone else they'd come against, and Judah would be no different."

That answer seemed to satisfy her. She looked at the others around the table. "Do you remember what King Hezekiah did in response?"

Everyone nodded, and most answered, "He prayed."

"Yes, along with all of Judah. And that's what we should do. In fact, I've already gone to the Yasha and laid it out before him, much like King Hezekiah spread out the Assyrians' letter before Jehovah. But I believe we need to do more."

Broward cleared his throat. "I suppose it's always a good idea to pray, but we need to be practical. What sort of defenses do we have? None that I can see. We're not even under the protection of the League of Planets."

"You mean," said Jax, "Karkar could invade us, and the League wouldn't do anything about it?"

Broward shrugged. "We're isolated. Have no military allies. It doesn't help that Gannah's always been a pariah. We'd get no sympathy from anyone. In fact, I'm surprised the League didn't swoop in and claim the planet's riches for themselves when the Old Gannahans died. If Karkar were to take the initiative to do it now, well, as far as the League is concerned, so much the better. They'd have access to our resources and could control one more world."

Dmitry ran a hand along his shiny head. "So let me get this straight. A powerful and desperate planet wants to take us over. They're here scoping us out, even as we speak. And we have no means of defending ourselves. Do I have that right, or am I missing something?"

Adam's stomach plummeted. He had to be missing something.

"You have it right," Emma said, "except for one thing."

"What?" Broward said. "The Yasha's on our side? Why don't I find that comforting?"

Abba tapped his fingers on the table. "Everyone who believes in God thinks He's on their side." He stopped tapping. "But it's not a question of whether He's on our side. The issue is, are we on His? Do we live in obedience? Do our actions and attitudes honor Him, or make Him ashamed of us?"

Adam sought the Yasha in his meah, personalizing those questions.

Your heart pleases me, came the answer, *and I take pleasure in your obedience.*

Adam breathed easier. No, he wasn't perfect. But he was in the Yasha's good graces.

For a time, no one spoke as each conducted similar prayerful self-examination. Jax, bony elbows on the table, covered his face with his hands. Dmitry and Broward bowed their heads, and Ras lifted his hands and looked heavenward.

Adam glanced at his parents, who gazed at one another. Whatever they were thinking, they, too, appeared to have clear consciences.

Emma turned to the others. "What I think we should do—" She paused to allow each to finish his contemplations and turn to her. "What I think we should do is call a worship gathering tomorrow evening for everyone who's able and willing to come. We'll pray, confess any sins we need to deal with, and ask the Yasha for direction."

Ras's bushy brows lifted. "How are we going to do that with the Karkar here?"

"We'll invite them."

Adam's ears twitched.

Jax chuckled. "What will old Kughie think of *that*, I wonder?"

"I doubt they'll come, any of them," said Abba. "But we should make it plain they're welcome."

Jax's smile faded. "I told him I'd take him out to the mines tomorrow. We won't be back until the next day."

"I'll fly you out," Dmitry said. "That will get you there and back in one day."

Emma nodded. "That's good. We'll lay it all out in the open. Let it be known that we have no defense but the Yasha. The settlers will realize we must be serious about obedience to him, and the Karkar will be put on notice that they'll have to get past the God of the Universe to get to us."

Adam bit his lip. "Will they even care?"

"Not a bit," said Abba. "But when their plot against us is foiled, they'll know the reason."

Broward's brow furrowed. "Seems like we should be making other plans as well. Didn't the Old Gannahans leave any weapons behind we can reactivate? We can't just sit here with a target on our chests."

Ras shifted in his chair. "We're talking as if we know for a fact they're planning an attack. But how can we know that for sure?"

Emma turned to Adam. "My meah tells me it's true, but it doesn't function as well as it used to. How certain are you?"

He opened his mouth to answer but paused. Through his meah, he sensed Lileela struggling to listen. When he glanced toward the door, he caught a glimpse of something through the sidelight.

Seeing his startled reaction, everyone else looked too. "What is it?" they asked. "Is someone out there? Who's eavesdropping?"

"It's Lileela," said Adam, half rising.

Emma held up her hand. "Stay."

He sank back into his seat, and she rose and headed for the door. "I'll go talk to her. Pik, I'll allow you to adjourn the meeting." She looked through the sidelight then opened the door. "Lileela, wait."

She hurried out.

Adam followed Lileela in his meah, but she'd broken the connection and wouldn't let him back in.

Everyone turned to Abba, who let out a long sigh. "I think prayer is in order before we adjourn."

10

"LILEELA, wait."

She considered fleeing but knew it was useless. Cursing her clumsiness, she stopped but didn't turn at the sound of her mother's voice. Why had she allowed herself to be spotted? Worse yet, she shouldn't have reached out to Adam. It was safer to keep her distance.

Emma caught up to her in the hall. "What's the matter, sweet? Can't unwind?" Arm around her shoulders, she steered Lileela into the kitchen. "Let me make you a cup of sleepy tea."

That was Emma's cure for Lileela's restless nights when she was a child. While the water heated, Emma used to turn Lileela around and pretend to crank an imaginary handle on her back to "unwind" her. That would set her to giggling. Then Emma would give her a cup of deshe tea, and they'd sit in bed and talk about whatever was on Lileela's mind. The deshe never failed. When the last drop was drained, Lileela would snuggle against Emma and drift into a carefree sleep.

But that was a long time ago.

Lileela scowled. "It'll just make me sicker."

Emma drew water into two small pots. "Feeling the effects of this evening's blend already? Maybe I should make yours eseb instead. With honey." She put the pots in the quickheater, opened a cabinet holding an assortment of teas, then glanced at Lileela. "Have a seat."

Moving against her will, Lileela pulled out a chair. She should have turned and left the room. Said, "I don't want any tea," and gone back to bed. Why didn't she? While Emma was occupied making the tea, she could easily get up and leave.

If it were Aunt Skiskii standing there rather than Emma, she'd have done it. She didn't want tea, she didn't want to talk, and she didn't want to be within smelling distance of Gannah. Nor its naked-faced people with their stupid paranoia and unfounded accusations against everything good and Karkar. But somehow, when Emma spoke a command, free will flew out the window.

Emma placed a personal tea tray before her. It contained a cup with a strainer lid, a stirrer, the pot of eseb tea, and a jar of honey with a dipper, all made of pale yellow glass with swirls of milky white. Gannahan glass. So famous throughout the galaxy for its beauty and durability that the phrase *like Gannahan glass* meant something that looked fragile but couldn't be broken.

She prepared another tray for herself, but with deshe tea instead. The steamy fragrances rose, mingled, and seeped into Lileela's mind. It smelled like home.

Emma sat beside Lileela, so close that her permanently-bent right arm brushed against Lileela. Then she put her brown little hand on Lileela's pale one. They both had five fingers. "This must be very hard for you."

With her free hand, Lileela poured the contents of the pot into her cup. "What makes you say that?" She pulled away from Emma and scooted her chair over a few centimeters. After removing the strainer from the cup and laying it on the tray, she lifted the honey dipper and let the translucent pink stickiness dribble into the tea.

Emma watched, not answering.

Lileela's hand shook as she stirred the honey into the tea. She felt those green eyes bore into her, felt Emma's meah massage hers with weak fingers.

Weak, but wise. They knew where to press.

Lileela turned, weeping, and Emma took her into her arms.

Emma was so small. Not much bigger than Lileela herself, but strong and solid, like bundles of muscle. And her smell was so—so different from the Karkar, but just what a mother should smell like. She wanted to run away and never have to see this woman again. She wanted to melt into this person and become her.

She wanted to understand what was happening. What she felt, and why she felt it. She was a stranger to this place, to this body, to this mind.

Emma spoke in gentle tones. "What did you hear when you were outside the dining room?"

Lileela shook her head and made a moan as if to say, "I didn't hear anything." But she couldn't put words to the lie.

Emma picked up a napkin and put it in Lileela's hand, then kissed her head. "Better wipe your face, sweet. You're probably getting make-up all over me."

Lileela's mind slipped back into gear. What was she doing? She sat up. "Sorry." She dabbed at her eyes then looked at the napkin. No smears. Good thing she'd bought waterproof.

A glance at Emma's blouse told a different story. Okay, so it wasn't waterproof. Awash in a rush of embarrassment, she blotted her face.

But Emma ignored the stain on her clothing. "What does your meah tell you about the Karkar's intentions?"

Lileela gasped. What a question! But before she could launch into a tirade, Emma continued. "I don't mean Aunt Skiskii and Uncle Ogliziizl. I'm talking about the ore inspector and the financial ministers and those other people. I mean the official Karkar position."

Lileela reviewed her memory of every word the officials had spoken to her. She couldn't recall them having uttered a single one.

They'd treated her like an object. One whose value was measured in leaguepounds, not human worth. They were as likely to speak to her as they would to their shoes — and were less concerned with her welfare. Her stomach churned. "I don't know."

Emma poured her tea and set the strainer aside. "Let me ask you this, then. Let's just say our council had suspicions that Karkar might be planning to attack Gannah, and you happened to overhear part of their conversation about that. Based on your knowledge of the Karkar people and their feelings toward Gannah, would you think those suspicions preposterous? Or might they be justified?"

Lileela swallowed some tea, then let her breath out slowly. She wouldn't allow her mind and meah to connect. "I told you, I don't know."

"I suppose not. They wouldn't have confided in you, after all." Emma took a sip. "So do you find it strange, coming home after all this time? You've been living in such a different world for the past ten years. The past two-thirds of your life, in fact. I'd think you'd find the transition difficult."

Staring into her cup, Lileela shrugged. "It's a little different here, but I remember lots of stuff."

"Many things have changed. For instance, we now have a Ministry of Education."

That was new. Not wanting to care, she didn't look up. "What's that?"

"It's the formal process for certifying students in the various educational levels."

"I don't get it."

Emma smiled. "I'm not surprised. We didn't follow the procedure when you were here, and I'm sure they do things differently on Karkar."

Lileela took another sip. She didn't know much about the educational system on that planet, either, since she was never permitted to be a part of it. Barred from attending school because of her race, she'd had a series of tutors, none of whom cared whether she learned anything or not. Their only concern was that Uncle Ogliziizl paid them. Sometimes she had to throw screaming fits before they'd provide her with new study materials.

"Remember Jerry Maddox?"

Lileela paused, then nodded. She hadn't paid much attention to the adults when she was little, but she could pull a face out of her memory when hearing his name.

"He found the Old Gannahan records and put together a system for us that closely follows the original. The biggest difference is language proficiency. We figure over time, the New Gannahans will develop their own language, or at least, a new dialect of the Standard Tongue. So as long as they're proficient in the Standard and have a basic knowledge of Old Gannahan, that should be sufficient."

"So are you saying I'm expected to learn Gannahan?"

"You'll pick it up quickly. You're probably more familiar with it than you realize." Emma poured the remainder of the tea from the pot into her cup. "There are still seven educational levels, but most people only achieve the Fifth by adulthood, and that's all that's generally expected. In order to be appointed to a position of leadership, a person will have to go on to the Sixth or higher. And before training for the Nasihood, the applicant must be at the Seventh Level."

Lileela almost choked. "The Nasihood? You mean knights, like in the old days?"

Emma nodded. "Yes. Jerry Maddox is our first Nasi of New Gannah. He completed his final requirement almost two years ago. Jax Florida is in training now. And Adam plans to pursue it after he completes his Seventh Level. He'll be testing for that in the next few months."

Lileela's brain had felt overloaded before. Now, it functioned no better than the Karkar translators. "What does all this have to do with me?"

"You'll have to prepare for your tests, too. I expect you know enough to easily pass Level One, except for a couple of practical skills like lahab proficiency. Adam's volunteered to help you prepare."

"Lahab proficiency? You mean those ancient weapons?"

"Everyone carries a lahab, and it's important that you know how to use it."

"I had a fake one, with dull blades that wouldn't cut warm powlcurd. I remember playing with it and pretending it was real." She scowled. "It was fine for a toy, but I don't want to walk around armed like a Ga… like a Cephargian pirate." She'd nearly used a Karkar expletive degrading to Gannahans.

"Unacceptable as it may be on Karkar, on Gannah, it's required of every citizen. Your lahab is a weapon, a tool, and your official identification. You'll get yours once we take your photo and program the image into it, along with your personal information. There are a number of designs to choose from, and we'll let you pick one out tomorrow."

Lileela's stomach cramped, churning noisily. As she'd feared, this tea made it worse. "So I'm supposed to take these tests to pass the educational levels. And carry weapons. And wear Gannahan clothes, of course, since you wouldn't let me bring any decent ones."

"Karkar clothes are impractical for this climate and the activities you'll be doing. You can wear them for formal occasions, but for everyday use, you'll want to dress like a native." Emma smiled. "Not only that, but Karkar clothing doesn't have a lahab pocket."

Lileela fought a fresh onslaught of tears. "Why are you doing this to me? Why couldn't you have just left me alone?"

"Left you alone?"

Why did Emma's voice have that edge to it? Wasn't she supposed to be comforting her? Blotting her tears, Lileela looked up to find her mother's eyes glistening.

"What did you think, that you could stay there indefinitely? Sure, your aunt and uncle could have kept you for four more years, but what then?"

Something wasn't making sense. "What do you mean, what then?"

"If you remained past your nineteenth birthday, you would have been considered an adult under League law."

Lileela swallowed a wet, burning burp. "So?"

"So, as an alien living in League territory, you would have been required to pay your debt. Which would have been considerable. Even greater than it is now, because you'd have incurred four more years of living expenses. On Karkar, the cost of living is extremely high, especially at the standard you'd been enjoying. All those clothes, the jewelry, the pretty things you had there? Not to mention the food you ate, the tutoring expenses, your music lessons, spa bills, and everything else. They all went on the tab."

Lileela shook her head. "Aunt and Uncle took care of that."

"Yes, they did. They took care of recording every League-cent they spent on you. And at the end of each year, when they submitted their report for reimbursement, they took care of calculating thirty percent of the total as the annual fee for their efforts."

No. It wasn't true.

"First, you incurred expenses for the surgeries and therapy you underwent. Each year you remained on Karkar thereafter cost nearly a hundred thousand League-pounds. If you'd stayed another four years, between your passage costs to take you there to begin with, and medical and living expenses, you would have owed the League well in excess of two million. Oh, and I'm forgetting their annual interest of eighteen percent. All that would have been due on your nineteenth birthday. And you'd have had no way to pay it. That would have given them the legal right to force you into whatever service they chose. Being young and pretty, and an exotic species besides, I expect you'd be put to use in the entertainment industry, where you'd bring in a very good price for whoever bought the rights to you. When you grew too old or damaged for that, they'd find another use for you. You'd labor there until you died, with no hope of ever gaining your freedom."

Lileela's head buzzed. She flushed hot. Couldn't breathe.

"We've been negotiating with the League for years, but they've been dragging their feet, trying to keep you as long as possible so we'd owe more money. Which is fine, we don't care about the money, we just wanted to bring you home before you turned sixteen."

She was barely able to gasp out the words, "Why sixteen?"

"Because that's the age of majority on Gannah. If you're considered an adult on Gannah, you might have been considered an adult in League territory, too. We weren't sure about that, since Gannah isn't part of the League. But we didn't dare take any chances."

"If that's—" Her heart raced, she felt faint. She laid her head in her arms, and her voice came out muffled. "If that's the way it is, why did Abba send me there in the first place?"

Emma rose. From the sound of her movements, she was preparing another tea tray. "He didn't know what else to do. If you'd stayed, you never would have walked again. We don't have the facilities here to help you, but he knew Karkar did."

Lileela hadn't let herself relive her last days on Gannah. Not often, anyway. And the memory was unclear. She'd been angry with Emma for abandoning them, for going up to that starship and then getting lost on the way home. Emma knew everything, was all-powerful and wise. If she'd wanted to come home, she would have. Or at least, that was the way the five-year-old Lileela saw it. And in her hurt and resentment, she wanted to fight back. What hurt Emma more than disobedience?

As a child, she hadn't analyzed those feelings. She'd merely acted on them. And it ultimately led to this.

Emma took the teapot from the quickheater and arranged a third tray, setting it on the table just as Abba entered. Lileela's head was still down, but she heard Emma's activities and felt Abba enter the kitchen, even as she heard the council leave the dining room and make their way out of the apartment.

Adam was the last to leave. He came to the kitchen doorway, stood for a moment, pushed gently at Lileela's closed meah, then said, "Goodnight," and left.

She never lifted her head.

Abba sat one seat away. Big and warm and Abba-smelling, neither Karkar nor Gannahan but a homey combination.

"Worship meeting will be in tomorrow's Violet Evening." Abba spoke to Emma, his reedy voice forming the Standard language words almost perfectly. "Half before the second hour."

Gannahans measured time so stupidly. Why couldn't they just say *nineteen hundred* like everybody else? Who counted hours in color-coded divisions?

Emma nodded. "That will be good."

Lileela lifted her head. "Good? What's good? You take my whole life, wring it out like a rag, and then go sing and dance to your Yasha?"

Wishing she could move quickly enough to make a more dramatic exit, she pushed herself up from the table. "Count me out. I'll be in my room." She fled the best she could, gratified that her mother didn't follow.

But Abba did. He was behind her in an instant, and before she reached the stairway, he blocked her way. "I know this is difficult for you." He spoke in a hushed Karkar squawk.

She scowled. "Why does everyone say that?"

"Because it's true. But what we have done, we've done because we believed it best for you."

"Yeah, sure. Whatever." She tried to get around him, but he was huge. It was hopeless.

He put a hand on her arm. Six long fingers and a hard, massive palm. "Lileela, listen to me."

She looked down at his hand, then up at his face. A Karkar face, but etched with lines of sorrow and concern. Her heart skipped a beat at the contradiction.

"You may not like the situation, but it is what it is."

"You're right about one thing—I don't like it."

"Of course you don't. But you don't need to like it, you just need to deal with it. You're fifteen years old and still subject to your mother. Once you turn sixteen, you'll be under no one's authority but your own."

She narrowed her eyes. "Now that, I like the sound of."

"But you'll also be responsible to live under the laws of Gannah. Which means you'll have to fend for yourself. You'll have no privileges but what you earn, and no status apart from the value you provide to Gannah."

"Gannah?" In Karkar, the word rasped out in a hateful snarl. "Who cares about that? I don't plan to hang around any longer than I have to."

Abba nodded, looking more sorrowful than before. "That's your choice, once you're of age. But you'll have a long wait before another vessel comes along for you to escape on. Better make the most of your time here."

"Okay. Well, right now, I think my time would be best put to use sleeping, so if you don't mind—"

He paused as if he was going to say more then stepped aside. "Or even if I do."

She took a step forward, then looked up, confused. "Even if you do what?"

"Even if I do mind, you may go to bed without finishing this conversation. I can see you're not up for it tonight."

She turned away and started down the winding stairs, clinging to the rail and to her determination. "You might not see what you think you see."

"Perhaps not. I don't have a meah, after all."

He let her get down one twist of the stairs before he spoke again. "One more thing."

She stopped but didn't look up. "What?"

"I love you, Lileela. Goodnight."

She gripped the rail tighter. "Yeah. Goodnight to you too."

As she resumed her journey down the steps, she felt gravity pulling, felt like she was about to fall, the whole way down. Felt his eyes upon her and his bulk filling the opening at the top of the stairway. Finally putting her feet on the floor at the bottom of the staircase, she breathed a sigh of relief and headed down the hall and out of his sight.

What she had heard outside the dining room, what Emma had said in the kitchen, none of that was true. She'd had a good life on Karkar. It was a charming planet, with beauty and culture everywhere. No, it wasn't perfect, but nothing was. Particularly not Gannah, despite what these people might think.

She eased through the bedroom door and sniffed. Auntie lay on her side, no longer snoring, but breathing deep and rhythmically. Filling the little room with the odor of Karkar body chemistry mingled with artificially scented skin-care products. Expensive ones.

Lileela moved toward the cot. The Karkar were the most truthful when half-asleep or half-drunk. "Aunt Skiskii," she whispered hoarsely.

Auntie didn't move.

"Skiskii," she said again as she drew nearer. She gently shook Auntie's shoulder.

The woman made a sleepy moan, then a clicking sound with her mouth. "Wha—"

Lileela gave her shoulder a squeeze. "I have to ask you something, Auntie."

"Sure, baby, what?" Her words slurred.

"Did you get paid for keeping me?"

Another moan. "Of course, dear. Why do you think we did it?"

Lileela bit a knuckle to stifle a cry, then took a long, slow breath. "Thanks. Just wondering."

Skiskii made more clicking noises and went back to sleep.

Lileela crawled into the bed alcove and drew the curtain. Bumping against the book she'd left there, she picked it up and dropped it to the floor. Skiskii stirred at the thump but resumed her deep breathing a moment later.

Lileela's mind went upstairs to her parents in the kitchen, talking about her. To Adam, who'd gone home to wherever he lived now. To the children sleeping in other rooms nearby. To the Karkar officials, spending the night in the transport shuttle, and to their starship orbiting above.

When the timedial rolled into the first hour of Gray Dawn, she was still awake, staring at the curtain that separated her from the rest of the room and the faint suggestion of light that filtered through.

11

*B*OLE-BETUL Interstellar Airport boiled with traffic, and the Ministealth circled in the shimmering heat for more than an hour before obtaining clearance to land. During the wait, Faris and his team learned delivery of the *Glowworm*, the Photuris they'd been promised, was behind schedule. They wouldn't be able to take off until late afternoon.

Safiy gestured toward the plane's tail and the prisoners that lay in it. "What do we do with them while we're waiting?"

Faris nodded. "Better take a look, make sure they're not coming to."

Safiy rose to check on them.

"We'll have to keep them here," Faris went on, "until we can transfer them to the ship. Which means, I guess, we can't all disembark and enjoy the airport's amenities. One of us will have to stay with the Mini, keep an eye on our guests."

"The airport's got amenities?" said Adil.

Omar laughed. "Kind of. I could go for one of those wat wraps they sell on the concourse. Ever have one?"

"Yeah." Binyamin stood. "Don't know about that for breakfast, though. A cinnamon roll and a cup of coffee is more what I have in mind."

"And a restroom," said Safiy on his way forward. "The prisoners are still sleeping, everything's okay back there. Want me to babysit once we land, amir?"

From his expression, Faris got the feeling Safiy hoped he'd say no. "Thanks, but we should take shifts. I'll take the first one, then in an hour you can spell me. Next Omar, then Adil. If we're still waiting after four hours, Binyamin, Ishaq, then Ya'qub if we need him. But I hope we won't be sitting here that long."

Once they landed, Esam shut down the systems except for the climate control, and the men left Faris on board alone. By the time Safiy came to relieve him, his plans were made.

He rose, stretching, from the seat where he'd been dozing. "Dengel was starting to come around, so I gave him another shot about ten minutes ago. The woman shouldn't need attention for an hour or so, and the kids? I'm not sure. Don't want to overdose them."

"Don't worry, amir." Safiy gave a dismissive wave. "Leave them to me and go have some fun."

Fun wasn't exactly on Faris's mind when he grabbed his bag, gave Safiy a nod, and stepped out into the steamy African air.

It felt good to stretch his legs. He'd been cooped up too long, and nervous tension gave him enough energy to do handsprings all the way to the terminal. But that would have drawn attention, which he didn't need.

Eschewing moving sidewalks and escalators in favor of using his muscles, he strode through the concourse with no particular destination. Around him swarmed the dark Earthish faces of locals dressed in colorful garb—the occasional waist-high Glenmarrian crowned with a thick shock of brilliant red hair—towering Karkar with painted faces—and clusters of fleshy Eutarians in dark business suits, talking on messengers whether walking or seated. All avoided looking his way. The aura of Special Starforces had that effect.

But Philip Dengel hadn't felt it. Or if he had, he never let on. He'd spoken kindly to Faris, as a soldier would to a fatherless child on a war-torn street. And he'd offered Faris, not a smile and a candy bar, but living waters from which he could now drink for all eternity.

Jaw set, Faris approached the attendant at a bookseller's stall. "Do you have writing paper? And an envelope?"

The woman was Faris's height, her silky blue and purple head covering bringing out the color of her eyes. Brows lifted, she rummaged in a bin beneath the counter. "Paper? And a what?"

"An envelope. You know, what you put papers in when you deliver them to somebody?"

She pulled out a small notebook. "I have paper, but never envelope."

He pursed his lips. "How about some tape, then? So I can fold up the paper and seal it shut?"

"Ah." She nodded as she opened a drawer. "I have stickers, yes?" She laid a sheet of round gold seals on the counter, then reached back into the drawer. "You want pen, too? I have pen."

He shook his head. "No, ma'am, thank you. I have one of those. I'll just take the paper and seals."

"Ho-kay, the cost will be two leaguepounds twenty, plus a half leaguepound tax." She handed the items to him.

He slipped them into his bag and gave her a nod. "Thank you, ma'am."

He stepped back out onto the concourse. The scanner emitted two soft beeps as he passed, one electronic eye reading the cost of his purchases and the other his hand chip, enabling the total to be deducted from his Leaguebank account.

He felt a stab of regret at the sum he'd be leaving behind there.

The ID reader at the lounge entrance granted him admittance, and he passed through the doors. "A private table, please," he told the servebot. "I'd like to be alone."

Its head rotated once. "Table available. Please follow yellow stripe. Gold bot will seat you."

A line of canary yellow lit up along the floor, and Faris followed it through the dim room, around a divider, and to a small booth, where a gold-colored figure about twenty centimeters tall flashed on the table near the back wall.

As soon as it detected his presence, it spoke. "You would like this table, sir?"

"Yes, this will do."

"Very good, sir, please have a seat."

He tossed his bag onto the bench and slid in beside it, and the yellow stripe on the floor faded away.

"Would you like a menu, sir?"

He unzipped a pocket of his bag and pulled out a breakfast bar. "No, I'll just have a cup of Arabic coffee. Black."

"Very good, sir. A cup of black Arabic coffee will be brought shortly." The bot's lights went out, and it backed up and disappeared into an opening in the wall.

He stopped himself before tearing the wrapper of his breakfast bar. "Excuse me, serve-bot?"

His server emerged again, lights flashing. "Yes, sir. How may I help you?"

"I just decided I'd like a real breakfast." He slipped the bar back into his bag. "Yogurt, flatbread with za'atar, and… what sort of fresh vegetables do you have today?"

"Vegetables today are cucumbers, tomatoes, radishes, bell peppers, squash—"

"Stop. In addition to what I just said, I'd like squash, tomato, and bell pepper sautéed, with two soft-cooked hen's eggs on top. Can the kitchen do that for me this morning?"

"Affirmative, sir." The bot repeated his order. "Your breakfast will appear shortly. Would you like your coffee now while you wait?"

"Yes, please."

"Very good, sir."

Moments after the bot receded into the wall, a panel beside the bot door pulled back to reveal a steaming cup of coffee in an alcove. He removed the cup, and a scanner beeped, debiting his account for the price, which was displayed on a small screen above the delivery panel.

Five leaguepounds for one cup of coffee? What would the whole breakfast cost? He shook his head. No matter. He wouldn't need leaguepounds where he was going.

He lifted the cup and took a sip. Best coffee he'd had in a long while. It had better be, at that price. After another taste, he put the cup down, then pulled the notebook from his bag along with his pen.

He sat, pen poised over the paper. Borne on a breeze of soft music, the quiet murmurs of the diners around him invaded his thoughts. He felt the subtle air currents from the climate control system, detected the odor of every drink the travelers sipped, every ingredient of the foods they ate.

It was always like this at such times. When faced with life-or-death choices, his senses sharpened, his heart rate increased, and his muscles readied for quick action. He felt invincible in these moments, the possessor of limitless life and stamina, able to conquer all.

But he didn't feel invincible this morning. His senses might be enhanced, his brain more retentive, his body stronger and more resilient than the average human's. But at his absolute best, he was no match for the force he faced now.

It would be so simple to put the paper and pen away. Eat his breakfast, and enjoy it. Take possession of the Photuris and carry out the mission. It was a delight to obey orders, a comfort to trust his superiors' judgment. Following his training gave him a sense of wellbeing, oneness with the universe.

But when one superior's orders conflicted with another's, blind obedience was no longer an option. A choice must be made.

Could he ask Captain Abdul-Malik for guidance? No. Abdul-Malik didn't know all the facts. There was only one Captain he could consult.

He didn't dare pray aloud, but the bot couldn't hear his thoughts. "Give me wisdom, Lord."

A female customer at another table wearing Arabian Nights perfume ordered rooibos tea. The servebot said, "Very good, ma'am. Would you like a sweetener?"

"Yes, please. Stevia, five cc's."

"Very good, ma'am. A cup of rooibos tea with five cubic centimeters of stevia will be brought shortly."

Faris heard the soft whir as the bot retreated into the wall.

"I am not a servebot," he whispered. "I have a choice."

He ran his options again. Carried each eventuality to its probable conclusion, factoring in every conceivable variable. Calculated the odds of each scenario's likelihood.

"I see now, Lord. I hear and obey."

He put pen to the page and began to write.

12

WIPING sweat from his face with an already-damp towel, Adam glanced up to see Elise Finnegan watching from the gymnasium doorway. The flush that coursed through him when she smiled did nothing to help his overheated condition.

He replied with a wink, then moved his attention to the six perspiring boys, ages ten and eleven, performing cool-down stretches on the floor. The timedial on the wall indicated they still had a couple of minutes left to go, but they'd worked hard today, and it was hot.

And Elise was here.

"Time!" he called, and the boys stopped in mid-stretch.

Two of them flopped backward and sprawled spread-eagle on the floor. Three sat where they were, hair wet and faces flushed.

Nathan Samuelson, their self-appointed leader, clambered to his feet. He approached Adam and bowed. "Are we dismissed, sir?"

Adam draped the towel around the back of his neck. "Um, yes. Or would you rather stay and work out a while longer?"

In the traditional Gannahan attitude of respect, Nathan stood before Adam, looking at the floor. "No, sir. But our time's not up yet, and—" He lifted his eyes, a smile playing at his lips.

"And—" Adam tried to think where this was going. When it hit him, he thumped his forehead with the heel of his hand. "And I made you guys a promise, didn't I?"

The boys on the floor jumped up. "Yes, you did, you promised! You said if you ever dismissed us early, you'd run up the wall like a Nasi."

Adam's ears smiled. "And a Gannahan—"

"—always keeps his promises," they chorused.

He didn't need to see her to know Elise's interest was aroused.

"Okay, guys. I suppose I'll have to give it a try." Pulling off the towel and dropping it to the floor, he gauged the distance to the far wall, where a row of climbing handles ran along the right edge to the ceiling four meters above. But a Nasi didn't use climbing handles. And though Adam wasn't even a Nasi-in-training yet, he wouldn't use them either.

If he succeeded, he'd be glad Elise was there to see it. If he fell? Well, he'd put that out of his mind and focus on the task at hand.

He closed his eyes, breathing deeply, flexing and relaxing his muscles, recalling the action and mindset necessary to propel his body up the wall. If he could climb high enough, he'd grab the ladder rungs that ran along the ceiling, move hand-over-hand to the climbing grips along the wall, and climb down. If he couldn't reach the ladder, the consequences would be painful. In more ways than one.

He should probably put the mats down, just in case.

But Elise was here.

Forget Elise. Concentrate. You've practiced this, you can do it.

It took several moments before he overcame the distractions and brought his mind and body under total control. Finally, he opened his eyes. One more deep breath, and he took off.

He didn't feel his body, didn't know if he walked or ran, just concentrated on reaching that horizontal ladder at the ceiling.

The wall rushed toward him. In his mind, it tilted away as he leaped the chasm between the horizontal dimension and the vertical. One, two, three strides along the wall, and his body grew heavy. He stretched for the ladder, fearing he'd fall short and slide back to the floor — but somehow his legs propelled him one more stride, and his six fingers snagged a rung.

He grasped it as the wall tilted, became vertical again, and his entire weight hung from one hand. Dizzy from the world's sudden shift, he grabbed the next rung with his other hand, supported by congratulatory hooting and stomping below. Without missing a beat, he made swift, rung-by-rung progress to the grips on the wall ahead of him.

He placed one foot on a handle, then transferred his hands, one at a time, from the ladder to the wall grips. After that, it was an easy descent to the floor.

The boys bounced over, whooping with glee. "You did it! I can't believe it! Did you see that, he ran straight up the wall, how'd he do that?"

Adam bent down, hands on his knees, breathing heavily. "Yeah, I did it." His Karkarish face remained straight despite the giddy grin that bloomed within.

The boys continued their clamor. "How can you run up a wall like that? How do you do that? Teach me!"

His dizziness cleared, but he still gasped for breath. "Trade secret. I'll teach you when you're ready. *If* you're ever ready." Standing upright, he felt Elise's adoration even before he looked her way.

He clapped his hands. "All right, boys, the show's over. You are officially dismissed. Now, get your sweaty little selves out of here before I find something else for you to do." He extended both hands, and each boy butted the heel of his hand against his before scampering out of the gym, chattering excitedly.

Elise threaded through them as she crossed the floor to where Adam had dropped the towel. She picked it up and brought it to him. "That was pretty impressive. I didn't know you were a weaverrat."

He thanked her for the towel, then wiped his face. "I'm not a weaverrat. I might climb walls, but I don't weave webs." He lowered the towel and gazed at her over it. Her cheeks glowed pink — was it the heat? — and her blue eyes sparkled. Her hair, smooth and straight and bound in one long braid, shone like polished copper.

"No?" The corners of her full lips turned up, and her right cheek dimpled. "You could have fooled me."

"What do you mean?" They headed for the door together.

"You might not spin webs, but you've captured me." She glanced up at him sideways.

His mouth felt parched, and he aimed for the cooler in the hall. "How?"

"I don't know how, but you've managed it." She held out her hand. "Here, give me that."

He stopped at the cooler. "What?"

"The towel. I'll take it for you."

He handed it over, though he wasn't sure why. "I can do my own laundry, you know."

She giggled. "I know. But I want it." She put it to her face and breathed in.

"Yuck." He poured himself a glass of water. "It's all sweaty."

"I know. But it's your sweat. I like it."

Thirsty as he was, he could hardly drink, the way his throat seized up. He managed two swallows. "Then that's not fair."

"What's not fair?"

"I don't have anything of yours."

She lowered the towel and smiled while he drank again.

But before either of them had a chance to speak, two of their Karkar guests came around the corner led by Dmitry, who hailed him. "Adam!"

Adam turned to the invaders. Zidz towered behind Dmitry, along with Pink-and-Lavender. They wore translators.

Adam addressed Dmitry. "Did you get the devices working?"

"Yes, at least for now." The odd trio stopped when they reached Adam and Elise.

Seeing the Karkar eyeing Elise with interest, Adam stepped in front of her to block their view.

"Yes, they are functioning." Pink-and-Lavender cocked her head. "Your Mr. Dmitry is quite skillful."

The pale Outsiders had seemed so fascinating yesterday. Now he found them abhorrent despite their physical similarities to his father.

"Our guests are interested in our medical facilities," Dmitry said. "The toqeph hoped you'd be able to show them around."

That wasn't how Adam planned to spend the rest of his day, but when the toqeph "hoped" something, it was best to not disappoint her. "Of course."

Zidz stared at Adam. "You are a doctor, like your father?"

"I'm a medical student. And a researcher, like my father."

Elise slipped out from behind Adam. "If you'll excuse me, I must—"

Zidz stepped to the side as if to intercept her. "Ah, a young female. Lovely." He started to lift his hand as if to touch fingertips with her, then, apparently remembering the rule about physical contact with females, he lowered it. "My name is Mr. Zidz. And you are—"

"She's late for an engagement," Adam said.

"Elise Finnegan," she said at the same time, and bowed. "And Adam's right. I *am* late for an engagement." She shot him a look out of the corner of her eye. The engagement she referred to was theirs, to be married. But he refused to present himself to her father for branding until after he'd completed his education.

"Which we shall soon rectify." He flashed her a smile, then turned to Dmitry. "Please tell the toqeph I'll be happy to show our guests whatever they'd like to see."

Dmitry grinned, no doubt getting the drift of Elise's meaning. "I'll tell her." He bowed to the guests. "Mr. Zidz, Ms. Neen." Then he hurried away with Elise, leaving Adam to deal with the duplicitous Karkar alone.

They gazed at Adam with pale yellow eyes, their faces blank but their ears tilting with disdain.

"So why did the head Gannahan woman give us to you?" Zidz narrowed his eyes. "Why don't we get a real doctor?"

Adam finished the water in his glass. "Do you need one? Are you ill?" He set his glass in the rack beside the cooler.

"No," said Neen. "Despite the distressing circumstances, my health is holding up rather well."

Zidz rubbed his jaw. "But now that you mention it, we've all noticed—" He glanced at his companion. "All us men have noticed, anyway, that the hair-inhibiting lotions we customarily use don't work in this place."

Neen tilted her head in agreement. "Even the hair on our heads is noticeably longer this morning. My blonde roots are showing."

"Mr. Dmitry gave us primitive razors to shave off our whiskers." Zidz's ears jerked with disdain. "He said he employs that crude method daily, not only on his face but also his head."

"But is there nothing we can do medically?" the woman asked. "Must we be afflicted with this unreasonable hair growth for the duration of our stay?"

Adam pursed his lips. "I see your point. It must create quite an inconvenience for you."

"How right you are!" Zidz's ears lifted. "Have you ever tried to apply cosmetics over whiskers? It's more than an inconvenience, it's an agony. A stubble destroys the whole effect."

Adam stroked his beard. "As I see it, you have four treatment options."

"Oh, really? Four?"

"Yes." He counted on his fingers. "One, you may use the razors Dmitry gave you and apply your cosmetics as usual. Two, you may allow the whiskers to grow and apply the cosmetics to the upper half of your faces only. You could create some interesting looks that way, I'd think. It might catch on back on your planet."

The visitors stared at him with blank expressions, their ears stiff with amazement as Adam went on. "Three, you may allow the whiskers to grow, and abandon the use of cosmetics entirely. Or, four…" He was going to say, "You may leave Gannah immediately," but decided against it. "I guess I was mistaken. You have only three options."

Zidz's ears drooped in disappointment. "Has no one tried electrolysis? Or do those devices not work, either?"

Adam nodded. "There's that, yes, and other epilation procedures. But all are time-consuming and unpleasant, and the hair grows back so quickly, it's not worth the trouble. That's why most of us wear beards."

Neen snorted.

"So," said Adam, "I understand you want to see our medical department. Since we're here, first let's tour our athletic facility, since physical fitness is part of the medical program."

Gesturing for the guests to join him, Adam started for the weight room down a long, narrow hall. "I'll show you some of the equipment we use for building muscle mass, agility, and endurance."

Neen shuddered. "I'm not sure. Is it safe?"

Adam didn't stop walking. "Why wouldn't it be?"

"Who uses it? Who's in there?"

Adam paused at the door of the weight room as Zidz put a reassuring hand on Neen's shoulder. "I'm sure it will be fine." Zidz turned to Adam. "She's afraid of running into a crazed band of Nasi warriors. You notice how she watches so closely when people talk? She's trying to see if their tongues are purple."

Adam tried to hold back the smile from his ears. "There are currently only two Purpletongues on Gannah. The toqeph, whom you've already met, and Jerry Maddox."

"Who's he?"

"You'll meet him tonight. You are coming to the worship service, aren't you? Because he'll be leading it."

Neen paled beneath her face powder. "Is he terribly fierce?"

"That depends." Adam entered the weight room and turned on the lights.

Zidz stepped in after him. "On what?"

"On whether anyone gives him a reason to be. But you should have nothing to worry about where Jerry's concerned. My mother has killed way more people than he has."

13

*A*FTER six fidgety hours at Bole-Betul Interstellar Airport, Faris received word that the *Glowworm* was ready to board.

Hoping his men didn't sense his tension, he ordered them to move the captives from the Ministealth to an enclosed truck. Ishaq drove, Faris rode shotgun, and the others piled into the back with the prisoners.

As they rumbled toward the airport's interstellar sector, Faris took a deep breath and ran a hand down his bristly face. His plan was made. Would he have the courage to carry it out?

They passed soot-stained shuttles from orbiting starships disgorging their passengers. Faris peered between towering mechanical frameworks filled with busy inspectorbots and scrubbers at other grounded vessels. Through the haze, he finally spotted what he was looking for—the gates where ships in the Stardarter and Photuris class stood at their tall docking platforms.

He pointed to Gate IS-23, its sign barely visible at this distance. "There's our ride."

"Pretty thing, isn't she?" Ishaq steered toward where the ship glimmered in the sun.

A detail of uniformed men on the ground and the platform watched the truck pull up beside it. The brilliant reflection from its Pyetronium surface made Faris squint, and his stomach tightened with dread. It would be so simple to just carry out his orders and not worry about anything else. Was it really necessary to do what he contemplated?

Yes. His decision was made, and he knew it was right. He firmed his jaw as the truck drew near the docking platform.

According to what he'd been told, the little craft was specially outfitted for the mission with three independent confinement units. Each soundproof room had a bed, basic sanitary facilities, and a secure portal for transferring food and supplies. Through sensitive surveillance microphones, Faris and his men would be able to hear the faintest whisper uttered within each room, and they could communicate with the occupants. But otherwise, the prisoners would be entirely isolated.

A renewed awareness of their presence in the vehicle behind him—drugged, bound and blindfolded—eased the knot in his stomach a bit. He was keeping innocent people from harm.

As Ishaq stopped the truck where two of the guards directed, Faris's messenger jiggled. He answered. "What's up, Safiy?"

"The kids are moving around a little. Should we dose them again?"

The guard approached, electronic clipboard in hand. Faris gave him a wave and said to Safiy, "I'll take a look. Be right there." Cutting off the call, he spoke to Ishaq. "I've got to see to the cargo. Take care of the paperwork?"

Ishaq nodded. "Sure, amir."

While Ishaq spoke to the guard, Faris stepped out of the cab and went around to the back. He rapped on the side of the truck, and Safiy pulled back the canvas covering.

"Dengel and his wife are dead to the world, but one of the kids whimpered a little and the other one moved a minute ago."

Faris climbed in and checked their condition. All signs were good, and they responded only slightly to his touch. "They're still out of it," he said. "As long as we keep them bound and gagged, they're not likely to cause any trouble. Let's just move them the way they are."

The men covered the prisoners with tarps and laid them on baggage carts, then tossed their duffels on with them. Even a careful observer's suspicions wouldn't have been aroused.

Once on board the Photuris, the tarps were removed and the prisoners carried to their respective cells—Dengel in one, his wife in another, the two girls together in the third. There, the men removed their bonds and left them to awaken as the sedatives wore off.

After a few minutes of exploring the small craft, which HQ had thoughtfully equipped with everything a person could want for a sustained voyage, Faris called the men to assemble in the dining room. They took seats as instructed, appearing fresh and eager for adventure.

They had no idea.

"We have a change of plan, gentlemen."

"Sir?" Each raised his brows expectantly. Trusting. Ready.

He turned to Omar. "Are you up for a special assignment, Sergeant bin Ibrahim?"

"Sir!" He stood at attention.

Faris hated deceiving this man who looked up to him, would do anything for him. Ignoring his misgivings, he went on. "I'm sorry, but you're not going to be able to join us on this voyage. We have a mission here on planet that requires delicate attention. I've chosen you as one of a two-man team. I'll let you decide on the other. Anyone but Esam, since we need him to pilot this vessel."

A flicker of pride flashed across Omar's face but quickly fled as he recovered himself. "I'd like to work with Ya'qub, if I may, sir."

"Good choice." Faris nodded at the other men. "The rest of you are dismissed. Esam, you may prepare for takeoff. Let the others know what you need them to do."

"Sir!" They saluted and left without so much as a curious glance in Omar's direction.

When they were gone, Faris pulled from his bag three paper packets affixed with gold foil seals. They didn't look as suspiciously unauthorized as he'd feared.

"These are not to be opened." He looked back and forth between Omar and Ya'qub. "By either of you. Under any circumstances."

"No, sir," they said.

He took a breath. No going back now. "Our guest, Mr. Dengel, has contacts in Abidjan and Naimey. Written on two of these packets, you'll see coordinates for the locations where we believe they can be found. You will go to Naimey and deliver this packet to a man named Barnabas." He handed the first envelope to Omar. "Next, to Abidjan, to deliver this to a man named Titus." He handed him the second envelope.

"If you can't find these men where they're supposed to be, hunt them down. If they've moved, follow them. If they've been apprehended by local authorities, spring them. If anyone asks, you have a message for them from Philip the Evangelist, and it must be delivered to them personally."

A question flitted in Ya'qub eyes but didn't change his expression.

Faris lifted an eyebrow. "You're wondering if it really *is* from our guest? No. Of course not. But as far as you're concerned, it is."

"Yes, sir!" Ya'qub stared straight ahead, probably ashamed of having questioned what he was told.

"If you discover either of the contacts is dead, destroy the envelope designated for him. Finally, when that is accomplished, you will deliver this to Captain Abdul-Malik." Faris handed Omar the third packet. "Tell him you've delivered the messages to Barnabas and Titus as ordered, and that I've instructed you to put this into his hands, eyes only."

Faris pulled out the fourth and final envelope, thicker than the others. "This one, you can open. In order to keep this business properly discreet, you're not to use personal or official credit accounts. These currency vouchers are clean and anonymous, and there should be enough here to cover all your expenses." He handed the packet to Omar. "Any questions?"

"No, sir. Your instructions are clear, sir."

"Good. Again, I'm sorry you won't be joining us on our voyage. We'll miss you."

"It's our pleasure, sir," said Omar.

"We hear and obey," he and Ya'qub said together.

Faris nodded. "Thank you, gentlemen. You're dismissed."

After they left the dining room, he got a cup of coffee and sat at a table, calming his nerves through deep breathing exercises. He'd just committed treason.

Hoping Omar and Ya'qub wouldn't have to suffer too terribly for his sins, he sent up a silent prayer on their behalf.

ONCE Esam took the *Glowworm* through Earth's atmosphere and set its course for Station Two, the automated controls took over. Sensors would detect obstacles in the path and sound an alert so the pilot could take any necessary action. Other than that, it was just a matter of periodic monitoring. Faris had Esam train all the men to perform the routine so everyone could share the load.

To assure no one grew lazy, Faris required each to take his turn monitoring not only the flight but also the prisoners, whom he took to calling passengers as soon as they left Earth space. He also assigned the men a minimum number of hours each week on the ship's weight machines and in what competitive sports the small gym area allowed.

Finally, he required them to make use of the extensive electronic library—and not just for videos or games. Each man could make his own choices, but he had to read two novels and two non-fiction selections per week.

The men kept him apprised of the passengers' welfare, but he didn't look in on the Dengel family. Every moment of every day, their imprisonment ate at his conscience. "I'm saving them from a terrible fate," he reminded himself. But it was no comfort. Isolating them like this was torment, and he couldn't condone it despite his excuses.

Three days from Earth, Safiy worked out on an elliptical machine beside Faris. The men were the same height, had the same stride. They worked together in complete unison. And when they conversed, they almost always understood each other. He wondered if that meant they were friends.

Another few days, and everything would change. Everything. When that happened, would Safiy be his enemy? He'd be a formidable one. The sweat on Faris's brow didn't spring only from exertion.

Safiy's voice broke into his thoughts. "What's on your mind, amir?"

Faris hoped Safiy didn't notice the way he started. "Huh?"

"You've been quiet this trip."

He puffed upward, trying to deflect a drop of sweat from the edge of a nostril. "I don't talk when I work out."

"True. It breaks the concentration."

So why do it?

"But," Safiy went on, "you're quiet all the time, not just now. Have been since we took off."

"Huh," said Faris. "That just your observation? Or do the others think so too?"

"We've all noticed."

"Guess I'm just thinking." He forced a chuckle. "About that joyride Esam asked about."

Safiy glanced over with a grin. "Oh? Where're we going?"

"Not sure yet." The sweat poured more freely. "I've been wondering about Gannah"

Safiy laughed. "Ask a silly question—"

That was the end of the conversation. But that evening at dinner, Faris added another duty to the men's list of chores.

He peeled back the lid from his faux pasta travel ration. "I'm giving some thought to our passengers."

Safiy chuckled. "Thinking how fortunate they are to share in this fine cuisine?"

"Yeah." Binyamin stirred his ration with a fork. "We're eating like prisoners."

Esam gave his meal a sorrowful look. "Too bad they didn't stock the pantry with real food. We've got a kitchen, but nothing to cook in it."

"True, I've had better," Faris said. "But that's not what I meant. I've been wondering why these passengers are worth the League's attention. They're not violent, so why are they treated like dangerous felons instead of petty criminals?"

Adil nodded. "Good question. I've never heard of the Jeshi Samaki committing any terrorist acts."

"Me neither," said Ishaq. "But Dengel is a lawbreaker. Openly, and with no reason. What does he hope to gain by his defiance?"

"That's what I'm saying." Faris was relieved the men showed an interest in the topic. "Don't you ever wonder why these otherwise ordinary citizens seem intent on putting themselves in harm's way?"

"I figure they're brainwashed," said Adil. "Not in their right minds."

"Stupid and gullible." Esam stabbed a rubbery ball of rehydrated soymeal and lifted it out of its red, oily sauce. "They were raised by their parents to think wrongly and don't have the sense to see through the lies."

Faris sprinkled grated cheese food product on his meal. "Did you ever talk to one of them?"

Ishaq snorted. "Why would I want to?"

"To see what makes them tick." Faris shook a generous amount of naga jolokia sauce on top of the cheese.

Safiy nodded. "In the words of Sun Tzu, 'If you know your enemies and know yourself, you can win a hundred battles without jeopardy.'"

"Enemies?" Adil licked sauce off the corner of his mouth. "I don't think of them as enemies, just loons."

Faris glanced at each man's face, trying to discern his thoughts. His loyalties. "Does the League waste resources sending a Special Forces team to capture simple crazies and ship them to Station Two? We treat enemies like that, people who are a threat to our peace and security. Not people who are harmlessly deluded."

Binyamin shrugged. "They don't seem very dangerous. Dengel just paces and prays. His wife's so depressed, she sleeps eighteen hours a day, and the kids huddle together and cry. None of them even looks for a way to escape."

"You're not questioning our orders?" Adil asked.

Faris's heart skipped a beat. "I'm trying to ascertain our opponents' motivation. Like Safiy said, that's Warfare 101, know your enemy. In fact, and with the captain's knowledge and approval, I've been doing a little research on this for the past several months."

He wasn't lying. Abdul-Malik was aware of his new penchant for Bible study and had made no objection. "I think, under the circumstances, we should familiarize ourselves with the ideas they're willing to die for."

Safiy nodded thoughtfully. "Makes sense to me, amir."

"I've been curious about their motives myself," said Adil. "I'll happily study their propaganda."

Binyamin got up to dispose of his empty container. "Other religions use the Bible too. Why does this Jeshi Samaki group get subversive ideas out of it when others don't?"

"It's not just the Jeshi," said Adil. "Groups all over the planet agree with them."

"Yeah," said Ishaq. "Organizations like the Saengseon Gundae in Asia. Ancient sects in across Europe and the Americas. It's pretty widespread."

Finished with his meal, Faris wiped his mouth on his napkin. This was going more smoothly than he'd hoped. "It's a persistent ideology, and if we're going to fight it, we need to understand what we're up against. I want us all to read these people's scriptures, find out what they believe and why they're so sure they're right."

"Aren't there different kinds of Bibles?" asked Adil. "Does it matter which we use?"

"I understand there are thousands of choices," said Faris. "But the version these criminals use depends on the language they're most familiar with. Some stick with their native tongue, but the Jeshi Samaki use a Standard Language translation called the Textus Receptus Based Version, or TRBV, and that's the one I think we should focus on. Definitely we should avoid any that are sponsored or authorized by the licensed religions, since the Jeshi and their ilk reject them."

"Yes, sir," said Ishaq. "Looking forward to it."

Esam tossed his container in the trash. "You look forward to everything."

Ishaq grinned. "Especially to a decent meal once we arrive on Station Two."

"So between now and noon tomorrow," Faris said, "read the first five books of the Bible. That's the old Jewish Law, but the Jeshi revere it as holy, too. See if you can figure out what's so special about it, and we'll talk about it after lunch."

They answered more or less in unison. "We hear and obey."

14

*L*ileela sat between Emma and Aunt Skiskii on folding chairs in the front row. Several hundred New Gannahans filled the risers that circled the glade in the thick, muggy evening.

This outdoor chapel hadn't existed when Lileela was a child, and it wasn't a brilliant idea now. The meeting would have been a Beehee's hooha more comfortable indoors. But no, they had to traipse a cross-county kilometer on a graveled track through the fields, traverse a stream over a rickety wooden footbridge, then thread through dense trees and even denser insects, to reach this clearing.

And for what? For the privilege of sitting on flimsy little chairs that could barely hold a Karkar? For the sheer delight of allowing a million tiny winged creatures crawl on your sweaty skin? For the pleasure of passing out in the humidity? Yeah, brilliant.

The only good thing was, the toqeph and her family were, as usual, among the last to arrive, so they wouldn't have to wait long for the show to begin.

Oh, another good thing. Small children remained at home, with their mothers or caregivers attending the service virtually if they chose. Therefore only Lileela, Adam and Ra'anan sat in the toqeph's section with their parents and Auntie.

Crude torches on tall poles circled the perimeter behind the last row of bleachers, marched down the aisles, and stood at attention around the circular central stage. The broad space between the front row and the stage remained unobstructed. As the toqeph and her family arrived, a bunch of older kids lit the torches one by one, using an open flame on a long stick.

Skiskii let out a gasp. Striking a flame was a criminal act in a domed Karkar city. Lileela leaned forward to look around Skiskii at the other Karkar visitors in the next section. Their ears stood stiff with horror, and the flight attendant, Liilo, looked like she was about to faint.

Being midsummer, it wasn't even dusk yet at this hour. The torches' purpose was not luminescence, but scent, which was supposed to chase away the insects. If it did, its effect wasn't immediate.

Before the last torch was lit, a man rose and climbed the steps to the platform. Lileela had been told Jerry Maddox would be leading the worship service, but if that's who this was, she would never have recognized him. Though short, as were all these non-Karkar people, he was broader of chest than she expected, with the thick, powerful limbs of an Old Gannahan. Didn't Mr. Maddox used to be a scrawny thing? She shook her head. It had been so long, she might be confusing him with someone else.

Once he started to speak, though, she recognized his voice. Yes, this was the man she remembered. His hair was still a straight, stringy brown and his beard straggly, but something had changed. Not just his physique, but his demeanor. He had a new confidence, an aura of authority. Was it because he was now a Nasi?

The circular stage made its slow revolutions, enabling him to face all parts of the audience in turn. His voice was amplified so all could hear.

Lileela hadn't been to a worship meeting since she was five years old, but she thought she remembered what went on. When she'd tried to explain it to Skiskii, though, Auntie didn't seem to understand.

Lileela had trouble describing it because she didn't fully understand it herself. The Gannahans worshipped the Bara, the Creator, whom they sometimes called the Yasha, the Redeemer. She knew this entity to be real, because there had been times he'd communicated with her through her meah. But she wasn't sure how to explain worship. "They sing songs to him and talk to him," she'd explained, "and someone talks about what his Book says."

Skiskii had looked at her blankly, even for a Karkar. "What's his book? And why don't people just read it for themselves?"

"Well, they do, usually. Many people read it every day."

"Then why do they need someone to tell them what it says?"

Lileela frowned, trying to think how to explain. "It's a special book, and it's not always so easy to understand."

"Then what good is it?" Skiskii's ears jerked with annoyance. "And will this Yasha person be there at the meeting? If he is, then maybe he should explain it himself. Or maybe he should just write more plainly to begin with."

"He won't be at the meeting."

"I thought you said the people will talk to him there? Does he do audio conferences?"

Lileela rolled her eyes. "He's not *actually* there. Not physically or virtually. Just in spirit." This had never seemed odd to her, since she regularly communicated with people at a distance through her meah. But she supposed it might be hard for a Karkar to understand.

"Young lady, are you playing games with me?" Skiskii put her hands on her hips. "What exactly *is* this thing you're dragging me to? Sounds pretty risky to me."

"It's not. You and the delegation won't be expected to do anything, just sit there and listen, and nobody will be in danger. Think of it as— as a lecture, like at the university, where somebody gets up and talks."

"Well, if that's all it is, why didn't you just say so?"

Looking back on it, Lileela should have warned her about the torches. To Skiskii, those were dangerous indeed. So was the wide sky above, with no dome for protection. Auntie kept glancing upward and all around, obviously feeling exposed and vulnerable.

Lileela also might have warned her that the speaker was going to be a Nasi knight. But since his purple tongue wasn't visible from this distance, what Skiskii didn't know wouldn't hurt her.

It never occurred to Lileela to warn Skiskii about the one thing that truly was dangerous: the Yasha himself.

ADAM scanned the crowd, looking for Elise. He spied her parents two sections away, with an empty chair beside them at the end of the row. They must be saving it for her.

He waved a swarm of gnats away from his face. At least they were lighting the torches. That should help. He glanced at the empty chair beside Mrs. Finnegan. The meeting was about to begin. Where was Elise?

Though not all the New Gannahans yet embraced the custom, Mr. Finnegan had agreed to seal the engagement of his daughter to Adam in the traditional manner. Emma had spoken with him about it, and the necessary arrangements were made. All that remained was for Adam to approach him.

Which he would, when the time was right.

The reward of betrothal to Elise kept him focused on his studies. Not that he needed the incentive. He'd always loved to learn and felt driven to achieve. Even among the Old Gannahans, it was rare for a person to reach the Seventh Level in only twenty years.

There she was, moving past a girl lighting a torch down at the front, now gliding up the aisle, face turned toward the toqeph's row, searching. Smiling at Adam, face brightening at his smile in return, and moving on to sit beside her mother.

Adam's smile remained after he returned his attention to the center of the glade, where Jerry mounted the platform.

ADAM scanned the crowd, looking for Elise. He spied her parents two

BROWARD held Marianna's hand. Silly, perhaps, but he still thrilled at her touch. An unexpected benefit of the weird Gannahan proscription against touching—once the ban was lifted by marriage, even the most casual contact sent chills down the spine.

Her son, Jax, sat on her other side, with his oldest daughter beside him. His wife and younger children stayed home because the little ones couldn't be up so late. Jax was a dutiful son. On Gannah, that meant being subject to his mother even after he had a family of his own. The convoluted family hierarchal system didn't make a lot of sense. But it was the Gannahan way, so when Broward became one of the newest of the New Gannahans, he adopted it as his own.

He'd even accepted the Gannahan religion. Or at least, he didn't object to it. He'd never been the superstitious type, but it wouldn't hurt to go through the motions. Especially since it meant so much to Marianna.

He gave her hand a squeeze. He'd walk barefooted through crushed glass for her, or fight Cephargian pirates, or anything else she asked, just for the privilege of sitting here with her.

A pain stabbed his heart at the thought that their happy marriage, along with everyone else's on this planet, might be short lived. Before long, the Karkar would wipe them all out and rebuild Gannah in the image of their own world.

Though Jerry's words were supposed to be encouraging, Broward had a hard time concentrating on them. How could anyone think tiny Gannah, not even village-sized by galaxy standards, could repel the power of a highly developed planet bulging with a population of billions? With no more effort than flicking a fly, one Karkar warship could conquer Gannah before breakfast.

He didn't care much on his own account. He was old and didn't have many more years left. What's more, he'd accomplished everything in life he'd ever hoped to achieve, and more. How many people could say that? It would all have to end sometime, so why not go out with a bang alongside the people he loved?

But that was just it. He loved these people, he loved the potential he saw in the settlement, and he hated to see it cut short by the Karkar. The war between Karkar and Gannah had been over for centuries. Why couldn't they let it rest?

Jerry droned on. The evening was warm, and Broward's eyelids grew heavy. It might not be bad if the Karkar ship just blasted them now and got it over with. He could go from this cozy chair to his eternal sleep without ever opening his eyes.

Marianna pulled away her hand, stirring him from his drowsiness. He hadn't heard the end of Jerry's talk. He looked at the people around him, trying to gauge their reaction to the things Jerry had said. Their expressions were sober, but not without hope. And certainly not filled with terror, as he'd half expected.

He hadn't been sure what to anticipate. But he hadn't figured they'd rise from their chairs and break into song.

ALONE in the toqeph's section beside Lileela, Skiskii squawked in disgust. Lileela watched too, but with a different response.

The singing had started innocently enough. It was just singing, right? Even if it was in the old Gannahan language. But then Jerry came down from the platform, people left their seats and filed into the open area in the center, and they danced. It was quite a sight.

They lifted their arms, they bowed to the earth, they swayed and they clapped. Not strictly in unison, as they would if the moves were choreographed and rehearsed. It was more like they each responded to the same voice in a way that was uniquely their own.

Lileela itched to join them.

She caught a glimpse of Ra'anan, and it was like seeing herself in another life, the one she might have had if not for her injury.

Yes, if she'd lived on Gannah all her life, she'd have been down there singing and dancing with the rest of them.

Abba stood out like a tree in a powlfield, shaggy head and shoulders above the others. When he raised his six-fingered hands, they reached to the height of the flickering torches. That's what filled Skiskii with disgust. That a Karkar, her own flesh and blood, would behave in such an unseemly manner.

Skiskii just didn't understand.

Lileela didn't quite, either. But unlike Skiskii, she knew what it was like to not belong. To be alien to both your mother's people and your father's. To hunger for acceptance.

At any cost.

Even dignity.

She tried to recall the old story she'd heard as a child. The one that prompted these people to cast away pride and act like blithering idiots. The one about the Creator who loved the Earthers so much that He sacrificed all dignity to join them.

Hearing the song and watching the movements, she couldn't remember the story's details. But her meah told her it was true. The Creator of the universe loved her, and accepted her, just the way she was.

Waves of revulsion vibrated from Skiskii. Based on the noises coming from the Karkar's row, they all felt the same. Lileela leaned around Auntie to see them. Sure enough, their ears tilted back flat against their heads and their yellow eyes reflected the torchlight in hateful sparks.

They didn't belong on Gannah. They were aliens here, and always would be. The Creator had given this planet to Emma's people, and these proud giants couldn't take it from them.

There was still much she didn't understand, but she knew the Yasha was real. She saw him in the beauty of Gannah, and in her parents' love. She saw him in the upturned faces, and felt him in her meah.

She rose from her chair and stepped off the riser.

15

*T*HE song ended and another began, but Lileela didn't know the words. Pulled out of the music's flow by the unfamiliarity, she glanced toward the near-empty seats just as Kughurrrro strode up to Skiskii in the flickering torchlight. The other Karkar were on their feet as well, preparing to leave the meeting.

Lileela stepped away from the pulse of the dance to watch.

Kughurrrro no longer wore his translator, but she could hear his Karkar roar from where she stood. "We've seen enough. Gather your things, we're going back to the ship. Immediately."

Skiskii tried to argue, but Kughurrrro reached out and grabbed her chin. "I said immediately."

Despite the muggy night air, Lileela's blood chilled. He had no business treating Auntie that way. As Lileela moved toward them, he yanked Skiskii's translator from her neck and flung it to the ground, grinding it under his gigantic foot. She couldn't hear the words he growled, but his actions spoke plainly in any language.

She'd taken only three steps when Emma spoke to her meah. *Stay where you are.*

Lileela turned and spied Emma in the crowd, eyes closed, reaching heavenward and swaying as she sang. Had she even spoken?

Lileela turned back to watch the Karkar exodus. Skiskii cast a furtive glance behind her as she followed Kughurrrro.

Let them go.

Lileela looked again at Emma, who opened her eyes and met Lileela's gaze. *All we can do is tell them the truth. They must make their own choices.*

Lileela stood between the fleeing Karkar and the singing Gannahans, knowing she must make a choice as well. Catching Skiskii's eye at last, she raised her hand and waved.

If Skiskii responded, it was too subtle a motion to be seen in this light. To all appearances, she left without saying goodbye.

※

BROWARD was too old to dance, and he wasn't much of a singer. So he didn't join Marianna and Jax when they rose and moved into the open part of the glade.

A few others dotted the seating area as well. In the fading light their faces were indistinguishable, but he recognized some of them by their shape or posture.

The Karkar were easy to spot. Never the sort to hide their feelings, they were plainly disgusted.

From what Broward had heard in his half-asleep state, Jerry had given a masterful talk. Without accusing the Karkar of anything, he used the scriptural illustration they'd discussed at the council meeting about that Jewish king, Hezekiah, bringing the Assyrian letter to God and pleading for help. He related that to Gannah's commitment to follow Jehovah, the God of Israel, and the Yasha's promises to reward his people for their faithfulness.

Finally, Jerry reminded his listeners that they couldn't take anything for granted. Gannah trusted the Yasha to protect them, so they must be serious about their obligations to him. From the Yasha's perspective, there was no such thing as secret sin. He saw it all, and it must be dealt with.

Jerry called for all believers to examine themselves, confess any sin they'd been harboring, and submit themselves to their Yasha. Then, under his protection, no power in the universe could harm them.

Did the Karkar take exception to the concept of sin and repentance? Broward had a hard time with that himself. These Yasha-followers made way too much of it. Sure, there was evil in the galaxy, but most people were inherently good. They should be given credit for that, not browbeaten for every little error.

Perhaps the Karkar were offended at the suggestion that they were the enemy. If so, was their offense legitimate? Did they really intend to take over Gannah, or was the threat merely in the toqeph's imagination?

Broward sighed. He'd known the toqeph for decades, and experience told him to trust her judgment. If she saw the visitors as a threat, it was a good bet they were.

The settlers were really getting into this worship stuff tonight. Many bowed to the ground in the traditional Gannahan manner, repenting of whatever sins they imagined themselves guilty of. All seemed totally absorbed in their adoration of the Yasha.

What would it be like to feel that way?

Movement near the toqeph's section caught his eye. Lileela had remained seated beside her aunt for a while but joined the singers a short time ago. Now, the Karkar had apparently reached the limit of their endurance and were getting up to leave.

The geologist approached Lileela's aunt. He certainly was upset about something. She joined her people as they strode away.

Broward brushed an insect off his arm. He'd seen the visitors' behavior at the airport and in Qatsiyr. Intelligent as the Karkar were in most things, they were clueless about navigating in this society. He also knew their night vision was poor. Would they find their way back through the twilit woods? Though the whole stand of trees was barely 250 meters across and about twice that wide, it would be dark by now, and confusing.

But who cared? It was their choice to leave in a huff, so let them find their own way back. And if they were, in fact, plotting to take over Gannah, they deserved to get lost or eaten by animals.

Broward rose and stretched the kinks from his back. He'd be glad to see them leave the planet, but not in body bags.

Moving slowly at first, then faster once the stiffness in his hips worked out, he made his way down the risers, then headed for the path that led through the woods. Once he left the range of the torchlight, it took a moment for his eyes to adjust, but he managed to make out the trail in the dusky light.

The sound of singing fading behind him, he plunged into the trees.

The Karkar weren't the only ones who'd never been in the woods at dusk. He hadn't expected the leafy limbs to block the remaining light so effectively. The air vibrated with insect trills. Diurnal birds fluttered and cooed as they bedded down, while others awoke to begin their nightly hunt. Unseen animals moved about, calling to one another with low, unsettling voices.

Chilled despite the muggy night, Broward pulled out his lahab and switched on the flashlight feature. It made the shadows dance around him, but at least he could see the path. Peering down the trail revealed no hint of the Karkar lumbering ahead of him. With those long legs, though, they could move at warp speed. They might already be out of the woods and across the stream by now. Was it worth following them?

Fifty meters in, he stopped. He should go back. Stories of animal attacks came to mind, and he gripped his lahab tighter. He wasn't comfortable with the weapon and would probably cut himself trying to use it, but having it in his hand gave a little comfort.

He heard a noise and spun toward the thickest part of the woods. Not just a noise — lots of noises. What kind of animals were those? Thumping and rustling in the gloom, shrieks and growls reverberating in the night like banshees or —

Or a herd of Karkar lost in the dark. "Hello?" he called. If it was the Karkar coming at him, he'd be okay. If it was animals, he hoped they'd kill him quickly.

The sounds intensified as they neared.

He called again. "This is Captain Broward. Did you lose the trail?"

The racket was now plainly Karkar voices, but his heart nearly jumped out of his chest at the sight. Their massive shapes looked like trees leaving their roots and moving toward him through the shadows, all squawking and cackling and yammering at once, tripping, running into stationary objects, and crushing small saplings as they came.

The stumbling forms took shape as they approached, and some of their squalling resembled Standard Language words. Blind in the dark, they were terrified, convinced they'd never make it out of the trackless Gannahan forest alive.

Once he understood what they wanted, Broward answered them. "I didn't bring lights for each of you, this is the only one I have. But if you can follow me, I'll lead you out of the woods."

Kughurrrro's Standard speech was hard to follow, but he managed to make Broward understand that some of their party was still missing. Broward cast the light into the trees on first one side of the trail and then the other, and all of them called. That was a sound he never hoped to hear again. It was a wonder the whole congregation didn't leave the glade and come running to see who was being tortured.

Finally the last two Karkar made their trembling appearance, scratched and torn.

Broward pulled out his messenger. "I think this has a light in it too." He fumbled for the right sequence of buttons to turn it on. "Do you each have messengers? Do yours have lights?"

Kughurrrro let him know that of course they had messengers, but their devices didn't have the flashlight feature. They didn't need such things, because their society wasn't so backward as to not provide safe lighting for their citizens.

That's what it sounded like he said, anyway. Broward shrugged. "Okay, then. I'll take the lead, and Mr. Kughurrrro, you take my messenger and bring up the rear. And maybe you'd better each hang onto the shoulder of the person in front of you so you don't get separated again. Will that work?"

The geologist took the messenger as they all made affirmative noises and stood together in a tight pack, trying to decide whose shoulder to hold. Broward didn't attempt to sort it out for them but waited until they'd organized themselves.

Finally they were ready to move. With the pilot's monstrous hand heavy on his shoulder and the lahab's light dim on the path ahead, Broward made his way down the trail, leading the shuffling train like a prisoner chained to his fellow inmates.

He felt positively ridiculous.

SHORTLY after Lileela and her family got home, reverberations from the departing transport shuttle shuddered the ground. They'd seen its takeoff lights in the distance and knew the visitors were leaving ahead of schedule, so the vibrations didn't alarm them. But it rumbled like an earthquake, and its thunder could be felt in the chest as well as heard in the ears.

Skiskii must have returned to the toqeph's suite for her belongings, and from the disordered look of things, she'd packed hastily. Had that terrible geologist been in the bedroom, overseeing? Lileela shuddered at the thought of him violating her sanctuary.

Spying something on the floor halfway under the pullout bed that no one had bothered to fold back into a couch this morning, she bent to pick it up. Aunt Skiskii's skin cream. Yes, she'd packed in a rush. She never would have left it otherwise. Lileela opened it and took a sniff. Odd, how different it smelled now. Not at all as pleasant as it used to.

Would she ever see Auntie again? Or Uncle Ogliziizl? Her eyes filled with tears and her head with confusion. After what Emma had told her last night, she could never go back. Whatever her future held, it wasn't a return to Karkar.

Dressed in her nightclothes, Ra'anan scampered in. "Wanna kiss you goodnight."

Lileela sat on Skiskii's bed. "Of course." She took the little girl into her arms. What a strange feeling, to have a little sister. Strange, but nice. "You had to give up your bedroom for me, didn't you? And now you're stuck sleeping with the baby."

Ra'anan giggled. "We're not together. She sleeps in a baby crib."

"But still, why don't we ask Emma if you can sleep with me instead?"

Lileela could sense Ra'anan imagining the scenario and liking the possibilities. But her expression was dubious, almost pouty.

Lileela patted the couch where they sat. "You could sleep here. We'll change the sheets and you'll be all set. You wouldn't have to share a room with a baby, and I wouldn't be so lonely in here all by myself."

Ra'anan's green eyes filled. "Are you lonely?"

"A little, sometimes."

"Well—"

What was holding Ra'anan back? "Don't you want to stay with me?"

"I do! But, I couldn't sleep on this, out here in the middle of nowhere." She wrapped her little arms around Lileela's neck. "I want to sleep in a real bed, with you."

That wasn't quite what Lileela had in mind. But on second thought, the alcove was roomy enough for two, and Ra'anan was small.

And it was the Gannahan way. The only people who slept alone were unmarried adults.

Which Lileela would be, in just a few months.

For now, though, she could use the company. "Sounds good. Let's ask Emma."

16

*T*EN days out from Addis Ababa, Faris called the men together in the *Glowworm's* dining room. "Gentlemen." Nerves taut, he looked from one to the other, wishing he could read their thoughts. "We come to a moment of decision."

They always gave him their attention, but now it was undivided for sure.

The men had shown an active interest in the Bible study project. From their daily discussions, it was apparent they were beginning to question some of their preconceived ideas about the book. But none seemed ready to follow the God of the Bible.

Though Faris couldn't anticipate their response to what he was about to say, the Spirit prompted him to make his move now. He took a deep breath to try to calm his pounding heart.

"I'm going to tell you something, and when I do, you'll each have a choice to make concerning your loyalties."

Safiy frowned. "What are you talking about, amir?"

"Just this. I am, even now, committing a treasonous act. And I'm about to ask you to join me."

Their eyes widened, but they didn't interrupt as Faris paced. "We're not ordinary people. Since our Petrie-dish conception, we have been an integral part of one of the League Starforce's most ambitious objectives, that of engineering a race of superior beings. We are the beneficiaries of the best of their provision, education, technology, and medicine. We were created for one purpose: to do the bidding of our creators. Promptly, without question, and to the best of our ability."

Their eyes followed him as he paced. "I have no choice in that purpose. It's who I am. I must serve my superiors, and I'll die fulfilling that duty. But I've realized something recently. There is one who is superior to League High Command. And that, I've come to understand, is the one I must serve."

He looked at each astonished face in turn. Since they were apparently too busy processing his words to interrupt, he went on.

"Philip Dengel is not an enemy, gentlemen. He is a wise and innocent man. One who a year ago shared the truth of God with me and brought me to saving faith in Jesus Christ. I must not be used as an instrument against the Dengel family any longer."

Each man's jaw clenched, Adil and Ishaq flushed, and Binyamin's mouth dropped open. But, as products of their training, they obediently waited for their commander to finish.

He drew a deep breath. "I am going to ask Esam to change this ship's course away from Station Two. I will go to the passengers and let them out of their cells. And I will do my level best to get them to safety. But I can't do this without your complicity."

They exchanged nervous glances with one another.

"And so I ask you: to whom do you give your loyalty? To the League, or to me? If you choose the League, then you'll have to kill me, or at the very least, arrest me and take me to Station Two with my friend and brother, Philip Dengel. If you choose to take my side, then you'll be making yourself a traitor and an enemy of the state, to be hunted by your brothers in arms.

"So what will it be, gentlemen? Are you with me, or against me?"

For several seconds, no one spoke. No one moved. If anyone made a sound, Faris couldn't hear it over the blood roaring in his ears.

Then Safiy rose. "I'll take that joyride with you, amir." He came and stood beside Faris, facing the others. "Two against four's decent odds."

Ishaq and Binyamin stared at them, their gazes pinging between Faris and Safiy. "Wh—"

Esam and Adil looked at each other then rose together. "Make that four against two, brothers."

Ishaq and Binyamin watched them go forward and stand with Faris and Safiy while some of the tension eased from between Faris's shoulders. God be praised, he might not die today after all.

He swallowed a lump of gratitude as he spoke to the two who remained. "I won't have you violate your consciences, men. Do what you know is right."

"What's right?" Binyamin said. "How can there be any question what's right? You're committing treason, insubordination, theft of government property, conspiracy—"

Ishaq hopped up. "This is the commander we're talking about." He gestured toward Faris. "He's never led us wrong before, has he? If it's a question of who we love and trust the most, there's no contest. Are you going to kill the man who slogs along beside us through thick and thin, who's put himself in harm's way for us a dozen times already and would do it again in a heartbeat? What has the League ever done for us—"

"Except give us our lives?" Binyamin rose, and so did his voice. "And make us soldiers, and feed us and clothe us and—"

Ishaq interrupted. "And treat us like property, like an investment?"

"We *are* their property. They created us for their use, and they've invested a fortune in each of us."

Ishaq took a sudden step forward, then strode to the front of the room with the others. "Faris treats us like men, like brothers. I don't know what he's doing, and I don't like it any more than you do. But I'm not going to turn my back on him after he's had my back for so long. I'd be dead by now if it weren't for him, and so would you."

Binyamin's eyes widened. "What's with you people? Are you all insane? I can't believe this!"

"I can't either, my friend," said Faris. "Maybe I am crazy. But crazy or not, I'm grateful to have these good men by my side, and I'd like to have you, too."

The instant Binyamin looked at the floor and put his fists to his temples in frustration, Faris motioned the other men. When Binyamin lifted his gaze, they were moving to surround him.

He turned from one to the other, wide-eyed. "What is this?"

Faris felt for him. "I know what I'd do in your position. If I couldn't fight my way out—which you can't—I'd lay low and then blow the whistle just as fast as I could get to a communication device." He nodded at Safiy, who locked gazes with Adil, and together they approached Binyamin.

Faris steeled himself against what he must do to his comrade. "If you would surrender your messenger, please."

Casting his glance from one sad, stern face to another, Binyamin slowly removed his messenger from his pocket and extended it to Safiy, dangling by two fingers. He dropped it just before Safiy's hand reached it, but Safiy didn't grab for it. Instead he snatched Binyamin's wrist, letting the messenger clatter to the floor.

Binyamin reacted like lightning, jabbing Safiy with his elbow and following with a strike to the neck. But all the men had the same training. Safiy countered, saving his larynx from being crushed by the elbow, and the rest reacted with blurring speed. In a few vicious moments, Binyamin was pinned to the floor by four men, and Faris injected his neck with a dose of sedative remaining from the Dengel kidnapping.

When Binyamin's body relaxed, the others rose, watching his prone figure. Faris hoped he'd stay down.

No doubt they all did. Ishaq still fought for air after receiving a foot in the gut, and Adil and Safiy both wiped blood from their mouths.

Faris shielded the sedative's needle and pocketed it. "Adil, find something to bind him with." He turned to Esam, who felt his jaw tentatively. "Do you know how to disable the location signal so we can't be tracked?"

Esam nodded. "Sure thing, amir." He winced and fingered his jaw again.

"Good. Do it. Then point us toward Gannah. Once we've got Binya secured, I'll get our guests out of their rooms. We'll put Binyamin in Dengel's cell until we figure out what to do with him." He paused a moment to think, and the others waited for him to finish before they went to do his bidding. "Put something in there for him to do. A loaded e-reader, maybe some games. We're not trying to punish him, just keep him from getting in our way. Once he's secure, we'll sit down and talk. I've got the shape of an idea, but we'll need to see what Dengel wants to do as well."

He looked down at Binyamin. "I regret he won't be joining us."

Adil returned shortly with some cord for Binyamin's hands and feet. None too soon, because he was starting to stir. They bound him and set him on the floor against the wall to wait. Faris left Safiy, Adil and Ishaq to keep an eye on him, then headed for Dengel's cell.

How could he face his friend after what he'd done? But he couldn't get there fast enough to put an end to this atrocity.

At the cell, he spoke into the microphone. "Brother Philip. I know you can hear me, but I can't hear you, so you don't need to answer. It is Faris. I'm going to open the door and come in. Don't be alarmed."

Heart pounding, he punched in the code. The door opened, and Faris stepped through.

Dengel sat on the bed, looking at the opening. Seeing Faris, he ran his hand across his face and slowly rose. "Is it—? Yes, it is you. The young man from Cairo. Faris-with-no-surname."

He looked Faris up and down. "A soldier, are you? Special Starforces?" His expression was the picture of confusion. "What—"

Faris swallowed. "I led the team that kidnapped you. And I'm sorry." To his embarrassment, his voice broke. "I had orders. I didn't know what to do."

Understanding seeped across Dengel's face. "I see." He nodded. "Of course. You had no choice."

Faris's jaw tightened. "That's what I thought at the time. But now, I realize I do. And I've chosen to turn traitor and make myself an enemy of the League. I, and four of my men with me. We're all outlaws now, and we must flee. But first, let's go release your family."

Dengel staggered. "My—my family? You mean, they're here too? Where are they? Are they all right?"

Acid of shame churned in Faris's gut. "Yes, we were ordered to take them too. They're scared half to death, but they haven't been harmed. Come, I'll take you to them."

Dengel followed him out of the cell and across the corridor to an identical freestanding cubicle. As before, Faris activated the microphone and spoke. "Mrs. Dengel? My name is Faris. Your husband is with me. I'm going to open the door now, and he will come in."

Faris punched in the code, but when the door opened, he allowed Philip to go in alone. When both Dengels emerged shortly thereafter, tearful and clinging to one another, Philip asked, his voice pinched, "Our children?"

His wife trembled and she made no effort to wipe the tears from her cheeks. "My girls? They are well?"

Faris nodded. "Right over here." He ushered them to the next cubicle. "Don't worry, they're both well." He activated the microphone, warned the children the door was opening, and then allowed the Dengels to enter.

The cries that came from within brought tears to his eyes. He stepped away from the open doorway and turned his back so as not to intrude on that private moment.

"The Lord has answered our prayers!" was the cry of every glad voice within the cell. He was glad the reunion took several minutes, for it gave him time to get a grip on his emotions before the family finally emerged. All four faces glowed with joy. "Thank you! Thank you, sir!" Mrs. Dengel grasped Faris's hand.

Philip held the younger child in one arm and wrapped the other around his wife. "You are a good man, and a brave one. You have made the right decision."

"I just wish I'd made it sooner." Faris released Mrs. Dengel's hand and turned to Philip. "But we're not home free yet. Come, let me introduce you to our fellow conspirators. We need to discuss our next step."

17

ROWARD carried a fresh cup of hot deshe into the sitting room and set it on the table beside his favorite chair. A relic from his starsailing days, the chair didn't fit the décor, but it fit his fanny perfectly.

He'd just settled into it and picked up his tea when Marianna came through the door and shot him a smile. "There you are. Why'd you run off before the meeting was over?"

"Long story." He set down his cup. "Which I'll be happy to tell you. And I should also tell the toqeph when she returns."

Marianna gave him a kiss, then sniffed the air above his steaming tea. "In that case, maybe you'd better hold off on that stuff, or you'll be falling asleep in front of the toqeph."

Broward smiled. "Thank you, but as wound up as I am, that's not likely."

She sank into a dainty wingback. "Did you hear the Karkar transport leave? Sounded like the end of the world. Looked like it, too, the way it lit up the sky. I thought they weren't going until tomorrow."

"Change of plans. I spoke with them before they left. That's what I wanted to talk to Dassa about."

"She left the clearing quite a while before I did, since I stayed to help with the cleanup. Which reminds me—did you know those Karkar creeps smashed their translators and left them scattered on the ground?"

Broward nodded. "Yes, I saw."

"Anyway, Dassa should be home now, if you want to see her. But what's going on, anyway? First Jerry talking about the Yasha protecting us like Jehovah fought for Israel in the Old Testament, then the Karkar stomping out of the meeting with you following. And now they blast out of here a day early. Is there something going on I should know about?"

"I'm not sure." He put his hands on the chair arms to launch himself upward. "Come with me when I talk with the toqeph. It will save me the trouble of repeating myself."

The toqeph's suite was around the corner from the Broward apartment. As he strolled arm in arm with Marianna, Broward looked over the balcony to the greatroom below, remembering his first visit here ten years ago. He loved the palace of Gullach. Though lightyears different from anything else in his experience, it felt like home.

At the end of a short hall, Broward pressed the buzzer in the doorframe. If it were daytime, he'd have just walked in, as he was here on official business. But after hours, it was customary to give the toqeph's family their privacy.

A moment later, the door slid back and Pik's frame filled the opening. "Oh, hello, Captain, Marianna. What can we do for you?" He stepped back and allowed them to enter.

"Is Dassa available? I'd like to speak with her."

"Have a seat. She's in the office. I'll go get her." Pik started toward a door across the room, then turned and waved a hand in the direction of the blend cabinet. "Pour yourselves a glass if you'd like. Anything behind the left door is fair game."

Broward smiled. "Thanks, don't mind if I do." All Gannahan blend was good, but the stuff in Pik's cabinet was top shelf.

Pik passed through the doorway, and his heavy feet clumped up the spiral stairs to the toqeph's office.

Broward ambled to the cabinet. He pulled out a stemmed glass and lifted it, along with one eyebrow, in Marianna's direction. "How about it?"

"Nothing too strong for me, as late as it is."

He laughed. "It's just fruit juice."

"Just fruit juice my eye." She took the goblet. "The kind of fruit juice that gets your blood racing."

Broward pulled out a bottle, already unsealed and about half full. He examined the label, then turned it so Marianna could see it as well. "Any idea what this says?"

She shook her head. "I don't read Old Gannahan. But it was on the left side of the cabinet, so let's give it a try."

Broward pulled out the stopper. "What if it's too strong?" He poured three or four centimeters into her glass.

"Then I'll take just a sip and give the rest to you."

She tasted, then licked her lips. "Better get your own. This is good."

While he took a second goblet out of the cabinet, she wandered to a nearby table and pointed to a brown brick-like object laying on the glass surface. "I don't remember seeing this here before. What is it?"

"That's Pik's dad." Still carrying the bottle and empty glass, he moved toward her. "See the engraving on the side?"

"What in the world are you talking about?" She set down her blend and picked up the brick. "I see some writing, but I don't recognize the characters. They're not Earthish, Standard, or Gannahan."

"It's Karkar. And according to Pik, it spells out his father's name, birthdate, and date of death, along with the Karkarish version of *beloved husband, father, and grandfather*."

She turned it over in her hands. "So it's like a little tombstone?"

"Not quite. When a Karkar dies, his body is dehydrated and compressed into a brick, then incorporated into a decorative wall in a memorial garden. But Lars asked that his brick be sent home to Gannah with Lileela when she returned."

Marianna yelped and dropped it onto an upholstered chair. "That's his body?"

Broward shifted his glass to the same hand that held the bottle and picked up the brick, which he replaced on the table. "What's left of it, yes."

She wiped her hands on her pant legs. "What's it doing here? Shouldn't it be in a cemetery or something?"

Broward chuckled. "It's no more macabre than keeping an urn of ashes on a shelf. But as I understand it, Pik wants to set it into a wall somewhere in one of our construction projects. He just hasn't decided the best place for it."

"So in the meantime, it sits on his end table?" Marianna picked up her glass and took a deep drink. "Lovely."

"You're going to finish your blend before I ever get a sip of mine." He shifted his glass to his free hand.

Pik's reedy voice floated through an intercom system Broward didn't know the suite had. "Captain?"

Broward jumped, nearly spilling the blend as he poured it.

Pik's disembodied voice continued. "The toqeph will see you upstairs. You can come too, Marianna."

"Uh, okay." Broward looked up and around the room, trying to locate the source of the sound. Not finding it, he and Marianna shrugged at one another. "Be right there," he said to the ceiling.

Broward went to the sideboard and set down the blend. Marianna put her glass beside his, and they headed for the door Pik had disappeared through earlier.

Broward squinted when he entered the round stairwell. In contrast to the soft lighting in the sitting room, the entrance to the offices blazed with light. Though he'd often been a guest on the main floor, he'd never been invited to the toqeph's inner sanctum before.

They reached the top and stepped into a bright hall, which gradually circled around and met itself back at the stairs. Subtle electronic hums and pulses formed an audio background, punctuated with an occasional low beeping.

Most of the planet had a rustic feel, even to the point of being backward. Here, though, it looked as modern as a starship bridge. Broward squeezed Marianna's hand. He supposed he shouldn't be surprised, since Gannah had space flight capabilities long before Earth did. But this place surprised him nevertheless.

Pik stood outside a doorway. "Come on in."

Broward gave Marianna's hand another squeeze and led her toward Pik and into the room he indicated.

It was, in fact, reminiscent of a ship's bridge, except he had no idea what any of this equipment was. The only thing he'd ever seen before was Dassa, and even she looked unfamiliar in this setting.

The floor, walls, and ceiling all seemed made of light. It wasn't the sort of brightness that hurt your eyes, but the illumination was sharp and complete, leaving no possibility of shadow.

In the midst of the large, round room, Dassa sat cross-legged in an egg-shaped enclosure, open in front. Because the seat was clear, it gave the illusion that she floated a half-meter above the floor. A band of light and energy surrounded her like Saturn's rings, flowing with colors.

She nodded at Broward when he and Marianna came in. "Captain. I'd like to thank you for rescuing our guests earlier tonight."

He bowed, speechless. How did she know?

Her green gaze didn't waver. "Is that what you wanted to see me about? The Karkars' departure?"

"Yes, Madam Toqeph." He bowed.

He and Dassa had a long history together, and under ordinary circumstances, they were on a first-name basis. But this didn't feel ordinary. Not at all. He hadn't realized he'd let go of Marianna's hand, but he wasn't holding it any longer, nor was she standing beside him. He was aware of her somewhere behind him, probably hesitating at the doorway.

"Good," Dassa said. "I'd like to hear about it, but I must stay here to monitor events. That's why I invited you to come up instead of meeting you downstairs."

Broward wouldn't have minded a chair, but he didn't want to ask.

She held him steady with that gaze. "You led them through the woods and then all the way back to the shuttle? Why?"

Shouldn't he have? He swallowed. "I saw them leave and was afraid they wouldn't be able to find their way back. Turns out they were already lost by the time I went after them."

Dassa nodded. "I heard them. They were terrified. Did they ask you to accompany them the rest of the way, or was that your idea?"

"I got the impression that's what they wanted. They'd removed their translators, so I had trouble understanding them."

"But they did talk to you?"

Her manner conveyed a sense of urgency, not accusation. Though he took comfort in that, this still felt like an interrogation. "Yes. There was no lack of speaking on their part, but most of it was incomprehensible."

"Were you able to pick up why they were in such a hurry to leave?"

Broward considered a moment. "Not really, no. I only know they could hardly wait to return to their ship."

Dassa didn't respond. She seemed to be focusing on an odd, shimmering cloud hovering before her.

Marianna crept up behind him and clasped his hand. "Are they — are they really planning something, do you think?"

Dassa didn't glance up. "There's no question about it."

The outer ring shifted a little higher than the others and changed colors. The room's walls flickered, faded, and then a projection of outer space covered them, filling the room with a wrap-around panorama such as a person might see from a starship observation deck.

The view changed and grew clearer until it concentrated on one quadrant, in which an orbiting ship could be seen. A League vessel of Karkar origin, from the crustacean-like shape of it. A spot of light moved toward it.

Broward studied the stars, trying to get an idea of what they were looking at. It seemed familiar. Then he gasped. "That's a real-time image. It's Gannahan space directly above our coordinates, with the Karkar vessel overhead, and the transport shuttle on its way back to meet it."

Dassa studied the projection. "That's correct."

Marianna held his hand in both of hers.

Broward stared. "I had no idea we had the capability of doing this sort of thing."

"Because you didn't need to know."

He tore his eyes from the projection and watched the flowing colors surrounding Dassa. "What else can that do?"

She ignored the question and spoke to Pik. "The girls are going to look for me in a minute. Would you mind going downstairs to see what they want?"

Pik nodded and left the room.

"I suppose you know," Dassa said to Broward, "that the toqeph had a palace in each of the provinces, and he paid a visit to each one every year."

"So I've heard."

"What isn't so commonly known is that each palace has a command center just like this one. Between his meah, his Nasi advisors, and these technologies, the toqeph could know at any given moment what was going on everywhere on Gannah or in space above it."

Broward found that a little unsettling.

"Almost like God." Marianna's voice was hushed.

Dassa shook her head. "Not even close. But some of my forefathers didn't discourage people from making that connection."

"So this stuff" — Broward gestured toward the colorful rings — "has been here all along?"

"Atarah Nemuel Ragal first developed the system a couple hundred years ago," Dassa said, "and it's been refined and updated since. But Gannahan technology hasn't changed dramatically since the days of Atarah the Great."

"He was the king who attacked Karkar, right?" Broward asked. "Eight or nine hundred years ago?"

"And the one who brought Christ to Gannah," Marianna said.

"Right. One and the same. By his time, the Old Gannahans figured they already had the technology to do anything they wanted. They saw no reason to keep improving on it."

"If you have the ability to do all this—" Broward surveyed the high-tech room. "Why live in the stone age? Why not apply some of this sophistication to other purposes? Why, life could be—"

"Just like it is on League planets?" Dassa shook her head. "Gannah is Gannah, not Earth or Nob or Eutare or Karkar. The Gannahan people have always preferred simplicity. We'd rather depend on our minds and our muscles instead of gadgets. Personally, I'm a little offended that we use technology as much as we do. But it's hard to give it up once you've grown used to it."

Already familiar with her philosophy on that, Broward only half listened. Mostly, he was trying to figure out those rings of color. "So from up here, you can see what's going on all over the planet, not just in space? Did the old toqephs spy on the citizens?"

"No." She increased the image's magnification as the shuttle drew closer to the Karkar ship. "Or at least, not that I know of. It would be possible, I suppose, but why should the toqeph concern himself with such things? This system was intended only for monitoring what's going on in space, to keep apprised of any dangers. I believe the only time the planet itself was viewed was to monitor the weather."

"Don't your sun's famous MREs interfere with it?"

Dassa nodded. "They can sometimes create problems, but for the most part, it functions without interference."

Marianna moved closer to the screen, studying the image of the Karkar vessel. "So you're saying we had the technology to see you when you were lost in the Ruwach Gorge ten years ago, but didn't use it?"

"Not exactly. No one knows how to operate it but me, and at that time, even I knew very little about it. I'm still learning its capabilities."

Marianna sighed. "Well, ain't that a fine howdy-doo."

Broward chuckled and gazed at her fondly. "Getting into the spirit of unsophistication, are we?"

Marianna turned her dark eyes on him. "You were here then. Just think of all we went through, not knowing where she was, or if she was even alive. And it was all unnecessary." She shook her head. "If I may say, Madam Toqeph, maybe you should teach someone else how to operate this equipment in case something like that ever happens again."

"It won't," said Dassa, "because I have no intention of ever leaving the planet again. But I will teach Adam to use it. It will be part of his preparation for succeeding me. Traditionally, I believe the toqeph's heir and a few select Nasi advisors were trained in its use. Few others even knew it existed."

Broward scratched his neck. "So how did you learn about it?"

Dassa sighed. "I found it when we were renovating Gullach. There are still a few things I haven't figured out."

Pik's footsteps could be heard coming up the stairs, and Broward and the others looked toward the doorway as he approached and then filled it to the brim.

"Ra'anan wanted to know if she could sleep with Lileela."

Dassa's brows rose. "Lileela wanted this too?"

"She was the one who suggested it. I told them I was certain you wouldn't mind. For tonight, at least. If they want to make the arrangement permanent, they can speak with you about it tomorrow."

"Hmm." Dassa nodded. "Good." She turned back to the projection on the wall, where the transport shuttle neared the Karkar vessel. The image was so clear the bay doors were almost visible.

Thinking about the belligerence of the occupants of the shuttle, Broward frowned. Then he looked at the flowing rings surrounding Dassa. "Is any of that, um, defensive weaponry?"

"Yes. But—" Dassa shrugged. "I have no idea what most of the weapons are, or how they work. And it's not the sort of thing I feel comfortable experimenting with."

Broward pursed his lips. "If you have proof we're in danger, maybe now would be the time to try." Remembering whom he was speaking to, he made a slight bow. "Madam."

If she thought him out of line, she gave no indication. "Oh, we have proof."

One of the rings changed colors and shifted its angle. A faint hissing sound filled the room, followed by low voices. Dassa seemed to be controlling these events, but Broward couldn't see how she did it.

"This recording was made earlier today," she said, "when Dmitry flew Jax and the geologist out to the mines and back. Mr. Kughurrrro could scarcely have made Karkar's intentions any more clear."

She turned up the volume so they could all hear.

18

*J*AX'S eager voice came into audio range in mid-sentence.

It sounded like he was giving a discourse on Gannahan history.

"….river forms the border between Periy and the desert of Midbar. Back in antiquity, there was no Yadad River, and Midbar wasn't a desert. The climate was different then, and the land below what's now the Yadad was fertile, like Periy. But then there was some sort of major upheaval, history's a little sketchy about what, exactly, but everything changed. The Great River up north of here, that's the one that runs into the old capital city of Ayar, it split in two, with the southern branch of it becoming what we now call the Yadad."

The geologist's alien voice broke in, with the translator superimposing Standard Language words over a muted Karkarish babble. "Midbar. Where have I heard of that land before?"

"We talked about it on the way to the mines," Jax said, "when you asked where machalatsah ore comes from."

"Macha—oh, yes. That amazing metal that expands and contracts dramatically with the temperature. Quite rare, isn't it?"

"Yes, extremely. It's found only on Gannah, and even here, there's not very much of it."

Kughurrrro moaned, perhaps with desire. "How I would love to see such a thing. You say it comes from the desert of Midbar? Could we stop and visit those mines as well?"

It sounded as if Jax hesitated, then Dmitry's voice broke in. "Sorry, Mr. Kughurrrro, but not today. We're pressed for time."

The Karkar growled. "This is such a beautiful planet with so many delightful things. I dearly wish to see where such amazing metals come from. Mr. Dmitry, could you not make a detour to please your guest?"

"I could not, Mr. Kughurrrro. It's just not possible. Even if we had the time, we don't have the toqeph's okay."

"You need that woman's permission to take every breath? Why can you not make a decision on your own?"

Jax cleared his throat before answering. "We have more political freedom here than a lot of folks. There's laws on Karkar, too, aren't there? I mean, you wouldn't be allowed to take a Gannahan just anywhere on Karkar. Wouldn't certain things be off limits to guests from other planets?"

The geologist made a choking noise, which Broward took for a laugh. "I would not be permitted to take a Gannahan anywhere at all. I marvel that that little princess of yours was not executed upon her arrival. It is only because her father was the most revered man on the planet at one time. And now he is the most famous turncoat. Pah!"

"Turncoat?" Jax asked. "How do you figure?"

"How else can it be figured? He turned against his people when he hooked up with a filthy Gannahan swineherd. This settlement, with its Earthish outcasts and half-Gannahan piglets, is an abomination no Karkar should even speak of, let alone help to create." Kughurrrro's passion was evident despite the translator's electronic monotone.

For several moments, all that could be heard was a droning in the background, the mechanical noises of the aircoach. Then Jax spoke again. "Why are you here then, Mr. K? If it's so terrible for a Karkar to have anything to do with us."

"I and my associates are here at the request of the League of Planets and our worthy Karkar government," Kughurrrro said, "to see Gannah's debt to our people finally and fully paid. And it will be, you mark my words."

After another brief pause, Jax said, "We'd kind of hoped to establish friendly relations with Karkar, since Dr. Pik is one of you. I mean, you're practically related to us."

The sound that followed, likely an exclamation of extreme distaste, was indescribable. "We are not relatives, Mr. Jax. We are not friends. And we never will be. You seem like a pleasant enough young man, and if I had met you in other circumstances, I would most certainly have liked you. But you have taken up with that Gannahan woman. That, I cannot abide. If you wish to save yourself from the coming ignominy, I invite you to join us when we leave for our ship tomorrow."

"Does that invitation extend to me, too?" Dmitry asked. "Because I don't like the sound of that igno – igno-whatever it was you said. Maybe I shoulda done some more tweaking on that translator, 'cause it sounds like it's making up words."

After another choking Karkar laugh, Kughurrrro said, "The word is not made up, Mr. Dmitry. It means great shame or disgrace. Public contempt. Something your Old Gannahan heroes knew well how to inflict." He laughed again. "But Gannah will be made to suffer the same when Karkar collects its final payment on your debt."

"I, ah, I don't think I understand what you're saying, Mr. K," Jax said. "You've already been paid. The papers canceling our debt are signed by both your people and our toqeph. Electronic versions are already on their way to Karkar, with a copy to Earth for the League records. What more needs to be done?"

"That particular phase is, in fact, complete," said Kughurrrro. "The princess's medical and living expenses are settled. But we have seen a small portion of the riches this planet has to offer, and a much greater debt remains to be paid. If you wish to escape, Mr. Jax, my offer still stands. Otherwise, you can pay with the rest of your miserable little people. It matters not to me."

After a brief pause, Jax said, "The toqeph was right, Dmitry. About, you know, the Assyrians surrounding Jerusalem."

"Yeah, so it would appear. Well, at least now we know for sure."

"What is Assyrian?" asked Kughurrrro. "What is Jerusalem?"

"Just a little bit of history," Jax said. "Speaking of which, where was I? Oh, yeah. The Great River split in two, and the Yadad cut off Midbar from Periy. After that, the people who lived south of the river had no way to get back across. You know, to where there was food and stuff. This was before the underground monorail system connected the whole planet, and..."

✺

THE recording faded out.

Marianna had drawn closer to Broward while they listened, and, feeling her trembling, he put his arm around her.

"Did that Karkar geologist mean—" she asked. "What *did* he mean, exactly?"

Dassa concentrated on a strange, hovering shimmer before her. "Exactly what you think. They hate everything Gannahan except the planet's resources. And those, they want for their own. We have other recordings as well, of conversations amongst themselves when they thought we weren't listening. There's no longer any question as to their true intentions."

She shifted her attention to the image on the wall. "There they go. The ship just swallowed the transport, so they're—" She stopped, eyebrows lifted. "What's this? They're sending a transmission. Already?"

If there were controls within that egg-like contraption she sat in, they weren't evident from Broward's vantage point. But the rings in the console shifted, and another image appeared on the wall beside the starscape.

A Karkar on a ship's bridge looked out at them. Her hair was streaked shades of yellow and pumpkin, and the pupils of her eyes sparkled like orange sequins. "Hailing the planet Gannah. This is Captain Skyoriin of the League Starship *Huh*."

Dassa's face appeared beside the Karkar's, apparently the image the Karkar captain saw on her end of the transmission. "Captain Skyoriin, I am the toqeph of Gannah, Atarah Hadassah Hagah Natsach Pik. I had not expected to hear from you so soon."

"I'm surprised you expected to hear from us at all. This is not a scheduled transmission."

"Nor was our guests' departure a scheduled flight. We had a pleasant send-off planned for them tomorrow. I hope there's nothing amiss?"

The Karkar captain's ears flattened. "That statement is not consistent with my information."

"I beg your pardon?"

"They cut short their visit because you made it clear they were no longer welcome."

Dassa's brows lifted. "I'm sorry if they got the wrong impression."

The captain turned to someone off-screen, muttered something in Karkar, then faced the camera again. "Wrong impression? Not likely. You openly stated that you have a power at your disposal that is capable of destroying us. The inference was plain. Our presence was not wanted, and if we didn't leave of our own volition, we would be forcibly removed."

Dassa nodded. "Oh, yes. They were present when our advisor, Mr. Maddox, spoke at the worship meeting this evening. And, although he wasn't insinuating what they apparently thought, this much is true. If an enemy decided to attack us for some reason, they would not find us defenseless."

"We've scanned your planet, Madam Toqeph. We find no defenses."

"Ah." Dassa pursed her lips. "Did your scans reveal forgiveness?"

The captain blinked. "Pardon me?"

"Do your instruments detect gratitude? Can you measure our joy? There's a great deal of that here this evening. How about hope?"

The captain's laugh sounded like a small explosion. "Madam Toqeph, you're being ridiculous. You would repel an attack with hope?"

"No. I'm merely saying that power exists that your instruments cannot detect."

"And that invisible, ethereal force is what you rely on to keep you from harm?"

Dassa smiled. "It is the force we rely on for every beat of our hearts. What makes your heart beat, Captain Skyoriin?"

The Karkar snorted. "Electrical impulses, of course."

"Which come from where?"

"Chemical processes within my body." The captain made an impatient gesture. "What are you getting at, Madam Toqeph? Do you have the power to stop my heart, is that what you're threatening?"

Dassa shook her head. "Not at all. But I will say that if Gannah is threatened, we have a Protector whose power is greater than anything at your disposal."

The captain made some sort of gesture to someone nearby, then faced forward. "Again, I see no evidence of any such thing."

"If your instruments can be trusted." Dassa shrugged. "But I assume you hailed me for a reason. Or did you just call to say goodbye, since our guests neglected to do so?"

"After a fashion, yes. I wanted to warn you that, based upon the intelligence our team gathered during their visit and the saber-rattling they were forced to endure, we feel it's only fair to warn you that Gannah is to be classified by the League as an Offender of the Peace."

"I see." Dassa nodded. "A settlement of fifteen hundred souls, no space flight capabilities, and no apparent global defense system, is a threat to the mighty League of Planets."

"I didn't say you were a threat, I said you were an offender. Your very existence is an offense to us, Madam Toqeph. The fact that you live and breathe is an abomination."

"And the fact that our planet is rich in every resource while yours is stretched to the breaking point is the greatest insult of all, I imagine?"

"Yes." The captain took a deep breath, obviously trying to control herself.

Pik was right. Karkar hatred ran deep and strong.

"And since we're sitting out here with no one to defend us," Dassa said, "you feel you should take advantage of the opportunity to settle an old score."

"Fortune smiles upon Karkar at last. We must take the gift the Universe has given us."

"The Universe?" Dassa shook her head. "You put your confidence in the mindless creation? Ours is in the living Creator."

The Karkar's ears tilted. "What do you mean?"

"You take the gift the Universe has given you, and we'll take the gift our God has given us, and we shall see who's still standing when the dust clears."

"Your God!" The captain spat the words. "Your God doesn't exist."

Dassa's face sobered. "That is a dangerous attitude, Captain. I suggest you reconsider."

"Why? Your weak little myth might give you warm feelings in your tummies, but we live in the real world. And that's not always so pleasant."

"I agree. And you're in danger of seeing the proof of it. For our Jehovah God is not only real, but He owns your Universe."

Skyoriin made a choking sound and cut off the transmission.

Broward's heart hammered and the blood pounded in his ears. "Was she serious? You'd better figure out how to use that weaponry, and fast. That's a Class A-1-P up there. It's not a warship, but every starship is armed for defensive purposes. And that one has enough firepower to wipe out our whole settlement in two or three blasts."

Marianna wept. "I can't believe this is happening. I thought those Karkar were funny and strange, but nice enough in their own way. How could they do this to us?"

Pik's face looked gray. "For them, it would be a dream come true. Growing up on Karkar, I was raised to believe it was our destiny to one day get our final revenge."

Broward remembered Pik's initial reaction, more than three decades ago, when he learned the plague ravaged Gannah. From his point of view, their distress signal was a cause to rejoice, not come to their aid. "But didn't that already happen? The plague they created wiped out everyone on the planet, except for Dassa. Wasn't that revenge enough?"

Pik shook his head. "When you're as consumed with bitterness as the Karkar, nothing is ever enough. Even one Gannahan alive in the galaxy is too many. And now, that one is multiplying, and she and her offspring possess riches Karkar can't begin to imagine. Even something so elemental as fresh, breathable air is unobtainable on their planet at any price, but here, it's everywhere, and free for the taking." Pik ran his hand over his face. "We used to think Gannah was hellish, uninhabitable. Now, though, thanks to me, they know otherwise."

Dassa had been watching the shimmer again but tore her attention away and fixed Pik with her green gaze. "Thanks to you? Why do you say that?"

"Because I encouraged them to establish relations with us. Because I sent Lileela to them. Because I indebted us to them, and invited them to come here to see our riches for themselves."

"How many of those things did you do foolishly or without prayerful consideration?" Dassa asked.

His expression was as placid as any Karkar's, but something about him looked thoughtful. "None, Madam Toqeph."

"Then this is not your fault." She turned to the shimmer again. "They're sending a transmission to the League. And something else I'm not familiar with. It would appear—"

She looked up at Broward and Marianna, who clung to him. "I'm sorry, it's late. I should let you two get home."

Pik exchanged glances with Dassa then turned to Broward. "I'll walk you down."

Broward recognized a dismissal when he heard one. Knees weak, he guided Marianna out of the room, and Pik followed.

In the hall, Broward craned his neck to see his tall friend's face, trying to discern something from his expression. But as usual, it revealed nothing. "What's going on? What does she see in that shimmer, Pik?"

Pik gestured for them to precede him down the stairway. "I don't know. But whatever it is, I think she'd rather deal with it alone."

At the bottom of the stairs, Broward saw the blend they'd left on the sideboard. He was about to comment when Pik said, "Stay and have a glass, would you? Might as well finish what you started."

Broward glanced at Marianna, who squeezed out a weak smile. "Sure, might as well. It could be the last chance we ever get."

Heading toward the blend cabinet, Pik didn't contradict her.

19

SEATED in the *Glowworm's* small dining area, Faris glanced from one man to another as they discussed their next step.

Safiy scowled. "Why would the Cephargians allow us to fly in, fuel up, and leave unmolested? They'd kill for a ship like this. Literally."

"Even if they just stole it and let us go," Ishaq said, "they'd put us on some leaky old boat that would fall apart halfway to the next station. No, stopping at a Cephargian outpost would be suicide."

Faris nodded. "I agree. And I'm still loyal enough to the League that I don't want our technology getting into Cephargian hands. We should steer clear of them."

Ishaq shook his head. "What choice do we have? We can't pass Outpost Cepharge, because we've barely enough fuel to get us even that far. Going the other direction, we could reach Nob. But since the Nobians are in the League of Planets, we'd be arrested as soon as we docked. Our chances of talking our way out of trouble with the Cephargians might be better than getting away from the Nobians."

Philip, who'd been leaning back in his chair, sat forward as if wanting to say something.

"What is it, Brother Philip?" Faris asked.

Philip glanced around at the others. "As you're aware, I have no military knowledge."

Faris smiled. "I hear a 'but' coming."

"No." Philip shook his head. "No buts. However, there is a 'nevertheless.'"

Faris chuckled. "Let's hear it."

"Nevertheless—" Philip grinned. "I do not feel comfortable going to the Cephargians. As you said yourself, we might be outlaws, but we're not truly traitors. We should go to our friends for assistance, not our enemies."

Adil scowled. "We have no friends."

"The whole galaxy is our enemy," Esam said at the same time.

Philip shrugged. "Though the enemy is all around us, our God has people everywhere. Even—" He bobbed his head toward Faris. "—in the Special Starforces."

Safiy rubbed his chin. "You're saying we should just go flying into Nob like nothing's going on?"

Esam's dour expression softened with the lifting of his brows. "We just might get away with it as long as we don't look guilty. Besides, the Cephargians would want payment up front."

"Yeah, like our ship," said Ishaq.

Adil looked at Philip. "Or our guests."

Faris had been thinking the same thing. "But Nob would put the fuel on the League's tab. Wouldn't that raise a flag? Tell HQ where we are?"

Esam snorted. "On Earth, yes, every purchase is instantly tracked. But on Nob, receipts are dumped into a big, sloppy electronic file of reimbursable expenditures. They'll record the *Glowworm*'s registration and flight information, but that sort of thing doesn't get relayed to HQ unless they ask for it."

Faris grabbed this buoy of hope. "You mean they'd charge the League for our fuel without reporting which ship they gave it to?"

"That's exactly what I mean." Esam nodded. "I'm told the League doesn't ask for a breakdown of expenses unless the amounts seem questionable."

Ishaq's eyes widened. "That's crazy. Why would they allow that?"

"Because," said Safiy, "according to what I've heard, the Nobians refuse to use our Leaguesoft systems. They like their software better. HQ gave up trying to make them switch over for fear they'd pull out of the League altogether. I guess they figure they stand to gain more from Nobian commerce than they lose through poor recordkeeping."

Never prone to optimism, Faris frowned. "But the Nobians are generally honest, and they're sharp. If they pick up so much as a whiff of shady business, they'll detain us."

"So?" Esam shrugged. "We won't blink."

Safiy's expression was thoughtful. "Besides, according to Brother Philip, we have friends in high places."

Pursing his lips, Faris ran the options through his mind, praying for wisdom. It was crazy, but... He took a deep breath. "Okay." He scanned the faces around the table. "Are we in agreement, then? We head for Nob?"

They all nodded, murmuring things like, "I think that's best."

"Wherever we venture," said Philip, "we are in God's hands."

Faris nodded. "Then let's venture to Nob." He glanced at Dengel, whose expression was dubious. "Don't you think so, Philip?"

"I appreciate what you've done for me, and especially for rescuing my family. If they had been taken to the Center on Station Six —" His eyes filled with tears. "But we're stealing a League vessel and planning to fuel it under false pretenses. It isn't right. I can't condone it."

Faris sighed. "You're right. I don't like it either. I'd like to return the League's property and reimburse them for their losses, but I haven't been able to figure out how."

"Perhaps the Lord will show us the way." Philip's voice sounded less certain than his words.

THE fuel depot off Nob's western hemisphere was a kilometers-long, misshapen assembly of unfamiliar materials constructed in a design Faris could only describe as haphazard. Apparently Nobian designers followed the same disorganized philosophy as their accountants.

Computer-generated Standard Language instructions coming through the communications system directed Esam through a series of convoluted channels, dimly lit, and onto a platform. Instructions saying *Fueling Only* scrolled in bright orange letters three meters tall. *No Debarkation.* Other signs around the platform proclaimed what was probably the same message in other languages.

He let Esam do the talking as well as the piloting, while he prayed the exchange would go smoothly.

It seemed God had been behind all this so far. Of all the team commanders, it was he who was assigned the task of apprehending Philip. He'd been provided with this splendid little spacecraft. Most of his men willingly joined his mission, and Benyamin, angry but uninjured, had not been successful at thwarting their plans. It had to be more than just luck.

Logically, he should have nothing to worry about. Why would God have provided a way for Faris to rescue the Dengels only to allow their capture on Nob? But no one could know the mind of God, and Faris would take nothing for granted.

Thinking of the Dengel family, he patted perspiration from his forehead with his sleeve. Funny how holding innocent lives in his hands worried him more than a situation involving only him and his men.

"God is in control," was one of Philip's favorite adages. Though Faris couldn't argue, he found the going easier when he called the shots instead of leaving his fate to some unseen entity.

Outside, the depot bot scanned the *Glowworm's* identification codes. On the communication screen, an image appeared—a human attendant in the booth looking over the electronic information on her handheld.

The Nobians were the least Earthish-looking of all the citizens of the League. This one was greenish-tan, smooth and hairless, her small ears rimmed with a spiral of gold running through an even arc of pierces. "Point of origin, Earth. Departure date, 2923.05.12. You're making good time. Destination, League Station Two? A bit off course, aren't you, mister?"

"Yeah." Esam grinned. "A little bit. Had to make a detour. Not so official that it goes on record, you know?"

"Hmph." Her dark, deep-set eyes glared at them through the monitor. "Makes no nevermind to me what you Earthers do, just so you don't bring your trouble here." She looked back at her check screen. "Hazardous cargo, illegal substances, or contraband?"

"I'm carrying only what it says there. Seven men, one woman, two children, all Terrestrials, and the standard supplies and equipment."

"You don't plan to drop anything off?"

"Just the used Pyetronium canisters."

"Good. Okay, I see. This is a League-owned vessel, so we transfer the charge to HQ's account. All right, then. Doors open?"

"Yes, ma'am, and ready for the exchange."

She nodded and punched something into her computer. "Preparing to load. Is there someone on the fuel deck to assist?"

"Yes, ma'am, we're ready."

"Just to warn you, we've recently added a security feature to prevent drive-offs. It's a scrambling signal that interferes with your controls. If you check your panel, it looks like you have no maneuvering capabilities, because you don't. Once you're fueled and the payment is approved, we'll stop the scramble and you'll have function as before."

Esam peered at the dashboard. "Yeah, I see what you mean. Wise precaution. Get a lot of ships through here that take off without paying?"

"You'd be surprised what we see. Stolen vessels, pilots whose accounts are overdrawn, wise guys trying to charge their fuel to the League when they're not authorized, that sort of thing. We got burned too many times, so now we do a check on every ship. If you don't check out, you don't fly out, it's that simple."

"Hey, I don't blame you." Esam shrugged. "How do you know, though? You can verify the Leaguebank account's valid and such, but do you have a list of every ship that's authorized to take on fuel at the League's expense?"

"Yeah. But we run into problems when a vessel's too new, because our lists aren't updated very often."

"Ours is fresh from the factory. Are we on the list?"

"The system's checking, sir."

"So what happens if we're not?"

Her lower face turned up in a lipless smile. "Then you'll be visiting us on the Holding Platform until we get clearance. Or instructions to detain you." She glanced down at her screen. "Oh, there you are. It says manufacture of vessels in this category should be complete by 2921.01.30, which was more than two years ago. Says all Photuris ships will be League-owned and operated." She looked up. "Like I said, this isn't updated very often. But you look legit, I wouldn't worry about it. Don't see any reason why you'd get flagged."

Someone else came into the booth then, and she turned away to speak to him.

The indicator on the control panel showed the fueling had begun, but Esam contacted Ishaq on the fuel deck. "Everything okay?"

"Roger. On your end?"

"Yeah, so far. You understand the filling system okay?"

"Do I look like I need my hand held?"

Faris's nerves were too strained to listen to the banter. He leaned back in the seat, closed his eyes, and tried to block it out. He succeeded, until the woman in the booth spoke up again.

"What do you know, we've just gotten a fresh list, and I'm told there are some new alerts out. Something about a missing League vessel. The information is uploading now."

Faris's heart almost stopped. Probably Esam's did too, but he kept his voice even. "Well, good. Maybe your new information will tell you that our ship's been moved out of the factory and into circulation."

"I'm sure it will. But it'll take quite a while for the whole database to be updated. In the meantime, you've already been approved, cleared about a minute ago. Once the fueling is finished, you can be on your way."

Faris didn't figure he was visible on the woman's com screen, but he stayed cool just in case. It might arouse suspicion if she saw him get down on his knees to pray.

Amazing how long it took to refuel a little Photuris. Finally, though, the depot bot pulled back, the fuel doors closed, and the scrambling signal released its hold on the steering control.

"*Glowworm*, you're cleared for departure," intoned a computer-generated voice, and the message on the electronic sign changed to "Thank You For Stopping at Nob Fuel Depot West."

Faris let out a long sigh as the ship slipped away from the dock. "Well, that was interesting."

At the controls, Esam grunted. "So's this crazy depot. Why'd they have to make it so hard to navigate? I'm not used to making tight turns like this."

"You didn't cover that in the test of the prototype, huh?"

Esam tossed him a withering look. "Do you mind? I'm trying to concentrate."

Faris remained seated until they'd negotiated the labyrinth and left the station for open space. Then he rose, patting Esam's arm. "Good job, buddy. You didn't blink."

"Of course not." He looked up at Faris. "Now what? On to Gannah?"

"As fast as this little bug will take us there."

20

AFTER a day like she'd just had, Lileela should have slept like a luglit with its belly full of zikzak. But every time sleep's sweet release crept over her mind, her body would jerk, or Ra'anan would stir beside her.

Ra'anan. So honest, so innocent. All she cared about was pleasing her parents. If they were happy with her, all was well in her world.

Lileela couldn't recall ever having a talent for pleasing people. Aunt Skiskii liked dressing her up like a doll, and Uncle Ogliziizl liked the profit he gained from caring for her. But did she please them? Did they love her?

And what about her parents? If they'd ever been happy with her in the past, it was a sure thing they never would be again. She was too Karkarish. Had no practical skills to contribute and no interest in learning any. A burden to bring home and a burden to keep. She'd have to leave the planet as soon as possible to relieve her family of the trouble.

But where would she go, and how would she get there?

Lileela rolled over, her back to her sister and her face to the curtain. She envisioned the empty sofa bed sprawled on the other side, reminding her of Skiskii and the life she once knew.

But she never really knew it, did she? That comfortable life she thought was hers was all a lie.

Thinking about the worship meeting that night, a longing swelled within her, one she couldn't identify. A longing, and a fear—a fear of losing what she longed for before she'd figured out what it was.

Without opening the curtain, she slid under it and out of the alcove into the shadowy room. She had no plan. She merely felt restless, needed to move. Passing the yawning sofa bed on her way to the door, she slipped out into the hall. Where could she go?

The boys slept in the chamber across the hall, the one her grandfather, Abba Lars, used to live in. Her eyes misted. If he hadn't gone to Karkar with her, would he still be alive? He'd be really old, yes. But he'd been healthy here, and his strength started to fade as soon as he left Gannah. He only lived a couple of years after they arrived on Karkar, just long enough to see that she got treatment and was put into the care of Aunt Skiskii.

Next was the baby's room, with Ra'anan's things still in it. And at the end of the hall, Emma and Abba's chamber. The door was open and the room dark. They were still up, obviously. Did they ever sleep?

She walked to the stairway and paused, looking up, listening. She thought she heard voices, and one was Abba's. Who were the others? And where were they? Probably the front room.

Last night when she'd sneaked upstairs, she learned things she wished she hadn't. Maybe it would be better if she went back to bed. She yawned. Yes, she was tired. Bed was where she belonged.

Nevertheless she tiptoed up the stairway, gratified that her movements made no sound. Near the top, she paused. Yes, the sounds were coming from the front room.

"It would be unwise," Abba's reedy voice said. "With defensive missiles, the consequences of a mistake are considerably worse than merely cutting yourself with your own lahab."

"I don't see what we have to lose." The answering voice sounded like Captain Broward's. "We can't just sit here twiddling our thumbs while they're up there preparing to attack. If we wait for them to make the first move, it'll be too late. We must act now."

A chill ran through Lileela as if she'd been plunged in ice water. She sank down and sat on a step.

"I share your frustration," Abba said. "But we can't tell Dassa how to proceed any more than she should tell me how to treat injuries or you to command a starship."

"Oh, all this talk of war and strategy." A woman's voice broke in. "I just hate it, hate that this is happening. I thought we'd be safe out here, away from the League and everyone else. Oh, Edwin—" It sounded like she was on the verge of tears. Who was she? The woman Broward had married, Jax Florida's mother? "What's going to happen?"

Whoever she addressed, Abba answered. "Unless I miss my guess, nothing. Not tonight, anyway. How do you see this playing out, Captain?"

Broward didn't respond for a moment, and Lileela imagined him furrowing his brow in thought. "A Class A-1-P vessel isn't permitted to use its weapons without League HQ's specific instruction, unless the commander has reason to believe the ship and its crew, or some entity within the ship's jurisdiction, is in danger. For instance, say we were orbiting a planet—like we did Beeheehoohaa years back, when we administered that infantile influenza vaccine. And a Cephargian pirate ship wandered into the area, with the likely agenda of targeting one of the waystations above Beeheehoohaa. We'd have been justified in discharging our weapons to repel the Cephargians without contacting the League for prior approval."

"But only if the pirates fired first," Pik said.

"Yes," said Broward. "Only if they were the aggressors. We'd need approval to pre-empt an attack."

"And you figure Captain Skyoriin is under the same constraints? She'd have to get approval before discharging her weapons?"

"I'm sure of it."

Jax's mother spoke up again. "But they'd never approve it, right? Because they know we're not a danger to anyone."

After a long pause, Abba spoke. "We know they sent a transmission to League HQ, but we don't know what the transmission contained. They may have manufactured some justification for what they intend to do. If they've put the League on notice that Gannah is an Offense to the Peace, could they later claim it was necessary to discharge their weapons in order to keep war from breaking out?"

Lileela's stomach churned. Were they talking about the Karkar ship? The one she'd just left, and that Aunt Skiskii and Uncle Ogliziizl were aboard even now? What in the name of Kankakar was going on?

"Yes," Broward said, "but if they want to be above reproach and do it by the book, they'll have to wait for authorization to proceed."

"Above reproach?" Jax's mother's voice squeaked. "If that was their goal, they wouldn't be talking the way they are. I think they've already decided to attack no matter what League HQ says. They'll shoot first and make excuses later."

"I'm inclined to agree," Broward said. "My guess is, they're going through the motions of contacting the League just to cover their tails. But they'll most likely fire on us before an answer comes back, saying we left them no choice."

Trembling, Lileela bent double, face in her hands. She didn't want to hear this. Why hadn't she stayed in bed?

"Quite possible," Abba said. "And if that's the case, Dassa's wise to not experiment with our own weapons systems. If we launch something at them and miss, or fail to knock out their firepower, that would be all the justification they'd need. They'd have us, fair and square."

"So we just wait, is that it?" asked Jax's mother. "Sit here and go about our little lives as if nothing's wrong, while those—those—those monsters—no offense to you, Dr. Pik, but that's what they are, they're monsters—" Her impassioned speech dissolved into sobs.

"They are, in fact, behaving like brutes." Abba's voice was husky. "I make no excuses for them, beyond the fact that I understand their motives. Which, I'm ashamed to admit, I once shared. Thank the Yasha, He's opened my eyes and changed my mind, as I pray he will do theirs. But no, Marianna, I don't think we should go about our little lives as if nothing's wrong. I think we should do as Jerry said tonight. Give it to the Yasha. Our lives are in his hands, not Karkar's. We can trust him to do what's right."

"But what *is* right?" Broward's voice sounded tight, with sharp edges. "You said it yourself. We each see *right* from our own perspective. If it's determined by faith, whose is greater? The Karkar's faith in the Universe, which does seem to be smiling upon them? Or ours in the Yasha?"

"As Jerry reminded us tonight," Abba said, "the measure of our faith is less important than the object of it."

Lileela trembled. What gave this Yasha the right to decide their fates? Shouldn't Gannaha be allowed to decide what's best for themselves?

But what *was* best? No matter what scenario Lileela envisioned, someone she loved was likely to die a horrible death. Either everyone on Gannah, or the Oglis aboard that ship.

She couldn't stand it. It wasn't fair. Not long ago, she was a spoiled little rich girl on Karkar. Lonely and out of place, yes, but essentially without a care. Doing whatever she wanted, getting her own way, and usually being the center of attention. Yes, it was all a delusion, but it was a nice one. It suited her perfectly, and she wanted it back.

She rose, wanting to scream, to pound and kick, to hurt and be hurt. You can't damage a Karkar with your fists—not when you're as small as Lileela. She'd learned that long ago. But if you were really frustrated, you could let loose on one and pound until they'd had enough, and then you could scream to your heart's content at the indignity of wearing the mark of a six-fingered hand across your backside. Every muscle tensed with the thought of how good it would feel to explode like that, to carry her frustration to a satisfying conclusion.

But here, they wouldn't understand that behavior. If she hit one of the children, she'd hurt them, and if she hit an adult— No, the consequences wouldn't be worth it. Nor did she want to alienate her family. Not after all they'd done for her.

Soundlessly, she descended the spiral staircase, walked down the hall, and slipped into her room where Ra'anan breathed in innocent sleep behind the curtain. In the faint luminescence of the baseboard glowlights, Lileela sank onto the sofa bed and clutched the pillow. It still smelled of Skiskii, and she flung it down.

Then she struck it with a trembling fist. It made little noise, and Ra'anan didn't stir. She hit it again, and again, and paused. Still no change in Ra'anan's sleep sounds.

After stuffing her mouth with the sheet to muffle her cries, she pounded the pillow with both fists, over and over, as hard as she could.

No one stopped her. No one cared what she did to that pillow. Her childhood was gone and her adulthood was over before it began, gone in a blast from space. And no one lifted a finger to stop the destruction.

She tore at the sheet with her teeth and pounded the pillow until she'd dampened the bed with her tears and sweat, then lay, breathing hard, atop it all.

Aunt Skiskii's ship was up there somewhere, aiming its guns at her head, while Emma and Abba did nothing.

But why should she care? She didn't want to live anyway. She was born on Gannah, she might as well die here.

Once her breathing slowed, she rose from the couch, then eased through the curtain and onto the bed.

"Leela?" Ra'anan mumbled. "That you?"

"Yes, sweet. Sorry, didn't mean to wake you."

"Ya d'nt." The little girl's slumber picked up where it left off.

Taking Ra'anan in her arms like a stuffed toy, Lileela listened to the child's unfettered breathing and slid into asleep.

21

"*G*OOD morning, girls."

Emma's voice jerked Lileela from sleep.

Beside her, Ra'anan yawned. "Morning, Emma."

The curtain opened, and Lileela moaned, crossing her arms over her face. No way was she ready to wake up yet.

Beside her, Ra'anan sat up. "Hey, Leela, I slept with you all night."

Lileela grunted, wishing she'd slept as well as Ra'anan.

The little girl climbed over her sister's recumbent form while Emma bustled about beyond Lileela's closed eyes. "We have a busy day ahead of us." From the sound, Emma stripped the sheets off the sofa bed. "Lileela, are you with me?"

Squinting, Lileela uncovered her face. "Where else would I be?"

The horror in Ra'anan's meah at such insolence brought Lileela fully awake in an instant. "I'm sorry, I was half asleep." She spoke rapidly, trying to erase the effect of her words. "What I meant was, yes. What're we doing today?" When she'd rubbed the heaviness from her eyes, she could see her mother's sharp glance.

"Abba and I have a Council meeting in a few minutes, and Sylvia's coming to help you get the little ones up and fed their breakfast."

"Uh-huh." Lileela sat and yawned. She hadn't the faintest idea how to make breakfast. On Karkar, you took a package out of the cabinet and opened it, but on Gannah, everything was complicated. And getting the little ones up? What did that even mean?

Emma grabbed some clothes she'd apparently brought in with her and handed them to Ra'anan. "Here, sweet, why don't you wash and dress before Lileela wants the bathroom."

Smiling, Ra'anan took the bundle, bobbed a little bow, and scampered out. Not a care in the world.

Lileela watched Emma, who'd gone back to disrobing the sofa bed. Was she supposed to bow and ingratiate herself like Ra'anan? She hoped not, because she didn't feel like it. She didn't ask to come here, nor had she invited the Karkar ship, nor—

"Want to help me with this?" Emma's eyes flashed green.

Lileela slid off the bed. "Oh, uh, sure." She tugged the nearest corner of the bottom sheet, yanking it from under the mattress. "We have servebots for this sort of thing back home."

She winced inwardly. For someone whose meah wasn't supposed to work right, Emma's unspoken rebuke could sure sting.

"I mean—" Lileela bit her lip. "Back on Karkar. Where menial labor is a thing of the past."

Emma spoke through her eyes more than her meah. *Then who does it?*

"That's work for robots and such."

Emma's brows lifted.

Lileela flushed. "We have human servants too. People who are, um, disabled, or—"

Emma finally spoke aloud. "Or foreigners? And debtors? You mean, people like you?"

How could a loving mother make her daughter feel so bad? Lileela looked at the floor, then realized she'd unconsciously made that little Gannahan bow. "I guess you could say that."

Emma took the sheet from Lileela and dropped it to the floor with the rest of the bedding. Then she took Lileela's hands and pulled her down to sit on the couch with her. "You have much to learn about living on Gannah. But you're a smart girl, you'll learn quickly."

She studied Lileela's face, her expression full of concern. "I'm sorry I wasn't here when you had your accident, and I'm sorry for everything that's happened since. None of that was the life I would have chosen for my Lileela."

Lileela meant *heart's delight* in the Karkar language. Lileela's eyes filled.

Emma's hands around hers were warm and rough. "But here we are, and we can't go back. Like it or not, you are Gannahan, and you will be expected to behave like one."

Lileela wished Emma would quit looking at her. She couldn't return her gaze.

"Are you up for the challenge?"

Lileela lifted her eyes. Emma wasn't exactly smiling, but her face was no longer so stern.

"I— I'll try. But I don't know what I'm supposed to do."

Emma squeezed her hands. "Adam will help you. He'll be here in about an hour. In the meantime, Sylvia can help with breakfast and the kids. When Adam comes, you can go with him and leave the little ones with Sylvia."

Fingers of dread crept up Lileela's spine. Were the children going to be her responsibility thereafter despite Emma's assurances earlier? She didn't have the first idea what to do with them.

Emma released her hands. "Help me put this sofa back together, then I must go. You'll find all the clothes you need in the closet. They might not be quite up to your standards, but they should fit."

The bed collapsed easily and folded into a curved couch, which they pushed against the gentle arc of the wall. Lileela used to think the right angles and square shapes of Karkar buildings looked strange. Now, the lack of straight lines in Gannahan architecture seemed odd.

When Emma left, Lileela looked at the timedial on the desk. The arrow was still in the last hour of Gray Dawn—in normal-people's time, before 0700. Why so early?

Her suitcase lay on the floor, still mostly packed except for the cosmetics and undergarments she'd taken from it. Lileela sighed. Better hang her real clothes in the closet. If Gannah survived long enough, she might have the opportunity to wear them again some day.

Of course the closet wasn't electronic. But at least she could reach everything without climbing on a stepstool. Perusing the limited selection, she paused, cold horror seizing her chest for a second. Gingerly, she touched the brown striped jumpsuit.

This didn't belong here. It should be in the Gray Room. Emma must have put it in the closet to remind her to behave.

Every Gannahan floor plan included a drab little room in the center, where misbehaving children were sent to sit alone and contemplate their errors. Sometimes, if they'd been especially naughty, their punishment would include wearing the Garment of Shame when they went out in public. The brown-striped jumpsuit signaled that the wearer was in disgrace and should be shunned.

Lileela shoved the jumpsuit as far back as she could and moved the other garments in front of it. She'd been forced to sit in the Gray Room on too many occasions, and once, she had worn a small version of that jumpsuit a whole day. In public. For all the settlers to see.

But it would never happen again.

Whatever was required, she'd be a good Gannahan, as good as precious machalatsah, until she figured out how to get off of this horrible, backward world.

Hands trembling, she chose everyday clothes: gray tunic and black mid-calf trousers, both of which were shapeless and loose-fitting. Thick, gray socks that came to the knee. And drab, clunky shoes with flat heels. Thus dressed like a buffoon, she took over the bathroom from the ever-perky Ra'anan.

Since Lileela's curls were too short to confine in braids like the other Gannahan girls, she treated them to a generous dose of klg to keep them from billowing wildly. She hoped that by the time the bottle was gone, her hair would be long enough to control through other means. Because, of course, no decent hair product was to be found on Gannah.

She'd just finished conditioning her skin and applying the first layer of make-up when Ra'anan knocked. "Miss Sylvia's here."

Lileela opened the door, eyeliner in hand. "Does that mean I'm supposed to go to the kitchen?"

Seeing Lileela's half-finished face must have made Ra'anan forget the question. "Can I watch you do your eyes?"

"Do I have time to do it now?"

Ra'anan nodded. "Emma made breakfast a long time ago. Miss Sylvia just has to get the other kids up and dressed and then feed us."

Lileela started in with the eyeliner. "I think I can feed myself."

"Wait! Don't do anything yet." Ra'anan ran out, leaving Lileela to stare at herself in the mirror. The little girl bounced back a moment later with a stool, which she set down. "Okay." She climbed on the stool and looked into the mirror with Lileela. "Now you can finish."

Lileela smiled. Ra'anan was a cute kid. "So what's for breakfast?"

"Micken."

"I don't remember that. What is it?"

"It's a goop made out of all sorts of stuff, fruits and grains and things. Emma puts it on to cook at night and then it's ready in the morning."

Lileela wasn't sure what she'd been hoping for, but micken wasn't it. "Is it good?"

Ra'anan nodded. "Food's always good."

That wasn't true in Lileela's experience, but maybe it was just Karkar food she often didn't like. "I'll try it."

It was either that or go hungry until lunch.

"You'll like it." Ra'anan watched her big sister's artistry with keen interest. When Lileela finished and surveyed the final result, their gazes met in the mirror.

It was almost like looking herself in the eye. She shifted her focus to the rest of the eager little face, then back to her own. "So what do you think? Do you like the look?"

Ra'anan nodded. "I can't wait till I'm old enough to do that."

Lileela put her equipment away in a drawer. "When will that be?"

"Emma says when I'm sixteen and a dult. Then I'll be my own woman."

Lileela's ears smiled. "In other words, she doesn't want you to do it."

"She says it's for Karkar people, not for Gannahans. But I'm part Karkar just like you."

Lileela took one last look at the two of them side by side. "You know what? I think you look good without it. But when you're sixteen, you can decide for yourself."

And when I'm sixteen, I'll be my own woman too. That time couldn't come soon enough.

WHEN they first set out from Gullach, Adam pedaled his biwheel slowly so Lileela could keep up.

In physique, his sister was a Gannahan. In termperament, she was Karkar through and through. He tried not to let that disgust him.

He gazed into the hazy sky. Was the ship still there? Did his father's people—his sister's people—his own people, in part—truly want to wipe out the New Gannahans and take the planet for themselves?

Last week, life had been full of hope and promise. Now the blazing sun mocked him. Even if he lived long enough to complete the Seventh Level and marry Elise, Karkar would most likely bring their happily-ever-after to a swift and sudden end.

"Would you slow down already?" Lileela's sharp words came in gasps. "This hill is killing me."

Hill? It was a gentle slope at best. Nevertheless, Adam slowed. He'd been so wrapped up in his thoughts he'd forgotten she was there.

Her biwheel wobbled up beside his, and he glanced toward her, repeating her request in Gannahan.

Face flushed from exertion, she lifted her brows. "What?"

"You know what I said." Their meahs connected, and he was aware of her understanding.

"Yes, but why did you say it?"

His ears jerked with annoyance. She knew the answer. "I'm trying to teach you to say it in Gannahan as well as Standard."

"No need to get huffy about it."

He'd thought his tone acceptable by any standard. "Did I sound snappish?"

"No, but your ears about bit my nose off."

He chuckled. "Most people don't notice my ear movements. And if they do, they don't know what they mean."

"That's because they don't know many Karkar." She blew a wisp of hair from her face. "Okay, so tell me again why we have to ride these prehistoric vehicles?"

"Because, dear sister, we Gannahans use our bodies the way they were created to be used instead of letting machines do everything for us, making us soft and lazy. In fact, I usually don't ride a biwheel between here and Gullach. Most of the time, I run."

She groaned as they crested the rise. "Yeah, yeah, I remember. I was just hoping I'd heard you wrong. This is crazy. There's plenty of room at Gullach where you could tutor me, but no, you want to do it at your place in Qatsiyr."

Adam sighed. Why would someone as smart as she pretend to be dense? "You need to learn to use your lahab, and I'm taking you to the store to get one."

"The store used to be in the basement at Gullach."

"And now it's in Qatsiyr." Feeling her next question in his meah, he answered before she verbalized it. "Yes, we could take a train or a car, like you and Emma and the children did yesterday when you went into town. But that would be too easy."

She snorted. "Don't tell me, I know." Elongating her face in what Adam guessed was supposed to be a mockery of his, she intoned in a deep register, "Life is difficult. If we're to survive, we must be equipped to meet the challenges."

A cloud obscured the sun, and they both looked up, their meahs connecting again. When would the attack come?

Lileela returned to her normal voice. "Do you think we will? Survive, I mean."

"Yes. As the Book says, *The Lord is my light and my salvation: whom shall I fear?*"

Her biwheel wobbled as she shook her head. "I have trouble with that. Trusting the Yasha."

Adam felt a twinge of her pain. "How can you not trust the One Who holds all power in heaven and Gannah?"

She shook her head. "Everyone I've ever trusted has let me down. Emma left us. Abba sent me away, and Abba Lars died when I had nobody else. Aunt Skiskii and Uncle Ogliziizl only cared about the money they got from keeping me, and the whole Karkar race is two-faced. And I'm supposed to trust someone I can't even see?"

"Hmm." Adam brushed a bug from the back of his neck. "I see your point. But you were never really abandoned. I didn't shut you off from my meah, it was you who did that. The Yasha brought Emma home, and you're back now, too. So maybe the one you can't trust is you."

As soon as the words were out of his mouth, he wished he hadn't said them. He reached for her in his meah to apologize as he explained, "I mean, your understanding of things. Yes, people are untrustworthy, but that doesn't mean the Yasha is."

He feared she'd be offended, but instead, she seemed to consider what he said.

They communed silently as they pedaled side by side. But Lileela's thoughts and values felt alien. And when he tried to inquire about her experiences off planet, she closed her mind to him.

Allowing her to entertain her own thoughts, Adam pedaled ahead along the old Migrashah Road, the highway from the palace to Qatsiyr. Where it neared the city, it rose and encompassed the town's connected circles in an elevated loop. Exits from the highway led to the parking areas beneath each chatsr. Within the chatsrs themselves, only pedestrian or biwheel traffic used to be permitted.

Now, however, the road was so overgrown as to be little more than a wide dirt track in places. Many of the exits were in disrepair, and only one chatsr was inhabited. First Town, they called it. In the center of the cluster, it was the first chatsr built by the ancients and the first to be restored by the settlers.

Coasting down the ramp toward its gates, Adam gazed at the little settlement with pride. It wasn't yet restored to pre-Plague condition, but it looked like a living town. The building faces were repaired, even if many of the interiors still needed work. Weeds no longer grew between the broad paving stones, and the central courtyard was well tended. Most importantly, people lived and worked here, happily so, a fact that his Karkar relatives apparently couldn't appreciate.

What *did* they appreciate? Precious metals, gaudy cosmetics, and high-tech devices, among other things. But what about beauty and grace, love and devotion, satisfying labor, joyful obedience, and working together for the common good? Those were the true riches of Gannah.

As they entered the courtyard, he was delighted to sense Lileela's pleasure at the sight of the little town. Perhaps she was more Gannahan than he gave her credit for.

22

FARIS studied his friend's set face. "You're certain you want to do this?"

Philip nodded. "Provided it will put the rest of you in no danger, yes. Station 27 is the last League outpost before we enter unallied territory."

"That's my point. Once we pass Station 27, we should be home free. Why look for trouble?"

Philip pursed his lips, his face sorrowful. "*Man is born to trouble, as the sparks fly upward.* Though I seek peace rather than confrontation, I am called to take the word of life to those who have never heard it. The gospel is already widely known on Gannah, so why should I go there?"

His wife, Ayana, clasped his hand in both of hers, her expression imploring. "Because you'll be safe there."

Philip's expression softened as he gazed at her. "Ask Jonah how safe it is to flee one's calling." He lifted her hands to his lips and kissed them. "You and our girls can serve our Savior on Gannah in whatever way He has ordained. But I am commanded to evangelize, and the Starstation is fertile soil. There is no church there, no light, no one carrying the message. It is my duty to preach in that dark place."

Ayana pulled her hands away. "Would the Savior make me a widow, then? And our children fatherless? You will be imprisoned, abused, and likely killed. Is that your wish?"

"It is my wish to go where I am sent, to speak as I ought to speak, and if need be, to suffer as it is my privilege to suffer. Didn't our Savior Himself do so with joy?" Philip bobbed his head toward Faris. "And did our friend here not willingly risk the same in order to rescue us? I heard you make no argument then."

Faris frowned. "That's hardly the same thing. But I agree that if our Commander has given the order, we must obey without fear." He turned to Ayana. "I think we can best help by sending him out with prayer." He wanted to add, "not rebuke," but resisted the temptation. Philip was the preacher, not he.

Her eyes filled. "You are a good man, Mr. Faris. I do appreciate you and your people putting yourselves at risk for us."

He wasn't good, not by any stretch. But he tried to smile. "I regret leaving you in your cells so long, but I couldn't release you until most of my men were ready to stand with me."

Her face softened. "They aren't all believers, are they?"

He shook his head. "No. I hope one day they will be, but for now, their loyalty is to me, not to the Lord."

"Then let us pray," said Philip, "for your men's salvation, and a harvest of fruit from my sojourn."

Ayana put her hand on her husband's arm. "And for our family."

THE following day, Faris accompanied their guests to the transport deck. He, and Adil at the controls, averted their eyes while Philip kissed his wife and children. When their goodbyes were said, Philip entered the molecular transportation chamber.

The girls stifled sobs as the door seal sucked closed, and Ayana took their hands.

Faris turned to Adil. "You're sure we're close enough to the Station to get him there in one piece?"

"Pretty sure."

Ayana gasped, and Adil amended his statement. "Very sure. I've got a fix on an unobstructed location in the receiving lobby."

Faris nodded then contacted Esam at the helm. "Everything ready to go, Sam?"

"Roger."

The girls ran to the clear walls of the transport chamber and pressed their hands against it. "Papa!"

Ayana hurried to them, stooped down, and put an arm around each. "Wave goodbye now. Goodbye, Papa! See you soon!"

Adil selected activation mode on the MT panel and clicked Send.

An instant later, Philip disappeared from the chamber without so much as a flicker. "Papa!" the girls screamed.

"We'll see him again, girls." Ayana laid her hands on their heads. "Just like before. He goes, and he comes. As always, the Lord will bring us together again."

Faris's mouth went dry. Would the Lord bring Philip's molecules together again on Station 27? He'd never seen a transport process occur so abruptly, and he couldn't imagine the toll that must take on a body.

He glanced at Adil, whose expression revealed nothing as he watched the monitor. What was he looking at? Faris stepped to the console to see for himself, feeling Ayana's eyes upon him.

A businesslike array of data scrolled along the left of the screen, while swirling points of color arranged themselves beside them. As Faris and Adil watched, the points assembled and took a human shape. Just as it formed, it fell flat, as if to the floor, while the data described human vital signs, all in the stressed but safe range. The scrolling words read, "Transport complete. All biological systems intact."

Faris read the words aloud for Ayana's benefit, without commenting on the fallen man-shape. "It would appear he's reached Station 27 safely." Then he hailed Esam. "Transport complete. Get us out of here."

"Roger that."

A few moments later, while the shape on the monitor continued to lie still, the ship lurched and shuddered as the engines shifted into the Super-Fold Pyetroflex protocol. To save fuel, they hadn't made use of the SFPP mode before. But they hadn't had anyone on their tail before, either.

The girls squealed and fell against Ayana, who clung to them as she staggered at the uneven motion.

Faris steadied himself by holding onto the transportation console. "Everyone okay?"

Leaning back against the empty transport chamber, Ayana nodded. "My husband?" She slid to the floor, still holding the children.

"The monitor shows a successful reassembly. I'm sure he's feeling unsettled, but he should soon recover."

As the ship's shuddering evened down to a dull vibration, Faris put his hand on Adil's arm and glanced toward Ayana and the children, wordlessly asking him to see to the Dengels. "I'm going to talk to Esam."

The vibration calmed to a busy hum as Faris made his way to the bridge, speaking to the pilot on his messenger. "Esam?"

"Yes, sir."

"Were we spotted back there?"

"Affirmative. Soon as we came within range, the Starstation Rangers hailed us from the control tower, and at least two ships in the bays scanned us as well. Then once the MT activated, three others locked in on us."

"So we didn't exactly sneak in and out unnoticed."

"No, sir."

"Did you answer the tower's hail?"

"No, sir. I ignored them."

Faris frowned. Not good. "But they know who we are and who we dropped off?"

"I expect so."

Faris reached the bridge and closed the messenger connection, speaking to Esam personally. "Anybody chasing us?"

"Negative." Esam turned on the aft-view screen. Station 27 was already out of sight. "Not that they'd be able to catch us if they tried. None of the ships docked there have SFPP capability."

"Good. Once we're in Gannahan space, we can appeal to the Gannahans for asylum." A tingle of relief trickled through Faris's limbs. Were they truly out of danger? "What's the fuel situation? Can we go the distance in this mode?"

Esam shook his head. "We shouldn't have to. Another lightyear or two out, we can slow to standard Pyetronium flexion."

Any pursuit from Station 27 would be left in the stardust by then. Faris nodded. "Let's see what's ahead."

Esam switched the screen to the forward view. Nothing was visible but blurs as they slid along the time-space channel in their tiny Pyetronium shell.

He hated the thought that they'd rescued Brother Philip only to surrender him again. The poor man was likely being yanked from the floor and taken into custody even now.

Faris focused on the forward blurs and put what was behind out of his mind.

Feeling Esam's gaze on him, he turned. "What?"

Esam shrugged. "I never expected to go to Gannah, that's all. They're all a bunch of crazies there, aren't they? Misfits and outcasts trying to resettle the land of the bloody barbarians?"

"So I've heard. If it's true, we should fit right in."

23

SITTING at a table in the shade of a spreading elah in the palace courtyard, Lileela felt ridiculous. How could Mr. Maddox take this so seriously?

And how could his broad, muscular chest fill out that crude Gannahan tunic so interestingly? She studied the fine embroidery work on the shirtfront. His wife had done the design. What was her name? Katarina? What must it be like to be married to a man like that, so strong and mature? Her gaze ran along the curve of his jaw beneath the short, neat beard. The creases in the corners of his pale blue eyes, almost clear in the sun. The —

"Do you have a question?" he asked.

A glimpse of his purple tongue jarred her to full awareness, and she sat up straighter. "No."

His eyes smiled. "Do you have an answer, then?"

"Yes, of course. Thirty-two. The answer is thirty-two."

He pressed something on his tablet. "That's correct. And that's the last question in the arithmetic section. You came up with every solution perfectly."

What a surprise. It was a test for eight-year-olds.

"Next, I'd like to see your lahab proficiency."

That part, she wasn't so comfortable with. "I, ah—I haven't been practicing very long, you know. I just got back from Karkar a couple weeks ago."

Mr. Maddox's expression didn't change. "I'm aware of that. But no Gannahan can pass the First Level without exhibiting basic lahab proficiency."

Hoping for the best, she pulled out her blade. So far, so good. At least it didn't get stuck in her pocket. "What would you like me to do?"

"First, project your identification onto the flagstones, and I'll verify that the information is up to date."

That was easy. She complied, inwardly wincing at the image that accompanied the data. Emma hadn't allowed her to wear cosmetics for the photo, and the picture looked nothing like her.

Mr. Maddox nodded. "Now, using only your left hand, open the blade, pass it to your right hand and back to the left, then close it up again. Like this." He demonstrated with swift movements.

She had trouble opening and closing it with one hand like that. Swallowing her nervousness, she shifted the disc to her left hand and plied the button between her thumb and middle fingers. It took several frustrating tries before she succeeded in opening it. Then in passing it to her right hand, she cut herself. She dropped it to the flagstones and pinched the wound closed on her palm.

Mr. Maddox was unruffled. "Do you have a handkerchief?"

When she shook her head, near tears with embarrassment, he handed her his. "You were wise to not lick the blood, as some people do instinctively. With your Old Gannahan breeding, that could have serious consequences."

She pressed the cloth against the cut. "Well, yeah, I've got sense enough to know that."

He ticked off something on his tablet.

"Can I try again?"

"With the lahab proficiency?" He shook his head. "No. Cutting yourself is an automatic failure, as is the inability to open the blade on the first try with either hand. I won't be able to pass you without re-examination at a later date."

She stared. "You're not going to let me pass the First Level? I'm fifteen — almost sixteen years old!"

He lifted his brows. "When you demonstrate the appropriate competency, you shall receive the certification."

"That's not right." Still pressing the handkerchief to the wound, she closed the blade and slipped the disc into her lahab pocket. "I can't fail. By the blessed Kankakar, I should be at the Fifth Level by now."

"As you would be, if you hadn't been away for ten years. No one expects you to acquire a decade's worth of learning in—"

She rose. "This is ridiculous. I was privately tutored on Karkar. On Karkar, which is a lot better than this land of bumpkins. I got high scores on all my exams. I was less than a year away from the university level. How dare you say I'm incompetent to pass the First Level here, where people are idiots? How dare you insult me—"

He entered something in his table again.

"Now what are you doing?"

He finished making his notation, then looked up at her, his rugged face stern. "I have marked you highly competent in the First Level of arithmetic, Gannahan history, natural history, scientific principles, Bible, and Standard Language. Also the practical skills of personal hygiene, table etiquette, and time computation. However, you have failed to demonstrate basic lahab proficiency, and I've put you on special watch for lack of control and respect for your superiors. You are plainly not yet at the First Level in those key areas."

A flush of horror flooded her. "Special watch? What does that mean?"

"It means, Lileela, that we're through here." He rose. "I will not test you again until your mother certifies that you have been thoroughly taught common Gannahan respect. It is not my function to teach, but to assess. And it's my assessment that you would benefit from some strict lessons. If any of my daughters behaved the way you have today, their mother would make the punishment swift and painful."

Visions of wearing that brown jumpsuit flew into her mind, and panic rose in her chest.

"I have just sent your mother the results of the examination along with my recommendations."

"No!" She fell to the ground in the traditional Gannahan position of abject submission. Under Adam's tutelage, she'd practiced the four degrees of bowing and learned the appropriate uses for each, but this one came almost by instinct. On knees and forearms, with her forehead pressed to the ground, she wept. "Fail me if you must, but please, Mr. Maddox, don't tell Emma to punish me!"

She felt him looking down at her. Imagined his hard face, his powerful frame taut with anger—and a thrill of fear and longing tightened in her middle.

"It is not my place to tell your mother to do anything. I can only make recommendations. But I can tell *you* what to do. Get up."

She slowly rose but was afraid to look at him—which made it easy to keep her gaze on the flagstones, as was appropriate for the posture.

"When your mother reads my report, she'll determine the best action to take. In the meantime, go to your father. Tell him what happened here today, and ask him to explain how you should have behaved differently. Perhaps he'll be able to persuade your mother that you acted more in ignorance than defiance." His tone suggested that he himself was not convinced of that.

Keeping her gaze on his feet, she bowed deeply and swallowed a throatful of tears. "Thank you, Mr. Maddox."

From the rustling of his garments, it sounded as if he tucked his tablet into a pocket. "There, that's an improvement."

She bowed again. "Thank you, sir." After taking three steps backward, she bowed one last time before turning, as Adam had taught her.

This Gannahan respect stuff was humiliating. It was more fun to flounce away in a huff, like she would have on Karkar. No, on Karkar, she would have carried on until she'd gotten her own way.

Realizing she still held Mr. Maddox's handkerchief, she wiped her eyes with a clean corner of it, both angry and fascinated with his refusal to be manipulated. That was a rare trait on Karkar. Surely there must be a way around it, though—other than submission, of course.

This place deserved its reputation for barbarism. How could she bear to confess her faults to Abba and ask for correction? This was insane.

And if Emma took Mr. Maddox's recommendation and punished her? No, she wouldn't think of it. She'd twist sweet Abba's heartstrings. He'd convince Emma to go easy on her—and, like a good Gannahan wife, Emma would do whatever her husband said.

Hurrying back to the apartment, she ignored everyone she passed. She yearned to be free of these cruel constraints, to be her own woman. But in order to achieve emancipation, she had to pass the minimum educational levels. And in order to do that, she had to subject herself to this hateful hierarchal system, shackling herself with the very chains she sought to cast off.

She paused before the door to the apartment. Who would be there to greet her? A stern, angry Emma? A sad, disappointed Abba? A swarm of little siblings to distract their attention? All of whom behaved better than she did?

She sighed. This was all so confusing.

ADAM kept his pace slow and steady for Elise's benefit. He could jog all day at this rate but wasn't sure Elise could keep up if he pushed harder.

At least she could run the distance. Unlike Lileela, who refused to even try. Said running, even if she didn't have a limp, would be unseemly. Huh. As if she'd know unseemly if she tripped over it. She'd sure gotten some strange ideas living on Karkar.

"Do you think she'll pass?" Despite her exertions, Elise sounded only a little short of breath.

He glanced over at her in surprise. "How did you know I was thinking about Lileela?" It's not like she had a meah, after all.

She grinned. "You sighed. You know, that *What am I going to do with that sister of mine* sigh?"

"I did?" He chuckled. "Well. What *am* I going to do with that sister of mine?"

"So you don't think she'll pass?"

He shook his head. "No way in Gannah can she pass lahab proficiency. Not without a miracle."

"So what? She can keep working on it, then take that portion again when she sits for the Level Two exam, right?" She paused for a few breaths. "Academically, you said she's already prepared for Four at the least, so surely she won't be held back for long."

"I don't remember. Is there a test for attitude? Because if there is, she'll fail that too."

Elise laughed. "She's not much like you, is she?"

"Nor the rest of us. Living with the Karkar has turned her into one."

A rivulet of sweat tickled his spine, and they fell silent at the mention of Karkar. The ship was still up there, hanging like an axe poised over their necks. The reminder of that reality darkened the mood like the sudden chill of an impending storm.

They rounded the bend that marked the approximate halfway point between Qatsiyr and Gullach. The palace was visible ahead, but not recognizable as a building. Did architects on other planets design structures to blend into the landscape?

There were so many things he'd like to know. More than anyone could learn in a lifetime.

Elise's breathless voice broke into his thoughts. "When will you get your results?"

"Next week. Maybe the week after."

"Why so long? You turned in your treatise ages ago."

"It's only been ten days. Problem is, there are no impartial judges. Not many people are qualified to make the determination." He wiped a bead of sweat from his brow before it ran into his eye. "And those who are, all know me. So they're taking their time, looking as hard as they can for errors, determined not to give me the benefit of any doubt."

"That hardly seems fair."

"No. But there's no way to make it fair. The community is too small for me to be anonymous."

"You've already passed all the exams, right? You've just got to wait for your paper to be accepted?"

"Right." The familiar longing struck again, even in the midst of running. "Got that wedding dress made yet?"

She might have flushed, but it was hard to tell, as she was already florid from exertion. "What I have is for me to know and you to find out." With a spurt of energy, she moved ahead, her coppery ponytail swaying from the top of her perfect head. Damp clothing clung to her feminine curves and made Adam's yearning grow all the more. One day soon, he'd find out all she had.

He let her pull ahead just for the pleasure of watching her. It was the best view in all Gannah.

She tossed a look back over her shoulder. "What's the matter? Can't keep up?"

He laughed and increased his speed. "Keeping up will be no problem at all."

"YOU said *what?*" Abba's voice squawked.

Sitting on the sofa in her room while he stood before her, Lileela flushed. "I told Mr. Maddox it was insulting."

He stared down at her, saying nothing, ears tipped sharply backward.

Desperate to win him over, she took a deep breath. Full disclosure was probably the best course. "And that I had better tutors on Karkar than anything here on Gannah, and it wasn't right to hold me back just because I can't handle a lahab." She looked up at him with wide eyes. "I suppose I shouldn't have said that, huh?"

He shook his head. "No." He lowered himself to the sofa beside her. "There's no shame in failing lahab proficiency, especially when you've had so little time to learn. The shame is in your response."

At the word *shame,* she cringed. "I'm sorry, Abba. This is all so strange to me." She put her hand on his arm and allowed her eyes to well with tears. "I really messed up today. I was so nervous, I couldn't remember everything Adam told me about bowing and stuff. I just reacted without thinking."

His expression was unreadable, but his ears tilted out sadly. She forced the tears to spill over. "I'm so sorry, I acted like a complete idiot. Can you forgive me?"

"Forgive you? Of course. But that isn't the issue here. The matter at hand is correction."

Lileela's tears turned genuine. "I've been trying, but I just don't fit in here! What am I supposed to do?"

He gathered her into his arms. "We know it's difficult for you, and we expect it to take time. But it's you who must change, not the rest of Gannah. You simply cannot act here the way you did on Karkar."

His sympathy seemed real enough, but this wasn't going the way she'd hoped. Gripping his shirt in both hands, she sobbed into his chest. "It's so hard! I can't do it!"

He expelled a sound only a Karkar could make, an exclamation of scornful disbelief.

Shocked, she looked up at him. "What do you mean?"

"It's not that hard, and you can do it. You simply don't want to."

Tears certainly weren't getting her anywhere. She rose. "Of course I want to!" She twisted her face piteously, a technique that never failed to move Auntie. "I just need more time, that's all. Help me to learn, Abba!"

He nodded. "You're right. You need help, and you shall get it. Now that Jerry has alerted us to the need, your mother and I will both take a more personal interest in your education."

Lileela's mouth turned dry, but Abba didn't give her the opportunity to speak.

"Partly for your benefit, but also for the rest of the family."

That came out of nowhere. "The rest of the family?"

"The example you've been setting is proving detrimental to your younger brothers and sisters. Their behavior has been degrading steadily over the past several days. Though we've been dealing with it, it's hardly fair to punish them for displaying the same actions and attitudes they see you getting away with."

Suddenly lightheaded, she sat back down.

"Your mother is upstairs monitoring the situation with the Karkar vessel."

Elbows on knees, Lileela put her head in her hands. How she wished she'd never left that ship.

"Barring unforeseen circumstances, she should be free in about half an hour. When she comes down, she'll explain her plan for bringing your education up to date. In the meantime, you will wait for her in the greyroom."

Her head flew up. "What?" Her heart pounded. "Why are you doing this to me?"

Abba's ears twitched. "The proper response would be to get off the sofa and promptly obey."

She stared. He couldn't be serious.

"I'm not speaking theoretically."

Trembling, she rose. Just like that? She was supposed to comply with this ridiculous request without question?

"I did say *promptly*, did I not?"

The lahab-edge to his voice plunged into her gut. She bowed. "Yes, Abba."

She started to leave, but another sharp command stopped her.

"But first, an apology is called for."

Pausing, she turned. "Apology?"

"Yes. That's where you admit your error and express your regret for causing problems."

She caused problems? None of this was her idea.

"Have you been taught the protocol for that?"

She stared at him. Adam had explained the procedure, but she'd never intended to *make* an apology. Just accept one.

"Lileela?" He put his hands on his knees as if preparing to rise.

Careful to keep the distaste she felt from showing on her face, she assumed the prone position and forced out the prescribed words. "I am sorry, Abba, for my unseemly behavior. My shame brings dishonor upon you and upon all Gannah."

Forehead pressed to the floor, she waited for his response. But instead of accepting her painful apology, he merely said, "The rest?"

She gritted her teeth. "Your penalty is just. You are wise to punish me."

"Rise."

She stood, eyes averted according to the stupid rules.

"Your words are proper, but your tone is not. I shall inform your mother that she has much work to do."

Though she wasn't sure exactly what that meant, the words made her stomach lurch. "Yes, Abba." She took three steps back, bowed, and left the room.

Her legs trembled as she climbed the spiral staircase to the main floor, then passed through the curved hall. On the right yawned the greyroom.

A dim light came on overhead when she entered, casting just enough glow to reveal the shape of the room and its sparse furnishings: a hard bench in the middle of the floor and a closet against the back wall.

She sat on the bench with her back to the doorway. Before her, the closet loomed. A mental image of its contents burned into her mind. The stout switch lying wickedly along the top shelf, and the array of brown striped jumpsuits in various sizes hanging on hooks.

All the years she'd secretly yearned to see her mother's face. Now, it was the last thing she wanted to see.

She heard the front door open, then a babble of high, young voices. "Ra'anan," Sylvia's voice said, "take the boys into the playroom, would you, while I put the baby down for her nap."

"Sure, Miss Sylvia. Ittai, Hushai, would you like to do some puzzles?"

Little voices chirruped happily and little feet scampered down the hall, then stopped abruptly at the doorway behind Lileela. In the background, Sylvia trod heavily down the stairs.

The sudden hush in the hallway was palpable. "That's Lileela," one of the boys whispered. Hushai, from the husky timbre. "Why's she in there?"

"What did she do?" asked the other in hushed tones. Yes, that was Ittai's lisp.

Lileela should have noticed sorrow for her in their meahs, but instead, she got the impression of morbid satisfaction.

"Keep going," whispered Ra'anan. "When a person's in the greyroom, we don't look at them, remember?"

Lileela detected no pleasure in Ra'anan's meah. Only shame.

Little Ra'anan was ashamed of her.

Lileela wanted to melt to the floor and flow away into the cracks between the cold stone tiles.

24

*F*ARIS studied the three-dimensional holographic projection of a hmmmjckt board. The Karkarish strategy game would hold an endless fascination for him if he'd allow himself to get lost in it.

Binyamin was good—very good. And with little else to do these days, his skill had long since surpassed Faris's.

The image flickered as a change was made on the board. One of Binyamin's pieces moved to a new territory, acquiring more lands.

Faris stroked his chin. Should he counter that move? He had soldiers in the area. But Binyamin knew that. Did he intend to sacrifice his farmer for some larger purpose? Perhaps Faris should let the farmer prosper there until he figured out Binyamin's motives.

At his messenger's buzz, he glanced at the text from Esam. "Message from Station 27. Dengel OK. See me on bridge."

He activated communication with the detention cell. "Binya, my friend. Something's come up. We'll have to put this game on pause for a while."

"No problem." Binyamin's reply filtered through a speaker on the console. "Anything I can help you with?"

Faris sighed. He hated keeping his comrade locked up like this. "No, but thanks for the offer. Just sit back and enjoy your vacation."

"Some vacation." Bitterness edged Binyamin's voice. "Would you enjoy it?"

"No. I would not."

Though the visual was turned off, Faris envisioned Binya's dark, angry face and the tension of his posture. Looking for an opening, poised to act at the first opportunity—and ruthlessly efficient when it came. His every thought would be focused on escape and bringing the traitors who'd wrongly imprisoned him to justice.

Faris rose. "I'll be back to finish the game later."

"You know where to find me, *Commander*." The last word was laced with acid.

Spending time with Binyamin always made Faris half sick with shame. Sending Philip to Station 27 made him feel even worse. But as he headed for the control center, a glimmer of hope buoyed his steps. If Philip were, in fact, in one piece, this mess would almost make sense.

He approached Esam. "What's the good word?"

Esam turned toward him and activated the comm screen. "This just in. Thought you'd want to see it."

"Good news?"

"In part. But not so good in other parts."

"Let's hear it."

Philip's face filled the screen. He sat in a traveler's room on the Starstation, not in a prison cell. An economy room, from the look of it, but it was far better than Faris had feared.

"Brother Faris," Philip said. "I am well. I met a brother here, a Karkar." Philip smiled. "Can you believe a Karkar is a brother? He was connected somehow to Dr. Pik. I have no time to tell you the whole story. I just want you to know I am in good health, taken under the six-fingered wing, so to speak, of Mr. Kohz, at whose feet I literally appeared upon my arrival, and who considers me an answer to his prayers. The ministry he has labored in fruitlessly for two years is now up and running, and we have established a church of seventeen souls. Thank you, thank you, Brother Faris, for delivering me here. The Lord bless you for your courage.

"Communication between this far outpost and League HQ is slow. No one here is aware of my arrest and escape, nor of your theft of the Photuris. Though news of the incident will come through eventually, for now, I can live and move about the Station openly."

Dengel's expression grew serious. "But while the work prospers and the Kingdom of our Lord grows in amazing ways, I must warn you of what Kohz has told me. He learned through contacts on his home planet that a

Karkar ship, well armed, has been dispatched to Gannah. Officially, they're on a trading venture, but he has it on good authority that their true mission is to take over Gannah for themselves. Kohz tells me that Karkar's resources are perilously strained, and desperate measures must be taken to assure the people's survival. With their ancient enemy now vulnerable, they see this aggression as the perfect answer to their problem. Kohz himself agrees. In fact, he believes Gannah to be God's gift to Karkar. He expects his old friend and mentor, Dr. Pik, to cooperate with the Karkar and deliver the planet to his people."

Dengel shook his head. "I don't know what you'll find when you arrive, as I pray you will soon, and safely. But be forewarned, it may not be the safe haven you expect. Only a miracle can save them. But our God is in the miracle business. Are not the things He is doing here proof of that?

"And now, a message to my family." Philip opened his arms as if to embrace them. "My dearest Ayana, the distance between us cannot hinder my love for you, for we are one body, one soul. May the whisperings I placed in your ear before we parted remain there until we're united and made whole once again. To Candace, my precious firstborn, I know you are fearful. I remind you to trust your mama, trust Commander Faris and his men, and above all, trust our Savior, who is with you always. And Priscilla, my sweet baby, I remind you of all these things as well. I love you, and God loves you. He has given you your mama, your sister, and these friends to help keep you while I am away. I look forward to the day when I can wrap my hungry arms around all three of you, for they ache with emptiness.

"My prayers are with you all, as I know yours are with me. The God we serve is mighty." Philip bowed his head and the transmission ended.

Staring at the blank screen, Faris felt Esam's eyes on him but didn't meet his gaze. "Can you give a copy of this to the Dengels so they can play it as often as they want?"

"Sure thing." But he made no move to do so.

Faris shifted his glance toward him. "What's on your mind, Sam?"

"You know I'd follow you to the end of the galaxy, Commander."

"That's what you're doing."

Esam nodded. "Yes, sir. That's what I'm doing. And I've never asked why."

"No. You hear and obey." Faris felt a chill. Were all the men having second thoughts?

"You and Dengel, you get your commands from someone above. Someone who seems to have people everywhere. Someone who can drop Dengel into the lap of one of them, though none of us had any idea he was there."

What was Esam getting at? "That's true…"

"Well, sir, based on what I get from the Bible you've been having us read, along with what I see with my own eyes, I think I should follow Him too." Esam rose and saluted. "I'd like to report for duty, sir, if you can tell me how."

IT had been a long time since Pik had held his wife in his arms like this. Not since the *Huh* had taken up orbit around Gannah. She'd work herself to death if he'd let her.

He pulled her closer. She made soft, contented noises and snuggled against him.

That evening, after putting the children to bed, she'd gone up to the office as usual. She'd spent every night up there for the past couple of weeks, intermittently monitoring the Karkar vessel and dozing in her chair. Realizing she'd keep going day and night until he put a stop to it, he'd followed a few minutes later.

In her usual place behind the colorful, circular console, she looked up briefly. "Do you need something?"

"Yes." He waited for her to look up again.

Finally, she did, like a person waking from a nap. "What?"

"I need you to take a break from being the ruler of Gannah, protector of the world, instructor of my children, trainer of the Nasi, and all the other responsibilities you carry so capably, and just be my wife."

At first she looked startled, as if she'd forgotten he had a function other than her assistant. Then she frowned.

"Have you forgotten your duty to promptly obey your husband?"

She instantly rose, manipulating a control that created an opening in the console for her to pass through. "No, Pik. Of course I haven't forgotten." Joining him outside the rings of color, she bobbed in a respectful bow. "My apologies. I've been distracted lately."

He peered down at her. He'd learned long ago that as a Gannahan, she responded more happily to a severe voice than a sweet one. And thanks to his recent frustrations, sternness came easily tonight. "Yes, you have. But a moment ago, it looked as if you were going to argue. You were about to tell me you were too busy to bother with me, weren't you?"

She kept her gaze properly averted. "I would never say that."

"But you thought it."

In an inbred response to her guilt, she bowed deeper than before. "I am at your disposal, my husband."

He used to hate seeing her act like that. Over the years, however, he'd learned to enjoy the role of a Gannahan husband, for she relished the game. "Ah, so you *did* think it?"

Her flush was so deep her ears flamed red, and her voice was subdued. "Briefly. But I was in error."

"You most certainly were. What do you think I should do about that?"

One corner of her mouth turned up. "Whatever you deem appropriate, my husband. Your judgment is always wise."

"Then come with me." He turned and headed toward the stairs, gratified to hear her following obediently. She might be ruler of all Gannah, but he ruled her. The planet held no better aphrodisiac.

As they lay together now, glowing with mutual satisfaction, his mind wandered lazily through the array of difficulties they faced. He could examine them without fear as long as she lay against him.

Starting with the least of their problems, he mentioned the unusual number of beetles attacking the third-year powl crop. They discussed the eradication methods and laughed about the antics of the children who'd been sent into the fields to capture them. From there they moved to the issues of Tamah's whining, Hushai's penchant for being the center of attention, and Ittai's fits of temper.

"I've seen changes in Ra'anan since Lileela came home," said Dassa. "She got lippy this morning, and I sat her in the Gray Room for two hours. She was sweet as ever afterward, just like her old self. I hope that will be the end of it."

Pik stroked her hair, unbound from its braid and lush between his fingers. "Getting Lileela under control should help the others as well."

"I'm sure it will." She sighed. "I feel sorry for her, in a way. Mostly, though, I want to lay a switch across her back. If you'd have let me do that two weeks ago, we'd be seeing some progress by now."

Pik shook his head. "In the society where she's been living, only animals, servants, and prisoners can be struck. It's too demeaning for a Karkar child."

"So you say."

Pik chuckled. "Not that wearing the Garment of Shame isn't the ultimate in humiliation."

"Exactly. If I gave her a choice, she'd take a whipping every day for a week rather than wear that suit."

"When I was her age, I'd have felt the same."

Dassa laughed. "You Karkar and your obsession with fashion and self-esteem."

"So you agree? My way will be more effective than what you wanted to do?"

"Yes, my husband. Your counsel is wise." She yawned and sat up. "But I should get back to the monitors."

He grabbed her arm. "No, you should not."

"But what if—"

"Are you arguing with me? Lie back down and go to sleep."

She sighed. "I'm serious. I need to—"

He pulled her down and stopped her words with a kiss. "You need to obey your husband, or you'll be spending the night in the Gray Room."

She put her arms around his neck and kissed him back. "You leave me little choice."

"None whatsoever."

As she lay in his arms, he listened as her breathing became slower and more rhythmic. Just when he thought she'd fallen asleep, she stirred. "Don't you wonder, though, what they're doing up there, what's going to happen?"

He let out a long sigh. "Every hour of every day. But they're under continual monitoring by the computer systems whether you're up there or not. I forbid you to give it another thought. Let the Yasha worry about it for tonight."

She rolled over and yawned. "Yes, my husband. You are wise to correct me."

His ears smiled.

25

$\mathcal{A}$DAM rang the bell at the Finnegan apartment.

After a moment, the door slid open and Elise's mother stepped back with a welcoming gesture. "Come in, Adam."

He entered, his gut in a turmoil.

"I hear you've passed your Seventh Level." She closed the door behind him. "Congratulations."

"Thank you, ma'am."

Her smile seemed forced. "My husband's ready for you." She glanced at Mr. Finnegan standing nearby. On a table beside him, a long-handled tool extended from a charging unit plugged into a power port.

"I'm ready too." Adam bowed deeply, partly in respect, but also to keep his gaze off the implement beside Mr. Finnegan.

She flushed, her eyes filling. "You're a dear boy. No. A dear man." She glanced at her husband again. "I'll leave you two alone." She hurried out of the room, and Adam turned toward Elise's father.

Mr. Finnegan cleared his throat. "Well."

Adam set his jaw. "Good evening, sir."

"Evening, son." The older man looked as uncomfortable as Adam felt. "We're glad to see you."

Adam managed a smile. "I've kept Elise waiting a long time."

Mr. Finnegan chuckled. "She thinks so."

Adam allowed himself to glance at the pole extending from the box. Why put this off any longer? He switched to the Old Gannahan language. "I would speak with thee, sir."

The older man sobered and gave the traditional response. "Speak your piece."

Adam tried to swallow, but his mouth was dry. "I love thy daughter as my own life, and I revere thy family as my father's. If I may wear thy noble name, our children will carry it proudly."

Mr. Finnegan's face drew tense, and the words came out clumsily. "I would delight to see my father's name pass to thy and my daughter's children."

Adam knelt on one knee. "I would seal my troth, if thou wouldst permit." He lowered his head and pulled his ponytail to the side, exposing the area behind his right ear.

Mr. Finnegan's voice sounded hoarse. "I grant thy request with joy."

Adam kept his breathing even and willed his heart to beat slowly. The man who would be his father-in-law stepped to the box and withdrew the pole, releasing the scent of red-hot iron.

Adam stared at the floor in front of him while the older man neared. Heat radiated from the tool, and Adam braced himself.

Mr. Finnegan stood behind him. "Bear bravely the name Finnegan, and let not thy children bring it shame."

A sudden, searing pain assaulted the side of Adam's head, and he sucked in air, biting off a cry. The sizzle of burning flesh was loud by his ear, and his mind and stomach rebelled. Nevertheless he remained firm, and after two seconds, the searing iron left his skin.

But the pain intensified. If his head had not already been lowered, he might have fainted.

With quick movements, Mr. Finnegan replaced the tool into its holder, then pulled a poultice of eseb leaves from a bowl of ice on a table nearby and pressed it against the wound behind Adam's ear.

"Rise, my son. Thou art an honor to thy family and mine."

Adam rose shakily, and his father-in-law, stifling a sob, wrapped him in a long embrace.

Adam held the cool cloth to the burn. The pain was worse than he'd expected, and he felt weak all over. "I appreciate you agreeing to follow the Old Gannahan custom." Speaking again in the Standard tongue, he was relieved his voice sounded stronger than he felt. "I know it was difficult."

"I understand how important it is to you, but—" Forehead beaded with sweat, Mr. Finnegan unplugged the box from the power source with trembling hands. "That's got to hurt like the dickens."

Adam held the cloth to the burn. "Oh, it's not so bad."

That might have been the first lie he'd ever told.

"You look like you'd better sit down. I've got some good blend I've been saving for a special occasion."

Gingerly removing the poultice and turning it over to the cooler side, Adam sat. "I'd say this is one."

Mrs. Finnegan must have been listening, for she entered carrying a tray with three glasses and a bottle. Her eyes were red and she held a handkerchief along with the tray.

"Ah, thank you." Mr. Finnegan kissed her forehead. "It's over, love."

She wiped her eyes then waved the hankie in front of her face. "But the smell!"

Her husband picked up the bottle. "I've known you to make worse smells than that with your cooking." He pulled back, chuckling, as she tried to slap his arm.

She sat on the sofa and turned to Adam. "You poor, dear boy. What customs the Old Gannahans had. I swear, I don't understand why you have to follow them. The toqeph said it's not the law, it was just the usual practice, so you wouldn't be violating any rules by not doing it."

Mr. Finnegan poured the blend. "We menfolk don't expect you ladies to understand. Just like it is in every culture, we do crazy things, and you women flutter about it." He handed a glass to Adam. "To my new son."

When Elise's mother gave a sob and covered her eyes with the handkerchief, Mr. Finnegan set down the bottle, sat beside her and put his arms around her.

Adam's head throbbed and his stomach churned. He took a sip of blend to calm himself.

Mrs. Finnegan sniffled. "I always did think of you as part of the family, the way you and Everett were so close."

"I'm sorry. You've lost so much." *And all for the sake of my ungrateful sister*, he resisted adding. "I miss Everett too."

Eyes filling, Mr. Finnegan cleared his throat. "Nothing to be done about that. He was a good boy, and we all loved him. But he knew the Yasha, and the Yasha took him home." He lifted a glass. "Let's drink to Everett, and to his best friend Adam, and to his sister Elise. All my children, each one loved."

Handkerchief still wadded in her hand, Mrs. Finnegan picked up her glass. "And if those horrid people on that ship up there decide to wipe us out, we'll all be together again soon."

Her husband frowned. "Let's not drink to that."

A clap of thunder buried his last word, and all three of them turned toward the window. Howling winds drove the rain across it with such fury the whole building seemed under water.

Sudden storms weren't unusual on Gannah, but this was the most sudden and ferocious Adam had ever seen. Before anyone could speak again, another sharp crack stunned Adam's already-throbbing ears, and he set down his glass before he dropped it.

THAT wouldn't cover much." Lynne Lucas studied the undergarment, her expression amused.

Lileela snatched the panties out of her hands. "It doesn't have to. That's why it's called *under*wear." She tossed the garment with the rest of her clean laundry on the folding table, then glanced toward the kids in the busy playroom attached to the laundry facility.

She wasn't sure what they were doing, but all four seemed occupied and content.

Laundry and child care. Who'd have thought she'd ever perform such labor willingly? But with the playroom to keep the little ones occupied, Ra'anan to oversee them, and a friend for company, it was a tolerable way to spend part of an afternoon.

Lynne picked up the underwear again. "Let me see that." She spread it out on the table, then, giggling, held it up as if to see how it would fit. "Can I borrow this for a few days?"

"What?" Lileela tore her attention away from the children. "You want to borrow my panties?" That might be pushing their newly re-established friendship a bit too far.

"Yeah. For a pattern. I want to try to make some like it for myself."

Lileela found matches for two little socks she'd laid aside, then looked up at Lynne. "You *make* underwear?"

Lynne pulled a pair of her own out of her basket and folded them. "What do you think, they grow on bushes like berries?" She giggled again.

A sudden deep, reverberation shook the floor and a ringing crash boxed Lileela's ears. Both girls turned to the playroom, where all the children had frozen in place like statues. Then little Amadeus Ayo let out a shriek. "Mama!" The next second, the playroom erupted in howls.

Lileela and Lynne joined the mothers rushing from the laundry area to the children as the rumbling continued around and over them. Lileela found Ra'anan sitting on the floor with Tamah on her lap and Hushai and Ittai pulled close on either side. None of them were screaming, but little Tamah whimpered, her lip extended, and fear widened all their eyes.

Lileela's meah sensed Ra'anan looking to her for assurance. She might have found that new experience gratifying if she had any help to give.

The mothers stared at one another over the wailing heads. "What is that? What's happening?"

Lileela noticed none looked her way. She had only Lynne to lock gazes with.

"It's not an attack from the Karkar ship." The oldest of the women answered everyone's fears, including Lileela's. "There'd be smoke and fire from that."

"Would we smell smoke down here?" asked Marilyn O'Dell, one of the younger mothers.

A couple of the others answered at once. "We'd hear the fire alarms, at least." They cast cautious glances Lileela's way, as if she had something to do with this.

"It almost sounds like thunder," said Marilyn, "but I've never felt thunder rock Gullach like that before."

In addition to the continuing rumbles, Lileela thought she could hear a frantic drumming, like rain driven before the wind. "I'm going to find a window and see."

She hurried out of the playroom, through the laundry area, and into the hall, where the glowlights came on. Ordinarily, sufficient illumination came through the door at the top of the stairs that the motion-sensitive lighting didn't activate during the day. But while she'd been doing the laundry, the afternoon had grown as dark as the hour before Gray Dawn.

Lileela stumped up the stairs to the door to look through the glass. When she reached it, all she saw was her reflection with a backdrop of furious waves. Then a lightning bolt sizzled to the ground like the flick of a fiery tongue. Between her surprise and the percussion of the blast, Lileela was almost thrown to the floor. The crying downstairs rose in volume.

Clinging to the handrail, Lileela made her way back down on shaking legs and rejoined the others in the playroom. "It's a storm, all right," she told them. "I guess. I mean, I don't know storms like you all do, but I've never seen anything like this one."

ON the tractor, Pik looked up from harvesting sheber. Something seemed wrong, but he couldn't put his finger on it. Had he heard thunder? He scanned the fields ahead, but saw nothing out of place. Reaching the end of the swath, he turned and started a new one.

And stared at the sky.

Behind and above, it was a sunny afternoon. But to the west, it was midnight. A blackness strobing with flashes rolled its shadow across the fields at an alarming rate.

Pik powered down, set the brake, and climbed off the tractor to disengage the harvester. He'd make better time without it. The task took only two minutes, but by the time he climbed back up to the seat, the blackness had taken over the western powl field.

Releasing the brake, Pik slammed the tractor into gear and bounced toward the equipment barn at the machine's top speed. His ears tilted back. The cloud raced toward the barn faster than he did.

The wind that fluttered his beard was more than just the breeze of his passing. He heard the thunder above the tractor's purr, and the cut sheber stems lifted off the ground and swirled about him.

Though lurching across the field at this rate nearly threw him off his seat, he hung on and coaxed the machine to its limits. He kept his eyes fixed on the shelter, not the storm. But before he'd crossed half the distance, the building was enveloped by the encroaching blackness.

Could he make it to Gullach? Pik glanced north toward the palace, but a massive clatter drew his attention back to the barn. From his bounding perch, he watched the shrouded building disintegrate into a mad swirl of flying debris.

A wall of rain roared toward him. Pik jumped from the tractor and dashed across the field to a depression in the ground twenty meters away, where he threw himself down, hands over his head.

26

*B*ROWARD stood beside Jerry Maddox in the toqeph's tower room. Despite the raging storm, everything here was light and peace.

Except for Dassa, whose dark expression revealed concern as she sat in the egg-shaped chair within the encircling console. "Weather conditions, even severe ones like these, shouldn't knock out our communications."

"True." Jerry nodded. "But it appears to be an issue with some of the individual messenger units, not the technical system as a whole."

Brows lifted, she pierced him with her intense green stare. "Is it the messenger units, or the people themselves? Perhaps they're not responding because they're not able to."

Jerry shrugged. "Either is possible. If the people were caught outside when the storm hit, their messengers could be damaged by water or some other cause. Or—"

"Or the people themselves could be damaged." She pursed her lips. "Is there any way to tell? Can we see if the units are functional and just not being answered? And can we locate them?"

"I'll check with Dmitry. He should be able to tell me."

"Approximately how many people are unaccounted for?"

"Twenty-two."

Broward's stomach did a flip-flop. Twenty-two missing, and the storm still raged.

"Is Pik one of them?"

Broward marveled at her directness.

And at Jerry's calm reply. "Yes, ma'am. And so is Elise Finnegan."

Was it their irrational faith that enabled them to take this so well? Or their Nasi training? Broward had little understanding of either, but both obviously had the power to change people.

In any event, why had the toqeph summoned him? He felt superfluous. But until she called on him to speak, he'd remain silent.

She stared into space for a moment, then turned her gaze back to Jerry. "Adam doesn't seem unduly alarmed. I will leave Elise's retrieval to him. Meanwhile, get with Dmitry and see what you can do about locating the others. If it's feasible to send out rescue parties, arrange it. But as you can see—" She brought up a satellite photo on the surround screen. "These conditions will be with us for quite some time."

Broward gaped. The images showed massive storms pummeling the entire planet, with extensive flooding already along western coasts, though two hours ago, the skies above Periy had been clear and sunny. How was this possible?

"If you can locate the people and reach them without risking more than you're saving, then by all means do it. But don't worry about Pik. I believe—yes, I'm quite sure he'll find his way home before long. Don't spend your resources on him."

"Yes, ma'am." Jerry bowed, stepped backward three steps, then turned and left the room.

Openmouthed, Broward continued to study the astonishing weather images until he felt Dassa turn her gaze on him. Then he faced her, snapping his mouth shut, and bowed. "How might I help, Madam Toqeph?"

"I need a starship captain's knowledge to interpret some information." The image on the screen changed to a view of space and the Karkar ship, with a stream of data scrolling beside it. "I see changes here, but I don't know what it all means."

Though Broward saw the data flow, his attention was drawn elsewhere. "The sun! It looks—"

"Yes. We can assume the massive turbulence we see there is causing our meteorological problems. But my question is, what's it doing to the Karkar ship?"

Broward tore his eyes from the sun's image and back to the vessel, which seemed to be bobbing on a sea of emanations from the solar surface. He'd never seen anything like it in all his years in space.

He tried to focus on the data read-out. "It's quite garbled. Hard to tell what's going on in there, but they're having a rough ride, that's for sure." He stepped closer to the screen, but changing the proximity didn't lessen the confusion. Some of the information flashed on and off, and other figures contradicted one another.

"It appears their propulsion systems are knocked out. The numbers are all over the place, but if I interpret them correctly, their Pyetronium's been deactivated somehow. When the data is visible, flexion capabilities read zero point oh two percent, and it has to be at seventy-five minimum to even think about folding." Broward pointed to the numbers. "And their conventional propulsion capability is out as well. See here? They don't have enough power to leave orbit, let alone get home to Karkar."

Dassa nodded. "Is there anyone alive in there?"

"These are the life readings." With his hand, Broward circled a wavering series of numbers. "I don't know how many were aboard to begin with, but—"

"Sixty-one."

With his finger on one of the figures, Broward turned to Dassa. "This number was sixty-one before?"

She nodded. "That's correct."

"A larger crew than I'd expect for just a transport mission." Broward shrugged. "But then, that was never truly their intent, was it?" He turned back to the screen. "So they've suffered casualties, since the number now reads forty-nine. They're experiencing tremendous turbulence." Envisioning the horror and helplessness they must be feeling, he shuddered.

"How are their life support systems faring?" Dassa's voice revealed no joy at the enemy's suffering.

He watched the data. "Seem to be holding steady. They're relying on their back-up systems, but those are still solid. Enough for basic survival purposes, at least. The atmosphere has the right pressure and gaseous mix, but the temperature seems a little low for optimal comfort. Water systems—" Pointing to part of the read-out, he tried to make sense out of the numbers. "Do you know what these were historically? I need a baseline."

She made a few motions and a static set of numbers came up to the right of the scrolling data. "These are the averages from yesterday. And this—" A third display appeared beside the previous one. "—is from last week."

Broward examined the notations. "Their water purification system might be malfunctioning." He looked at the current figures and compared them again to the old. "Yes, that's what this represents. Purification processes are reduced eighty percent."

Dassa leaned back in her chair. "So in your judgment, the ship is crippled but still capable of keeping them alive for a short time?"

Broward eyed the image of the furious solar activity. "Yes. But that could change any moment. I'm amazed there's anything left of that ship at all." He knew what he was seeing, but couldn't comprehend. This was huge. The most significant natural phenomenon he'd ever encountered. It was almost as if—

He turned back to Dassa. "Has anything like this ever happened before?"

"Closest thing was thousands of years ago, when the poles apparently shifted."

Broward's heart thumped. "What happened then?"

She changed the projection back to the weather satellite view, but its motion had ceased. Apparently it was no longer a real-time view, though it still showed heavy storms across the entire globe. "History tells of violent weather conditions and flooding across the whole northwest portion of the continent. Nothing worldwide, like this. Of course no one knew about solar magnetic disturbances back then, but later scientists assumed that that was the cause."

"Do you—" Broward broke off as the building shuddered and the rotating halo around Dassa's chair flickered several moments, then regained its glow. He staggered to the doorway and held on, not sure if the floor was moving or if he was merely dizzy.

Dassa's gaze went back and forth between the colors swirling around her again and the display shimmering before her. "Earthquake. Looks like we caught the mere edge of a ripple. The epicenter appears to be eight or ten thousand kilometers to the southwest."

Broward gasped. "And we can feel it here?"

"I'm not sure if that's what's happening." Dassa shook her head. "The sunspots are interfering with my data collection. In fact—" The weather projection disappeared from the screen. "I've lost touch with the satellites entirely."

The colors in the rings around her seat had changed and their motion slowed. The shimmer remained before her, and she poked it here and there as if pressing invisible buttons. Invisible from Broward's vantage point, anyway.

"We might have lost our solar power collectors as well." She rose, and the console surrounding her chair parted, allowing her to pass through. "There's nothing more I can do from here. I'll go see how the children are faring. At least I know they're safe in Gullach."

Broward released the doorframe and stepped aside so she could pass. He noticed the worry lines creasing her face. Until recently, she'd seemed ageless.

"Thank you, captain, for your expertise. Your contributions have been vital to the New Gannah."

He followed her down the hall toward the stairs. "But I—"

"If not for your decision to come to our assistance when the plague struck two decades ago, there would be no New Gannah at all."

Descending the winding steps, Broward well remembered that eventful time. "Just doing my duty."

"That's all that's asked of us, Captain Broward. We do our duty and leave the results to our Commander."

Goosebumps skittered across his arms. Those were no idle words—she truly meant them. And for the first time, he understood how right she was. The lives of the New Gannahans and the Karkar people alike were all in the Yasha's hands.

With a wave of relief, he realized he wouldn't want it any other way.

The next worship service—if they survived that long—he'd be among the first to get up and dance. He felt lighter on his feet already.

THE wind screamed in Pik's ears as he lay in the hollow, hands protecting his head. Flying debris scoured over him, and he didn't look up for fear of getting hit in the eye.

He heard an approaching clatter, like a stack of lumber falling. Then for a few seconds, something pummeled him with a furious rhythm. He yelped in pain, but the wind tore his shrieks from his lungs and flung them to the ground, impotent. What had just pounded him like a madman on a drum? Turning his head to look downwind, he saw pieces of shed siding dancing a jig across the field away from him.

When he heard more of the same coming, he got up and ran blindly across the field, with the wind funneling him in the direction it wanted him to go.

Something loomed in front of him. He had no time to swerve, and with the gusts propelling him forward, he couldn't stop. He had no choice but to try to fly. He leapt over what materialized beneath him into a large tree trunk.

Even in a Gannahan windstorm, gravity will have its way. Not quite clearing the tree, he tumbled over it and sprawled in a shallow stream hadn't been there before.

Or maybe it had. He wasn't sure where he was.

THE rain pouring through Adam's hair soothed the burn behind his ear. Maybe. A little. Or maybe his fear for Elise overrode the pain. One thing was for certain: he would find her and bring her back safely, or die trying. He couldn't abandon his newly betrothed wife nor allow the Finnegans to lose their only surviving child.

She'd told him this morning she was going to pick shachorberries. When the storm struck, he'd tried her messenger to make sure she'd gotten home, but he got no response. Elise was still out there somewhere. And not answering her messenger.

Shachorberries grew all over the place. Where had she gone? He recalled her mentioning a big patch in the woods between the two sheber fields southwest of the palace, so that's where he headed.

Not that he could see where he was going in the torrent, but he had enough native Gannahan in him that his sense of direction was near perfect. Even with the wind trying to drive him off course, he was certain he was on the right track.

Tripping over something that blew into his path, he spun around as he fell. But he didn't hit the ground. A savage eddy of air sucked his breath from his lungs and lofted him a foot or two into the air. Twirling him in a pirouette, it dropped him, staggering and gasping, on his feet—which resumed their running as soon as he'd caught his balance.

His head hammered from the pain of the burn and the percussion of the thunder. Squinting against the lightning's flashes, he shielded his eyes from the rain as he trotted the three kilometers to the woods. True, in this kind of weather it was best to stay away from trees. But that's where Elise was, and he homed in on her like a missile on its mark.

Near the edge of the woods, he called. "Elise!" But a thunderclap covered the sound. "Elise!" he called again, and plunged in. The trees swayed and groaned, and the earth seemed to move beneath Adam's feet as he pounded down the trail. "Elise!" But she wouldn't be on the path, would she? If she could reach the road, she'd have followed it home. Where in this wild mess of blowing foliage and falling timbers was that berry patch she'd talked about?

Hearing the crack of splitting wood and the crash of a heavy object through the branches above, Adam threw himself down at the foot of a large rock as the forest fell down upon him.

27

ADAM crawled out from behind a screen of wildly blowing branches. Though he was scratched and shaken, the rock had borne the falling tree's weight, protecting him from being crushed. "Thank you, my Yasha." He gasped as he clambered over downed limbs. "But could you also please lead me to Elise?"

Standing in the deluge beside a yawning hole torn open by the uprooted tree, Adam tried to think. If she couldn't get to the road, where would she be hiding? She'd have done what he did—seek shelter against something high and solid. But which of the many boulders scattered about might she be crouched behind?

On the other hand, the best berries grew near the water…

Adam dashed through the torrent down the slope toward the shallow stream that flowed through the middle of the woods like an artery. He clambered over or skirted what obstacles he couldn't leap, until he slipped in the mud and skidded into a hollow stump. It crumbled wetly upon impact. Picking himself out of the woody pulp, he gazed through the blowing rain toward the stream.

What was that? Something was moving—against the wind, under its own power. And it had a human shape. He hurried toward it. "Elise!"

The shape paused, and through the pounding of the rain against the forest, Abba's reedy voice called faintly, "Down here!"

Adam galloped around a pile of branches and toward the figure, now clearly his father. "Abba! Elise! Do you see her?"

Abba resumed his movement and pointed ahead to where a fallen tree sprawled. "She's down here!"

Then Adam heard another voice—a woman's scream, carried on the wind. "Adam!"

He and Abba reached her as a lightning bolt hit the opposite bank with a ripping sizzle and an impact that made the ground quake.

It also illuminated Elise's pale face. She lay pinned between the tree and a hollow on the edge of the streambed where she'd apparently tried to take refuge. In ordinary conditions, the water here was only ankle deep, but the storm had bloated it to where she had to lift her chin to keep her face above water.

The thunderclap left Adam deaf for several seconds, but he didn't need to hear to run to her side. "Elise!" He climbed onto the tree trunk. With his back pressed against the bank, he tried to push the tree away with his feet. "We'll get you out, Elise. Don't worry."

She was saying something, and so was Abba, but he couldn't hear the words for the ringing in his ears. He concentrated on moving that tree.

When his father grabbed his leg, Adam looked up. What was he saying?

If anything, Abba was muddier than Adam, and sticks and debris bristled from his hair like quills. "Let me try that," he shouted. "See if you can get to her from below."

Adam nodded. "Good idea." He scrambled down into the stream.

It was only waist deep, but the current almost knocked him off his feet. Not waiting to see if Abba needed help climbing up, Adam dove, hanging onto a branch to keep from being swept away.

He couldn't see a thing in the silty water. Groping with his free hand, he felt something, but it moved away. Searching again, he found a hand. It grabbed him and pulled him beneath the tree. He could feel Elise's panic through her touch.

Her touch. How he'd longed for the day he would feel it! But now it held him under the water, under the tree trunk. Letting go of the anchoring branch, he flailed with his other hand, trying to get an idea of how Elise was pinned, how he might get her out. It appeared the trunk lay against her chest, wedging her against the bank.

When he could hold his breath no longer, he broke her grip and pushed away, making a desperate grab at something, anything, to save himself from the current's grip. Connecting with a sturdy branch and clinging to it, he pulled himself back toward Abba and Elise.

"Are you hurt?" he called to her.

"The water!" she screamed. "It's climbing! Get me out of here!"

She was right, it was rising. She gargled and choked on it.

Abba's greater size gave him better leverage than Adam, but he'd made no progress against the unmoving tree. Adam scrambled up beside him, hoping their combined strength could budge it. They only succeeded in pressing themselves into the soft bank. If they didn't get this thing away from her, she'd be completely under in seconds. She'd quit calling for help, but only because she had to close her lips tightly to keep the water out.

Nearly crying with frustration, Adam pushed beside Abba until Abba's feet slipped and flew up in the air, sending his head into Adam's lap. While he struggled to right himself, Adam noticed one of the straight twigs protruding from his hair was from a tubetree.

He sat up with a jerk. "That's it!" He snatched the twig and clambered over Abba to where Elise choked in the water. "That's it! Elise! Can you hear me?" He reached down and put his hand behind her head. He was able to lift it enough to get her face and one ear out of the water. She coughed and gagged.

"Elise! I've got a tubetree stick. You can breathe through it as the water rises. It'll give us time to move this tree."

As he held her head, the coughing quieted and her gaze fixed on his as she squinted in the driving rain.

"Can you do that? Can you breathe through the stick?"

She coughed again and nodded.

He placed the stick in her mouth and she sucked on it as if her life depended on it.

Which it did.

"Don't bite it off, just hold it and breathe."

"Um hum."

"I'm going to let go of you now, and your head's going to sink. But the stick's long enough, it won't go under. You ready?"

"Um hum." She closed her eyes and her hand came up from the murky flow to hold her nose.

Adam released her head, and it sank beneath the water, the muddy current combing her hair.

Abba had climbed off the tree and onto the stream's bank. As Adam turned toward him, he set a rounded rock on the ground nearby. Adam climbed up after him.

Abba had to shout to be heard over the storm as Adam approached. "I've found us a fulcrum. Now we need a lever."

"Ah!" Adam joined him in searching for an appropriate branch. They had plenty to choose from, but most were bent, too long to wield, or connected to something. It took several minutes to free a strong, straight elah limb of the right size.

When they returned to the bank, all Adam could see of Elise was the end of the tubetree stick protruding through the current. His heart raced with fear.

He and Abba placed the lever along the stone fulcrum with the end as low under the trunk as they could, and, their strength fueled by adrenalin, they pushed down.

The log moved, a little. More than it had before, anyway.

Abba brushed wet hair from his face. "I'm going to lift the log again. You get down there and pull her out."

Without wasting the breath to shout a reply, Adam leapt in. If he hadn't thought to hang onto a branch, he'd have been swept away.

"Wait until you see the log move," Abba shouted.

Adam gave an okay signal and prepared to dive.

Abba strained against the lever, and the rising water worked with him. Adam saw and felt the log lift, and plunged beneath it. Working by feel, he found Elise's hand and gave it a squeeze. As soon as he felt the tree's pressure release her, he found her face with his other hand, removed the stick from her mouth and pulled her downward.

Kicking and squirming, she wriggled under the tree, tearing her tunic. Before they caught their breaths, the current captured her and Adam both in its furious grip.

After a wet, battering ride of several meters, the water dashed them against a collection of flotsam jammed in a tangle of tree roots hanging from the bank. Adam twisted around so his body blocked the flow, protecting Elise from most of the force as she slumped against the jam, choking and clinging to him.

Even in this chaos, he tingled at her touch.

Arms around her, he shook the water out of his eyes and saw his father's hand reach down. The six fingers wiggled and Abba shouted, "Elise! Grab hold!"

She didn't seem to hear. Adam cradled her face in his hands. "Elise. Let Abba help you out of the water." He lifted her arm and placed her hand in Abba's.

She nodded, coughing, and turned to clasp Abba's hand with both of hers. Between Abba pulling from above, Adam lifting from the water, and Elise scrambling her feet against the pile of rubble, she rose from the current, streaming muddy water, and onto the bank.

Adam tried to climb out after her, but the angry stream pulled at him, trying to keep him in its grasp. After a minute or two, Abba reappeared and extended his hand again. With his help, Adam scaled the unstable pile of flotsam and staggered to high ground, where Elise lay on her side, making sounds like a cross between coughing and sobbing. He knelt beside her.

Seeing her upper body covered with Abba's shirt, Adam turned to his father, whose torso was now naked. "Thank you," Adam told him, then turned back to Elise. He wanted to take her in his arms, but now that she was out of danger, he wasn't sure of the propriety of it. "Elise, are you injured?"

She shook her head, but Adam saw she was shivering. They needed to get her out of this weather.

Abba knelt on the other side of her. "She's scraped up, but it doesn't look like anything serious. Nothing that should keep her from being a beautiful bride at your wedding."

"Oh!" Elise gasped and struggled to rise. "Is it official? You've been to see my abba?" She sat up, wrapping Abba's filthy, wet shirt around her.

He'd almost forgotten about the pain of the burn until she mentioned it. Now its throbbing seemed stronger than ever as he pulled his hair away from it. "We'd just sealed the agreement when the storm struck."

"Let me see." She got on her knees, and he turned so she could look at the mark behind his ear.

She gasped again. "Oh, Adam! I can't believe you'd do that for me!"

Letting go of his hair, he turned to her. "There is nothing I wouldn't do for you."

Tears and rain mingling on her face, she bit her lip. "Let me see again."

He showed her, and could almost feel her eyes examining the wound.

"What's that symbol? I thought it was supposed to be an *F* for Finnegan?"

"It is. But it's a *Fe,* from the Old Gannahan alphabet, rather than the Standard Language *F.* Finnegan isn't an Old Gannahan name." He looked toward her out of the corner of his eye, and smiled. "But it will be part of the ruling family's name in New Gannah."

"Oh, Adam! It's—it's—"

He turned to face her. "It's what?"

"It looks like it hurts! And—I want to kiss you." She lowered her gaze, and even in the torrent, Adam could see her blush.

"It's harder for me to kneel here without holding you than it was to kneel before your father."

Rising, Abba cleared his throat. "The immediate danger of drowning is past, but I think even the toqeph would say this is still an emergency situation."

Elise raised her eyes. Adam opened his arms, and she fell into them.

28

*U*NRELENTING legions of raindrops battered Gullach's porthole-shaped windows in wave after endless wave, and the wind seemed bent on blasting the world flat.

But within the safety of the toqeph's suite, Lileela and her family had much to celebrate. All the settlers were alive, and several had miraculous stories to tell. The furies still raged, but all the inhabited buildings remained standing. And Adam and Elise were finally engaged.

On Karkar, marriage was a legal matter transacted by lawyers and judges. It was commemorated only by the recording of a decree and the issuing of a certificate. Lileela had never heard of a celebration like this for a wedding, let alone for an engagement. It appeared this marriage business was one thing the Gannahans did better than the Karkar.

The dining room table had never been so crowded. Elise's parents were there as well as Lileela's entire family, including the children. Dortius and Sylvia Dmitry and Captain and Mrs. Broward attended as friends of Adam's family. The Finnegans had invited Elise's closest friend, Ami Sayami, and the Lucas family, which included Lileela's friend Lynne.

Lileela wished Aunt Skiskii could be here, though. Was she all right up there on the crippled Karkar ship?

Sitting beside her, Lynne watched Lileela pop a plump shachorberry into her mouth. "So you eat Gannahan food now, do you?"

Lileela nodded as she chewed. After swallowing, she said, "You're just now noticing, after the fourth course?"

With a mintstick from the centerpiece, Lynne poked a seed from between her teeth. "No, I'm just now commenting. It's weird watching you eat, though. I mean, the way you take such little bites, like your mouth doesn't open far enough or something."

"It doesn't. That's why us Karkar mostly eat chopped and pureed foods. We're not bone-crunching savages like you Gannahans."

Lynne giggled. "You're more Gannahan than I am, you know. And have you ever seen any of us crunch up bones?"

Lileela shrugged. "No, but my emma says the Old Gannahans used to do it. Next time we have fresh meat, she wants to show us how it's done. Abba says he doesn't think those of us with Karkarish mouths will be able to chew bones, though." She wrinkled her nose. "Not that I'd want to."

Lynne's younger brother, David, had been listening. "I killed and ate an arnebeth once, bones and all. The small ones get soft when you cook them, and the larger ones, you just break and suck the marrow out. I suppose I could have crunched them up, but I was afraid to try."

"That's just disgusting." Lileela shuddered. "Why would you?"

"Because it's good for you," David said. "Marrow is very nutritious, and the bones are full of calcium and other good stuff. You should talk to Adam about it. Didn't he just write a paper about that sort of thing?"

Lileela shrugged. "Maybe. He did some fancy study on health or something, but I don't know what he wrote about." She glanced down the table toward her brother. "I just know he was happy to pass the Seventh Level so he could finally get married."

The way he and Elise looked at each other sent an ache of longing through her middle. What must it be like to be in love? He kept his meah closed to her at the moment, but plainly, exciting things were going on inside him despite that placid face.

She took a sip of blend. It was good. The food was good. With the storm howling outside, she felt safe in the solid arms of Gullach and accepted by her family. But would she ever fit into this New Gannahan society? She'd surely never find anyone to fall in love with here. Some of the men weren't bad looking, but they were all such rustics.

Besides, they wouldn't want her. She wasn't pure and untouched like the Gannahan girls.

But she couldn't go home to Karkar now. Those bridges were burned. What in Kankakar could she do?

A lump rose in her throat, but another glance at Adam and Elise quelled her selfish sorrow. Even if she could never be happy herself, she could be happy for him, today.

Just then Elise cast her gaze down the table, but avoided Lileela's eye. "If everyone's finished with the blue course, let's go into the sitting room."

Why did Elise seem so uncomfortable around her? She'd have to ask Adam about it next time she had the chance.

But he not now. He rose with Elise. "Yes, I think it's time."

Lileela started stacking the dishes. "It's my and Lynne's turn to clear the table. Don't start the song without us."

He turned his pale amber Karkar-eyes to Lileela. "I wouldn't dream of it."

Elise's friend Ami rose. "I'll help you." She joined Lileela and Lynn carrying the dishes into the kitchen.

"This all seems so odd to me." Lileela scraped smashed berries from Ittai's plate into the scrap receptacle before handing the dish to Ami to rinse. "I'm used to bots doing all these menial things."

Ami gave her a puzzled look. "Menial?"

Lynn took the plate from Ami and loaded it in dishwasher. "What do you mean?"

"You know." Lileela waved another plate in the air. "Mundane, mindless tasks like cleaning. Normal people don't do that sort of thing on Karkar. It just seems so weird that everyone takes their turn here. I mean, look at the way the Finnegans cleared after the first course, and the Dmitrys after the second. And none of them are servant class. Why, Mr. Dmitry's a councilman!"

"By the way, it's not first course and second." Lynne rearranged things on the bottom rack to make room for more. "It's the red course, and then green —"

"Yeah, I know." Lileela put a bowl of leftover berries in the chillbox. "Then white and now blue. Which is just crazy, if you ask me. Who ever heard of eating things in order of their color?"

"How else would you do it?" Ami handed the last platter to Lynn.

Lileela thought for a moment. "I guess it doesn't matter, it just seems strange. But we can't cram much more into that dishwasher. Let's turn it on and let it work while we're in the sitting room. Then whoever's turn is next can empty it before loading the dishes after the yellow course."

"Yellow's not next," Ami said. "White is."

After filling the detergent dispenser, Lileela started the cycle. "I thought we already did white."

Lynne laughed. "This is a party, not a regular meal. We get two whites."

"Two whites, and two blues." Ami counted on her fingers. "Then yellow at the end."

Lileela groaned in mock agony. "Three more courses? Where will I put it all?"

Ami hung the towel after wiping the counter. "That's why we move around between courses. To let it all settle and make room for more."

Lynne dragged Lileela by the hand toward the front room. "Don't you just love this, though? Eating and drinking, singing and dancing, all the way to the first hour of Black Slumber? I can't believe you never had parties like this on Karkar. You just sat and slurped your mushy gruel, then got up and went your merry ways?"

"Well, not quite." They'd joined the others, and Lileela didn't feel comfortable talking about life on Karkar with all these Gannahans. She climbed onto Abba's Karkar-sized sofa between Ra'anan and Lynne and sat cross-legged, since her feet didn't reach the floor.

"Okay, we're all here now." Ami took her place beside Elise. "I can't wait to hear this song, Adam."

He held a stringed instrument, kind of like a primitive Karkar garxhaaaa, but without speakers and no need to plug into power. He held the instrument as if he knew what to do with it and strummed a few chords. "Emma went to put Tamah to bed. But while we're waiting, we can sing some other songs."

Lost in Abba's big lap, Ittai yawned. The limitations of his Karkarish mouth kept his yawn small, but his brilliant azure eyes were barely open. Should she offer to take him downstairs too? She knew the children's bedtime routine now and almost felt competent to perform it.

But just as she was about to make the suggestion, Adam began a brisk song, and Ittai sat up straight. Seeing Hushai leap up and dance, Ittai slid off Abba's lap and joined him while everyone else sang. Lileela didn't know most of the words, but she picked it up quickly.

What Lynne had said was true. They did nothing like this on Karkar. Parties there usually involved stultifying conversation among adults about matters that were above her head. If there were others there her age, they sometimes played video games. Until they got a little older. Then they'd escape to whatever seclusion they could find, where they —

Lileela flushed at the memory. There were no rules on her planet against males and females touching.

But Karkar wasn't her planet anymore, was it? Gannah was. And though she was coming to appreciate it, she'd always be somewhat of an outsider here. Stained. Not fit to be a full part of all this.

They sang, some of them danced, and Emma returned, smiling. Abba poured more blend, and then Elise sat on the floor by Adam's feet and looked up at him in open adoration while he sang to her.

Following the Old Gannahan tradition, he'd written the song himself. His love was so evident Lileela brushed away tears as she listened.

She imagined herself in Elise's place, looking up into the face of a strong, handsome man as he sang words written just for her. Words he'd sing to her again and again, to a tune she'd learn to harmonize with, so their song would entwine itself throughout their marriage, growing and changing as their lives expanded.

What she wouldn't give to have never breathed any air nor drunk any water nor eaten any food other than Gannah's.

What she wouldn't give to be pure.

THE yellow course was a light, fruity confection of Sylvia's creation. And Sylvia was an artist. Each serving looked like a pale yellow flower in an individual dish, so lifelike and beautiful Lileela found it hard to bring herself to eat hers.

The rain still drummed against the windows. The night had moved deep into the late Blue hours. Hushai and Ittai were in their beds, and Ra'anan and Audrey, along with the youngest Lucas child, slept where they'd drifted off in the sitting room. Even Lileela's eyelids were heavy as she sat in the glow of the love around her. When the yellow course was finished, she was glad to get up and move around.

As guests of honor, Adam and Elise were exempt from cleaning duties, as were Abba and Emma as hosts. They went into the sitting room and spoke in low tones over eseb tea while everyone else cleared the table, loaded the dishwasher, and rendered the kitchen and dining room spotless. The job went quickly with everyone pitching in. And, novel though the practice was, there was a certain pleasure in working together.

Abba and Emma had gone downstairs to carry Ra'anan to bed by the time Lileela and the others entered the sitting room, each carrying a cup of tea. Audrey hardly stirred when her parents sat on either side of her.

"I'm so happy for the two of you." Mrs. Lucas beamed at Adam and Elise. "You're perfect for each other."

Elise locked gazes with Adam. "Thank you. We think so too."

Mrs. Finnegan wiped her eyes. She'd been doing quite a lot of that all evening, to the point where Lileela wondered if she had allergies or something.

"Adam spent so much time with us when he was growing up," Mrs. Finnegan said, "I almost thought of him as part of the family." She squeezed her husband's hand. "We're delighted that now he really is."

That's when Lileela remembered that Adam and Elise's brother, Everett, had been inseparable at one time. How odd he hadn't come to the engagement party. Had they had a falling out? "That's right, you and Everett used to be best friends. Where is he tonight?"

A silence fell across the room like a heavy curtain.

Lileela's mouth went dry. Should she not have asked that question?

She searched Adam's meah for an answer, and gasped. "He died?" she said. "How?"

Adam's face showed no emotion, but his voice grew husky. "In a mining accident."

"Oh." Lileela covered her mouth with her hand. Mining? Did he mean— "When? That is—"

"Yes, Lileela." Elise interrupted, her expression hard. "They were mining the ore to pay your debt. My brother died so you could come home. Him and Mr. Lawbby both."

Lileela stared at Elise. She remembered Mr. Lawbby. He and Mr. Dmitry used to do everything together, but she hadn't seen him since she'd come home. "Mr. Lawbby? And your brother Everett? They died?" She glanced to the Finnegans and then to Mr. Dmitry. "Oh! I'm so sorry. I didn't know!"

She felt her mother come in before she heard or saw her, and she wanted to run into her arms. But she stayed frozen in her seat.

Emma came and sat beside her. "I'm sorry too. We should have told you. But, well— No." She took Lileela's hand. "No buts. Being busy is no excuse. I should have told you long ago."

Emma squeezed Lileela's hand. "There was a mining accident, yes. But it wasn't in the zahab or nechosheth mines. We'd thought at one time those minerals might be too heavy to transport in sufficient quantities, so we investigated the possibility of adding some livingore to the payment. Since it's found only on Gannah and is the rarest metal in the galaxy, we hoped it wouldn't take much to equal the sum the Karkar government demanded."

Lileela glanced up at Abba standing beside Adam. His ears tilted sadly, but he didn't say anything.

"Four men opened the old livingore mine," Emma went on. "They hadn't been in the shaft very long before it collapsed. Two of the men escaped, but Everett and Lawbby died. Don't blame yourself, Lileela. It was my decision to open that mine. You had nothing to do with it."

Abba interrupted. "It was the council's decision."

"Half the council advised against it." Emma shook her head. "The final decision was mine."

Dmitry cleared his throat. "With all due respect, Madam Toqeph, those men volunteered for the job. You didn't send them to their deaths. We loved those guys, and we miss them. We'll miss them every minute of our lives until the day we join them. But what's done is done, and it was no one's fault."

Lileela fingered Emma's ring. The signet of her rule. The ancient token made of livingore, the metal that expanded and contracted to fit the finger of the ring's wearer. Emma's father and grandfather and great-grandfather before her had worn that very ring. She was glad they didn't send any livingore to Karkar. It would have been a sacrilege.

"But it *is* someone's fault." Lileela's voice broke. "It's mine. If I hadn't disobeyed Abba all those years ago and gone sledding on those chutes, I wouldn't have been injured. You wouldn't have had a debt to pay, and none of that would have happened." She clung to Emma's hand, staring at the ring and choking back a sob.

Emma put her arms around her, but she didn't deny the obvious. Those men had died to pay for Lileela's sin.

29

$\mathcal{M}$ARIANNA gaped. "We're *what?*"

Frowning at his reflection in the full-length bedroom mirror, Broward smoothed his hair with his hands. "I should shave my head, like Dortius."

She met his frown with a darker one. "You absolutely should not. But don't change the sub—"

"I'm nearly bald anyway. Why not get rid of what little—"

"Edwin." Hands on hips, she moved between him and the mirror. "I'll trim it short if you'd like, but I won't have my husband looking like a Cephargian pirate. Now, what was it you just said about those awful Karkar?"

One look into her ebony eyes made Broward melt. Every time.

He shouldn't make it too easy, though. He lifted an eyebrow. "Do you presume to tell your husband what to do?"

Her frown fled before the rueful smile that took its place. "Of course not, my husband." She made a respectful bow like a good Gannahan wife. Then, still bent, she looked up with a raised brow of her own. "But I am entitled to give my opinion, am I not?"

She was as cute as a Nobian kitbug, and he laughed. "Your counsel is always wise, and I value it." He kissed her forehead. "I guess I won't shave my head."

"Good." Then her frown returned, along with her hands to her hips. "But what exactly went on in that council meeting?"

Sighing, he turned. "I need a cup of deshe tea. Would you like one?"

"Sure." She followed him into the kitchen, her scowl speaking impatience.

Before she could start nagging, he answered her question. "Now that the storms have passed, the toqeph was able to contact the Karkar ship. They're in pretty bad shape up there."

While the water heated, he assembled the tea tray and brought it to the table.

Marianna sat with arms crossed. "I hope I'm not supposed to feel sorry for them."

"Of the original sixty-one aboard, only fifteen people are still alive." He shook his head. "And those won't last long. Their life support systems are failing, and the damage is too extensive for in-space repairs. What's more, they've been unable to contact anyone but us, since their signal is too weak to go very far."

"That's a switch. Usually it's communication with Gannah that's hampered, not messages traveling *away* from the planet."

"It's different, all right." He poured tea through the strainer into her cup. "But many things are strange in this quadrant of space. Most ships steer clear of it for that very reason."

"So the toqeph has invited them to come down to the surface?"

"She said the Yasha has already punished them, and she doesn't want to let the rest of them die up there."

Marianna drizzled honey into her tea. "Beats me why not."

"I see your point." Broward removed the strainer from his cup and sipped his tea without adding sweetener. "But I see hers too. Whether or not we agree, she's made her decision, and it's not open for discussion."

The corner of Marianna's mouth twitched. "Did she even give you a chance to advise? Or did she just do what she wanted despite your objections?"

"I should send you to the greyroom for such an attitude." He wouldn't, and she knew it, but her question bordered on disrespect for the toqeph. "The fact is, the council agreed unanimously. Without even much discussion. Once we saw what the situation was, we all knew what we had to do."

Marianna pursed her lips. "I suppose. If we've been forgiven by the Yasha, we shouldn't withhold forgiveness from others, I get that. It's a lovely idea, really. Except when it applies to *those* people. She could have made them beg first, anyway." Her brows lifted. "Or did they? Did they grovel? That would make it easier to take."

Broward took another sip. "She didn't say. But if you want to envision it that way, go ahead. It might be true, for all I know."

"Where will we put the survivors? Please don't tell me we're going to have to share our homes with them. That would be asking too much."

"No, they'll have a chatsr all to themselves. We've got a team checking out the damage to the residential buildings in the second chatsr, but the plan is for us to set them up in one of the sections that's already been made habitable. We'll have to haul some of their oversized furniture down from their ship as well as whatever food they have left. They should be able to live there fairly comfortably."

She pursed her lips. "For how long?"

Broward shrugged. "I have no idea. For us to absorb them into New Gannah, they'd have to swear to live by our laws. And I don't see that happening."

"I wouldn't believe them if they did." Elbows on the table, she rested her chin on her hands. "So they'll be like a foreign body imbedded in our midst, festering like an infection? That can't be good."

"I don't believe that's the way it will work. They're coming, though, and that's that. If we have reservations about something the toqeph decides, there's a procedure to follow to bring our concerns to her attention. But a little private grousing in the kitchen can grow into unrest throughout the settlement, and I won't allow that ugly monster to spawn in my home."

"You're right." She sobered. "I'm sorry. We don't want another incident like we had with Arick Bushati."

"We certainly do not." He sighed. "Following Gannahan law doesn't come naturally to us Earthers. But the Old Gannahans knew how best to live in this place, and we've all agreed to follow their ways." He took her hand. "I love you for introducing me to that uncomfortable truth."

"And I love you for reminding me of it."

STRAPPED in the shuttle seat, Adam breathed slowly and deliberately to keep his excitement under control. Abba used to do this all the time. Traveling all over the galaxy, helping people in distress. What a life that must have been!

Of course what Abba used to do wasn't *exactly* like this. But the whole thing did seem a little full-circle. First, Dr. Pik of Karkar went to Gannah's aid and rescued Emma from the dying planet. Now, the same doctor and his son flew from Gannah to rescue the dying Karkar. And in both cases, the Earthish Captain Broward was at the helm.

The Karkar ship captain had piloted the transport shuttle to the planet, bringing with her eight survivors who were able to travel unaided. Captain Skyoriin herself could barely function, but she'd somehow managed to get them there safely.

Abba, Adam, Jax Florida and Myles Lyfar helped get the survivors from the shuttle onto the bus. Adam was disappointed that Skiskii wasn't among them, and he could see Abba was too.

"Didn't you say my cousin is still alive?" Abba had asked the captain as he helped her into the bus.

"Yes. She's one of the ones still aboard ship. In the sick bay."

While Abba and Adam examined the patients in the bus, Myles drove them to the clinic in Qatsiyr. They were dehydrated and suffering from hypothermia, but all would likely recover quickly with proper treatment. Abba left them in the care of Dr. Jane Verpleegkundige with Lileela to translate and assist, while he and the rescue party flew back to the ship to bring down the rest.

Now, in the Karkar shuttle, Adam willed his heart to slow its racing as Captain Broward maneuvered the craft through the bay doors and into the Karkar vessel.

He shouldn't be so excited. After all, Lileela had spent months on this ship and considered it no big deal. The other men seemed to be taking it all in stride. But Adam had never been off Gannah before, and the thrill of the experience coursed through his whole body.

The bay doors folded closed, and the shuttle was sealed in. Though orbiting Gannah, they were on Karkar soil. Adam's ears grinned at the thought.

Since the ship's atmosphere could no longer sustain life, they wore full envirosuits with oxygen canisters. Adam looked at the data screen as he prepared to disembark. He didn't understand all the characters, but he could see the temperature in the shuttle bay was colder than a Gannahan winter.

Shuffling in the ungainly suit, he followed Abba through the small craft's portal and into the bay. The area was barely lit, but the team was armed with flashlights. Two other shuttles loomed in the dusk in adjacent bays, but Skyoriin had commandeered their fuel cells for other purposes, so they weren't operational.

Adam stared at what looked like rectangular mountains towering against the far wall. Once he directed his flashlight beam in that direction, he realized they were hoppers mounded with the raw zahab and nechosheth ores from the surface. The sight made his skin prickle beneath his suit.

But Abba wasted no time sightseeing. His voice filtered strangely through the earpiece in Adam's suit. "First we find the sick bay and prepare the patients for transport." He walked as he spoke, and the others followed. "We'll worry about furniture and supplies once they're safe."

Though they'd been given directions, Abba pasued to study a diagram displayed on the wall just outside the shuttle bay. "I hope the elevators work, because we need to go up several levels." With a gloved finger, he pressed a button on a wall panel, and a door opened in front of them. So far, so good.

They entered the lift. Adam felt lightheaded for some reason. The others seemed no more comfortable in their gear than he, and between the unfamiliarity and the darkness, they moved clumsily. Then, when Järn Hand stumbled exiting the elevator, Adam tripped over him and fell at a weird, slow speed.

"There's not much gravity up here." He picked himself up. "Did they warn us about that?"

"No," Abba said. "They didn't mention it."

"I think it's a recent development." The captain turned around slowly as if searching for something. "The transport settled down normally."

"Maybe they've got the gravity generators running in the shuttle bay, but not up here," suggested Myles.

Järn Hand nodded. "Good. Low gravity will make moving furniture easier."

"Not good." Abba's voice was clipped, and he moved quickly down the hall. "It's death to our patients."

A pang of guilt swept through Adam as he followed. He'd been thinking of this expedition in terms of what he could learn and experience. He hadn't even thought about the people they'd come to help. Could they save their lives?

"What's that over there?" Jax directed his light toward an area to the left.

"Ah, sissgx. Perfect!" Abba headed toward the array of small vehicles lined up in a corral. "I'm glad you spotted those."

"If siskich, or whatever you said, means carts," said Jax, "you're right. This is great. But will they work in this low gravity?"

Adam felt oddly bouyant as he followed the others to the vehicles. Jax had a good point. The vehicles wouldn't go anywhere if their wheels didn't touch the ground.

"I think with our combined weights, they'll be fine," said Broward.

"But what about transporting the patients?" Abba climbed into the nearest one. "If we all pile into one, we won't have room for anyone else."

"There are six of us." Jax clambered into the vehicle beside Abba. "Let's see what happens if we ride two in a cart."

Myles studied one of the sissgx. "Yeah, I think there would be room in the back for two stretchers on these larger ones. Some of them are just two-seaters, though."

When Abba started up his vehicle, Adam and the others moved out of the way so he could try it out. Apparently familiar with the controls, he immediately moved forward.

"Looks like it'll work. Since these were made for use on starcraft, they might be designed to operate under weak gravitation. Let's each take one. That way we'll have plenty of room to carry all the patients and supplies."

He explained how to turn them on and the basics of their operation. Adam, for one, was thankful for the instruction, because it was unlike anything he'd ever seen.

Once they got the hang of it, the carts saved them valuable time. The sick bay was deep in the ship's interior, and they followed what must have been a kilometer of passageways. Abba stopped twice to check directions on one of the signs that appeared at every intersection, and once he had them turn around and go back the way they'd just come.

Despite his space suit, Adam was chilled before they arrived at the sick bay. The dark, alien emptiness made the hair stand up on the back of his neck. It must have been awful up here, tossed by the space storms and helpless as a log going over a waterfall. He'd rather deal with surface weather any day than be trapped in such an artificial contrivance.

It was huge, though. The Karkar didn't like to be cramped. Their affinity for overstated elegance was also evident, despite the damage. But it was still a prison, and Adam was already looking forward to escaping into the freedom of Gannah's atmosphere.

Abba eventually located the spacious sick bayt, where he promptly zeroed in on the patients. All clustered in one ward, they were anonymous in identical envirosuits. Striding to the first occupied bed, he checked for monitors or charts or anything else to indicate the patient's status. "Did no one keep records?"

He pulled out an oxygen mask and checked to make sure it functioned. "Captain Broward, what do the air pressure readings look like? Would it be safe for me to remove the patient's helmet?"

Broward found a gauge on the wall and shone his light on it. "Not optimal, but it should be fine as long as you've got the oxygen handy."

Adam helped Abba unfasten the helmet and remove it from the Karkar on the bed. He didn't recognize the man, but despite his massive size, in this low gravity his head seemed no heavier than a child's.

Abba spoke to him in Karkar, but the man only groaned. Abba covered the patient's face with the oxygen mask while he spoke again then lifted the mask so the man could answer.

His voice was muted and gasping, but Abba must have understood him because he tipped his head in a Karkar nod and replied. He replaced the mask, asked another question, then lifted it for the response.

He returned the oxygen to the man's face one more time and then translated. "The ship's doctor was the first casualty, so they had no one to treat the injured and ill. When people grew too weak to function, they were brought here. For all practical purposes, apparently, brought here to die, though until recently someone did look in on them from time to time and try to give them food and water. And carry out the dead."

Adam gasped behind his helmet. "They've had no treatment?" He found a store of glucose/electrolyte solution in a nearby bin and grabbed a bag. Though icy, it could easily be warmed in a quickheater. "They could have been rehydrated, at least. There's plenty of this stuff here. I can't believe no one even tried to help them."

"No one knew how." Abba affixed the mask to the patient. "In this cold, we can't remove their suits to examine them. We'll have to get them into the shuttle before we can even see what's wrong. Anyone spot any stretchers around here?"

Adam took a step away, intending to start looking, when Abba stopped him. "Do you have that list I gave you?"

"Oh, yes." He pulled it out of a zippered pocket. "Right here. I'll get right on it."

Adam located a bin that looked suitable for carrying supplies, then shone his light in cabinets and drawers. He couldn't read the Karkar-language labels, but many were also marked in the Standard Tongue, and in most cases he knew what he was looking for anyway.

Abba moved to the next patient, who turned out be Skiskii. When Adam heard Abba speak her name, he paused his search to watch. She responded to his words with a low mumble that even Abba couldn't understand. He made sure the suit's oxygen was functioning, then fastened her helmet back in place. "Stay with us, Skiskii. We'll get you the help you need."

Adam sent a prayer for her to the Yasha. Then with a jolt, he realized he should be concerned for all these miserable people. But the only one he really cared about was his cousin — and only because Lileela was so fond of her.

He wondered how all those years ago Abba, a Karkar, could have worked so hard and long to find a way to save his people's ancient enemies. He hadn't even known the Yasha in those days, so he wouldn't have been acting out of love for Him. Did unbelievers sometimes do His will without knowing it?

Now, Abba was trying to save people who truly were his enemy. But despite their treachery, he truly cared about them. It was humbling to see him work with such compassion and competence. Abba acted as if nothing about this was strange as he spoke to each patient to determine his or her condition. He'd help the men load the patient on a stretcher, then move to the next bed as the others carried the stretcher to a cart and fastened it in.

Adam found everything on the list and filled two bins with the supplies, then found places for them in the carts. It seemed to be growing colder the longer they were there, an observation Broward confirmed after consulting the gauge on the wall. And when Adam knocked over a box of instruments, they floated to the floor, hardly making a clatter. By the time all the patients were ready to be moved, his feet barely touched the ground.

They got lost on the drive to the elevators, so the trip back was longer than the first leg. Adam gritted his teeth. Even after they arrived at the landing craft, it would be hours before they made it back to Gannah.

Helping Myles move an over-long stretcher into an elevator car, he wondered if that motionless, suited body strapped to it was even alive anymore. At least once they got onto the shuttle, they'd be able to remove the envirosuits and get the rehydration process started. Adam swallowed nervously. Most of his medical training was theoretical. He didn't have much practice with real people. Would he make a fool of himself in front of Abba? Even Captain Broward had more experience than he did.

Abba might have been thinking along similar lines. They loaded the patients into three elevator cars to carry them down, and when they met again in the hall outside the shuttle bay, he spoke to the captain as they picked up a stretcher. "Do you still remember how to do an IV?"

Broward grunted as he rose. The gravity was, in fact, greater on this level, and the Karkar bodies lay heavy on the stretchers. "Probably. Why?"

"I figure Adam and I can examine the patients while Järn, Jax and Myles go back to get beds and other things we'll need for them. If you can assist us on the shuttle while they're gone, it might help save some lives. I'd like to get them stabilized before we break through the atmosphere."

They set their patient's stretcher on the floor, and Broward stood upright with a groan. "I'll be happy to do what I can. At my age, I'm certainly better suited for nursing than moving furniture."

Adam lifted the head of another stretcher while Myles took the foot. How old was the captain, anyway? He must be well into his seventies, less than a decade younger than Abba Lars had been when he'd gone to Karkar with Lileela.

Adam thought about Abba Lars as he and Myles carried the first patient toward the shuttle. Would his grandfather still be alive if he hadn't left Gannah? Adam felt fortunate to have known him. Few of the New Gannahans in Adam's generation had ever met their grandparents.

He and Myles laid the stretcher across a row of seats and secured it. The Karkar patient moaned inside his envirosuit. Would these Karkar die on Gannah yearning for home, like Abba Lars had died on Karkar?

After making sure the stretcher was secure, Adam straightened up. Though the Yasha had been born on Earth and died there to save the Earthers, he freely extended that same eternal life to any extraterrestrial who believed in Him. That knowledge had transformed Gannah and given its people new purpose—both the Old Gannahans and the New. But without faith in his Creator and Redeemer, the only immortality this dying Karkar could know was to have his death brick put in the memorial wall on his home planet.

As Adam passed Abba and Jax securing Skiskii's stretcher in place, he smiled behind his helmet. He'd just thought of the perfect place for Abba Lars's brick. Once they were back on Gannah, he'd talk to his father about it.

30

"*T*HIS has gone cold. Are you trying to kill me, making me sit in ice water?"

Neen's impatient whine made Lileela's teeth hurt. "I'll warm it for you, Minister." She bit back a growl as she manipulated the lever to add more hot water. Two minutes ago, Neen had yowled about being scalded.

Though Lileela hadn't decided yet what sort of career to pursue, she'd definitively ruled out nursing.

The clinic was hot, miserable, and crammed with nine oversized patients. It didn't help that Jane kept the temperature tropical to aid their recovery. But the worst part was those patients hadn't bathed in days.

Oh, but no worries there. One of Lileela's duties was to help them undress, one by one, and climb into a warm bath, where, after washing, they soaked until their body temperatures rose to a normal thirty-seven point five Celsius.

But whether they were stripping, soaking, drying, or lying in beds equipped with makeshift extensions to accommodate their length, they demanded more of this, better that, more comfortable what-have-yous, and above all, prompt attention. It was enough to give her a headache.

Turning away from Neen to stand in the doorway of the ward, Lileela fanned herself as she watched Jane bending over Digghok. "Where are we going to put the rest of them?"

Jane cleaned a seeping wound on the mechanic's massive chest. "By the time the new arrivals get here, we'll have moved all these to their quarters."

"I hope our accommodations will be more suitable than this sorry excuse for a hospital." Digghok spoke in a growling Karkar, which Lileela dutifully translated. "I'm surprised the great Dr. Pik would permit such a substandard facility to operate."

"They're bringing down some of your own furniture from the ship." Jane tossed her swab in the waste container. "You should be comfortable enough in your new apartment." She picked up a tool from a tray nearby. "I'm going to have to clip that closed."

Digghok made a tent over the wound with his many-fingered hands, his ears grimacing. "I'd like a real doctor to look at it, if you don't mind."

"A real doctor is looking at it." Jane's brow puckered upon hearing the translation. "If you leave it gaping like that, it can't heal properly. But if you prefer to leave it open, inviting in all sorts of Gannahan germs—"

Digghok eased his arms back down by his sides. "Tell the woman to go ahead," he told Lileela. "But make sure Dr. Pik checks her work when he returns. At least he was trained on a civilized planet."

Once Lileela relayed the message in the Standard speech, Neen's snarl drew her attention back to the bathing chamber. "Where'd you go, you little mongrel?"

As Lileela contemplated how to respond with dignity, Captain Skyoriin, in a tub behind another enclosure, uttered an angry expletive. "Show some gratitude, Minister. If not for these barbarians' aid, we'd be doomed. The least you can do is call the little creature by its name."

A deep sigh came from Neen's direction. "You're right, Captain. I apologize. But I don't recall what it's called."

Lileela limped to Neen's enclosure. "You do too. On the flight here from Karkar, you said I have the same name as your grandmother. And I'm not an *it*, I'm a person."

Neen's ears stiffened. "Well, then, *Lileela*. If you're a person, why are you acting like a servebot?"

Lileela picked up the ear thermometer and checked Neen's temperature. "We have no servebots here because we consider it an honor to serve those we love. Are you ready to get out, or would you like to soak a little more? Your temperature's up to normal now."

Neen's pink and lavender hair lay wet and limp on her white scalp, the graying blonde roots showing. Her wan, expressionless face hovering above the water was as naked as the rest of her. It was devoid even of eyebrows, since most Karkar women had them surgically removed so they could replace them with artificials in whatever size, shape and color their mood dictated.

"You love me?" Neen's voice suggested amusement. "I'm sorry, dear, but you're not my type."

"No, I don't even like you. I'm just saying that's why we don't have servebots. Do you want to get out or not?"

Neen's ears tilted backward. "Does your father know you're talking to me like that?"

Lileela wanted to push that unnatural head under the water and hold it there for about ten minutes. "Do you see him here? How would he know? But look, I'm trying to help you. Why do you have to be so difficult?"

Skyoriin's laughter bubbled from the next enclosure. "Watch it, Neen. She's half Gannahan, you know. Better not get her angry. But Lileela, dear, I feel warmed through. You may help me out if that would please you."

Neen fluttered a six-fingered hand in a "go ahead" gesture.

Lileela went around the privacy screen to the captain and inserted the ear thermometer. "Temperature's normal." After slipping the instrument into a pocket, she took two towels from the warmer and set them on the chair nearby. She pressed a switch, and the water began to swirl out of the tub. Another switch caused Skyoriin's seat to lift. "Make sure you hang onto the rails. I can help steady you, but I can't hold you up if you start to fall."

The captain rose, water streaming from her body. When she was upright—that is, when her jewel-embedded belly button hovered before Lileela's eyes—Lileela handed her a towel. "Wrap this around your top half, and I'll give you another to wrap around your waist. Watch you don't get the IV tangled."

Skyoriin complied, keeping her gaze on Lileela as if daring her to look at her nakedness. Lileela busied herself arranging the mat, turning on the heat lamp and checking the progress of the water's draining. When the level had gone below the opening, she unsealed the door and swung it wide. "Okay, let's bring you out here to dry. Don't trip over the threshold."

When Skyoriin uttered a groan and wavered on her way to the chair, Lileela helped her to the seat beneath the heat lamp, praying the captain wouldn't collapse and crush her in the fall. "Are you okay?"

"Mmm. Just a little light-headed when I stand." Skyoriin sank into the chair. "I've never been so weak. You people must be poisoning me or something."

"Lileela!" Neen's whine caused Lileela to grit her teeth. "I thought you were going to help *me* get out!"

One of the male patients in the beds bellowed, "I need more water. And make sure it's filtered."

Lileela bowed her head. Hard to believe she used to think this was normal behavior.

Worse yet, that she'd acted this way herself. *Yasha, forgive me!*

TWENTY hours later, Kughurrrro, wrapped in a blanket, leaned back in the recliner. The apartment he shared with Zidz was small and plain, but adequate. It even had heat, which he had cranked up to thirty-two Celsius.

"Are you warm enough?" he asked his roommate. "They've provided us with extra blankets, if you need one."

On the sofa, Zidz didn't look up from his computer. "No, I'm comfortable."

Listening to the soft music coming from the speaker behind him—not Karkar music, but pleasant enough, in its own way—Kughurrrro stared at the wall opposite his chair. He'd never heard of upholstering walls, but according to that Jax person, it was typical here. The panels of padded fabric were oddly attractive and provided soundproofing as well as insulation against the climate outdoors.

Zidz's voice broke into his contemplations. "How many of us are left? Fifteen?"

"Yes." Kughurrrro sighed. "Just fifteen. I believe three are still interred in that miniscule, substandard clinic, and the other twelve are housed in these strange apartments."

"Eleven," said Zidz. "The Ogliziizl woman is staying with her half-breed cousin and his family."

Kughurrrro nodded. "Yes, I knew that." His eyes felt too heavy to hold open, and he gave up the struggle. "She might be nearly as unbalanced as he."

Though his eyes rested, his mind remained active. After several minutes of silence, he spoke again. "On that alien substitute for a computer you have there, are you able to access Old Gannahan history?"

Zidz yawned. "What? Oh." He stirred on the couch. "It's so warm in here, I was starting to nod. Pleasant, isn't it, to be warm at last?"

"This planet *might* be pleasant, if it were Karkar territory." Nevertheless, he did feel overly warm. Opening his eyes at last, he threw off his blanket.

"I might be able to locate some history." Zidz yawned again. "What were you looking for, specifically?"

"I'd like to know if the Gannahans ever took prisoners."

Zidz snorted. "Of course not. Everybody knows that."

"It's common knowledge, yes. But often what we call common knowledge is a common fallacy. I should like to know the truth of the matter."

"But would the truth be found in the Gannahans' own records?" Zidz tapped at the computer.

"Just see what you can find." Kughurrrro took a long drink from his water bottle. "I believe their records will verify ours. That is, that their policy did not provide for prisoners of war."

Zidz's ears frowned. "I don't see the logic to their data system. It will take some time to figure out."

"Time? We have plenty of that." Sighing, he set down the water. "But I agree. Their logic is so hard to follow it almost seems as if they have none. But yet, we had them in our grasp, and now we are in theirs. That couldn't have happened by chance. Their plans are so devious I can't even see them in hindsight, let alone anticipate what's coming. If they've taken prisoners previously, I'd like to know what they did with them, what their purpose was in keeping them alive."

Zidz lifted his gaze. "You consider us prisoners?"

Kughurrrro's ears frowned. "You don't?"

"I hadn't thought about it, but no. They saved us from certain death, though it meant humiliating themselves through their servile behavior. They've given us generous provisions and comfortable accommodations. I see no chains, no bars, no fences—we can come and go about the settlement as we please. How is this imprisonment?"

"All this supposed kindness and freedom? It is a deception. It must be. There's no reason for them to treat us this way unless they have something to gain from it."

Zidz's ears swiveled in a Karkar shrug. "I'll see what the records show, but I don't think they'll yield anything useful. In the meantime, I'll continue to enjoy the benefits of their deception, if that is the case."

"Hmmph." Kughurrrro rose. Between the intravenous hydration at the clinic and the fluids he'd been drinking, his bladder was finally filling properly. "I don't trust them. It's stupid to treat your enemies kindly. And whatever else they may be, the Gannahans are not stupid."

31

IN the palace courtyard, Lileela sat at the table in the shade of the spreading elah. Though she felt confident she'd done well on the exam, she held her breath as Mr. Maddox made notations on his tablet.

His eyes made one last pass across the screen. Then with a nod, he closed the notebook and looked up. "Congratulations, Miss Lileela. You've passed the Fourth Level."

Feeling her face flush, she rose and bowed. "Thank you, Mr. Maddox."

"No need to thank me. I'm just the examiner." He stood, pocketing the tablet. "The credit goes to those who have taught you. And to you, of course, for your diligent efforts. You've made amazing progress. Your mother is very proud of you."

"I hope so."

Mr. Maddox moved toward the walkway leading to the palace entrance. "She's pleased, there's no question about it. She just remarked on it this morning."

Since they were going the same direction, Lileela walked with him. "Did she really?"

"She did indeed. As a parent myself, I know how that feels. Nothing pleases us more than to see our children be happy and succeed in life."

"I suppose so." But Emma had so *many* children. How could she care much about any one of them? Especially one who was always so difficult?

At the foot of the long, curving stairway, she moved behind Mr. Maddox to get out of the way of a group of people coming down. That left her following him up the steps. And that made her feel obligated to look down at the creamy stone risers rather than watch his smooth, rounded posterior as he climbed the stairs in front of her. Not that she would have minded studying the sight, but it didn't seem appropriate.

She was making progress, yes. But she was still too worldly to fit into this society, where virtue was such a passion. In her case, Gannahan virtue was as reachable a goal as flapping her arms and flying to Karkar.

Yielding to the inevitable, she lifted her eyes. Her gaze lingered on the object of interest for a second or two, then rose and ran across his strong back and broad shoulders. Too bad about that scraggly ponytail, though. It spoiled the look.

At the top of the steps, he turned. "How is your aunt doing? Getting her strength back?"

She finished her climb. "Yes, thank you. She was a bag of bones when they brought her down from the ship. She's getting stronger, but she still cries a lot. She misses Uncle Ogliziizl something awful."

Mr. Maddox shook his head. "I'm sure she does. It's a tragic situation." They passed through the entrance and turned together toward the toqeph's apartment. "Did I hear she's eating Gannahan food?"

"Yes. She asked Emma if she could stay here forever, even if the rest of the contingent does manage to find their way back to Karkar somehow. When Emma agreed, Auntie decided it was time she learned to eat like a Gannahan."

Mr. Maddox chuckled. "I imagine that delayed her recovery a bit."

"Yes, but just a day or two. Now she's eating everything—in small bits, of course, because she can't bite and chew very well—and drinking blend like a—like an I don't know what, but she's putting it away in serious quantities. Abba says she's still hydrating, but I think she likes the buzz. Even though it's non-alcoholic, it gives a feeling of well-being."

"It does indeed. Quite a heady feeling for one who's not used to it. But it's probably good for her, after all she's been through."

They reached the apartment, and Mr. Maddox went in with her. Why was he here? Oh, that's right, there was a council meeting this afternoon.

Skiskii's shrill voice met them at the door, but she was nowhere in sight. It sounded like she was with the children in the playroom.

Lileela turned to Mr. Maddox. "When may I schedule my test for the Fifth Level? I'd like to pass it before I turn sixteen this Frostmonth. If that's possible."

"I can arrange for the examination a week or two before your birthday, if you think you'll be ready for it by then." A faint smile brushed his lips as his blue eyes studied her face. "I suspect you will be."

Looking at those lips, she blushed. "Yes, sir. I'm nearly ready now. There are just a couple subjects I need to get up to speed on. And, of course, those two papers to write." She bowed. "Thank you, sir. But for now, I'll go see if Aunt Skiskii needs my help with the children."

He returned her bow with a pleasant nod as she took three steps back, bobbed again, and turned to leave. Did he watch her departure as she'd watched him climb the stairs? She swayed her hips a little, just in case. She could always blame it on her limp.

Behind her, she heard him enter the dining room. Apparently he wasn't watching.

In the playroom, Tamah slept in a heap on the floor. A rag doll, glistening with drool, lay under her round little cheek, while her six tiny fingers held the doll's crumpled tunic.

Across the room, Auntie and the boys were engaged in a noisy game involving the Standard, Old Gannahan, and Karkar alphabets. From the way they played, it seemed points were acquired not only through knowledge of the letters but also through the volume with which the names and respective sounds were pronounced.

"DOUBLEYOO!" yelled Ittai.

Hushai hollered at the same time. "That's a *W*!" He stood nose to nose with Skiskii sitting on the floor. "OOOOOWU WU WU WU WU! Say it, Auntie!"

Ittai climbed on her back. "Wu wu wu wu ooooowu."

"There is no Karkar equivalent," she said in her clearest Standard speech. Which wasn't very clear. The last word sounded like *ee-kiddo-lent.* "I cannot say 'luh.'" With Ittai clinging to her like a monkey, she leaned forward and wrote a Karkar character on the marker board. "This is a Ghx. Can you say that, boys? Ghx, as in 'ghxixchl'." She sketched a quick line drawing.

Ittai giggled as he slid off her back. "That's a bird, Auntie. And that starts with B, not Ghx."

Standing in front of the board, Hushai studied the picture. "She's right, Tai, it's a ghxixchl. But why does a Karkar ghxixchl have only two legs?"

Lileela approached. "Because only Gannahan birds have three legs." Picking up another marker, she drew a third leg on Skiskii's creation, extending from its breast. Underneath it she wrote a Gannahan character. "Now it's a tsippor, and that starts with—"

Ittai scowled and erased the bird with his fist. "Don't wanna tsippor! Auntie, make me a ghxixcl again!"

Lileela put her marker down. "Fine. You can have all the ghxixchlirt you want, but I'm going to put Tamah in bed before you two start running around and she gets stepped on."

Skiskii's ears stiffened. "Oh, my, I forgot all about her, she was so quiet." She twisted around to see. "Look at that, isn't she precious. I'm surprised she can sleep. We've been pretty noisy."

Bending down to pick up Tamah, doll and all, Lileela spoke softly. "She's a good sleeper."

Tamah's eyes fluttered when Lileela lifted her, but then she laid her head on Lileela's shoulder.

"How did your test go?" Auntie asked in un-quiet Karkar. "Did you pass? I'm sure you did. You're such a smart girl, you could have passed with only ten fingers." She chuckled. "Well, I guess that saying doesn't mean much on this planet, does it?"

Lileela nodded and mouthed the words, "I passed." She lifted a finger to say, *I'll tell you in a minute,* then turned and carried Tamah out of the room.

Auntie's voice followed her. "I'll draw you another ghxixcl, Ittai."

"Ghx!" The boys gargled like little Karkar. "Ghx, ghx, ghxixcl!"

Before Lileela had taken two steps down the hall, Tamah lifted her head, still heavy with sleep. She pointed back toward the playroom and let out a whine.

Lileela patted the baby's back. "Go to sleep, sweetie. Nap time's not over yet."

Tamah's whine rose in volume. She clutched the doll with one hand and reached toward the playroom with the other, nearly throwing herself over Lileela's shoulder.

Lileela's ears scowled as she continued down the hall, trying to shush her sister. She should have let the kid sleep on the floor. At least then all the shrieking would be confined to one room.

And Tamah was harder to hold than a greased slahj. How would she get down the stairway? She needed to hang onto the handrail, but she also had to hold the squirming little beast with both hands.

Emma emerged from the kitchen carrying a tea tray. "Wait just a minute." She set the tray on a table in the sitting room, then turned back to Lileela, hands extended. "I'll take her. Would you mind carrying the tea into the dining room for me?" She relieved Lileela of her noisy burden.

"Sure." Ears tilted backward and nose wrinkled, Lileela felt her shoulder, wet with tears and drool. "She was sleeping on the floor in the playroom and I tried to put her to bed."

Emma smiled. "You did the right thing. I'll see if I can get her back to sleep. While I'm doing that, would you please tell your auntie the boys will have to clear out while the council meets? She can take them to play in the courtyard if she'd like. Just remind her to keep out of the sun, or she'll burn again, and your Abba will not be pleased. And then, once I get baby down, would you mind staying downstairs in case she wakes up?"

The way Tamah carried on, it didn't seem likely she'd get back to sleep, but Lileela didn't argue. "Of course. I can do some of my reading."

"Thank you." Emma turned toward the stairs, then paused. "Congratulations, by the way. Jerry told me you passed your exam with the highest scores possible. And he absolutely loved that story you wrote."

Lileela grinned. "Really?"

Emma shifted Tamah to a hip and gave Lileela a hug with the other arm. "Your Abba and I are both very proud of you. You'll be a fine Gannahan. But I must get Tamah back to sleep, or she'll make life miserable for all of us." She turned and started down the stairway. "Won't you, little Tamah? When baby's cranky, we're all cranky." Her crooning mingled with Tamah's cries as they wound down the steps. "So let's finish our nap, shall we?"

Lileela grinned. If someone had told her she'd be a fine Gannahan two months ago, she'd have wanted to slap them. Now, though, she could think of no higher praise—and no one she'd rather hear it from. What had happened to her? It must be true what they said on Karkar, that Gannahan air, food and water were toxic. They not only upset the digestion, but also poisoned the mind.

She picked up the tea tray and carried it carefully into the dining room, where Mr. Maddox and Mr. Dmitry sat talking. At her entrance, they looked up and smiled.

She flushed to her toes with pleasure. Who knew poison could taste so good?

BROWARD clenched his jaw against a yawn as Ras Tewodros droned on.

"... washed away, and approximately sixty-nine percent of the powlroot crop was lost due to flooding. Loss to the pod crop was less severe. Though the young pods couldn't be harvested, the mature seeds can still be reaped and shelled, with a loss of only about thirty percent."

Dassa nodded. "It's a set-back, to be sure. Especially since some of the families who have been self-sufficient have suffered heavy losses as well and will have to rely on the general stores for the next year."

Jax lifted his hand. Once the toqeph looked his way, he spoke up. "One plus. The storms riled up the wildlife something terrible. That wouldn't be a good thing, except it's given us opportunity to increase our stores of meat. We also keep finding injured ones and so put them out of their misery. Between that, coming across fish collecting in drying-up pockets as the floods recede, and crazy hezir going on the rampage and having to be killed, we might be powl poor this winter, but we'll be protein rich till spring, at least."

"So long as we can keep the freezers functioning." Dmitry ran his hand across his bald head. "With the collection satellites knocked out, power's going to be a serious problem. The storage cells are being depleted faster than they can be recharged. If we don't cut back even further on our energy consumption, we'll be in big trouble."

"That's one of the things we're here to discuss." Dassa turned to Pik. "I believe you drew up a list of suggested austerity measures?"

"I did. I've got them right here."

While he pressed the code for the viewing screens to emerge, Jax lifted a hand again but spoke before being acknowledged. "On the subject of the satellites being out, I'm wondering something. If I may, Madam Toqeph."

She smiled. "You don't need my permission to wonder, Jax. What's on your mind?"

He flushed. "It's just that, well, I'm wondering about the Bushatites. Didn't you say that before the satellites went out, we could see that the entire planet was affected by those storms?"

The toqeph nodded. "Compared to what I saw happening elsewhere, we got off easy here in Periy."

Broward watched the emotions play across Jax's face. Of course he'd be worried about the Bushatites. His sister and her husband were among them, as well as any children they might have produced by now. Marianna prayed for them every day, but since the planet came under that terrible meteorological siege, her pleas for protection had been especially fervent.

Ten years ago, the toqeph ruled that the settlers should make no attempts to contact the renegades. Bushati had left under false pretenses and started a new settlement without permission—with stolen supplies, no less. "They took off on their own," she'd said, "and they can stand or fall on their own. Whatever happens to them now is up to the Yasha to determine, not us."

Nevertheless, Broward sympathized with the family they'd left behind, and he knew the toqeph did too. He shifted in his seat. "Should we send out a party to see? I mean, not necessarily to check on the Bushatites, but to assess what damage the rest of Gannah sustained."

Jax glanced his way with a smile of gratitude. "I'd be happy to get a group togeth—"

The toqeph shook her head. "Thank you. Perhaps later, but for now, we have too many things to do here at home. We must—"

A flashing blue light on the wall above the sideboard, accompanied by an intermittent, low-volume hum, interrupted her.

She and Pik met gazes. Though his face was placid as usual, her expression showed puzzlement. "You're sure you found all the Karkar survivors?"

"Positive," Pik said. "We ran a sweep of the entire vessel. Besides that, the captain confirmed that all were accounted for."

The toqeph rose. "Then who's hailing us?"

His sleepy spell suddenly ended, Broward exchanged questioning glances with the other council members.

At the sideboard, the toqeph pulled a small controller from a drawer. As she returned to her seat, the display screen on the room's east wall emerged. "I am Atarah Hadassah Hagah Natsach Pik, Toqeph of Gannah. Who hails us?"

A face came into view on the screen.

The man was young and clean-shaven, with dark hair shorn like a League soldier's. He wore a uniform. Special Starforces, from the insignia on the collar.

And his eyes glowed a vivid azure. Like a Gannahan's.

32

*A*dam watched through the observation window as the strange vessel descended through billows of smoke and flame. In all his twenty-one years, he'd only seen three vessels come to Gannah, and here was a fourth, just two months after the last.

What would this arrival bring?

Elise stood beside him. Though glad of her company, he hadn't wanted her to come. He didn't trust these people — whoever they were — and would rather keep her far away until he knew more about them.

But when he'd told her of his concerns, she wasn't impressed. "Silly, do you think the toqeph would let those people come to the surface if they were dangerous? Other woman are coming too — Marianna and Sylvia and Katarina. I'm sure there's nothing to worry about."

He shrugged. "I suppose not." But how could Emma know? The solar flares had rendered most of the monitoring equipment useless, and her meah didn't work properly, either. But somehow she seemed to know things. How much of that went along with being the toqeph and how much came from her relationship with the Yasha?

Whatever her reasons, she'd allowed the visitors to land. But it didn't escape Adam's notice that she'd made sure the prison cells beneath Gullach, though never used since the settlers arrived, were ready for occupancy if necessary.

The descending ship was small, something they called a Photuris. Once Broward heard that, he almost drooled. Apparently he'd heard of the species and thought it remarkable.

As Adam watched the sleek monster shimmy downward toward the landing pad, he agreed. Though hardly bigger than the Karkar transport shuttle, this mysterious traveler had come all the way from Earth in just a few months. The technology that permitted a solid object to fold into a different dimension and then emerge in another part of the galaxy was magical. If not for the medical heritage passed down through five generations on his father's side, he might have wanted to study physics instead of medicine.

Elise quivered beside him, shielding her eyes from the glare despite the tinted windows. The spectators wore sound-deadening headphones — a lesson learned from their last experience with intergalactic guests — and stared, rapt, as the fantastic craft settled on the pad.

Once the ship set down and its savage roar tapered off to a dull growl, the watchers removed their headphones. They replaced them in their boxes, which Järn then hauled away to wherever they were kept. By the time he returned, it looked as if the craft was powering down.

"There go the ground anchors." Emma turned from the window. "They'll disembark soon. We should go down and greet them."

She led the Council into the elevator, and the door slupped shut behind them. Adam, Elise, and the rest of the non-Council members remained where they were and watched.

The wind blew a swirl of grit against the windows, and Adam realized with surprise it wasn't caused by the ship. The darkening sky and a new rumbling confirmed it. It had been sunny when the Photuris had first come into view, but a storm now rolled in. After the cataclysm they'd just endured, Adam wondered what new troubles might be in store.

He felt Elise's gaze and glanced down into her questioning blue eyes. Guessing she wondered the same thing, he smiled reassurance. The Yasha had kept them safe so far and he wouldn't let them down now. "Just the usual Gannahan welcome."

She chuckled. "I suppose so. Hope they like it."

Despite the threatening weather, the Council went outside to await the visitors under the entrance's canopy.

A door on the craft opened upward and a stairway unfolded downward, with a lightning bolt in the background illuminating the action in a manic strobe.

A man emerged escorting a woman with two children. Then, as another flash lit the scene, four more men exited the craft surrounding another, who kept his hands behind his back.

Marianna Broward gasped. "Why is that man handcuffed?"

With a flush of embarrassment at his naiveté, Adam realized the man was a prisoner.

Katarina Maddox leaned forward for a better view. "Now what are they doing to him?"

Sylvia answered above another rumble of thunder. "They're putting him in leg irons. I guess they had to take them off to get him down the stairs."

"Leg irons?" Elise shivered. "What kind of a criminal are they bringing here?"

Adam watched as the strange party moved across the tarmac toward the building, their clothes whipping in the wind. "I guess we'll find out."

BROWARD would have loved to get inside that ship and take a look around. Better yet, take it for a spin. Before coming to Gannah, he'd followed the progress of the Photuris's development and hoped one day to be able to see the fairy-tale technology for himself. Now, unable to hold back a grin as he gazed at the real-life beauty gleaming in the fading light, he put his hand over his mouth so as not to look like a lunatic.

Not that anyone was likely to notice his expression. The Council members all watched the visitors, and the newcomers were intent on reaching the safety of the airport before they got wet.

The curtain of rain drew across the stage of his view from the west, and before the visitors had crossed half the distance, it nailed them. As he watched from under the canopy, Broward felt the storm's mist. In the space of just a few seconds, the travelers looked half drowned.

The leader—named Faris, according to what he'd said in the transmission—fell back and helped with the prisoner while another man ushered the women and children ahead of the rest.

Once they were all together under the roof, Faris stepped forward and saluted, streaming water from every fold. "Thank you, Madam Toqeph, for allowing us to land on your fair planet."

Dassa returned his salute. "I'm sorry the weather is not so fair." She had to raise her voice to be heard above the torrent drumming the cover above. "Let's all get inside, shall we?"

Pik pressed the button to open the door, and they followed Dassa into the lobby. The council lined up behind the toqeph while the drenched visitors stood in puddles of their own making behind their leader.

Dassa got right to the point. "I have extended you the liberty of visiting Gannah, and here, everyone is free until found guilty under our law." She turned her gaze to the prisoner. "I must ask you to unbind our guest."

Broward expected an immediate objection. But Faris merely nodded to the four guards, and they removed the man's bonds.

While they did so, Dassa turned to the woman standing with one arm around each of the shivering girls, who looked to be about eight and ten years old. "You're soaked, and you have nothing to change into, do you?"

Clinging to one another, all three shook their heads, eyes wide.

"We'll take care of that." Dassa turned back to the soldiers, but gestured toward Pik. "This is my husband, Dr. Pik."

He bowed, and the soldiers nodded.

"If you would go with Dr. Pik and the rest of the council," she continued, "they will take you to the airport lounge. I'll take the ladies to get some dry clothing, but I'll return to you shortly." She reached toward the woman. "Ladies?"

The woman tossed a glance toward Faris, who nodded. Then she and the girls followed the toqeph.

Pik stepped forward and addressed the men. "As the toqeph said, my name is Pik. And you must be Commander Faris." With respect to the visitor's Earthish tradition, he shook Faris's hand.

The commander introduced the rest of the men, each of whom, oddly, bore only one name: Safiy, Ishaq, Esam, Adil, and the man who recently had been in chains, Binyamin.

"We are fugitives escaping from the League of Planets' domain. We seek asylum."

Pik asked no questions and offered no assurances. "Come with me, if you please." He gestured for Faris to follow him.

ADAM turned as Emma entered the lobby. The woman and children who'd arrived on the Photuris stood beside her, drenched to the skin.

Emma spoke. "Elise."

Elise stepped forward and bowed. "Madam Toqeph."

"Would you be so kind as to take Mrs. Dengel and her daughters to your parents' house? I would like them to make our guests welcome in their home. But first, stop at the store and get them some clothes. What they're wearing is all they own."

"Certainly, Madam Toqeph." She bowed, then turned to the visitors. "We'll get you taken care of right away." She tossed a quick smile to Adam, then went to do the toqeph's bidding.

Adam glowed with pride that Emma had chosen Elise to help. But his attention was on the toqeph, who addressed him and the others. "The rest of the visitors are on their way to the lounge. We'll meet them there."

She turned to Katarina Maddox. "You are prepared to record the exchange?"

Katarina bowed. "I am, Madam Toqeph."

"Very good. If any part of the proceedings should be censored before distribution, I'll let you know, but I sense no guile in these men."

She glanced up at Rip Tischtuch, mayor of Qatsiyr. "Do you have housing available for them in town?"

He nodded. "As long as they don't each want a private room."

"If I allow them to stay, they can share. All right, let's go see what they have to say for themselves."

Emma turned toward the elevators, and everyone followed her out of the lobby.

Adam's ears frowned. Was it wise to trust these men?

Every Outsider is not an enemy, Emma said through her meah. *If they are brothers in danger, we must be quick to give them succor.*

Adam flushed. The communication was faint, but its message was clear. But how would they be brothers?

Her silence answered that he must wait and see.

33

*T*he councilmen headed toward the airport lounge. As the toqeph had previously instructed, each escorted a guest, keeping the visitors sufficiently separated that communication among them would be hindered.

Broward accompanied Ishaq, a short, baby-faced man who would have looked to be about fifteen but for a thick, muscular physique. He reminded Broward of images of the Gannahans of old. Assuming the Special Starforces uniform he wore was legitimately his, he had to have been at least in his late twenties.

And be skilled in hand-to-hand combat, he thought. *He could overpower a septuagenarian like me before I could scream.*

Broward's lahab lay heavy in his pocket, and his hand twitched with the desire to pull it out in case he needed it. But other than the visitor's obvious power, youth, and strangeness, he seemed to pose no threat as he walked by Broward's side.

A short distance ahead, the man who had been shackled spoke to Jerry, his escort. "You are a Purpletongue." It was the first words he'd spoken. Obviously, he liked to get right to the point.

Jerry nodded. "I am."

The two men were roughly the same size. Both trained warriors. But Jerry's training had been more theoretical than practical. He'd killed animals, but never a man. He'd never even fought a man, except in sport. How would he fare against a seasoned warrior?

And how did the Old Gannahan Nasi train for combat, since they didn't war amongst themselves? Considering their bloodthirsty reputation, he probably didn't want to know the answer. But Binyamin had no problem asking questions. "I thought all the Nasi were dead."

"The toqeph is not dead. Nor am I."

"There are Nasi among you settlers? How is this possible?"

Jerry didn't so much as glance at his guest. "We undergo the training and complete the requirements, just as the Old Gannahans did."

After several strides in silence, Binyamin spoke again. "What requirements are those?"

"One only learns that when qualified to fulfill them."

After that, no one spoke until they arrived at the lounge, where pots of tea awaited them. Did the toqeph expect these Outsiders to ingest Gannahan tea? Wouldn't it make them sick?

It was a fairly long walk, and thanks to the uniforms' remarkable fabric, the men's clothes looked nearly dry by the time they entered the lounge. Pik invited them to sit, each visitor separated from his comrades by his escort.

Before taking their seats, they glanced at their leader for direction. When he pulled up the chair beside Pik and sat, they followed his example.

Even Binyamin, who presumably had no reason to cooperate. Imagining the scene should he, or any of the other guests, decide to revolt, Broward nervously ground his teeth. Just how much of a Nasi knight was Jerry, really? Broward would be more confident once the toqeph returned.

Pik poured himself a cup of tea and offered one to Faris. Taking his cue, Broward and the other Council members did the same with their guests. When Faris accepted, each of his men did too.

Except for Binyamin, who shook his head and waved his hand over the cup. "No, thank you."

Faris tossed him a glance, but if Binyamin saw, he chose to ignore it.

About the time the tea issue was settled, Dassa breezed in, followed by the others who had watched the landing from the lobby upstairs.

PIK looked up as Dassa entered, followed by Adam and the others. Her stride was purposeful, her manner brisk.

Rising, Pik swallowed a lump of shame. Now the truth would come out.

He should have told her years ago. And he would have, except…. What if she already knew? What if she knew, but graciously chose not to mention it? He couldn't very well re-open the wound.

At the visitor's first contact, the young man's brilliant Gannahan eyes glowing from the viewscreen had sent Pik's guilty heart plummeting to his feet. How old must the soldier be? A quick calculation—and the stocky, powerful frames of all five of these men—gave credence to his fears.

What an idiot he'd been back then. The memory of his self-centeredness made his stomach churn. What had he done for the sake of fame and filthy lucre?

Dassa took her seat, and they all sat, Pik wishing to be invisible.

She avoided his eye. "Let's get down to business then, shall we?" She turned her attention to the man named Binyamin. "The first thing I'd like to know is why you were in shackles."

Faris cleared his throat. "If I may—"

She lifted a restraining hand in his direction but kept her eyes on Binyamin. "I'd like to hear from this man first."

Binyamin sat straight as the soldier he was. "I was incarcerated, ma'am, because I was a danger to the others."

"And how were you dangerous?"

"I would have killed them if I'd had the chance."

Her expression didn't change. "Would you kill them now if you had a chance?"

"At this point, it would serve little purpose." He sat up straighter. "I would rather bring the traitors back to Earth to be delivered to justice. I would like to return the Photuris they stole. And I'd like to apprehend the suspect they freed and deliver him for questioning, as was our mission."

Elbows on the chair arms and hands clasped, Dassa pursed her lips. "So your commander and these men are traitors, and you alone remain faithful to the League?"

"Ma'am, that is correct." He locked eyes with her. Not an easy feat.

She nodded. "Tell me about this mission that you say was derailed."

How the man didn't squirm beneath that stabbing green gaze, Pik couldn't imagine. His training must have included the ability to remain cool under torture, because Pik was already squirming and his interrogation hadn't yet begun.

"We were to pick up Philip Dengel and his family from the compound where they were hiding." Binyamin spoke clearly and concisely. "Then take him to the detention colony on Station 2 for questioning. The wife and children were to go to the Multicultural Pleasure Center on Station 6. Those were our orders." Binyamin tossed Faris an accusatory glare.

The Pleasure Center? Pik's stomach rolled, and a chill gripped his body. Only Adam and Jax, who didn't know about the League's facilities for legal enjoyment of every conceivable aberration, lifted curious eyebrows. The others knew that what the woman and her daughters would have faced there should not even be imagined, let alone endured.

Dassa appeared unfazed. "These orders were fair, just, and properly given, and you had no reason to question them. Is that so?"

Binyamin nodded. "I do not question my orders, ma'am. I hear and obey."

"So if your commander told you to take a knife and slit your comrade's throat, you would do so and think nothing of it?"

"Yes, ma'am. I would know he had good reason. I would not waste precious moments trying to figure out why."

"But your commander" — she gestured toward Faris — "is a traitor, you say."

"Yes, ma'am."

"So now, instead of obeying him without question, you want to kill him?"

His jaw tightened. "I only want to carry out my orders."

"Whose orders?"

"The League's orders, ma'am. Captain Ahmed Abdul-Malik gave them to Commander Faris, and Commander Faris relayed them to us."

Dassa picked up the pot and poured the tea through the strainer into her cup. "Did you witness the captain give these orders?"

"No, ma'am."

"But you believed Commander Faris when he told you that's what the orders were?"

Binyamin's brows crinkled, just a little. "Yes, ma'am."

"Why?"

Pik knew Dassa better than anyone, but even he couldn't guess what she was getting at.

Binyamin shook his head. "I'm sorry, ma'am. Why what?"

"Why did you believe him? Didn't that sound like a terrible thing to do, taking that woman and two little girls to Station 6? Or did your captain routinely send you on missions that involved the kidnapping and torture of innocent women and children?"

He sat up straighter. "We aren't told the reason for our missions, ma'am. We just carry them out. Our unit is a tool, like a scalpel in the hands of a surgeon."

Dassa took a sip of tea. "Using that analogy, your captain is the hand and League HQ is the head. And the scalpel can't have a mind of its own."

"That's correct, ma'am." His shoulders relaxed a bit.

She put down her cup. "All right, so you had your orders. You picked up the Dengel family and you took off in the Photuris. When did things start to go wrong?"

"Shortly after we left Earth, Commander Faris ordered us to read the Bible."

Pik made a Karkarish squawk of surprise, which he camouflaged with a cough.

Dassa remained unmoved. "Did he give a reason?"

"He said it would help us understand the enemy."

Pik glanced sideways at Faris, who seemed to be studying his hands clasped in his lap. There was more to this situation than met the eye.

On multiple levels.

"And what did this research reveal? What did you learn?"

Binyamin rubbed his nose. "I learned that the unlicensed teaching that Mr. Dengel propagates is very narrow. The deity that stands as its figurehead is said to be the only such entity in the universe, and people who worship it are forbidden to acknowledge any other."

"But you don't believe this?"

"No, ma'am."

She took another sip of tea. "Why not?"

"No one can know for sure what's true. Just as there are many kinds of people, there are many ways of seeking. The whole truth is too big for any one religion to hold it."

"What's the point of seeking something if you can't find it?"

Binyamin's brows rose. "Beg pardon, ma'am?"

"If the truth can't be found, why bother looking?"

"We can find bits of it, ma'am. We just can't say we have the *whole* truth."

Dassa cocked her head. "Or perhaps there is no such thing as truth. Perhaps truth is in the eye of the beholder."

"Yes, ma'am. Perhaps it is."

She rested her arms on the table. "What if one or more of the other men disputes your statement about why you were incarcerated? If there is, in fact, no such thing as truth, should I not make my decision upon what seems best to me rather than trying to ascertain the *whole* truth?"

Binyamin's eyes widened. "I've given you the whole truth, ma'am. And they won't deny it."

"Why would Commander Faris, or any of the others, confess to these things? It would put them in a very bad light. I'd think they'd try to talk their way out of it."

"They'd admit it, ma'am, because that's what happened, and they won't lie to you."

Her gaze surveyed the other visitors. "Is that true? You are all trustworthy traitors?"

Faris spoke first. "It is, Madam Toqeph."

"It was just as he said, ma'am," the others murmured.

"Hmm." Her fingers tapped the table. "Interesting."

Pik didn't know what she was driving at, but he had the sick feeling she'd find them more trustworthy than he.

Dassa sat up a little straighter. "You all respect the authority of the truth and what it requires of you."

She turned to Binyamin. "I understand Commander Faris's actions were a blatant insult to the oath of allegiance to which you're both sworn. But do you concede the possibility that he acted on a truth, an authority, if you will, that supersedes that oath?"

Binyamin took a deep breath. "I had not considered that a possibility, ma'am. And I'm still not convinced. But I suppose it might be."

She nodded. "Good. Now, please finish your story."

He shifted his position. "The commander told us to read the Bible, and we discussed what we were reading. Then one day he announced that he'd made the decision to serve the God of the Bible instead of the League High Command. He said Philip Dengel wasn't an enemy, he was a servant of that same God, and he couldn't turn him over as ordered."

He tossed a glance toward Faris. "He asked if we'd join him. He made no excuses. He just said he was going rogue, and I think he was willing to die right there if it came to that. One by one, though, everyone agreed to go along with it. Everyone except me. I don't know what they thought about all that God of the Bible stuff, but they all believed in the commander."

Binyamin's eyes glassed with tears. "But I couldn't turn my back on the League. The Commander knew I'd try to stop them, so he had me thrown in the brig."

He shook his head. "Though they kept me fed and all, I never saw another soul until they trussed me up and hauled me down here today." He gazed at the faces around the table. "I saw the wife and kids leaving the Photuris, but where'd Dengel go? Why'd he stay on board?"

"I think we'll let the commander answer some of those questions now." Dassa turned to Faris. Still avoiding Pik's eye. "Let's hear the story from your point of view."

34

*F*ARIS took a deep breath. The shadowy galactic puzzle called Gannah was no less inscrutable in person than in legend.

How had these backward, unassuming people disabled the Karkar ship? And how could the region where they lived remain relatively untouched by the cataclysm that had ravaged the rest of the planet?

The toqeph, her green gaze boring into his mind, waited for his response.

"The events as Binyamin related them are accurate, as far as he saw them." He took a sip of tea, which seemed to calm him. "But he couldn't tell you what happened after we freed the Dengel family and put Binyamin in a cell. At that time, we set our course for your planet, Madam Toqeph, because we'd heard that Gannah does not forbid the worship of Jesus Christ. But as we neared Station 27, Mr. Dengel asked us to leave him there. He said he was called to preach the gospel to the lost and refused to flee from that duty. When last we heard, he was safe on that station in the company of a handful of other like-minded people."

The toqeph nodded. "You are a follower of Christ, Commander?"

"Yes, ma'am."

"How did that happen?"

"I had occasion to meet Mr.. Dengle a couple of years ago under—" He glanced around the table at his men. "Under circumstances that are probably best not divulged at this time. During our brief association, he helped me to see what I've tried to help my men see. That Jesus offers us freedom from the grip of sin, which we can't possibly neutralize ourselves.

He embodies a perfection far beyond any human engineering. He is the truth we all instinctively long for, the way to everything we require, and the life we yearn to live. Since Mr. Dengel introduced me to Jesus, the Messiah has been the captain of my life."

The toqeph's eyes glowed warmer and the corners crinkled in a smile. "So when you were ordered to capture Mr. Dengel and his family, what was your response?"

Faris swallowed. "I had to obey. But all the while, I was praying for a way out. And I came up with a plan.

"One of my men, Omar Ibrahim, was a practicing Muslim. Even before I was sure what I was going to do, I knew he would oppose any plan I devised. So first, I had to get him out of the way."

A glance at the faces of the rest of his team showed they were putting the pieces together even as he explained.

"Before we took off on the *Glowworm*, I sent him and another of my men, Ya'qub, on an errand. They had no reason to suspect the mission was not officially sanctioned.

"Providing travel expenses from my personal funds, I first sent them to two leaders of the underground church who would be concerned for Dengel when he disappeared. The messages reassured them that Dengel was safe and that he would remain so as long as I had any control over it. The third message was to go to Captain Abdul-Malik, but only after the first two were delivered. I insisted these all be delivered personally in order to keep Ibrahim and Ya'qub busy as long as possible. The message to the captain confessed that I had taken the prisoners, stolen the ship, and defected. I explained that my men were not willing participants—I did it wholly without their knowledge. And I gave him my reasons for everything I did."

He smiled weakly. "He got a pretty clear gospel message, I think. And I've been praying that the Spirit will get through to him. I like the captain, he's a good man. I hope he'll come to know the Lord, though it would take a miracle to accomplish that."

The toqeph returned his smile. "It takes a miracle to accomplish that for anyone, Commander. If the Yasha can give a wild Gannahan eternal life, he can do the same for a tough old Earther."

"I'm praying that he does just that. But even so, I'm still a criminal. If they catch up with me, I have no hope of leniency."

The toqeph nodded. "So what of your men, Ibrahim and Ya'qub? What will happen to them?"

Faris sobered. "They interrogated them both, I'm sure. And I regret that. But they're good men, well trained. And they're innocent of any wrongdoing, merely following orders they had no reason to question. I have no doubt they've been exonerated by now."

Feeling Binyamin's eyes boring into him, he cast a glance his way. "I'm sorry. I didn't know what else to do."

Binyamin curled his lip. "Follow orders. That's what else you could have done. You—"

The toqeph raised her hand. "Enough." Her quiet voice commanded respect. "You've had your say. Now it's the commander's turn."

Though Binyamin said no more, he didn't avert his angry glare.

"In your note to your captain, did you tell him you were going to Gannah?"

"No, ma'am. I didn't know at the time where I'd go. I'm sure they'll figure it out, though." He set his jaw. "I don't want to make trouble for you. If they send someone after me, I'll go willingly."

She waved a gesture of dismissal. "We don't get much traffic out here. But if anyone comes inquiring, we'll deal with it."

A lump rose in his throat and his eyes burned. He swallowed. What was the matter with him? "We thank you for your hospitality, Madam Toqeph. We're completely at your disposal. And if you want us to leave, we'll leave. But may I ask a question?"

She nodded.

"There's a Karkar A-1-P orbiting your planet. It's crippled and abandoned."

"That's not a question."

"No, ma'am. My question is what happened?"

She leaned back in her seat. "What else did you see from up there, Commander?"

He exchanged glances with the men. Did she truly not know?

"It looks, ma'am, as if your planet has recently suffered some sort of, um, disturbance. A major one. Above the atmosphere, you have thick clouds of magnetic dust floating everywhere, and a dead ship drifting along in a sea of nonfunctioning satellites. On the surface, you have — well, what used to be one large landmass, as I understand it, is now broken into at least three separate continents."

All the Gannahans in the room, including the toqeph, either sat up straight or fell back in their chairs, eyes widening.

"You didn't know?"

The toqeph shook her head. "We knew about the massive MREs, of course. They created the most widespread, violent meteorological activity in recorded history, destroyed the Karkar ship, and knocked out our satellites. We knew there were major earthquakes as well, but once our surveillance sats went out, we couldn't see what was going on beyond our own region." She leaned forward, her voice incredulous. "The land mass has actually separated?"

"Yes, ma'am. Comparing what we saw when we arrived with the photos of the planet in the database, the change is quite dramatic. Seeing a global catastrophe like that, we were surprised anyone survived."

She stared at the table in front of her, apparently stunned, and no one in the room so much as shifted his weight.

"If I may ask, ma'am. How many of you died during the event?"

She looked up as if surprised at the question. "None. We lost no one. In fact, we gained a few."

Faris raised his brows, and she smiled. "Three babies were born during all that mess, including a set of twins. And we invited the surviving Karkar down to the surface. Their life support systems were failing, and they wouldn't have lasted much longer."

"What were they doing up there, if I may ask?"

Her smile faded. "You may not." She took a breath. "Before I open the floor to anyone else's questions, I have one more line of inquiry I'd like to pursue, Commander."

The bearded Karkar beside him stiffened, and Faris glanced at him out of the corner of his eye. His face was as impassive as any of his race, but Faris felt anxiety pulsing from him in waves.

"You and your men have only one name. Not a first and last name like most Terrestrials. Why is that?"

Though her green glare, sharp as a knife, sliced through Faris, it was the Karkar beside him who tensed as if in pain. What was eating him?

"We are prototypes, ma'am. Genetic experiments. Conceived in a laboratory and raised in a special facility. Since we have no families, we have no need for familial designation."

"So in all the official records, you are just Faris?"

Faris nodded. "We each have a serial number, like any soldier. But only one name."

The toqeph scanned the faces of Faris's team one by one, looked long and hard at the old Karkar, then turned her gaze back to Faris. "How many of these genetic experiments are there?"

"As I understand it, ma'am, they created twenty of us at first. With some of the genetic experiments in the past with other animals, the subjects grew normally at first but their systems tended to disintegrate shortly after reaching maturity. Before making any more humans, I believe they wanted to be sure we could sustain a full lifetime, for one thing. Also, they wanted to monitor certain traits to see if they turned out as hoped and if they could be further enhanced."

The Gannahans stared at the team members like they'd suddenly changed color. Faris and the others glared back, wordlessly daring one of them to say something.

But only the toqeph spoke. "So there are twenty of you?"

"No, ma'am. Some turned problematic and were euthanized early on. One succumbed to complications following an investigative medical procedure, and two died in accidents. Last I knew, there were fourteen of us still living. That's why each eight-man team had one Normal on it, to balance it out. That is, Omar ibn Ibrahim on my team, and Jorge Yamato on the other."

The toqeph tapped the table with her fingers, making the ring on her index finger flash with reflected light. The ring's stone was the same shade of green as her eyes.

Her mouth grim, she turned those eyes on Safiy. "Do you know, you look so much like my brother Areli that I did a double-take when I first saw you?"

He paled. "No, ma'am. I would have no way of knowing that."

She raised her brows at Binyamin. "From your build, you could be a native Gannahan."

"Yes, ma'am." Binyamin cast his glance at Esam, then Adil, and back to the toqeph. "We've all been told that."

"And you, Commander." She turned back to him. "Your eyes are the same color as my father's and his father's before him."

Finally she turned to the Karkar, who trembled with tension.

"Do you have any idea where these men's genetic material came from, Dr. Pik?"

As if in slow motion, he rose, gray-faced, to his full seven-foot height. He stepped away from the table. "Madam Toqeph. If I may beg your gracious indulgence." He prostrated his gigantic self beside her chair, speaking face-to-face with the floor. "I beg a word with you in private. If you would, Madam Toqeph."

She stared down at him, her face a mixture of emotions Faris could neither sort out nor describe. Everyone at the table watched, frozen.

"Yes, Dr. Pik, I will have a word with you in private. In fact, I will have many words." She rose swiftly. "Gentlemen of the Council, please instruct our guests concerning the basic laws of Gannah. Then Adam, Mr. Maddox, and Mr. Tischtuch, you will take our guests to Qatsiyr and show them to their quarters. See to it that they're well supplied and comfortable. I will speak more with them later. Mr. Binyamin?"

He sprang to attention. "Madam!"

"Can I trust you to behave yourself? You will not harm Mrs. Dengel or her children, nor attack your commander or comrades, nor try to abscond with the ship?"

He made a small bow. "You can trust me, ma'am, to do no harm."

"I will personally hold you to that." She turned to the younger of the two women. "Katarina."

"Madam Toqeph." The woman rose and bowed.

"Draft your news report honestly, but leave out the end, about the genetic engineering. We'll complete that when the issue is resolved." She included everyone in her gaze. "This meeting is adjourned."

Without glancing down at the Karkar, she spun on her heel. "Get up, Dr. Pik."

Before he'd clambered from the floor, she'd left the room.

Her messenger, however, remained on the table. As the Karkar headed for the door, brushing off his clothes as he went, it chimed.

The Purpletongue rose and picked it up. "This is Maddox. The toqeph just left."

He listened for a moment then said, "I'll let her know, and I'll be there myself directly. Thank you."

Pocketing the messenger, he turned to the man called Tischtuch. "Rip, you and Adam will have to get the guests settled without me. I'm sorry to leave you all so abruptly, but Captain Broward and I are needed elsewhere."

The old man Broward lifted his brows. "We are?"

"Yes." Maddox glanced to one of the women. "You and Marianne both." Turning away, he gestured for them to follow. "Miami and her two children, along with a handful of others, have just come out of the tunnels. They walked here all the way from Yapheh. They're at the clinic in Gullach."

The woman gave a cry then covered her face with her hands, and the council member named Jax let out an undignified whoop.

35

PIK caught a glimpse of Dassa disappearing around the bend. His long legs caught him up to her just as she entered the elevator, and he slipped through before the door shut.

She looked straight ahead as the elevator started downward, and he cleared his throat. Without deigning to look up, she cut him off before he could get a word out. "Save it for when we get home."

Below ground, they exited in silence, made their tense way to the depot without speaking, and climbed into a Gullach-bound pod like a couple of grim-jawed mutes. Pik slid the door shut and set the destination. The vehicle stirred to life, built speed, then sliced along the single rail through the dark toward the palace.

Unmoving, Dassa stared out the window at the blackness.

Pik wanted to fall at her feet again, this time in tears. But he kept his dignity and his seat during the interminable five-minute trip.

At the depot beneath Gullach, they exited to find several people gathered in the vicinity. The group turned, some hailing them. "Madam Toqeph! Dr. Pik!"

Dassa raised her hand. "I'm sorry, not now."

Everyone bowed. "Of course, Madam. Dr. Pik."

Pik had never seen a crowd like that at the depot level unless a group was traveling to Qatsiyr for some reason. But these weren't boarding. They just stood around talking. It seemed odd, but only vaguely. His main concern was how to fix things with Dassa.

Was that even possible? What he'd done was unconscionable. How could he have rationalized such a thing? How would he feel if someone stole samples of *his* DNA and sold it to the League of Planets?

And for what? All he'd gained was a prestigious position at Earth's branch of the Centers for Disease Control in Paris—which he soon abandoned anyway. Shame over his actions had burned in his breast all the years since.

Would she throw him out of the apartment? Remove him from the council? Banish him to a distant part of Gannah? Gannahan law didn't provide for divorce, but.... He swallowed hard. There was no law against a woman killing her husband for good cause.

True, the provision was there to protect her against unconscionable violence. The wife was obligated to obey her husband, and he was obligated to discipline her if she failed to please him. But if he went too far, she was allowed to defend herself. Did that right extend to wives whose husbands betrayed them?

Following her upstairs to the residential area of the palace, he envisioned the small circle on the floor under a skylight in Gullach's tower. When a person was convicted of a capital offense, or so he'd been told, the criminal would be made to stand in that circle. And there, the toqeph would carry out the sentence.

He remembered how Dassa had swiftly dispatched the two muscle-bound Cephargian pirates decades ago. She'd have no trouble with his scrawny neck.

Pik felt the surrounding people's eyes boring into him as he was swept along in her wake. He imagined their gossip once he and Dassa were out of earshot.

Finally they arrived at their apartment. He started to speak as they passed through the door. But, as if deaf, she strode through the front room and clattered down the spiral stairway.

Ears frowning, he followed her down the stairs, along the hall, and to their bedroom.

As soon as he stepped inside, she closed the door and turned to face him. Hands on hips, head tipped back to meet his gaze, her eyes glowed with a ferocity that took his breath away. Five decades of sorrow—most of it caused by Pik and his people—lined her taut face.

"I have been violated by you." Her voice was cold and controlled. "I have been humiliated, betrayed, and lied to by you. And I have resented you for it. Even hated you at times. But never." She spoke through gritted teeth. "Never. Have I been so thoroughly disgusted, so horrified, so cut to the quick by your behavior as now."

Pik tried to speak, but again she lifted her hand.

"Just—just keep that pathetic squawk of yours still. I don't want to hear your voice." She turned away and spoke to the wall. "I don't want to see your inhuman, plastic face. I don't want to—"

Did her voice break?

He took a step closer, hand outstretched tentatively, but she spun around.

"You've degraded me today beyond anything you've ever done before. How could you?" Her face was flushed and her eyes narrowed with fury. "How could you prostrate yourself like that?"

Pik's jaw dropped as far as a Karkar jaw could fall, and kept on falling. "What? What do you mean? You're the toqeph, I was—"

"I'm your *wife*! A man does not *ever* prostrate himself before his *wife*! It's the greatest insult possible." She turned away again. "I'll never be able to face the council. And Adam—"

Pik struggled to follow. She wasn't upset that he'd sold her genetic material, but she was appalled that he'd tried to apologize?

She covered her eyes with her hands. "He saw that. You've ruined his life as well as mine. How can he and Elise ever hope to have a healthy marriage after seeing his parents play out such a travesty?" Her voice broke for certain. "How can he— be— the man Elise will need him to be—" The toqeph of Gannah was sobbing? "—after the example you've set?"

Pik's mind grappled with this surprising development, shuffling through everything he knew about Gannahan relationships between the sexes. He'd felt from the beginning that he was an inadequate husband, but it was worse than he thought. He couldn't even follow what she was talking about.

He'd only seen her so emotional one time before, and that was years ago, when—

You look enough like my brother Areli that I did a double take when I first saw you…

Your eyes are the same color as my father's…

Pik didn't look, smell, sound or feel like a Gannahan. But it was time he acted like one.

"Haddassah." He spoke as sharply as his reedy Karkar voice could manage. "Stop that harping at once."

"Harping! How dare you—"

"I understand you're displeased with me, and with good reason. But my being a substandard husband does not entitle you to be an unfit wife."

Gasping, she raised her arm as if to give him a wholehearted slap, but dropped it. She turned away and covered her face with her hands again. "Look what you've done. You've turned everything upside down."

He took her by the shoulders, tense and quivering beneath his hands. "Come over here and sit down."

She shook her head and tried to brush him away, but he gripped harder. "Whatever else I am, I'm still your husband."

Feeling the fight drain out of her, he turned her around to face him. "Come."

He guided her to the bed where he sat, then pulled her down beside him. "I'm not a native Gannahan, and I don't understand all the nuances of being one. Once you compose yourself, I need you to tell me where I've erred. And how I can make amends." He handed her a handkerchief from the bedside table.

She took it and wiped her eyes. "You can't make amends. The damage is done."

"That was my thought, at first. And then I realized we were talking about two different things."

Staring at the floor, she sighed. "What were you talking about?"

So she was going to make him say it aloud, was she? Very well. It was time he made full confession.

"When you were my patient on the *Barton*. All my examinations and tests. I took samples of your DNA, and—"

She shook her head. "I know. I mean, I didn't know you were going to try to create a new race with it, but I knew—"

"I didn't intend to do anything other than sell it. Use it to further my career. But you knew that?"

She backed away from him on the bed and pulled her feet up to sit cross-legged. "I knew you'd taken samples. And I knew you got a lot of professional mileage out of being the first medical researcher to get his hands on a live Gannahan. I didn't care about the details, for what was done, was done. All I cared about was that you'd saved my life and restored me to health."

Pik's ears twitched ruefully. "And that the Yasha required us to marry."

"Well, yes, there was that too." She shrugged. "That was another thing I didn't want to think about at the time."

He took her hands, handkerchief and all. "But you married me anyway. Me, the researcher who provided those Frankensteins with the material they needed to create their monsters." He looked down at her hands, and with his thumb, rubbed the ancient Ring of Atarah passed down from her forefathers. "A man who's so unfit to be your husband, he doesn't even know when he's doing something wrong."

He raised his gaze. "What *did* I do wrong? Other than what I did all those years ago, I mean?"

To his surprise, her eyes filled again, and she turned her head away. In all the years he'd known her, he'd seen many quail at looking *her* in the eye, but he'd never known her to flinch from another's gaze.

"My meah must be more damaged than I realized. I had no inkling that you hated me."

His heart plummeted. "What?"

"The way you fell on your face like that. In front of the council and in front of our son. No man would do that unless he hated his wife with a perfect passion."

She started to rise, but Pik pulled her back down. "I do not hate you."

She finally met his gaze, her brilliant green eyes questioning. "Then why would you humiliate me like that?"

He let go of her. "You mean prostrating myself?"

"Yes!"

He shook his head, trying to clear it. "Isn't it customary to bow to the toqeph?"

"Not when the toqeph is your wife." Her lips pursed as if she were exasperated beyond words. "How long have we been married? And you still don't know that?"

His mind raced through his memories of all the council meetings and other official dealings in which he and Dassa had been involved. It was true—he couldn't recall another time he'd had occasion to bow to her like that. Others had, but not him.

He reviewed the protocol. Children bow to adults. A man bows to any woman who is not his wife. Except in greeting, a woman never bows to a man unless he has authority over her, but she falls on her face before her husband at the first hint of his disapproval. It was a system he neither fully understood nor approved of. But Dassa was determined to make it a part of the New Gannahan society, just as it was in the Old.

"So you're saying that a man should never prostrate himself to his wife, no matter what her standing. And if he does, it's the bitterest insult imaginable?"

"Yes, of course. How could you not know that?"

"There's no reason I would know that. As far as I was aware, when the toqeph is displeased, falling on one's face is always the recommended protocol."

"It is! But not when the toqeph is your wife!"

She flopped backward onto the bed and covered her eyes with the crook of her arm. "With all due respect, my husband, I fear you have irrevocably undermined my authority. I must resign my rule. But Adam is not yet Nasi. I shall have to make Jerry temporary ruler, though he's not Atarah's heir."

Pik couldn't believe his stiff-with-amazement ears. "Have you lost your mind? Why would you say such a thing?"

She removed her arm from her face and glared up from him. "Because, my husband, you have humiliated me. I thought we'd already established that."

He took her hands. "Sit up."

She did, though her frown remained.

He continued holding her hands. "I have studied Gannahan law and history for many years. I have lived on Gannah for more than two decades, served on the ruling Council for the entire time, and have tried to integrate Old Gannahan customs into my life and my marriage. And this is the first time I've ever heard that this is supposed to be such a terrible insult. If I didn't know it until you just now told me, how would anyone else?"

Her expression turned thoughtful while remaining displeased.

"Do you seriously think they're appalled by *my* behavior?" He gave her hands a squeeze. "Don't you figure they're more alarmed by your response to it?"

She scowled—the way she did when unwilling to concede he was right. Her eyes probed him as if trying to find a hole in his logic. When she tried to pull her hands away, he held them tighter.

"I think I know what the problem is," he said.

She scowled deeper. "What, my husband?"

His ears lifted in amusement. "Your words are respectful, but your expression is not. If we're going to be good Gannahans, let's do it right."

She bit her lip. "Yes, my husband. My behavior has been shocking. I apologize."

He shook his head. "It's I who wronged you." He gave her a long look, almost fearing the answer to what he was about to ask. "What would be done to an Old Gannahan husband who had betrayed his wife as I did you all those years ago?"

She studied his face, her expression unreadable. "I cannot imagine a Gannahan man doing what you did. But it's a moot point. When you betrayed me, I was not your wife, and we were not on Gannah."

She pulled her hands away and rose. "I gave it a lot of thought at first. How could I marry someone who had violated me so? The touching, the examining." She paced, gesturing with animation. "The robbing my body of not only its dignity, but its very identity, the source of what makes me, me? And sharing your findings—and the fruit of your theft—with the galaxy? There was nothing on Gannah I could compare it to, and at first, I didn't know how to deal with it."

She stopped pacing and sat again. "Until I recognized the situation for what it was."

The woman was full of puzzles today.

"And what was that?"

"Eight centuries before, Gannah attacked Karkar. And though the fighting had ceased, no treaty was made, the war had never officially ended. I was, therefore, a prisoner of war. As such, I was treated quite well and had no cause for complaint."

"So you married your captor? You've been suffering from Stockholm Syndrome all this time?"

She shrugged. "I'm not familiar with the term, but no, probably not. I married you because the Yasha commanded it. And after I got past the resentment and allowed myself to get to know you better, I saw that His commandments are not grievous." Smiling, she reached up and ran her finger along his jaw. "Now what was that you said a moment ago? You know what the problem is?"

He kissed her finger, then clasped her hand. "I believe I do. For one thing, I don't think you've gotten over your resentment as well as you thought. You shoved it into the back of the cabinet but never disposed of it. Seeing the living and breathing evidence of it brought it all back, and it made you angry. Which is quite understandable."

Pulling her close, he felt the tension in her body, and it confirmed his theory. "But that's not all. That living and breathing evidence made you feel as if your father's eyes were watching you, your brother Areli was sitting across from you, and all the Old Gannahans were judging you, to see how you ruled their planet."

She stiffened even more.

"On my part, I was horrified at what I'd done. I wanted only to apologize, to let you know how very, very sorry I am. And when I expressed my remorse in the best way I knew, you saw it from the perspective of the Old Gannahans."

He stroked her hair. "I'm sorry for what I did thirty years ago. I'm sorry for not confessing it earlier. And I'm sorry for upsetting you today. But honestly, no one there could possibly have considered it offensive. They're not Old Gannahans. Not even the ones with your DNA."

Gradually, she relaxed in his arms. "I believe you're right, Dr. Pik. I did react rather foolishly, didn't I?"

"You did. But my fault is far greater. For that reason—" He gave her a squeeze. "Although you made an embarrassing scene this afternoon, tossing our dirty laundry all the way between the airport and our apartment, I won't punish you as you deserve."

"Thank you, my husband." He heard a smile in her voice. "You are both wise and merciful."

She looked up at him. "And I mean that, seriously. But I would like to say one more thing, if I may."

"Certainly, my wife."

"I feel obligated to point out one error of yours I didn't mention."

The smile left his ears with a jerk. "And what might that be?"

"You said you were unfit, a substandard husband. But that's not true. You are an exemplary husband, one whom I'm proud to be possessed by. I am deeply grateful to the Yasha for commanding our union."

Ears lifting high, he lowered her to the bed. "Amen."

36

*L*ileela's lahab whirred through the air, then sliced through the arnebeth's throat. The little beast fell to the muddy ground, long ears limp and head at an impossible angle.

Lynne Lucas gave an appreciative whistle on her way to the scene of the crime. "Nice! A good, clean kill, no suffering."

No suffering. So why was it flopping like that?

Lynne picked up the creature by one back foot, holding it low so the blood pulsing from the neck wouldn't splash her. "Oh, wait, you should be doing this." She glanced up at Lileela and motioned with her head. "Come on over here. You want to learn to do this or not?"

Lileela uprooted herself from where she stood and limped toward Lynne across the spongy, uneven ground. "Do I *want* to learn? Not particularly." She retrieved her lahab, cleaned it, and slipped it back into its pocket before taking the animal's carcass from Lynne. "You're sure I need to do this in order to pass the Fifth Level?"

"Yes. You won't have to demonstrate, but I have to certify that you've done it. Besides, Mr. Maddox'll be able to tell from the way you answer his questions." Lynne snorted. "I'm surprised you passed the Fourth without doing this. I think he went easy on you."

"Oh, yeah. Real easy." Lileela shuddered at the memory of the "instruction" Emma had given her at his recommendation. The chafe of that brown jumpsuit still made her skin crawl.

Lynne chuckled. "Hey, we all go through that. The rest of us just get it out of our systems before we're fifteen. Haven't you seen your little brothers sent to the greyroom?"

"Yeah. But they've never had to wear that awful suit for a week while everyone shuns them except when an adult stops to ask why they're being punished, and then they have to bow and tell them what they did and apologize for bringing shame to their family and all of New Gannah."

The arnebeth's paroxysm having ceased, Lileela lifted the body by its long, fluffy gray tail and headed for the campsite. "Even you treated me like a pariah that week."

Lynne followed her. "I had to, you know that. If I'd talked to you while you were being punished, or even looked at you, I'd have been sent to the greyroom myself. And I don't like it any better than you do."

Lileela sighed. But enough on that subject. "So now what am I supposed to do with this thing? Undress it?"

Lynne chuckled. "Dress it, you mean."

"Peeling the skin off seems more like undressing, if you ask me."

Lileela stopped, holding the bloody arnebeth at arm's length. "Can I do it here? It's too messy to carry."

"You can do it anywhere you want."

Lileela looked around. The wooded area between Gullach and the outdoor chapel was so littered with fallen trees and broken branches, it had been a challenge for her and Lynne to find a clear area big enough to set up their camp. But the clutter did make it easy to find a horizontal surface.

She sat on a fallen trunk and laid the carcass beside her. Lynne straddled the tree to supervise. "You've seen it done, so show me what you've learned."

Lileela flicked open her lahab. "Well, the head will be easy." She sliced through the remaining skin, muscle, and tendon, and the head dropped to the ground with a small, sickening thud. She focused on the mechanics of what she was doing and tried to forget this had been a living creature two minutes earlier. "Next I cut off the feet, right?" She grabbed a front paw.

Lynne nodded. "Right. Cut through the ankle joints."

Imitating what she'd seen Lynne do yesterday, Lileela severed the feet and dropped them to the ground with the head. Next she pulled the pelt from the still-warm animal, which was no simple feat. Finally, her hands slimed with blood, grease and hair, she held her breath and inserted her blade into the creature's soft abdomen.

"Before you pull the guts out, do you want to review the anatomy?"

"No, I think I've got that down pat." Lileela gritted her teeth, trying to summon her inner Gannahan, and pulled out the internal organs. She wasn't sure which was more nauseating—the feel, the sound, or the smell. How could anyone want to be a doctor?

"You're pretty good at that," Lynne said. "I was real squeamish the first few times I did it."

"Huh. Like I'm not?" Lileela completed the horrible task, then held up the finished, smeary product in a hand as messy as the carcass. "I need some water." She slid off the tree trunk—on the opposite side as the pile of guts—and headed for the stream, much reduced since the storms ended but still twice its former size. "This is disgusting."

Lynne hopped down and walked beside her. "You get used to it."

"I hope I never have the chance. I don't ever care to do it again."

At the rushing water, Lileela washed the carcass, then laid it on a broad elah leaf. Next she washed her lahab and her hands while Lynne searched for a few late shachorberries.

Lileela looked up. "Do I hear thunder?"

"I didn't hear anything." Lynne looked at the sky in all directions. "But it is pretty dark over there toward the west."

"Oh, good. We need more rain. Do you suppose it'll last a month again?"

Lynne popped a berry in her mouth. "It wasn't a month. But it sure was awful. I thought it would never end." Brows lifted, she held up another berry between thumb and forefinger. "I only found two. I ate the first. Want this one?"

Lileela opened her mouth. Lynne popped the berry into it, and Lileela chewed. "Umm, sweet."

"Yeah, mine was good too. Too bad I couldn't find any more." Lynne looked up at the sky again. "Grab that arnebeth and let's get back to the camp before the rain catches us."

Holding the carcass wrapped in green elah leaves, Lileela led the way, shuffling through the maze of fallen timber to the clearing. "They're going to clean all this mess out of here this winter. I heard Emma and Abba talking about it. They have other things to worry about now, like crops and building repairs and things. But once the bigger priorities are taken care of, they plan to have crews salvage any good timber and haul out the rest."

"Sounds like a lot of work." Lynne clambered over a tree trunk while Lileela skirted the soil-clad roots rising from the ground. "My brother David will want to help. He'd rather be outdoors than in, and he loves the smell of sawdust. I don't know why. It makes me sneeze."

"I don't know if I've ever smelled it."

"You're kidding."

Lileela stooped beneath a low-hanging branch. "Don't tell me, let me guess. In order to pass Level Five, I'll have to identify twenty kinds of sawdust by their odors."

Lynne chuckled. "No. You only need to identify trees by their leaf, seed, and bark, and know what fruit or nuts they produce, what their wood was traditionally used for, and where they grow."

"And which lichens and mosses grow on them, what kind of insects lay their eggs beneath the bark, what animals and birds make their nests in them, what kind of fungus grows on their roots, and how to translate their names into six different languages."

Lynne let out a hoot. "Lileela, you are so funny! We don't need to know all that."

"Maybe not, but I can't believe all the stuff we *do* need to know. I stay up late every night pouring it all into my brain."

"Yeah, but you've got like a photographic memory, so you'll do all right. Jerrina told me she's been doing labs with you, too. Qualitative analysis and all that fun stuff."

"Yeah. I was hoping Adam would help me with the science part, but he's been occupied."

On an unobstructed portion of the path, Lynne walked backward to talk to Lileela. "Jerrina's a good choice to teach you, though. I mean, with her abba being the one who's going to test you, and all."

"I like Jerrina, she's smart. But her abba being the Education Minister isn't going to help anything."

"I like Jerrina too." Lynne spoke over a rumble of thunder. "I wish she could have come camping with us. We'd have—"

"Watch where you're going!"

Lynne looked behind her, but too late to keep from falling over a branch in the path.

Both girls laughed as Lynne picked herself up. She was muddied, but that was the worst of the damages.

Still laughing, Lileela brushed a wisp of hair away from her face with the back of her hand. "I'm usually the clumsy one."

Lynne brushed off the seat of her pants. "You move slowly, is all, and carefully. Not clumsy. In fact, my little sister Audrey's always trying to imitate the way you walk. She says she wants to 'float like Leela.'"

"Float, huh?"

"That's what Audrey says. But whatever you call it, we'd better do it a little faster, or we'll get wet."

Lileela hastened her pace to keep up, but Lynne reached the campsite ahead of her and closed the tent's window flaps.

"Put our lunch in that pot." Lynne nodded toward a battered old pan they'd found in the woods. "Cover it with water to help it cool, and then help me bring some firewood into the tent to keep it dry. When the storm's over, you can build us a cook fire and roast us some grub."

The darkening sky cast a pall over the woods, and dry leaves blew before the breeze while Lileela unwrapped the arnebeth and laid it in the pot. She covered it with water from one of the buckets the girls had carried from the stream earlier. Lynne gathered up an armful of firewood. But instead of helping her, Lileela carried the pot into the tent.

"What are you doing?" Lynne came in and laid down her load. "We can't cook it in here."

"I know. But I don't want some animal stealing it while we're inside." She started out the opening, intending to grab another armful of firewood, but Lynne tugged at her tunic.

"We've got enough already, and the rain's starting." The sudden pattering of drops on the tent confirmed her words. "Just seal up the door, we'll be fine."

After fastening the opening, Lileela sat on her bedroll and looked upward. "I've never been in a tent in a storm. It's just fabric. How's it going to keep us dry?"

Lynne shrugged. "It's a special kind of fabric, I guess. Don't know how it works, but unless it rains for days on end again, we should stay dry as dowb in a cave in Midbar."

Lileela wrinkled her nose. "What's that supposed to mean?"

"Even a Second Level knows that much."

"I know Midbar's the province south of here, and a desert. And a dowb's a big hairy creature with huge claws and teeth. But I'd rather be a woman in a Periy palace than a beast in a desert cave."

"Okay then." Lynne wrapped her arms around her legs. "We'll be snug as two Gannahan ladies in Gullach. But it doesn't have the same ring to it."

"Zhsiu ghysidaaaax," Lileela said in Karkar, then laughed when Lynne jumped at the raucus sound. "It means *We'll be comfortable*."

"Well, it's not very comfortable on the ears."

The rain drummed steadily and the wind buffeted the little tent, but it seemed sturdy enough. Lileela lay on her side, bedroll supporting her head, and looked up at her friend. "So, you've been sixteen for two weeks now. What's it like? Being your own woman, I mean?"

Lynne grinned. "I like it. It's fun having an apartment all to myself. But I still see my family all the time, since I work with them in the shop. Emma talks to me just like she talks to her friends, she never harps at me anymore. But what's really cute is the way Abba bows to me sometimes. You know, the little head-bob? And calls me ma'am, with a little half smile like he thinks it's nice that I'm a lady, all grown up." She lay on her back. "Yeah, I like it."

A flash of lightning outside brightened the tent's interior for an instant, and Lileela waited for the thunder, silently counting the seconds. She didn't quite make it to three before the percussion of the crash shuddered through the ground and rang in her ears. "It's right above us."

"Sounds like it." Lynne lay down head-to-head with Lileela.

"How long are you going to live alone like that? I mean, you and Dale are going to get married, aren't you?"

Lynne's face settled into a satisfied smile. "Yeah, in a while. His mother won't let him yet, though. She says he's got some growing up to do first." She rolled onto her back, knees pointing upward. "What a pain that a man has to listen to his mother all his life. I mean, Dale's almost nineteen years old. He should be able to make his own decisions. The mother being able to boss her son around must have caused all sorts of problems in Old Gannahan marriages, wouldn't you think?"

"I guess Emma's lucky Abba's mother died before they were married, or it never would have happened."

"I can't figure out how it happened anyway. How could a Karkar marry a Gannahan? What's the story there?"

Lileela stared at the ceiling, expecting to see water seeping through it. But the inside remained dry. "I never heard. All I know is, the Yasha told Emma to marry him after Abba came to believe in the Yasha and agreed to follow him. I don't know the details, but you're right, it sounds like a good story." She rolled on her back too. "Odd that I never heard it."

"I'm sure there's a lot you didn't hear in the ten years you were gone. You'll have to ask your abba sometime."

Lileela closed her eyes. "I think I will."

They listened to the storm for a few moments, then Lileela spoke again. "Isn't it funny that on Gannah, it's the fathers who talk to the daughters about marriage and—well, and sex and stuff. And the mothers aren't supposed to discuss it? On Karkar, neither men nor women talk about marriage much, but they talk about sex all the time, both men and women. And they're no more embarrassed about it than we are to talk about the weather."

Lynne turned toward Lileela with a curious look. "Really? So you — you know all about it?"

Lileela blushed. "No, not *all* about it. Not from personal experience."

She had more experience than she cared to admit—not to any Gannahan, at least. Strictly speaking, what she said was true. She'd made explorations in that arena, but her knowledge was not extensive.

After another thunderclap, she went on. "What about you? I mean, I know once Dale turned sixteen he couldn't touch you, but when you were both kids, there were no rules against it. Did you ever, um, you know — "

Lynne gasped. "Lileela! The very idea!"

"Did you hold hands? Did you kiss?"

Lynne chuckled. "Oh, is that all you mean? Well, no. We weren't interested in each other in that way then. That all started about a year ago."

"I was just wondering, because Adam said he and Elise kissed when they were younger. And now he'll never be able to kiss her again until they're married. Isn't that terrible?"

"Oh, I don't know." Lynne rolled onto her side to face Lileela. "I think that self-control thing is very sweet, and the anticipation makes it *really* exciting." She shivered. "Being married wouldn't mean half so much if you could act like you were married beforehand. I don't see why anyone would want it any other way."

Lileela snorted. "Then you're a lot more Gannahan than I am."

Lynne laughed. "Of course you're more Gannahan than I am. Genetically, anyway. But we're all Gannahans, you and me and everybody our age and younger. In another generation or two, our kids and grandkids'll be just like the Old Gannahans. Except for looks, like eye color and build."

"And in some cases, a different number of fingers and toes." Lileela grinned. "But seriously, you don't find all the rules and things too restrictive? Don't you just want to break out and do what you want?"

Lynne sat up. "I already do what I want. I love my family, I love my job, I love Gannah, and I love the Yasha. And I love Dale. When his mother finally lets him marry, I'll love being married. I'm just not sure—" she made a face—"I won't like his mother telling him what to do. I hope she'll lighten up by then."

Lileela matched Lynne's expression. "I don't blame you. I wouldn't like that either."

"What *would* you like?" Lynne rummaged in her pack for her water bottle. "In a husband, I mean. Are you interested in anyone?"

While Lynne drank from her bottle, Lileela pursed her lips in thought. "Don't think I haven't been scoping out the possibilities."

Lynne half-choked on her water.

"But no. For one thing, they all have mothers."

Lynne sputtered her next mouthful all over her bedroll.

Though Lileela found Lynne's antics as amusing as Lynne seemed to find hers, she kept her face Karkar-straight. "Abba says the rigid Old Gannahan family hierarchies worked better than you'd think. Supposedly, it was a pretty good balance of power. A man's mother could tell him how to deal with his wife, but she herself was under the control of her husband. So her husband could tell her to back off if she intervened too much. All that oversight kept anyone from going too far."

Lynne wiped spilled water from the front of her tunic with her hand. "That might work in theory, but I wonder how it was in practice?"

"I don't know. But what do I want in a husband? Well—" She sighed. "I need someone who wouldn't think less of me because of the things I saw and did on Karkar."

Lynne sobered.

"And I think that pretty much rules out everyone on the planet."

37

*P*ropped on his elbow, Pik gazed down at Dassa. "There is one thing I must insist upon."

"And what is that, my merciful husband?"

Pik sat up. "You're hoping for a light sentence, is that it?"

"Sentence?" Her green eyes flashed. "I thought you said you weren't going to punish me."

"Not to the degree I should. But I can't ignore all those things you said earlier. You'd lose respect for me entirely if I didn't do something about that."

"Oh. That's true." Her face stricken with remorse, she rose from the bed and prostrated herself. "I spoke as only a wicked woman speaks, and my behavior brings shame upon you and upon all Gannah. Whatever punishment you invoke will be less than I deserve."

Pik wanted to take her into his arms but didn't dare break protocol again. "Rise."

She stood before him, eyes downcast, awaiting his judgment.

Who invented this system, anyway? "No punishmenrt, just a little damage control. I want you to explain to everyone who was at the meeting today why you flew off the handle. Go ahead and tell them that I sold your genetic material. Don't sugarcoat it, let them know it was an unconscionable act." Though seated, he was at eye level with her. "But make sure you say that when I did obeisance, I acted in ignorance. You were angry without cause. Your main objective is to apologize for your extreme overreaction."

She nodded. "That is wise, my husband. I shall be happy to obey."

"But I want you to apologize to each person individually. Not just to the group."

Dassa bowed again. "Of course, my husband. You are wise and just."

He took her shoulders and kissed the top of her head. "What about merciful? Don't ignore that."

Her face softened as she lifted it to his. "True. You are merciful above all else."

The door buzzer sounded, and Pik groaned. Duty called at the most unseemly times. He reached toward the panel above the bed and activated the intercom. "Yes?"

"It's Jerry. Is the toqeph available?"

From her expression, it looked as if she were trying to ascertain something in her meah but without success. At the same time, she felt for her messenger and came up short there, too.

Since she was apparently too occupied by her search to answer Jerry, Pik responded for her. "Yes. Come in, we'll be right there."

Dassa continued searching for her messenger. "I must have left it in the lounge. I remember laying it on the table."

"If I know Jerry, he picked it up for you." Pik opened the door.

She followed him down the curving hall to the stairs. "He seems quite excited, but I sense it's in a good way."

Jerry stood in the front room. When they entered, it looked like he wanted to keep his face expressionless but lacked the Karkar gift for deadpan. It didn't take a meah to know he wondered what was going on between them.

He bowed, perhaps more deeply than the occasion required. "Madam Toqeph. As soon as you, ah, adjourned the meeting, you received a call." He handed Dassa her messenger.

She took it. "Thank you. I get the impression it's good news."

"Very good news. A short time ago, Miami Hakkatan led a group of Bushatitites out of the rail tube. They'd walked all the way from Yapheh and came out at the first useable exit they found. That is, at the chatsr occupied by the Karkar."

Swept with a rush of delight, Pik laughed. "An answer to our prayers!"

Dassa's face lit up. "How many came? Where are they now?"

"There are twelve. They are all in the clinic here at Gullach. Dr. Jane's checking them out, and Edwin and Marianna are there too. But I've kept everyone else away for now."

"Excellent." Several years' worth of care seemed to fall away from her. "Let us go."

She headed for the door, but Pik stayed rooted. When he cleared his throat, she and Jerry stopped and turned toward him, brows raised.

"I believe there was something you wanted to speak with Jerry about." He gave Dassa what he hoped was a meaningful look. "If I may, I'll go on ahead, and you can join me at the clinic when your conversation is finished."

Dassa's nod was just enough of a bow to satisfy the wifely requirement without relinquishing her royal authority. "Of course. Thank you for reminding me."

Ears smiling, Pik bent and kissed her as he passed.

He felt Jerry's gaze follow him all the way out the door.

LILEELA slapped the desk with her hand. "I'm never going camping again. Ever."

Katarina Maddox lifted her brows. "Why not? I thought you girls had a good time."

"We did. But look at what happened while we were gone. I turn my back for one minute, and starships come in manned by genetic experiments, Emma and Abba get in a big, screaming fight in front of everyone—"

Mrs. Maddox frowned. "I was there. There was no screaming whatsoever, and it could hardly even be called a fight. They had a disagreement, is all."

"Whatever." Lileela waved her hand. "The way I hear it, they were pretty public about it, and that's *never* happened before. And then the Bushatites came back! Lynne and I come home from a little two-night camping trip, and the whole settlement's changed. What might happen if I go again?"

"You'll have a good time, that's what. Your adventure had nothing to do with these other things. It's just a coincidence."

Lileela leaned back in her chair. "I know. It was just weird." She looked at Mrs. Maddox's notes. "This news report is going to be huge. Where do we start?"

"I've already started." Mrs. Maddox pulled up the four-page document that had already been distributed. "But, lacking details, I could only give a general summary of the events. Now we'll have to dig deeper, do a few interviews. I'm thinking of running a segment in each of the next several editions. That is, a story on the Bushatites and what happened with them since they left, a profile of the visitors, and so on. In addition, of course, to the usual news and announcements." She smiled. "Such as an update on the royal wedding plans."

"Of course." Excited as Lileela was about Adam's wedding, these recent events had driven it from her mind. She scanned the list of items to be investigated further. "Why are some of these highlighted?"

"Jerrina and I have those covered. Hers are in yellow, mine are in blue. There's plenty here for you too. Do you see anything in particular that interests you?"

"Oh, I don't know." Jerrina's tasks all seemed to involve the Bushatities—reviewing the history surrounding their leaving ten years ago, interviews of the people who returned. Mrs. Maddox had assigned herself some of those interviews as well, and also planned to explore the details of how and why Abba had collected and sold some of Emma's DNA.

Lileela tapped the list. "I see you plan to speak to Mrs. Dengel, but how about the other visitors?"

Folding her hands across her stomach, Mrs. Maddox leaned back in her chair. "They're available, if you're interested."

Lileela returned her gaze, wondering why Mrs. Maddox was looking at her that way. "Sure, I'd be happy to interview them. What sort of things should I ask?"

On the tablet, Mrs. Maddox brought up a page of questions. "Here's a place to start. If you think of anything you'd like to add, go right ahead."

Lileela flushed, though she wasn't sure why. "I'll just stick with what you have here. Should I interview all of them? Or just the leader?"

"Until we get to know them better, I think it would be best if you interviewed them as a group rather than individually. I'll arrange a meeting and have Ras be there with you. He'll be there as a chaperone, but the interview will be all yours, as will be the write-up."

Lileela's stomach fluttered. "Thanks." It's not as if she'd never met Outsiders before. Still, something about these genetic hybrids both drew her and frightened her. She hadn't even seen them yet, but just thinking about them gave her a thrill.

How Gannahan were they, exactly? More than she? What must it have been like growing up with no parents? She could almost relate to that, but unlike them, she at least knew where she came from.

From what she'd gathered, these were strong, vibrant men, each with the thick, powerful Gannahan build she'd so admired in old movies and photos. Burdened with neither the gangly, exaggerated length of a Karkar nor the fleshiness of the Terrestrials, these were *real* men. The sort she was instinctually attracted to.

Mrs. Maddox watched her with interest, as if she could sense what Lileela was thinking. Lileela flushed deeper. Too bad she couldn't control her blushing the way she controlled her facial expressions. "When do you think we should do the interviews?"

Mrs. Maddox turned to her calendar. "How about tomorrow morning? You can write up the article in the afternoon, I'll edit it tomorrow evening, and we'll include it in the next morning's edition."

"Do you think I'll be able to get it ready that soon?"

Mrs. Maddox patted Lileela's hand. "I'm sure you can. You're an excellent writer. I'll let you know when I've arranged the meeting. In the meantime, how about going through today's messages and sort out the notices and requests for help?"

Hoping that mundane task would ease the excitement that tightened her midsection, Lileela opened the inbox. "Sure, I can do that."

Damaris Song just discovered she was pregnant. The Gaskin twins passed their Second Level tests. Denis Armistead took a fishing trip and returned with a record catch, which he and his family cleaned and flash-froze. The fillets would be available at the Lucas's store until the supply ran out.

Lileela frowned at the next message. "A greyroom report? Why do we have to publish those things?"

Mrs. Maddox came and looked over her shoulder. "Enid Vigneron again?" She shook her head. "That poor lady. Caught between her son and her husband. It just doesn't seem right."

Lileela read the message. "No, it sure doesn't. The son disobeys his father, and the mother is punished? That's crazy. Especially since the son is an adult. And what do you mean, Enid Vigneron *again*? Does this happen often?"

Mrs. Maddox sighed. "Unfortunately, yes. The boy's always been a problem. He was just a toddler when we all came to Gannah. It's good the educational system wasn't in place when he was young, because he probably would've had trouble passing the levels, and then Dieter would punish poor Enid for his failures. I don't think the boy's stupid, but he's different. His biggest problem is, he does what he wants and doesn't care what others think. I don't mean to say he's a bad man, because he's not. But he's never been interested in the family business, and it drives Dieter to distraction."

"Dieter Vigneron?" Lileela recognized the name. "Isn't he the one who's been doing all that work with fruit blends? Abba said his blends are as good as some of the Old Gannahan stuff."

Mrs. Maddox nodded. "Yes, that's the guy. He and his family moved into an old blend shop in Qatsiyr shortly after you left Gannah, and he's devoted his life to studying the art. He started out learning the traditional methods, identifying the organisms that enable the juices to ferment without producing alcohol, and trying to duplicate some of the old recipes. But lately he's been doing some experimentation with ideas of his own, and the results are showing considerable promise. It's a lot of work, though, and the whole family works with him. Except for Orville, who always seems to have his head in the clouds. Dieter will send him out to gather five bushels of berries, and he'll come back with just one, along with stories about what minerals he found in a cave or some unusual clay he dug up."

Lileela leaned back in her chair and crossed her arms. "When he does things like that, Mr. Vigneron takes it out on his wife? And it's okay for him to do that?"

"Yes and no." Mrs. Maddox sighed. "As you know, Gannahan law holds the mother responsible for her children's behavior. But once a boy's an adult, should she still be responsible for what he does? I don't know."

"Well, I know." Lileela's heart thumped with fury. "She shouldn't be. Her husband's making her wear the Garment of Shame because his twenty-five-year-old son doesn't do what he says? He should take it up with his son, not blame his wife."

"I tend to agree." Mrs. Maddox shook her head. "But I think he's within his legal rights."

"Then the law should be changed." Lileela scowled at the form awaiting the information, which would then be uploaded into the official record. "I hate to publicize that sort of thing. It's bad enough that her husband treats her that way, but it's worse that we have to tell everyone about it. If I fill out this form, it will be recorded for all posterity."

"As I'm sure you know," Mrs. Maddox said, "that's part of the disciplinary process. Public shame helps deter repetition of the offense."

"That's for sure." Lileela still burned with embarrassment at the memory of her own recent punishment. At least she was still a juvenile, and children's greyroom experiences weren't entered into the record. "But in Mrs. Vigneron's case, the shame should be her husband's, not hers. The way he's treating her is terrible."

"Isn't it better to let the world know what he's doing instead of sweeping it under the rug?"

Lileela's brows rose. "What do you mean?"

"If a man mistreats his wife, he can be taken to task. But no one will call him on it if they don't know. Making people aware of the problem can be the first step toward resolving it."

"But how can he be prosecuted if what he's doing is legal?"

"I'm not talking about official prosecution." Mrs. Maddox gave a conspiratorial smile. "Have you ever heard of the Old Gannahans' Black Night Right Squads?"

Lileela thought she knew her history. "Umm… no."

"I didn't learn of them myself until a year or two ago. There's not much mention of it in the official histories, but they were fairly common. And—" She cleared her throat. "Unsanctioned, I guess you'd say."

"Really?" Lileela had thought everything Old Gannahan was official, regulated, and painfully proper. "What do you mean?"

Mrs. Maddox drew her chair closer to Lileela's. "If a man became aware of something going on that didn't seem right, he'd get together a group of others to go take care of it in the middle of the night."

Lileela gasped. "Vigilantes?"

Mrs. Maddox shrugged. "Not really. What they did wasn't usually illegal. Sometimes it wasn't even violent."

"You mean sometimes it *was* violent?" Lileela's eyes widened.

"Sometimes. Like in the case of a man who mistreated his wife. The law allowed him to punish her, but if he went too far, did it too frequently, or for no good reason—"

"Like with the Vignerons, you mean?"

"Yes, exactly that." Mrs. Maddox nodded. "If a man went too far, his wife was allowed to defend herself, but women don't usually want to do that. They'd rather their husband would just quit abusing them. So sometimes one of the neighbors, or maybe a relative of the wife, would organize a Black Night Right Squad. They'd go to his house in Black Night, pull him out of bed, drag him outside, and beat him to a pulp. And they let him know they'd do it again if they had to, and keep doing it until he learned his lesson."

Lileela gaped. "That wasn't illegal?"

Mrs. Maddox shrugged. "I don't mean to say it was condoned. But apparently the magistrates often allowed it." She began to stand. "I'm getting a glass of water. Would you like one too?"

Lileela hopped up. "Oh, please, sit down, I'll get it."

"Why, thank you." Mrs. Maddox settled back into her seat.

Lileela headed toward the water cooler. "Tell me more about these night squads. You said they weren't always violent?"

"That's right." The chair squeaked as Mrs. Maddox leaned back in it. "Sometimes they good deeds, like doing work for someone who was injured, for a widow, or a woman whose husband was away for an extended time. Whenever the Old Gannahans saw an injustice and were capable of righting it, they'd take it upon themselves to do whatever was needed. Anonymously, if possible."

"What did they do, wear masks?" Lileela moved carefully as she returned with the water so as not to spill it.

"Oftentimes, yes. I think they did."

"And here I thought the Old Gannahans were a bunch of stodgy old fuddies." She handed Mrs. Maddox a glass. "So do the settlers do that, too? I mean, is a gang going to pull Mr. Vigneron out of bed some night and beat him up, do you think?"

Mrs. Maddox shook her head. "I don't believe so. Maybe someday the old Black Night Right Squads will organize again. But in the meantime, it wouldn't surprise me if someone went and had a talk with Mr. Vigneron."

"Just a talk?" Did she mean her husband? Mr. Maddox's stern look made Lileela wither, but what effect would it have on a man?

Mrs. Maddox smiled. "It's possible." She put her hands flat on her desk. "However, we have a lot of work to do." She leaned over and looked at Lileela's screen. "What other messages do you have there?"

"The Han family's looking for help with their root harvest. The elder Han hasn't recovered from the injuries he received in the storm, and Wayne's wife just had a difficult childbirth. With that in addition to caring for his father and two other little ones, she isn't able to work in the fields." Lileela entered the information. "And David Lucas found the items Klast Otazky was asking about. He just brought in a carton of 60-centimeter woven bootlaces from the ruins of a town called Par. They're available at the store, along with a batch of winter socks in all sizes that he recently found as well."

"Oh, good," Mrs. Maddox said. "Jerry needs some new ones. I'll run over to Lucas's this afternoon and get some." She turned back to her own computer then paused. "That's not cheating, is it?"

"Cheating?"

"Getting the socks before the announcement is made. I wouldn't want to take them from someone who might need them more."

"I wouldn't worry about it." Lileela filled out the form. "Weren't the Nasi entitled to first preference and the best quality of everything?"

"Why, yes, I believe you're right." Mrs. Maddox took a sip of her water. "I guess I don't need to worry about it, then."

"No, I don't think any Black Night Right Squads will be coming to your house to take the socks back."

Mrs. Maddox laughed. "I suppose not." She punched a code into her messenger. "I'll check with Ras to see when he's able to chaperone your interview with the visitors."

"Thank you." Lileela's stomach fluttered. "As you know, I'm available any time." She partly hoped she could do it immediately, and partly wished she didn't have to do it at all. A flush of heat coursed through her, as well as a sense of urgency. "But if he has no preference, the sooner, the better."

38

*F*aris watched the girl on the other side of the table. The green eyes and tight dark curls—especially the eyes—told him she was the toqeph's daughter, though she'd only introduced herself as Lileela.

Wearing the typical Gannahan wardrobe but with her face painted like a Karkar, she made an intriguing picture. Despite her being almost as small as a child, the figure sculpting her modest clothing indicated something quite different.

She handled herself well, looking each of the men in the eye and speaking without a stammer. Even if she did blush when it was Faris's eye she looked in.

He was used to that. But most people couldn't hold his gaze as long as she did. On Earth, no one else's eyes glowed like his, and it tended to unnerve people. As a youth, it used to even startle him, sometimes, when he'd look in the mirror. Her eyes flamed with that same Gannahan fire, though, so that must not be her problem.

Now interviewing Binyamin, her glance moved from Binya to her tablet and back to Binya as she spoke. She must have felt Faris's eyes on her, because she glanced his way, briefly, before returning to her screen, blushing again.

She spoke to Binyamin. "Am I to understand you're beginning to think the others might be right? That the God of the Bible is the highest authority?"

Binyamin didn't look Faris's way, either. "The evidence does seem to point to that conclusion, miss."

"Do you resent them for imprisoning you?"

"No, miss. They did exactly what I'd have done in their situation. I'm just grateful they were able to subdue me without resorting to lethal force. I wouldn't have wanted to die without knowing what I know now."

The girl nodded. "Of course not. No one wants to die."

"No, miss, that's not what I mean." Binyamin's words echoed Faris's thoughts. "We're prepared to die at any time, on every mission. But now I realize we weren't given all the facts. That is, that when we die, we'll have to stand before a Holy God and give account for our sin. I wasn't prepared for that."

"So if you die tomorrow —" She let the question dangle.

Binya bowed his head. "I'm not sure, miss." He looked up at her. "I'm still working through it. But I've been thinking about it a lot the past couple of days."

All the men chuckled, including Faris, and the girl smiled with understanding.

Except for Binyamin, who had refused the tea offered at their first meeting, they'd all developed stomach upsets hours after their arrival on Gannah. Their distress increased immensely upon eating their first meal there, and Binyamin's began soon after.

At the onset, Faris accused the Gannahans of poisoning them. The one named Jax, who had apparently been assigned to look after them, rubbed the back of his neck and answered slowly. "Yes and no."

"What's that supposed to mean?" Faris tried to stand upright, gritting his teeth against the knife-pain in his gut.

"Well, you've been drinking and eating our food and things. They're not poisonous in the usual sense. In fact, I imagine they're more healthful than anything you've ever had before. But the thing is, y'see, when a person who's not used to it ingests anything Gannah-grown, it tends to make them sick for a while."

Clutching his stomach at a spasm, Faris sank into a nearby chair. "You might have warned us."

"I thought so too. But the toqeph said not to. I'm not sure why. But don't worry, it'll be over in a day or so, and then you'll be able to eat or drink anything on the whole planet without getting a stomachache, ever again. 'Cause there's no diseases or anything like that here, you know. And nothing's poisonous."

Jax chuckled, and if not for his having to make a dash for the bathroom, Faris would have decked him.

"Not really, anyway," Jax called as the door closed behind Faris. "It'll just feel like it for a few hours."

Those "few hours" had numbered more than twenty, each filled with an absolute and unremitting agony. Not a one of Faris's men thought they'd survive.

Being the last to start what Jax called the acclimation process, Binyamin still looked a little peaked as he sat beneath young Lileela's exotic green gaze.

"Yes," she said, "I understand you've recently been quite ill. I was sick myself when I came back to Gannah a few months ago. But it wasn't so bad for me, because I lived the first five years of my life here."

Faris spoke out of turn. "You've been off the planet?"

She glanced at him and then down at her tablet. "Yes. I was on Karkar for ten years. For medical treatment."

Ah. That explained the lavish use of cosmetics. That Karkar ship floating out there must have brought her home.

Faris still had unanswered questions, but the girl turned back to Binyamin. "So what are your plans? Now that you're acclimated, do you plan to stay with the others? Or will you take the ship and return it, and yourself, to the League?"

"I'd like to head out, miss, if I may. And as soon as possible."

Did she perk up with interest? Whatever was going through her mind, she paused, consulted her notes, and looked at Binya again.

And stammered for the first time. She must be moving off the planned agenda onto one of her own. "Would you be, um, willing to, maybe, take on, ah, a passenger? I mean, passengers?"

Binyamin's brows lifted, along with those of everyone in the room. Including the girl's chaperone, who until then had sat in heavy-lidded silence.

She flushed again, deeper than ever, and Faris could not only feel her embarrassment, but he almost thought he understood her thoughts. She'd lived as a Karkar through her formative years. She didn't enjoy the rustic life here, she wanted to return. But she was ashamed to beg—and probably didn't want her overbearing mother to know her plans.

Faris decided to toss her a lifeline. "Are you inquiring if the *Glowworm* could be used to transport the stranded Karkar back to their planet?"

She grabbed it, turning grateful green eyes to him. "Yes! That's exactly what I meant."

Her eagerness confirmed his suspicions. "There might be space for them, now that you mention it. How many Karkar are there?"

She seemed to be drinking him in with her eyes. Reading him, somehow. Didn't the Old Gannahans have some sort of telepathic power? He could almost feel the probing.

"Fifteen," she said, never breaking eye contact. "But one, my father's cousin, will be staying here."

Hadn't the child ever been taught it wasn't polite to stare? Almost breathless in the grip of her scrutiny, he found himself wanting to wash her face, slowly and gently, to see what it looked like under all those cosmetics. He imagined her closing her eyes as the facecloth in his hand massaged around them, while his other hand cupped the back of that curly head. "So we'd be talking berth for fourteen?" He tore his gaze away from her two fire-lit emerald magnets and addressed Binyamin. "That could be arranged, don't you think?"

"Or maybe..." she said weakly, "maybe fifteen."

"In case the cousin decides to go?" Faris asked, still looking at Benyamin, who seemed unaware of the subtext behind the questioning.

"Yes," she almost whispered. "In case."

"It would be close quarters," Binyamin said. "Especially since the Karkar are so large."

Esam spoke up. "I think it could be managed, though we'd have to do a little rearranging."

Ishaq frowned. "What's this *we* you're talking about? I thought the rest of us were here for good?" He glanced toward Lileela. "Assuming we're allowed to stay, I mean. The toqeph hasn't told us definitely that we're welcome."

Though no longer reading from a script, Lileela seemed to have found her old confidence. "Oh, she wants you, all right."

"How do you know that?" asked Safiy. "Did she tell you?"

The girl shook her head with the attitude of the teenager she probably was. "She never tells me anything. But I know, because she obviously wanted you to drink the water and eat the food."

Faris and the others blinked at her in confusion.

"There's an old adage. *I've breathed the air, I've drunk the water, I've eaten the food grown in Gannahan soil. I am Gannah.* That is, once you've tasted Gannah, you'll never want to leave. Yes, I'm certain of it. My mother wants you all to stay." She glanced at Binyamin. "But I don't expect she'd keep you against your will. Most everything here is voluntary. More or less, anyway. That is..." She tossed a glance toward Faris and colored again before turning her attention back to Binya. "You should probably stick around for a little while. Like, maybe until after Frostmonth. Just to see if you like it. And then if you still want to go, maybe you could take, um, some people with you."

What was Frostmonth? And why did she want to wait until then before slipping away?

Binyamin nodded. "As I said, miss, I would like to return as soon as possible. But I will respect the wishes of the toqeph."

"Yes," said Safiy, "she's been such a pleasant hostess so far, what with abruptly running out of our first meeting, then poisoning us."

Faris laughed with the others. "I can understand her being upset, though, at her husband selling her DNA. And then we show up as living proof of his treachery? I wouldn't have blamed her for killing him, and us, on the spot."

"I think—" Lileela began then shook her head. "No, I think we can conclude this interview. Unless, of course, any of you have something else you'd like to add?" She looked from one to the other, allowing her gaze to linger on Faris last and longest.

"Your questions have been quite thorough," he said. "I can think of nothing pertinent you didn't cover." He chose not to bring up the impertinent.

Safiy lifted a hand off the table. "I'd like to say something."

She turned to him. "Of course. What would you like to add?"

"I just want to underline what Binyamin said, that the evidence points to the existence and supremacy of the God of the Bible. When you read the book, it sounds pretty fantastic. At first I was sure it was just a collection of myths, stories ancient man dreamed up to explain what they couldn't understand. But the more I read, and the more I thought about it, the more I realized there's really something to it. That's why, when the commander told us his plan and asked us to join him, I didn't quite believe, but somehow, I knew I would at some point."

He nodded at Binyamin. "I was probably where Binya is now. Leaning toward belief, but not quite there yet. It's all so different from what we were taught, and it goes against instinct. But it connects with something deeper than instinct. Something I think we're all born knowing, but don't know we know, until we can't hide from it anymore."

Faris nodded. "That's it exactly."

The others murmured their agreement, except for Binyamin, who remained silent and thoughtful.

"Our coming here," Safiy went on, "to the land of our origin the way we did, and at the time we did, was just too perfect. Obviously, it was planned and executed by a far greater mind and power than anything humanity possesses. I'm convinced we were brought to this place by God for some purpose, and it would take an act of God to get me to leave."

Adil nodded. "Well said, brother."

"I'm with him," said Esam.

"Me too," said Ishaq. "Except for one thing."

"What's that?" Lileela voiced what Faris was thinking.

"It wouldn't take an act of God to get me to leave. All it would take would be a word from Him. I am at His disposal, to send wherever He wishes. Even if it means leaving Gannah." His expression turned regretful. "But I hope He will never ask that of me."

The other men sobered, and most nodded. Faris was surprised to see Lileela's face cloud.

"Well," he said, "I think we're all in agreement. Our lives and allegiances have been forever changed." He turned to Lileela. "Will you put that in your report?"

"I will, Commander." She closed her tablet. "I most certainly will."

39

IN the toqeph's sitting room, Pik saw Dassa grasp their youngest son by the jaw and turn his face toward her. "Look at me, Ittai."

When she used that voice, she meant business. Pik was relieved when Ittai quit whining and obeyed.

Once she had his attention, she let go. "You've been a very good boy all evening, and you made your abba and me proud. Don't misbehave now."

Despite his little Pik-shaped face, his lower lip turned downward in a way no Karkar's could, and his eyes narrowed.

"Ittai." She spoke sharply. "Don't start."

Her manner might seem harsh at times, but Dassa did manage the children better than Pik would have if it were up to him.

Or rather, better than he did *when* it was up to him. He'd never forgive himself for the way he'd let Lileela run wild a decade ago.

"I told you to go with Hushai and Ra'anan and get ready for bed." Dassa turned Ittai around and directed him toward the hall. "Now go. I'll be there shortly to tuck you in."

He seemed to consider his options for a moment, but only a moment before he turned to face her. "Yeth, Emma." He bowed, then started for the stairway.

Emma sighed. "I need a cup of tea."

After she left the room, Pik turned to Lileela. "As I was saying, the evening went very well. The food was great and the concert was lovely. That Ayo family has enough talent to make a splash anywhere in the galaxy. We're fortunate they chose to bring their considerable gifts here instead of trying to cash in on them elsewhere."

Lileela handed Pik a cup of tea. "What a shame about Baako's brother, though, that he died in Yapheh. It's terrible what went on there."

Pik sank into his favorite chair, setting his tea on the table beside his father's brick. He laid his hand on it briefly. "Yes, it is a shame." Ama Ayo's death, along with Bushati's and all those others, were the result of his lack of leadership, just like Lileela's injury. And his father having to die alone on Karkar. "But the shame is mine. If your emma had been here managing things, they wouldn't have left." None of them. Not Lileela, not his father.

Lileela plopped onto a nearby sofa and pulled her legs up under her as Dassa often did. "No, Abba." She bobbed her head in a small bow. "I mean, with all due respect, my abba, I believe you're mistaken. We each make our own choices, don't we? And bear the consequences?"

Pik's ears smiled. "You sound like your em."

As if on cue, Emma returned with her own tea. "Poor little Ittai is overtired. I should have let him stay home. There was no need to keep him up so late."

"I disagree." Pik shook his head. "I see no need to treat him like a baby. He's old enough to learn to behave."

"Yes, I'm sure you're right." She smiled at him. "As usual." Pouring tea through the strainer into a cup, she glanced up at Lileela briefly. "Tamah was no trouble? She went right to sleep for you?"

"I laid her down, she cuddled up with her snuggly, and I haven't heard a peep since." She glanced at the timedial across the room. "That was hours ago. Must have been some concert."

"It was delightful. I wish you could have been there." Dassa set the strainer on the tray. "Did you get your write-up finished?"

"Yes. I want to let it sit a bit and then give it a final once-over before submitting it. Mostly, I've been studying."

Dassa sat beside Lileela. "Katarina tells me you're a natural for the Information Dissemination position. Do you like the work?"

"I do. Mrs. Maddox is pleased, really? I mean, she seems to like me, but I was afraid she was just being nice."

Pik shook his head. "If Katrina Maddox is unhappy with your work, she'll most certainly let you know. She's no shyer about that than her husband."

He chuckled when Lileela wrinkled her nose. "And we all know how reticent *he* is."

Emma squeezed Lileela's hand. "You're doing fabulously. When you first came home, it didn't seem possible that you'd be ready to be on your own by your birthday." She gazed at Lileela with obvious pride. "But look at you now. I'm so happy for you, I could burst."

Lileela's eyes filled. "Thank you, Emma. I don't know that I'm doing *that* well."

"I didn't say you were perfect, now, did I?" Emma took a sip of tea, then set down her cup. "But you're making wonderful progress. And if you keep going the way you are, it will be with great joy that I release you into the world." She stood. "But now, I'd better go down and tuck the kids in before they think I've forgotten them."

Ears smiling, Pik watched his wife until she disappeared from view, then turned his attention to Lileela. "She's right, you know. You've grown quite Gannahan lately." Seeing her expression, his ears lifted in amusement. "Does that offend you?"

Her face twisted in an Earthish grimace, and Pik couldn't decide if it detracted from her beauty or enhanced her charm. She was, truly, a composite of everything lovely in all the races that made up her heritage.

"Seems like it should," she said, "but, no, it doesn't. I guess that means I'm becoming a real Gannahan." She repositioned her legs. "But you're the amazing one, Abba. You grew up on Karkar—and I know what that's like. I can easily see how Aunt Skiskii and the others thought you'd gone mad. Coming here is so far beyond anything a Karkar would even consider. And to marry Emma, who's as much your opposite as it's possible to be. How have you managed to make all that work?"

Warming to the subject, Pik rose and then took a seat beside her on the sofa. "Maybe the answer to your question is the same as the answer to what I'm about to ask: why have *you* changed so much since coming home? Why aren't you still kicking and screaming about wanting to go back to Karkar?"

She looked at the floor. "I didn't kick and scream."

"Only on the inside." He put his arm around her. "But I heard you. And I understood completely. I grew up on Karkar too."

She sighed as she laid her head on his shoulder and wrapped her arms as far as they'd reach around his middle. "Do you know how many times I yearned to do this? How many times, when I was on Karkar, I wished I could climb up into your lap and play with your beard?" She disengaged a hand and, looking up with a mischievous smile, gave his whiskers a gentle tug before embracing him again.

He swallowed hard. "Not as many times as I wished for that too."

"Why did you do it? Why did you marry Emma? Like they all said, you had it made on Karkar. Why would you turn your back on fame and fortune and come to this desolate place?"

He hesitated. It was hard to put into words.

"Did you do it for love? I mean, I know you like Emma and everything, but—I mean, I can't see why anyone would give up *everything* for her."

A throaty Karkar laugh exploded from his chest.

She looked up at him. "I'm serious!"

"I know, Leela. It's just that— What do you know about love, anyway?"

She pulled away. "What do you mean? Just because I'm not sixteen yet, you think I'm stupid? Of course I know what love is."

"Yes, you do. You know what love *is*. But do you know what it *means*?"

Her face puckered. "What's the difference?"

"Love *is* the most powerful, motivating force in the universe." He shifted his position to almost face her. "What love *means* is that it changes us. It makes us more like the object of our love. It empowers us to do things we never could do without it."

"Hmm." Her expression turned thoughtful. "I guess I never thought about it that way."

He sent up a silent prayer for help finding the words. "What do the Karkar love?"

She giggled. "The Karkar."

"Exactly. So they'll do anything and everything they can for themselves and for their planet. And no matter how devious or how cruel their acts, they justify it as being necessary."

She tipped her head in a Karkarish gesture. "That makes sense."

"And the first Gannahans were the same way. They did what they did, first to survive, and then when they'd been overtaken by bloodlust, to satisfy their need to kill. They didn't care if they destroyed planets or wiped out races, they did it for love of themselves."

"That's terrible." She shuddered. "Though I suppose it's true." She looked up at him. "But then Hoseh the Wise met the Yasha?"

Pik nodded. "He learned what the Creator God did for the Earthers."

"You mean the gospel story, right? How God went to Earth in the form of a Terrestrial baby, and grew up as an Earthish child, and lived and died like an ordinary man?"

"The Yasha—or as the Earthers call him, Jesus—was far from ordinary. He was perfect. I don't mean he wore nice clothes and always had his beard trimmed neatly. I mean he never sinned. Never. Not even when he was Ittai's age. When his mother told him to get ready for bed, he said, 'Yes, Emma,' and did it, no matter how tired and cranky he felt."

Lileela giggled. "And he never mouthed off to his education minister, and he never told a lie, and he never made out with girls when he was a teenager."

Dassa had told Pik she suspected Lileela felt guilt on that score. He tried not to show his concern. "Why? Did you make out with girls?"

She flushed. Deeply. "No, Abba. Did you?"

"Yes, I confess that I did. It was the thing to do, growing up on Karkar." Looking at Lileela, the reality of what he was saying sickened him. "And it might have been the thing to do in Nazareth where Jesus grew up, too. But he didn't do it. Do you know why?"

Her eyes widened. "I'm not sure."

"I believe that, even in His humanness, He was motivated by the love of God. Because He *was* God, that love was strong enough to overcome the temptation."

"I don't see what love has to do with sin."

Abba nodded. It was a difficult concept, to be sure. "Think of a child, whose emma tells him to put away his toys, but he doesn't want to do. It's not because he doesn't love his emma, is it?"

"Of course not. All little children love their ems."

"That's right. But love of his own pleasure can sometimes be greater. It's human nature for us to want to make ourselves happy, not the people we love. But Jesus was different. Right from the beginning, he always chose to please his mother rather than himself."

Her expression thoughtful, Lileela unfolded her legs, stretched them over the arm of the sofa, and lay back against Pik's arm. "So if Jesus always obeyed when he was a kid because he loved his mother, how about when he was an adult? Did he still have to obey his mother, like sons do on Gannah?"

"I doubt it. But that's not what I'm talking about. I meant he was sinless because he loved his Father."

She hesitated as if mulling his words then said, "Oh, I get it. Whether he was a kid or an adult, he didn't want to sin because it would displease God."

"Absolutely. But he also had to be sinless because it was necessary to His mission."

"Mission? Like Commander Faris and his men?"

She had a good grasp of things. "Much like that, yes. God the Father sent his son on a mission, which he could only accomplish if he remained sinless. That's why the devil took such pains to tempt him, you know. Because if Jesus had messed up even one time, his mission would have failed."

"Yeah, well, I'd have never made it half that far. He was what, like, thirty then? I couldn't go thirty minutes without sinning, let alone thirty years."

"Same here." Pik shifted her head to his side, then stretched his arm along the back of the sofa, wiggling his fingers to wake them up. "Thankfully, he wasn't like you and me."

"But why was it so important that he not sin, anyway? I mean, those are pretty tough orders for his Father to give him, even though he was God in the flesh. Couldn't God cut him a little slack?"

"No. Because the only way to pay for the world's sin is with a perfect sacrifice. If Jesus was anything other than pure and holy, it couldn't fully atone for man's sin. It would be like the sacrifices the Jews used to make. Their offerings of imperfect animals couldn't do the job completely, so they had to make those offerings over and over. Jesus could only offer himself once, so He had to get it right the first time. One perfect sacrifice for everyone, everywhere. Because He loves them."

Lileela sat up and faced Pik.

He watched while her quick Gannahan mind whirred. "You're saying Jesus went through all that out of love? Love for *people*, not just love for his Father?"

"That's right. And in Hebrews 12, we're told that He did it all with joy."

Lileela's eyes filled with tears. "That's unbelievable. I mean, I know that's what the Bible says. But to love someone enough to go through that for them? I can't imagine."

"The amazing thing is, he did it knowing full well most of them wouldn't care. The majority of the people he died to save have refused the gift he paid so much to give."

Lileela bit her lip. "That would be like—in a small way, it would be like if I didn't care that Everett and Mr. Lawbby died so my debt could be paid, and went back to Karkar when I turned sixteen."

"Well, kind of." Pik considered this new thought. "Maybe more than kind of. You do have the right to leave Gannah any time after your birthday, just as a person has the right to refuse the gift of salvation. And both would be not only selfish, but ultimately self-destructive."

Lileela sighed. "It's weird. The thing we think will make us the happiest is, in the long run, the worst thing we could possibly do. And what we think is most restrictive is the very thing that frees us."

Pik blinked in surprise. "That, my dear, is profound. I wish I'd known it at your age."

She settled back against him. "I can't take credit. Emma's a good teacher."

Pik's ears lifted. "She is indeed. She's good at a number of things, I think."

Just then Dassa's steps padded on the stairs, and a moment later her voice came from behind them. "My, this is cozy."

Pik yawned. "Your tea's probably cold."

"I'm sure it is," Dassa said, but didn't bother reheating it.

Lileela sat up and folded her legs beneath her. "Lynne asked me something the other day, and I don't know the answer."

Dassa sat in Pik's chair across from the sofa, cross-legged like Lileela. "And what was that?"

"We were talking about how weird it is that a Gannahan and a Karkar would get married, and she asked me how it happened. I asked Abba just now, and he rambled all over the place without ever quite answering. I know the em's not supposed to talk about marriage and things with the daughter, but can you ask Abba to tell me? Maybe he'll do it for you, since he won't for me."

Pik and Dassa exchanged glances, then Dassa laughed. "This could be interesting." She bobbed her head in a respectful bow. "My dear husband, have you ever told our daughter the story of our romance?"

Pik chuckled. "No, I have not. I can't tell a tale I don't know myself."

Lileela looked back and forth between them. "What's that supposed to mean?"

"It means there was little romancing involved," Dassa said. "But you're right, this is your ab's venue, not mine." She rose. "It's late, and I've got some reading to do. So you two get this subject out of your system, and I'll take my tea to bed." She bent and kissed Lileela's forehead. "I look forward to reading your article in the morning. I doubt Katarina will have to edit it much."

She turned to Pik with a smile. "You'll be coming soon?"

He yawned again. "Soon enough." Though she was standing and he sitting, they were eye to eye—hers glowing greenly with contentment.

His ears lifted. "So should I make up something to satisfy her romantic inclinations, or tell her the truth?"

"The truth always wins in the end." Dassa gave Pik's hand a squeeze. "Good night, you two." Smiling, she glided out.

Arms crossed, Lileela glared at Pik from under a furrowed brow. "You weren't serious about making it up, were you?"

"Of course not. Gannahans don't do fiction."

She relaxed. "Okay, so what's the story? I mean, I know how you two met and everything. And now I even know how you took tissue samples and sold her genetic material to buy yourself a good position with the League Center for Disease Control. Whatever that is."

"It's—"

"I don't really care. Could you just get to the good part?"

"You're the good part. You, and Adam, and Ra'anan, and—"

"Okay, so you went with Emma to Gannah, found the Kankakar Jewels, and returned them to Karkar. I saw them on display in the Viewinghall at Agkztikkokikanon, with a video of you presenting them to the Kaaqakaanikakak Council." She frowned again. "Along with another video of the ceremony where the Council burned Emma's letter of apology to them, and burned her and Hoseh the Wise in effigy. And you stood there and watched. Like you approved of that sort of thing."

Pik had tried to put that memory behind him. "Yes, that was rude, to say the least. But—"

"But that's just what I mean. How could you go from that, to this?" She waved an arm, referencing Pik's Gannahan home, so far from Karkar in every respect.

"It's as I said before. Love for Emma, despite our differences, in combination with love for the Yasha, whom I finally came to know after a conversation with my father."

Lileela's eyes widened. "Abba Lars?" Her gaze went to the brick on the table beside Pik's chair. "You shouldn't keep him in the sitting room. He belongs in a wall somewhere." She stood and ambled to the brick.

"It's not him, of course," said Pik. "It's the compressed remains of his mortal shell. But you're right, the brick should be in a place of honor. And it will be. You know that building Adam's renovating in the second chatsr in Qatsiyr?"

"The one he's turning into a hospital?"

"A hospital and research lab. He plans to study the development and growth of children from conception to maturity. The Earthers brought physical problems with them the Old Gannahans didn't know, and he and I both believe we can eradicate, or at least alleviate, most of them if we can figure out how Gannahan medicine worked. Anyway, since Abba Lars loved children, Adam wants to incorporate the brick in the construction."

A grin spread across Lileela's face. "Really? That sounds perfect!" The smile turned instantly into a pout. "But I think you're trying to distract me again. Tell me how you wooed Emma. How you swept her off her feet and convinced her to marry you. And why you'd want to do such crazy a thing in the first place." She ran her finger around the edge of Abba Lars's brick.

"Very well, Miss Lileela." Pik sighed. "I see you can be as persistent as your em. Because, as you evidently aren't aware, the whole thing was her idea."

Her finger stopped moving along the brick. "No!"

"Yes. She pursued me relentlessly. Wouldn't take no for an answer. Made quite the silly fool of herself. She—"

The withering look Lileela gave him made Pik stop to laugh.

"Gannahans don't do fiction, remember?" she said.

Ears high with amusement, he went on. "Okay, so that's not quite the way it happened. But the truth is, it was her idea, not mine. Or rather, it was the Yasha's idea, and of course she was the first to pick up on it. I didn't get in the game until after Abba Lars challenged me to think seriously about the existence of God and the gospel portrayed in the stars. I read Hoseh's writings, I read the Bible, I recalled everything your em had told me, and I finally came to the conclusion that I had to believe it or deny the plain facts."

"You're the second person to tell me that today."

"Really?" Pik hadn't been expecting that. "Who was the first?"

"One of the starsoldiers I interviewed today, the one who'd been a prisoner. He said he's about ready to believe in God because the evidence points to His being real."

Pik nodded. "That's good. I imagine all their stories are interesting."

"Not as interesting as the one you're not telling me. So Emma knew the Yasha wanted her to marry you, but you didn't, at first. Did she tell you that was his plan?"

"No, she never mentioned it." He chuckled. "It wasn't until I finally understood about the Yasha that I put the pieces together myself. The more I studied it, the more I liked it. I just didn't realize she was thinking the same things. I thought it was all my idea."

His ears lifted high at the memory. "I could hardly wait to tell her. I was excited for her to know I believed in the Yasha, first of all. And I was dying to see the look on her face when I asked her to marry me. I didn't know what she'd do—slap me, for all I knew."

Lileela grinned. "So what *did* she do?"

Pik meshed his fingers and stretched his arms toward the ceiling, then brought them down behind his head. "Well, first I got to Earth as quickly as possible. Which wasn't very quickly. It was the longest sixteen months of my life."

"It took over a year?"

"Space travel wasn't quite as efficient then as now, and it seemed like everything that could go wrong, did. As if the Yasha was determined to keep me from reaching Dassa. And maybe He was. I think part of the reason for the delay was that He had to mature my faith a little, because all along the way, He kept bringing me into contact with other believers. Who knew there were so many out there? They helped me to learn more, so by the time I finally found Dassa in North America, I was no longer such a baby in the faith."

Pik leaned back and stretched out his legs. "I showed up on her doorstep, my heart pounding out of my chest with anticipation. When she opened the door, she looked happy to see me, which was encouraging."

"What did you say?" Lileela was wide-eyed.

His ears smiled. "Well, I always used to tell her, whenever she talked about her faith, that I didn't understand her. Because I didn't. So the first thing I said, even before *Hello*, was, 'I understand you.' She knew what I meant immediately. I thought she was going to throw her arms around me—and I wouldn't have minded if she did. But, even though she lived on Earth at the time, she was still a good Gannahan, so instead of hugging me, she just grinned like her face would split, and invited me in.

"I sat down in that tiny sitting room of hers and said, 'Do you know what I mean? That I understand you?' And she said, 'Yes,' and started to cry."

Lileela gasped. "No!"

"Yes. I'm not kidding this time. She cried. And I was so unnerved, everything I'd planned to say and do flew out of my mind, and I blurted out, 'We have to get married.'"

Lileela clapped her hands. "You didn't!"

"I did. And she said, 'I know.' *Then* she threw her arms around me."

40

*E*LISE was so adorable when she pouted. Standing in the unfinished room, with her kissable lips turned down at the corners and her golden brows pinched together above the bridge of her freckled nose, it made Adam want to take her into his arms.

Except that he couldn't. And besides, she was being unreasonable.

He glared at her. "How am I supposed to help with the decorations when I'm working on our apartment? The wedding's less than a week away."

She put her hands on her hips and her scowl deepened. "My point exactly. Less than a week to go, but a tonne of work to be done. Do you have any idea how —"

Adam raised his hand to stop her. "I'm sorry, Elise. It can't be helped. If it's too much, you might have to scale back your plans. I can't —"

"It's your wedding too, you know!" Her face flushed and her voice rose. "And *you're* the one who insisted on a traditional Gannahan wedding. We could have kept it simple, but no. You want the whole promenade thing, and the —"

Adam put down his tape measure and waved both hands in front of her face. "Hold it right there. *Who* wanted the traditional Gannahan wedding?"

She colored deeper. "*You* did!"

"I never asked for that. You're the one who brought it up. We all said, 'Are you sure?' and you said, 'Yes. Traditional all the way.' So now all of a sudden —"

"I said that because I knew it was what you wanted." Her eyes filled. "You're half Gannahan. You're the toqeph's heir, for crying out loud." The tears spilled over. "How could you not want a traditional Gannahan wedding?"

"For crying out loud is right." Exasperated, Adam searched for an almost-clean rag for her to wipe her face. "Even my parents didn't have a traditional wedding." He found a rag and handed it to her. "Why do you think I need one?"

She sniffled and gazed up at him with wide, wet eyes. "They didn't?"

"Of course not. They got married on Earth." He gestured toward a stack of lumber behind her. "Let's sit down."

Wiping her nose, she sat. "I'm sorry, I just thought you'd want it, that's all."

Adam shook his head as he parked himself beside her. This business of keeping his hands off her was getting harder every minute. "You're right, I do. But only if you do. If it's going to be a problem, we can forget it. Like Emma said, most of us here are Earthers, not native Gannahans, and she expects the New Gannahans to form their own customs. Marriage traditions are just that, traditions. They're not the law."

She bit her lip, and Adam could sense the depth of her thought processes.

"Okay. Well—" She shifted her position on the boards. "I want to go traditional. We're Gannahans now, both of us. We were born here, we're going to live and die here and raise our children to be real Gannahans. I want to do it right."

Adam brushed the sawdust from his lower pant leg where it had accumulated above his boot top. "It's not a question of right or wrong. All that counts is what you want to do."

"I want—" She took a deep, shuddering breath. "I want to be a good Gannahan wife to you." Her voice broke.

"You w—" Adam tried to reassure her, but she broke in.

"And I want to start being that as soon as possible." Still wiping her eyes, she rose and spoke with new determination. "So you keep fixing up our apartment, and I'll continue with the wedding arrangements. The beginning and the end of the route will be decked out for sure. If there's a big gap in the middle, then I don't suppose it matters."

Smiling, Adam rose with her. "It doesn't matter a bit. You will be an exemplary wife, with or without decorations." He bent to put his face in front of hers, not touching, and made a kissing sound. "That's for you."

She closed her eyes and smiled dreamily. "Umm, you're a great kisser." She puckered and made a loud, protracted sucking noise. "And that's for you."

"Delicious."

Smiling, Elise turned to gather up the empty lunch containers and put them in the basket. "Well, I'm going back to work now."

"Me too." He handed her an empty water bottle. "Do you know the time?"

She looked at her messenger. "Almost the third hour of Orange, why?"

"Emma was going to meet with the Bushatites this morning, then the men from the Photuris, and then with the Karkar. I was wondering where she was in the schedule."

Elise nodded. "Sure are a lot of things happening at once."

"Yeah. Like the Old Gannahans used to say, 'never a sprinkle, always a torrent.'"

"I thought that referred to the weather."

Adam shrugged. "That too. But she wants to have everything ironed out before the wedding." He smiled down at Elise, her face still blotchy from crying. "I guess we've all got a lot to do before then."

He waved his arm at the hollow room. "This time next week, we'll be snuggling right here in our sitting room."

PIK set Dassa's water glass on the tray beside the pitcher. "Ready?"

She nodded. "I suppose so."

The corners of those brilliant eyes were again creased with grief lines as she turned and ascended the two steps to the ancient Throne of Atarah.

When the settlers first moved into Gullach, Dassa had them convert the original throne room into their meetinghall. In the process, they'd taken apart the throne and dais, carried the pieces up the winding stairs to Dassa's office suite above the apartment, and reassembled it in the largest of the suite's rooms. But she rarely used it. Ordinarily, meetings were conducted in the dining room.

Now that New Gannah was growing, the Council—with Pik's full support—suggested she use the throne room while proclaiming judgment, receiving formal petitions, or holding an official hearing.

Today, her schedule was crammed with those tasks.

The morning's interview with the Bushatites had been taxing. Thirty-seven settlers, two of them pregnant, had illegally left Gullach ten years before with stolen equipment and food supplies. Twelve returned— starving, scarred, and hollow-eyed. Waking-in-the-night-screaming terrified. Jumping-at-sudden-noises jittery. Burdened with guilt and willing to pay the consequences, whatever they may be.

Dassa had ordered all who were twenty-six years old and above— that is, those who had been of legal age at the time they'd left—to appear before her this morning to hear their fate. The guilty survivors numbered a mere three. Jax's sister Miami, Danzig Oliphant, and Faye Ayo.

They allowed Jerry to lead them from the clinic area where they were temporarily housed, with Pik following. They filed up the stairs in silence, shuffled behind Jerry down the hall, entered the throne room, and prostrated themselves on the hard, gleaming floor before Dassa.

Watching them from his post by the door, Pik's gut tightened. He should be down there with them, begging for forgiveness.

Not that he'd make that mistake again. But for all these years, he hadn't been able to shake the feeling that he shared this guilt. He should have seen what was happening. He should have put a stop to Bushati's plans before they could be carried out.

It wasn't Pik who bowed before the toqeph, though. It was a rag-tag trio who had already paid dearly for their error. When he'd examined them upon their arrival, they looked and acted like the abused prisoners he'd seen on Bappas. People whose most grievous wounds were not physical.

Her expression pained, Dassa let the condemned hold their positions for an uncomfortably long time. "Rise," she finally said.

They complied, with difficulty. Standing guard on the other side of the doorway, Jerry twitched, apparently fighting the desire to assist. Pik had the same urge.

Miami and Danzig had to help Faye to her feet, and the three stood before the toqeph, eyes downcast.

Dassa questioned each one. Again. They'd already told their stories, but she made them repeat it: Their willingness to be misled by Arik Bushati against their better judgment. Their scheming, deception, and surreptitious departure under cover of night. Their theft of every working vehicle in Gullach so they couldn't be followed, and their plundering of more than their share of food supplies and seed for planting. Their trek to Yapheh in late winter, including the animal attack that killed five of their number.

Dassa made them recount again the difficulties that befell them as they tried to establish a new colony: warring with beasts, accidents, ruined harvests, and harsh weather. They recounted the cruelties of Bushati's reign of terror as he lorded over the dwindling group: the forced labor of children too young for the work, the deprivations, the floggings of those deemed rebellious.

And finally, Danzig told how he and a group of six men and women had murdered Bushati and two of his most ardent followers, then fled through the underground tunnels, destroying the entrance behind them to avoid pursuit. Twenty of them set out for Gullach, including children.

"And then," Danzig said, "the earth moved. Rumbling and grinding, again and again, off and on for many days. Walls and ceilings collapsed, floors fell beneath us, deep fissures opened around us. Some fell there, deep into the bowels of Gannah. We had no light, no water, no food. Foul things lived there." He wept. "I don't know how we found our way. We should have died underground. Died with the others."

He fell to his face. "I am guilty, my toqeph. I make no excuse, and deserve no mercy. Only say the word, and I will stand to be executed."

The two women looked at the floor, shuddering with sobs.

Pik involuntarily glanced at the circle inlayed on the floor beneath a skylight. The old toqephs had passed judgment in this room.

He turned his gaze back to Dassa. Could he stand here and watch her break these people's necks? They were traitors and thieves, yes, and murderers. They deserved to die.

And she'd killed before.

But Dassa shook her head. "Rise, Mr. Oliphant. No one will die here today."

Miami gasped, and Faye's sobs rose to a wail. "Madam Toqeph! Why do you spare us?"

"Why?" Dassa said. "Your crimes are great, but not capital offenses."

Miami bowed. "Madam Toqeph, we—" She bowed deeper. "We committed murder."

Dassa's face softened. "There is no such charge against you. What you describe was self-defense. A *good* Gannahan would have done it sooner."

Danzig's jaw dropped. "I guess I never did quite get what being a Gannahan was all about."

"I think not," Dassa said, "or you never would have fallen for Bushati's lies."

Suddenly stern, she surveyed their faces. "You have confessed your guilt of treachery, deceit, rebellion and theft."

When she paused, the condemned each nodded and looked at the floor. "We are guilty, Madam Toqeph."

"Under Gannahan law," Dassa went on, "the penalty is indentured servitude for life. And that just punishment, I do invoke."

Pik almost choked.

While everyone, including Pik and Jerry, stared in alarm, she raised her arm toward the trio, signifying her official judgment. "Danzig Oliphant, Miami Hakkatan, Faye Ayo. By your actions, you have forfeited your freedom to choose your home or your employment. You each, along with your families, shall be housed, clothed, and fed by the house of Atarah, and your medical needs attended to. You shall perform whatever services the house of Atarah shall require. You shall not change your residence without permission. Your children shall be free upon reaching the age of adulthood. But should you remarry, your spouse shall enter into your servitude. I, Atarah Hadassah Hagah Natsach Pik, Toqeph of Gannah, have spoken. This decree is immutable and shall not be altered."

Shock made way for understanding. Miami and Danzig prostrated themselves once more, weeping in gratitude. Faye merely fainted.

41

 ARIS and his men, including Binyamin, followed the retired starship captain into the odd little underground monorail pod. The youngest councilman, Jax, took up the rear, sliding the door closed behind him.

Though comfortable, the vehicle had an odor of antiquity, as if it had carried Old Gannahans beneath the planet surface for several lifetimes.

Faris's skin prickled with a thrill. He, Safiy, Adil, Esam and Ishaq had petitioned the toqeph for asylum. Benyamin had requested permission to leave. Within the hour, they'd hear their fates.

The pod hummed, shuddered a little, then whirred into smooth motion, accelerating along the track until the tube's walls blurred past the windows.

At this rate, they'd know where they stood in far less than an hour.

Gannah was riddled with perplexing contradictions. Its society was ancient and new, primitive and sophisticated, wild and disciplined, all at once. He wanted to burrow into its culture, explore its every nuance, swim in the spirit that pervaded the place.

He shifted his gaze to Binyamin's face, which reflected nothing of what went on behind it. Binya had kept to himself since arriving here — not that anyone could blame him. But Faris longed to know what he'd decided about Jesus.

No one spoke, not even Jax. Everyone seemed occupied by his own thoughts.

In less than a quarter hour, the pod slowed, entered a wide, lit chamber, and came to a gentle stop.

"Welcome to Gullach," said Broward as Jax rose and opened the door.

Gullach, Faris knew, was the New Gannahan name for the Old Gannahan palace of Gibah. According to some of the reading material he and the others had been given, *gullach* meant *redeemed,* and *gibah* meant *hill.* A simple name for a palace, to be sure, but fitting, since the structure looked almost identical to the natural hills in the vicinity. But Faris liked the new name better. Somewhere in that rambling pile of rock above him, he'd receive the toqeph's answer to his petition—and, he was certain, his redemption. A fresh start in a new life.

He exited the car with the others and waited while Jax consulted a notation on his messenger. Jax then nodded to Broward. "We can go ahead."

Broward nodded in return. "All right, gentlemen. The toqeph is ready to receive you."

Faris and the others followed Broward along the platform. It was very possible the toqeph might deny their petition and send them all away. The planet had just undergone a tremendous catastrophe. Much damage had occurred to the infrastructure, and food supplies were limited. How could the toqeph allow so many Outsiders to remain and consume their precious resources? Especially Outsiders whose very presence reminded her of past humiliations?

And especially since more settlers had arrived from another part of the planet.

That part puzzled Faris. No one had told them the details of that event, only that people had left a decade or so ago, and some of those had unexpectedly returned.

Limited resources or not, though, the toqeph's lovely green-eyed daughter had expressed certainty that her mother wanted Faris and his men to stay. Remembering her confidence—and her small shapeliness, and her blushing, furtive glances—he steeled his jaw against a smile.

With Broward at point and Jax at the rear, the procession made their way through what apparently was once an extensive rail terminal, moving ever upward until they passed through a wide entrance into Gullach's central hall.

It was no rustic hill on the inside.

Columns of polished stone rose in evenly spaced pairs to support a glassed-in balcony encircling the hall. Each graceful couplet of pillars framed an arched portal to another chamber or passage. In the center, inviting arrangements of furniture were scattered on one vast, round carpet, like cozy rooms without walls. On one edge of the circle, a boy was evidently getting a lesson on an ancient earth musical instrument called, if Faris remembered aright, a piano. Though the tune was childlike and the music unamplified, the sound was pleasant, even if the sight was incongruous in this alien place.

On the far side of the circular room, a broad stairway made of milky blue stone fell from a landing above like a cataract. Its steps flowed in even ripples and spread out to meet the floor in a wide apron. It was toward those steps that Broward and Jax now guided them.

Though the place wasn't exactly bustling, there were several people about, each of whom looked up as the group passed, their expressions curious.

At the landing, the men turned left and continued upward to the glass-sided balcony. There they rounded the gentle curve of the room's circumference, then turned down a narrower hall to the right—the first thing resembling a straight line Faris had seen since they'd piled into the tube. The hallway terminated at a doorway, which Broward opened with a touch of a button.

"The Chamber of Atarah." Broward gestured for them to pass through the doorway. "This is the toqeph's suite."

Faris stepped past Broward and entered the apartment, his men following.

The small foyer opened into a large sitting room. It was an uneven shape with fabric-covered walls. Before Faris could take in more than the usual quantity of details he was trained to absorb in an instant, Broward headed toward an alcove in the near wall. "This way, please, gentlemen. The throne room is upstairs."

They went around the corner, through a door and up a tall, tight spiral staircase toward a skylight high above. The sun's rays showered the men with brilliant stripes as they wound their way upward, and Faris squinted at the brightness that flashed between the steps as he rose.

The temperature rose as well, but once they reached the top and exited the narrow stairwell, the air grew more comfortable. Broward continued purposefully down a curving hall and paused before a tall double door. "Remember the protocol, gentlemen."

Faris and the others nodded. Jax had schooled them earlier, and they were exemplary students.

Broward pressed a button in the wall. It wasn't instantaneous, but in a moment the doors slid open, revealing a bright, airy space empty of furniture except for the ornate chair on a low platform across the room, upon which the toqeph sat waiting. Her Karkar husband and the Nasi, Maddox, stood just inside the doorway, facing them.

"The toqeph will see you," Pik said, and he and Maddox stood aside to allow Faris and his men to enter. When the door closed behind them, Faris realized Broward and Jax hadn't joined them.

No matter. He and the men knew what to do. Approaching the dais in a razor-straight row, they marched forward four paces, then stopped and went to their knees, pressing forearms and foreheads to the floor as instructed. Their movements were so precisely synchronized one would think they'd practiced it. Even Faris was surprised.

Seeing only the front of his shirt, which had fallen forward before his eyes, Faris waited several moments before the toqeph spoke.

"Outsiders, rise."

They did, with less perfect timing, and stood at attention.

What must be going through her mind as she surveyed them, with their obvious Gannahan traits? Did she loathe her Karkar husband for what he'd done? Did she hate them as well for reminding her?

Though her eyes shone greenly, her expression revealed nothing. "Commander Faris, Lieutenant Safiy, and Sergeants Adil, Esam and Ishaq, please step forward."

Once more in sync, they complied, then bobbed their heads in a bow. "Madam Toqeph."

"You have confessed to the following crimes: disobedience to your superiors; treasonous acts against the government of the League. The kidnapping and unlawful detention of one of your comrades. And grand theft of League property."

Faris's heart sunk to his knees, and probably the others' did too. But they merely bowed again. "Yes, Madam Toqeph. We confess to these crimes."

"In an attempt to escape justice, you have petitioned for asylum on Gannah, where you believe the authorities will not follow. Is that also true?"

This wasn't going the way he'd expected, but he couldn't deny the truth of her words. Faris and the others cast sideways glances at one another, then answered in ragged unity, "Yes, Madam Toqeph. That is true."

Her mouth had a grim set to it. "I have reviewed the facts and made my decision." She raised her hand toward them. "The Outsiders named Faris, Safiy, Adil, Esam and Ishaq. Because of the nature of your confessed crimes, I must deny your petition for asylum."

Faris gritted his teeth against the tears that burned his eyes.

She lowered her arm. "However, I will allow you to remain on Gannah until such time as your superiors demand your return. I will neither hide nor protect you, but will surrender you to any League entity that demonstrates the proper authority and presents suitable documentation for apprehension or extradition."

Faris held his breath. What exactly did that mean, then?

"Until such time as that occurs, you shall be permitted to live as full citizens of New Gannah."

He let out the breath. It meant he was free.

"I grant this," she went on, "under certain conditions. To-wit, you will return the League vessel *Glowworm* to its rightful owners. You will swear to abide by all our laws and give due reverence to the authority of Atarah as supreme ruler of this planet."

Faris tensed, wrestling a grin that threatened to slip out.

"You will submit yourself to the authority of the Nasi, Jerry Maddox, for training in the law, customs, and requirements of Gannahan citizenship. And you will henceforth live for the good of Gannah and not for your personal advancement." She eyed each man, one by one. "Do you agree to these terms?"

Each head bobbed. "I do, Madam Toqeph."

She almost smiled. "The decree will be transcribed and printed. You will each affix your signature, and it will be then entered into the record." She scanned each face again. "Be aware, however, that your past troubles me. Gannah is not lenient with those who renege on promises. I will hold you each to both the word and the intent of your agreement."

"We understand, Madam Toqeph." Faris bowed, and the others followed suit. They'd been created out of the stuff of this world for this very life of obedience. It should prove no hardship.

She nodded. "Very well." Then she raised her arm once more. "I, Atarah Hadassah Hagah Natsach Pik, Toqeph of Gannah, have spoken. This decree is immutable and shall not be altered."

The men each prostrated themselves. "Your judgments are wise, Madam Toqeph. It is my privilege to obey."

"And I am happy to welcome you to Gannah. Rise, gentlemen, and please step back. I have one more petition to rule upon."

Ah, yes. Binyamin's. Faris and his men rose, took three steps back and bowed, then assumed a parade rest stance.

Based on the quiver of her lips and the flicker in her eye, the toqeph seemed to find that amusing for some reason, but she straightened her face as she turned to Binyamin. "Sergeant Binyamin, please step forward."

He did. "Madam Toqeph."

"You arrived as a prisoner of these criminals but have been freed by my command. Though your companions petitioned for asylum, you request permission to leave the jurisdiction of Gannah and Gannahan space."

"Yes, Madam Toqeph."

"You feel duty-bound to your oath to the League, and you intend to throw yourself at their mercy, despite the fact that you now —" She studied him as if ascertaining the truth of her own words. "That you now are a follower of Jesus Christ, which is forbidden by your government."

He swallowed then bowed. "Yes, Madam Toqeph."

Faris wished he had a Gannahan meah so he could reach out to the brave, honest Binya. He'd never realized until this moment how much he cared for the man. Loved him like a brother—which he now truly was. Though what he proposed might be the right thing to do, Faris hated the thought of that righteous man going back into the lion's den.

Did the toqeph sigh? "I am inclined to grant your petition."

Binyamin's shoulders stiffened.

"But in order to do so, I must, as I did with your comrades, assign conditions."

"Yes, Madam."

"Despite the way your commander treated you, I would like you to help him fulfill the conditions of his agreement by returning the *Glowworm* to the League. But of course, that was part of your petition, so this is not an additional condition."

"Yes, Madam Toqeph."

"I also require that you allow our other Outworld guests, the Karkar, to go with you. It's my understanding that the pilot of their disabled vessel is able and willing to fly the ship if you are unfamiliar with it."

"Yes, Madam Toqeph. That would be agreeable."

"They will take it to Karkar, and there you will surrender yourself and the ship to League authorities."

"Yes, Madam Toqeph." He bowed without hesitation.

"And finally, I understand the vessel is too small to carry much cargo, but it has the capability to tow quite a load. That would slow your progress, but it would be possible?" She looked at Esam as if asking both him and Binyamin the question.

"Yes, that's correct, Madam," Esam said.

Binyamin nodded. "Apparently so, Madam Toqeph. I have no personal knowledge of that."

"Good. I would, therefore, ask that you tow the shuttle containing the precious ores that the Karkar and the League have accepted as payment for what we owe them."

When Binyamin seemed to hesitate, Esam stepped forward and bowed. "By your leave, Madam Toqeph."

She turned to him. "Speak, Esam."

"You were correct when you said such a load would slow the progress. The Super-Fold Pyreflex Protocol can't function while the craft performs a tow. It would take years to travel between Gannah and Karkar pulling such a weight."

The toqeph nodded. "Yes. So Captain Broward has informed me. But I won't have it said that we of Gannah don't pay our debts. And with the Karkar ship destroyed and no spaceworthy craft of our own, we have no other way to transport it."

She turned again to Binyamin. "As I see it, you have two alternatives."

"Madam?"

"The first is this: I will grant your petition only with the stipulations as discussed. That would mean you would share your ship with fourteen Karkar. And with their captain at the helm, you would be under their command. And, sad to say, you would have to endure those conditions for a period of several years. Moreover, you would have to eat their food, as I'm sure you haven't sufficient supplies aboard your craft to last, whereas I'm told their ship has abundant and renewable stores."

Binya paused then bobbed his head. "Yes, Madam."

"Your second alternative would be to withdraw your petition and request permission to remain here with your comrades. You would, of course, be subject, just as they are, to Gannahan law, and you'd be required to surrender to the League should they demand it." Her black brows lifted. "Do you need time to think about it?"

Binyamin took a deep breath and let it out. "Thank you, Madam Toqeph. But I believe— I believe it would be best for all concerned if I withdrew my petition."

Faris's grin finally escaped.

"If I were instructed," Binyamin continued, "on the procedure for requesting permission to remain with the others, I would like to do that, Madam."

The toqeph nodded. "The proper documentation will be prepared." She raised her hand. "Sergeant Binyamin. I have voided your petition to leave the jurisdiction of Gannah and Gannahan space. A new request will be prepared for your signature according to the terms of our discussion. And that request and its terms are hereby granted."

Binyamin dropped to the floor. "Your judgments are wise, Madam Toqeph. It is my privilege to obey."

42

$\mathcal{A}$FTER leaving the Karkars' hotel, Pik crossed the courtyard to the building that would soon house the new hospital. He entered through the small side door, which he already thought of as the private entrance, and up the stairs.

Spiral stairs, of course. The Old Gannahans liked circles and spirals. But these narrow stair treads were treacherous to negotiate on long Karkar feet. Tiptoeing for safety's sake, Pik climbed to the third-floor residence suite, where, happy to stand flatfooted at last, he found Adam attaching a vertical bracket to the wall in the sitting room.

When Adam had finished using the screw gun, Pik said, "You're making good progress."

Adam turned, brows raised. "Oh, Abba. I didn't hear you come up."

"I suspect you have other things on your mind."

Adam's ears lifted high. "I do indeed." He set the screw gun on a sawhorse and patted his pockets. "Did you try to message me? Did I miss it?" Apparently not finding what he was looking for, he started searching the room.

"No. I was in the chatsr so I thought I'd stop in."

Adam located his messenger on a window ledge, checked the screen, then slipped it into a pocket of his carpenter's apron. "You were— Oh, visiting our guests?"

Pik nodded. "Giving them the good news."

"Good news." Adam ran a roll-measure across the wall, then marked a spot. "You mean they get to leave with our other guests?" He marked another spot a little higher than the first.

"Something like that." Until the plans were official, it was probably best not to discuss them with anyone. Not even Adam.

Though they hadn't talked much about it, Pik had the impression Adam liked the Special Starforces visitors even less than he did the Karkar. And that bothered him. Did Adam object to their shady genetic origin? Or did he dislike Outsiders in general? Whatever the cause, the attitude was disturbing. Particularly in the man being groomed to be toqeph.

"I hear Elise has grabbed everyone she can get her hands on to help with the decorations."

Since Adam's back was turned, Pik couldn't see his face, but his ears didn't smile. "She's a little worked up over the whole thing. We should've—" He turned and set down the roll-measure. "I'm not sure why we didn't start sooner. I mean, we discussed our plans, but we never actually started anything until the official engagement. I don't think there's any rule that says you have to wait for the branding, is there?"

Pik shrugged. "You're asking the wrong guy. You had premarital counseling with Jax and Gillian, didn't you?"

"Yeah, we did." Adam picked up a bracket and lined it up along the marks he'd just made.

Pik stepped over and helped him hold it while Adam reached for the screw gun.

Adam felt in his apron for a screw. "Even that didn't scare her off. She's determined to go traditional all the way. In every aspect of our marriage." He set the screw in the nozzle then drilled it in.

"In that case," Pik said, "I'd better let you discuss this with your em instead of me."

Adam chuckled as he prepared to put in another screw. "I suppose you're right."

As Adam finished affixing the bracket, Pik strolled through the apartment. All the rooms were finished except for the wall coverings. In two of the rooms, he bent and peeled the protective sheet from the floor. The original surfaces were still in nice shape. There would be no need to do anything except clean them.

He went back to the sitting room. "Have you picked out the fabrics?"

Adam shook his head. "Not yet. And not for lack of effort. Elise found just what she wanted in a shop in the twelfth chatsr. They had a nice selection, but something had chewed every bolt of fabric in the place. Nothing was useable."

"You haven't found anything else?"

"Nothing that suits her fancy." Adam paused to drink from his water bottle. "I told her if she wants the walls covered before we move in, she'd better make up her mind. I'm tired of poking around the ruins looking for the perfect fabric."

"Be thankful she's not a Karkar. I had a friend whose parents split up over the color scheme in the dining room." Pik brushed sawdust off his elbow. "I must go and give the toqeph my report on my meeting with Kughurrrro and company. Just wanted to stop and see how you're doing."

Adam nodded. "Once Elise makes up her mind about the fabric, will you help me stretch it on the frames and snap them into the brackets?"

"Not sure yet. Depends on what else I have lined up then. I'll let you know."

Adam smiled. "Hope you can. Sometimes those extra fingers of yours come in handy."

Ears smiling high, Pik wound back downstairs and out into the Gannahan sun. Yes, he had quite a report for the toqeph.

He'd been surprised when she sent him to meet with the Karkar instead of summoning them to Gullach.

"Truth be told," she'd said, sitting on her throne after ruling on the Special Starforces guests' petitions, "I don't care to have them in my home. So if you would, I'd like you to be my emissary. You can speak with them without a translator. While you're doing that, I have one more hearing to conduct, and then I'd like to help Elise with the decorations."

Pik had looked at the timedial. "Good idea. I'll contact them and have them meet me in the lobby of their hotel instead of coming here."

He'd found them all assembled and ready when he arrived.

Kughurrrro rose and greeted him with a twelve-point touch. "Do you have glad news for us, doctor? We've been following the information disseminated by your primitive news services, so we know there's a new arrival orbiting the planet."

Greeting the others with twelve-points as well, Pik tipped his head leftward in a Karkar gesture of assent. "Your surmise is correct. The toqeph has sent me to inform you that it will be possible for you to leave as early as tomorrow afternoon."

The general jubilation that followed, not surprisingly, made Pik's ears ring for several moments afterward.

But he hadn't anticipated Kughurrrro's statement after the din died down. "Your offer is very generous, but I would like to be excused from the voyage."

The silence rang louder than the previous celebration as everyone stared at him with blank expressions, ears stiff with shock.

Pik finally found his voice. "You want to stay?"

Kughurrrro's ears quivered with embarrassment. "Yes, doctor. That is, if possible. Your cousin is staying, isn't she? Could the same courtesy be extended to me?"

After further discussion, Pik helped Kughurrrro file a petition requesting permission to emigrate while his fellow Karkar went back to their rooms in a high pique.

If Dassa denied the petition, poor Kugh would be shunned throughout the long, lonely trip home.

JAX tried to avoid squirming beneath the toqeph's sharp green gaze. Standing before her in this capacity was nothing like sitting around her dining room table at a Council meeting.

He and Gillian had felt honored when the toqeph asked them to serve as Ministers of Domestic Peace five years ago. They'd expected the training to be difficult, since the Old Gannahan domestic laws were convoluted and, for the Earthborn, not at all intuitive. But the practical aspects of their duties had proven equally challenging.

More and more couples were opting for traditional Gannahan marriage, and each needed to be thoroughly instructed in the process. Also, the law required refresher courses at certain points along the way. Couples who had completed their training sometimes came for advice and further counseling. And, of course, as the official Ministers, Jax and Gillian's own marriage was under continual scrutiny.

All that, Jax could deal with. But he didn't like having to file an official complaint and prosecute a case like this.

The toqeph gazed down at the parties before her. "I have reviewed the facts and have made my decision."

All five of them—Jax and Gillian on one side, and Dieter, Enid and Orville Vigneron on the other—looked up in nervous anticipation.

Rather, four of them did. A glance out of the corner of Jax's eye revealed that Enid, as was proper for one wearing the Garment of Shame, still stood with her eyes downcast.

"And I must say," the toqeph said, "I am disappointed in all of you."

Jax felt himself flush, and Gillian made a sobbing noise in her throat.

"Mr. Vigneron has acted within his rights and in accordance with the law." Her glowing gaze pierced Jax and Gillian. "I see no justification for the charges against him." She raised her hand. "The complaint against Dieter Vigneron for failure to properly maintain discipline is hereby dismissed."

Feeling short of breath, Jax caught Gillian's eye and tried to comfort her wordlessly. From the stricken look on her face, it didn't work.

Dieter's jaw jutted proudly, and Enid trembled. Only Orville appeared unmoved.

"However," the toqeph continued, "that doesn't mean things are all they should be in this family. As Ministers of Domestic Peace, Mr. and Mrs. Florida were right to be concerned."

Jax's heart rate began to slow, and Gillian took a deep breath.

"Dieter Vigneron."

He bowed. "Madam Toqeph?"

"Your family is unhappy, and I place the blame on you."

Enid started, and Dieter raised his brows. "Madam?"

"How many children do you have, Mr. Vigneron?"

"Four, Madam Toqeph."

"And would you say that, with the exception of your eldest here, they are all good children? Dutiful and obedient? They show proper respect and are well educated?"

"Yes, Madam Toqeph."

"Even your daughter, who is of age. She isn't obligated to continue working with you in your blend business, but she does nevertheless."

He started to frown but stopped himself and bowed. "Yes, Madam. She is a good girl."

"So if three of your children are all good Gannahans, then your wife must be a good mother."

Dieter's jaw worked.

"Mr. Vigneron?"

The toqeph's sharp voice cut through his hesitation. "Yes, Madam Toqeph. That—that does stand to reason."

"Have you ever praised her for that, Mr. Vigneron? You chastise her for one son's failings, but do you ever acknowledge the good work she does with the others?"

Deep red rose from Dieter's collar to his hairline. "Nnn—no, Madam Toqeph."

Jax was glad she'd never speared him with the look she now gave Vigneron. "You are not obligated to, under the law. But a good Gannahan husband praises his wife with liberality. He takes delight in her. He gratefully rewards her for the efforts she expends on his behalf."

Dieter said nothing. He merely flushed deeper, if that were possible.

The toqeph turned to Orville. "Orville Vigneron."

He bobbed his head. "Madam Toqeph."

"Are you aware that your mother is punished for your behavior?"

Orville glanced between the toqeph and Enid, then above his mother's bowed head to his father. "Yes, Madam Toqeph. I think so."

"Then you are not a good son. A good Gannahan son is respectful of his mother at all times. That includes making sure she doesn't suffer for his behavior."

Orville sniffled. "Yes, Madam Toqeph."

She nodded. "This is my recommendation. I will make it a part of the official record of this proceeding. Though it's not a royal decree, I do expect you each to take note and modify your behavior and attitudes accordingly. Understood?"

Jax didn't know if she was including him and Gillian in the statement, but both bowed and answered with the Vignerons. "Yes, Madam Toqeph."

The toqeph turned to Enid. "Enid Vigneron. You may look up."

The woman lifted her head. "You are a good Gannahan woman, and you have nothing to be ashamed of. I will not countermand your husband's orders, so you should continue wearing that Garment for whatever length of time he told you. But you should wear it with pride, for in your case, there is no shame in it. The shame is your husband's."

The toqeph turned to the sniffling son. "Orville Vigneron."

"Madam Toqeph?"

"I understand you've found some interesting things in your explorations. Tell me about them."

"I, uh, I found some nice rock, Madam Toqeph." He gave one last, long sniff. "And I learned how to dig it out of the ground, and to cut and shape it? And, uh, I paint it and stuff, and make pretty stuff out of it."

She nodded. "So I've heard. I would like to see some of those things."

"You would?"

Dieter snorted, then turned it into a cough. "Pardon me."

She glanced at him but didn't answer, then turned back to Orville. "Yes. I would like to see it. If you would bring some of your favorite pieces to me tomorrow, I would be very pleased. Could you do that?"

Orville bobbed happily. "Yes, Madam Toqeph! Yes, I'll do that, yes. Thank you."

"Very good. I look forward to seeing it." She turned to Dieter. "Dieter Vigneron."

He bowed. "Madam."

"If you're displeased with your son's behavior, take it up with him, not with your wife. You're aware of the law concerning laziness? Gannahans who can't or won't seek regular employment for the good of Gannah?"

"Yes, Madam."

"It would seem those laws are the ones that we're dealing with here. This is plainly not an issue of neglect on your wife's part."

"Madam Toqeph." Dieter's face was so red, his ears almost glowed. "You'd take my boy as a slave?"

She shook her head. "That's the last resort, Mr. Vigneron. The first step is giving him a choice. If he doesn't like his current occupation, he's free to choose another."

"But Madam, all he wants to do is play in the dirt."

"From what I hear, his games might be worth playing. That's why I want to see his creations for myself."

She sat up straighter. "I have spoken. Dieter, Enid and Orville Vigneron, you are dismissed."

They prostrated themselves. "Your judgments are wise, Madam Toqeph. It is our privilege to obey." Rising, they stepped back three steps, bowed, and left.

The toqeph turned to Jax. "Thank you for bringing this case to my attention. Filing a complaint wasn't the best way to do it, but the situation did warrant intervention." She smiled. "I hear good things about the Ministry, generally. The people hold you in high regard and value your counsel."

Jax and Gillian bowed. "Thank you, Madam Toqeph."

She waved her hand. "Enough of that, the hearing's over." She rose. "Could you use some help at the Ministry, do you think? Would you like another couple to work with you?"

Jax and Gillian exchanged glances. Reading her expression, Jax nodded. "I think we will, eventually."

"I wondered. You've seemed rather busy lately, and the workload is only going to increase. We'll discuss suggestions for possible assistants at the next Council meeting." She led the way out the door. "But for now, I have wedding decorations to make."

43

O N the morning of Adam's wedding, Lileela opened the closet, reached into the back, and pulled out the outfit she'd brought from Karkar. "Finally," she muttered. "An occasion to dress like a civilized person."

Her conscience slapped her. Okay, so it turned out the Karkar weren't all that civilized. But at least they had better fashion sense than anyone on this planet.

She pulled at a side seam to flare out the skirt. She used to love the way it fit snug in the hips but swirled around her lower legs, flirting with her ankles. Best yet, the fluid movement helped conceal her limp.

Laying the skirt across the back of the desk chair, she sighed. She'd have to wear the pants instead, though. On Gannah, skirts were menswear.

But that was all right. The pants were nice too. She slipped them on.

What the— Rising on her toes, she tugged harder. She wriggled and twisted, but with the same result.

"They're supposed to be snug, but this is ridiculous." After a brief pause, she tried again.

The third time wasn't the charm. They wouldn't go past mid-hip.

"This isn't possible!" She flung off her nightshirt, grabbed the blouse and slipped it on.

It wouldn't button across her bosom.

Hands shaking with frustration, she righted her nightshirt and pulled it back on, then stumped out of her room and down the hall. "Emma! Emma!"

Shrieking indoors was unseemly for a Gannahan, but the circumstances were extenuating. "Emma!" She pounded on her parents' door. "I have nothing to wear!"

❀

THE early autumn sun shone from a clear azure sky as Adam, resplendent in his cream-colored wedding dress, stepped up to Elise's door.

He took a deep breath, wiped the grin off his face with an eager, six-fingered hand, then knocked. "I have come for my bride," he called in Gannahan. "I pray thee, open to me."

The door flew open.

His grin returned, and widened.

Elise had never been so beautiful. The green of her wedding suit—green for fertility—made her blossom. "Is it thou at last?"

He bowed, then offered his hand. "Come away, my love. I shall take thee home."

Looking into his face, she took his hand.

He trembled at her touch.

❀

BROWARD stood with Marianna beside the road, examining a streamer hanging from a three-meter-high pole. "Surely they didn't decorate every step of the route between here and Qatsiyr."

Marianna laughed. "Elise wanted to, but she ran out of time. Even if it had been possible to plant all those poles and decorate them during the night, there wouldn't have been time to make all the bouquets. They just did the front and back ends. From the Finnegan place to the chatsr gate, and then from the park entrance to Gullach's courtyard."

Broward's eyes followed the line of garland-and-bouquet-bedecked spires marching along both sides of the highway until they disappeared around a bend. "And the courtyard itself."

Marianna took his hand. "Isn't it wonderful? I've never seen anything so beautiful."

Broward turned to her. "Do you regret we didn't have an Old Gannahan wedding?"

"No." She smiled. "I don't regret one thing about our marriage."

As he bent and kissed her, a shout could be heard farther down the road. "I see them! They're coming!"

Several children ran onto the road and peered toward Qatsiyr. "There they are!" The kids jumped and pointed. "I see them!" They took off running.

"Get off the road," their mothers called. "We need to stay in this side of the poles."

The children scampered back behind the curb. But once within the boundary, they ran along the roadside in the direction they'd been pointing. A number of others, adults included, hurried after them, clamoring with excitement.

Broward and Marianne followed at a more leisurely pace, arm in arm.

STANDING at the open entrance to Gullach's courtyard, Pik squinted against the sun as Adam and Elise walked toward him. Half the population of Gannah, dressed in bright party clothes, trailed behind. The other half lined the road. Both groups waved squares of white cloth, each representing a diaper to be changed in the couple's future. Royal blue streamers hanging from the poles fluttered in the happy breeze.

When the bride and groom reached the gates, they smiled and nodded at their parents as they passed through. Pik and Dassa followed Adam, and the Finnegans left their station on the other side of the gateway to follow Elise through the arch into the courtyard, with the rest of the people following at a respectful distance.

The delightful aromas that had teased his senses while he stood outside the gates did a number on Pik's salivary glands when he entered the yard. It occurred to him that he hadn't yet eaten today.

Nor had he slept that night. No one had. He and most of the men had been employed driving in the poles and affixing the decorations along the route, and the women had been busy in the kitchens. This wedding was the biggest event New Gannah had ever seen.

The groom led his bride and the rest of the party beneath the arbor through the length of the courtyard. On the far side, a long table stood in the portico beneath the mezzanine.

The wedding party mounted the two steps to the portico and took their seats at the table. Bride and groom in the middle. Family and friends of the groom on his side, those of the bride on hers. The rest of the guests filed in and lined up in the open space in front of the table. Musicians took their places a little apart, but most of the people stood waiting for the proceedings to begin. Tables and chairs filled the rest of the courtyard where the people would dine after the ceremony.

When the crowd was assembled, Adam rose and opened a bottle of the blood-red wedding blend that stood on the table in front of him. According to the label, that particular bottle had been made the year Old Gannah died.

Adam poured Pik's glass first, for he was the oldest. Pik rose to accept it. Next he filled the other parents' glasses in order of their age, then his own, and last Elise's, until all six were standing.

He then faced forward. "Before all ye witnesses," he said in Gannahan, "we drink this fruit, representing the mingling of the blood of our families."

Adam and Elise turned toward one another, and the parents faced them. When Adam raised the glass to his lips, they all drank together, draining their glasses.

It was a wonderful blend. Pik would rather sip slowly to enjoy it, but the wedding blend was to be drunk quickly, with the implication that life was short.

When all were finished, they put down their glasses. Pik and the bride's father each picked up a pod of te'enah. Pik took one fruit and ate it, then handed the pod to Adam, speaking in clumsy Gannahan. "I bequeath to thee, my son, long life and happiness with the wife of thy youth." Adam ate a fruit from the pod.

Mr. Lucas and Elise repeated the procedure. Then bride and groom exchanged pods and ate from the other's.

Next, Dassa picked up a roll and broke it. Handing half to Adam, she said, "I bequeath to thee, my son, a table laden with bread."

Elise's mother took a roll and performed the same ritual with her daughter. Then the bride and groom faced each other.

Adam gazed down at her. "Finnegan Elise Scott, art thou mine?"

She smiled up at him. "I am indeed."

Dassa moved toward them, Adam stepped back, and Elise allowed Dassa to fasten a red collar around her neck.

Dassa moved back to her place, and all four parents sat.

Elise turned to Adam. "Pik Adam Atarah, art thou mine?"

He nodded. "I am indeed." He bent, and she pulled a small brimless hat from her belt and affixed it on his head.

Picking up the bottle again, he poured the last of the blend into a fresh glass. "Thou shalt be called Finnegan Elise Scott Pik, now and forevermore." He took a sip from the glass and gave her the rest.

As she drained it, the onlookers cheered. Then the bride and groom kissed.

Pik took Dassa's hand and glanced down at her face.

It ran with tears.

IF Lileela had ever attended a traditional Gannahan wedding, she was too young to remember. This day, though, she'd never forget.

Seated on the platform beside Emma, she had a hard time seeing the ceremony, since her parents blocked much of her view. Too bad, because the whole thing fascinated her. She'd heard no talk about it being recorded, on video, but she hoped it was. She'd like to watch it again and again.

Elise's acceptance of the collar and Adam's wearing of the hat before witnesses somehow made the union legal and binding. No lawyers or judge, nothing a Karkar would consider official. Lileela craned her neck to watch the kiss that sealed their pledge. When the onlookers stamped their feet and hooted with approval, she and the others seated on the platform pounded the table with their palms.

The din faded away as the bride and groom took their seats. Then Daniel Lucas stood. As designated friend of the groom, it was his responsibility to superintend the proceedings.

He spoke to the people assembled below. "Good Gannahans! We celebrate today the union of Adam and Elise."

More stomping and hooting.

"First, we have some gifts to present." He reached beneath the table and pulled out a large box.

The gifts were not wrapped. In the traditional process, he handed each gift first to Aunt Skiskii beside him, who passed it down through each of the children, to Abba and Emma, and then to Adam. The newlyweds examined each gift, lifted it to show the guests, and thanked the giver. Then they passed it the rest of the way down the table through Elise's family and friends. At the other end, Elise's friend Ami deposited it in another large box, which would be later carried to the couple's new home.

Traditional wedding gifts were always handmade. The giver took pains to make sure it would be something unique and appreciated, and crafted it with great pride, for it was destined to become a family heirloom. But only those who sat on the platform gave gifts.

Lileela had made a book of Karkar love poems and song lyrics, which she'd translated into both the Standard Language and Old Gannahan. On luxurious, creamy paper Lynne Lucas had found in the family store, Lileela hand-lettered the poems in all three languages in the appropriate characters. For the cover, she created a collage of photos of Adam and Elise through the years, collected with the help of Abba as well as Elise's parents. Katarina Maddox helped her bind it—at the top, as with all Gannahan books—and it was, in Lileela's opinion, a thing of beauty. Seeing the genuineness of Elise and Adam's appreciation of it, she flushed with pleasure.

Once the gifts had been distributed, Daniel turned to the onlookers in the courtyard. "If you would, please join me in a prayer for Elise and Adam's health and happiness, as well as the Yasha's blessing on the food and festivities we enjoy today."

Lileela and the others on the platform rose, and Daniel said a brief prayer in Old Gannahan. It sounded as if he'd been practicing, because he didn't stumble over a word. When he transitioned to singing the blessing, everyone joined in. He led them in all seven verses.

Daniel allowed a brief moment of silent reflection after the last note, then resumed his speech. "Now, everyone, it's time to seat yourselves at the tables on either side of the courtyard, where the red course awaits."

The past few days had been a whirlwind. Besides working at the Dissemination Ministry and studying for her next exam, Lileela had helped with the decorations and food in preparation for the wedding. It was high time to kick back and relax.

She felt the tension ease as she reached for the bowl in front of her.

AFTER the red course—a tangy compote of spiced tappuwach, pickled hezir, and other delicious ingredients—everyone filled the dance floor.

Even Lileela, for she knew the steps.

She joined in the reel after the green course, too, but struggled to keep up with its lively pace and was nearly trampled.

Following the white course, Adam and Elise led the marriage dance. This was a married-couples-only event, for it was slow and tender, involving an intimate closeness seldom seen in public.

While Aunt Skiskii took her turn clearing the table and bringing out the blue course, Lileela sat watching the dance. Imagining herself out there swaying, pressed close against—

No. It wasn't appropriate to think of it.

After the dance ended and the couples pried themselves apart, everyone returned to the tables. But Adam's and Elise's places stood empty. They'd slipped away and wouldn't be seen again until tomorrow.

TWO courses later, Lileela stood on the edge of the dance floor. The sun had moved behind the building, and the courtyard lights burned bright. The dancers moved more or less in unison around the floor, following complicated steps that Lileela's limited range of motion wouldn't allow.

Although she didn't participate, she felt complete. This day was perfect. Adam was happy, and his glowing meah warmed her own. Elise had appreciated her gift. The clothes Lileela had borrowed from Emma fit well and made her feel mature.

With good reason. Next week, she'd take the exam for the Fifth Level, and she was confident of passing. Two weeks later, she'd turn sixteen, and Emma would put the white collar of emancipation around her neck. Mrs. Maddox had offered her a permanent position with the Ministry of Information Dissemination, and Adam would give her his old apartment in Qatsiyr.

Maturity had not come easily, but it had come. She was glad she'd stayed behind when the *Glowworm* left Gannahan space with the Karkar and her ransom. She'd been bought with a price, and her feet—and her heart—were solidly where they belonged.

Gazing across the undulating sea of dancers, she felt someone watching. She turned and scanned the faces of the crowd until her eyes met Faris's brilliant azure orbs.

His gaze held her in a grip that reached to her loins as he moved toward her through the laughing Gannahans.

Yes, this was where she belonged.

Author's Note

In the early 2000s I ran across a little nonfiction book called *The Gospel in the Stars* by Joseph A. Seiss, originally published in 1882. It became the inspiration for my first attempt at writing science fiction.

What started out as a short story became a novel (*The Story in the Stars*), which evolved into a four-book series. I never set out with that intent. I just wanted to illustrate some basic truths that apply to everyone, everywhere, no matter what stars they live under.

Karkar—its language and its people—merely represents me having fun. However, in creating the language of Gannah, I employed *Strong's Exhaustive Concordance of the Bible*, borrowing the Hebrew words used in the Scriptures for the concepts I wanted to convey and adapting (probably more like corrupting) them for the story. *Gannah*, for instance, comes from the Hebrew word for garden. Here are some others:

lahab – blade

meah – sometimes translated bowels or intestines, the word was used in the Scriptures to indicate the place where sympathy and soft feelings originate; the seat of emotions; the heart.

toqeph – authority, power, strength

Yasha – Savior

I don't anticipate mankind will ever travel through space as described in this story. I don't believe there is life, let alone human life, on other planets. And I don't believe that the biblical references mentioned in this book apply to extra-terrestrials. That stuff's pure fiction.

But the stars are real, and so is the Creator whose handiwork they show. That's what this whole thing is about.

Yvonne Anderson

www.facebook.com/OutofthisWorldFiction

If you enjoyed your flight to Gannah, please tell your friends – and I'd love it if you'd leave a review on Amazon!

Fly Through the Gateway to Gannah
For Some Serious Sci-Fi Adventure!

Book 1 – *The Story in the Stars*

Though heirs to an ancient cosmic feud, he must save her life, and she must… well, she doesn't want to think about it.

"The world-building in this epic is gorgeous, and the author created a place I want to visit again."

Book 2 – *Words in the Wind*

Marooned in a place where reality and fairytale are flipped, Dassa wonders if "home" ever really existed.

"A thoughtful and nuanced piece. It lives firmly in the world of social science fiction, and as such, is remarkably solid. I applaud the world building and the crafting of a distinct culture."

Book 3 – *Ransom in the Rock*

How much is a life worth? And who will pay the price?

"I'm impressed with the author's ability to craft such lifelike characters-without whitewashing them. A VERY intriguing read."

Book 4 – *Promise in the Prism*
(formerly titled *The Last Toqeph*)

Will Adam right an ancient wrong and lose his inheritance? Or ignore the truth and lose his integrity?

"The author deftly continues threads from the past 3 books, ties up loose ends, and brings the series to a satisfying conclusion. I was sorry to come to the end, as I have enjoyed my time on Gannah. Such a fascinating place. And the characters have become almost real to me."

More speculative fiction by this author:

The Four Lives of J. S. Freeman, a pseudo-autobiographical story that spans three volumes:

One of the most prominent names in the lore of the planet Umban, author J. S. Freeman is as mysterious and controversial as the island of Freemansland from which she came.

How does one rise from the shrouds of obscurity to become one of the world's most influential figures? In this series, Freeman breaks her long silence and tells the whole tale. Come and see. The truth she tells is better than her fiction.

Book 1: *Stillwaters*
Book 2: *Citizen*
Book 3: *Free*

"Anderson's trilogy is a good, solid, out-of-this-world, thought-provoking block of writing

9 781946 985033